Table of Contents

THE

COBRAS

ON

THE HILL

A

Fiction Thriller Suspense Novel

CHARLES E.A

THE COBRAS ON THE HILL
Copyright © 2025 by **CHARLES E. A.**
All rights reserved.

Published by Overlook Books

OVERLOOK
BOOKS

ISBN: 9798993404202 (Paperback)
Email: akalahucharles@gmail.com
For permission requests, please contact the publisher at the above address.

To my parents for instilling in me the belief that anything was possible. For your constant love and support. For how you faced the challenges of parenting head-on, even though no book could fully equip you for what was to come. And for that, I will be forever indebted to you.

When fiction blurs into reality, all that remains is the storm. And this storm begins with rain—merciless, unrelenting, and unforgiving. The rain battered the city like a curse, hammering windows until even glass seemed ready to break; it was as though the sky had cracked open.

I stood by the window, the kind of window meant for diplomats and secrets and not for men like me, men who knew too much and slept too little. My watch ticked with the kind of tension you feel in hospital waiting rooms. And there, in the middle of it all, stood like a statue of defiance carved from grief, was Emily.

She wasn't just standing in the rain; she was challenging it. Water streamed down her trench coat like it was trying to wash away whatever weight she carried, but Emily... Emily didn't budge. Her eyes locked on something, or someone, out there, like she was reading a silent confession only she could hear.

You don't meet people like Emily often. When I was told to keep an eye on her, the only information I was given was that she was in the midst of whatever was going down. So, yes. I made it a point to get to know as much as I could about her. And it didn't take long for me to realize that she had that rare mix of brilliance and beautiful dysfunction. Tenacity? That was her baseline. But tonight, something deeper had taken hold of her. Something that made obsession look like a vacation.

And from my observation, it wasn't just determination in her face; it was darkness. The kind that creeps in when you realize the truth you've spent your whole life avoiding has finally pulled up a chair and offered you a drink.

Around us, the place was swarming with so many government acronyms. FBI jackets brushed shoulders with CIA operatives disguised as FBI and Secret Service agents. Homeland Security, all moving in that slow, synchronized way that suggested they also had no idea what was coming. Everyone was here for the same purpose: to manage the chaos. But let's be clear: our reasons weren't the same. They were here to clean the blood off the floor and paste it into a report. While I was there to confirm an intel, something only a few knew.

Yes, I know; not doing a dame thing about it clearly makes me a bitch, but hey, I was only following a lead, given that what was about to go down wasn't just blatantly diabolical. It was a message.

So, I checked my watch. Again. The second hand ticked toward 7 PM like a countdown to the apocalypse.

And then, silence.

Not the kind of silence you enjoy. No, not the peaceful kind. Rather, the kind that grips your lungs and makes the hairs on the back of your neck stand. The kind that makes your ears ring and your skin prickle, like the universe itself, had just hit mute on reality.

That's when they revealed it.

The body.

Lying on the crimson carpet of a podium that had once hosted some of the most powerful voices in the country. A place where promises were made, and lies dressed up in patriotism were sold like hot dogs on the Fourth of July. But now, this hallowed stage is cradled with a crime so calculated, so intimate in its brutality that it brings the nation to its knees.

Lifeless eyes stared at the ceiling, at that massive, golden chandelier, still swaying like it knew it had witnessed too much. The air smelled like fear and betrayal. The blood wasn't just blood. It was a statement, pooling dark and thick, the kind of red that made you think of expensive wine and bad decisions. It looked almost elegant, if death could ever be described that way.

By morning, the entire nation had heard about it.

Some called it a murder. Others, more dramatic and maybe more accurate, called it an assassination. But no one could deny it—someone had just shaken the foundations of power, and the tremors were only beginning.

TV anchors leaned into their microphones like they were narrating the end of the world. "Capitol on lockdown," they said. "Federal agencies everywhere." They didn't mention the part about trust disintegrating faster than a cheap umbrella in this same storm.

Rumors flew like startled birds. Who was behind it? Why? What did they know? And who else had to die?

Colleagues began watching each other the way one-eyed cats watch dogs. Loyalty was now a luxury; everyone suddenly had a poker face they didn't know they owned. Friends, real ones, not the handshakes-and-smiles kind, started to cancel dinners, ignore texts, and vanish behind "security clearances."

But this story, this real story, it didn't begin here, at the Capitol, with blood and blinking red lights. No, its seed was planted weeks before. Long before, Emily found herself frozen in the rain. Before federal agents started treating each other like potential threats. Before, the world tilted, and trust fell off the edge.

So, let's take a step back.

Let's rewind to the part where everything still looked normal, at least on the surface.

Because that's how all tragedies begin.

Quietly.

CHAPTER

A Nation Mourns

"Optimism is a mystery—born of nature or nurture, no one can say. It lights our path through life but never reveals the certainty of where it ends."

It was February 15th, 2023, just one day after Valentine's Day, and the world seemed to be rubbing the sleep out of its eyes. The morning sun, still bashful from yesterday's romantic overindulgence, slipped its golden fingers through the sheer curtains of the kitchen, spilling soft light onto the polished oak counter. It gave the entire room a soft glow, the kind that made you pause and feel like something meaningful might happen, even if it was just breakfast.

Mrs. Eleanor, an elegant woman in her mid-sixties with silver-streaked curls pinned in place like a gentle crown, was humming along to a forgotten Sinatra tune as she flipped pancakes with a kind of graceful authority. She wasn't just making breakfast; she was orchestrating a mood. The scent of warm batter and freshly brewed coffee drifted through the air, filling every corner with comfort and expectation.

At the dining table, Emily sat, half wrapped in a cozy cardigan, her gaze drifting between her coffee mug and the soft light dancing on the tablecloth. She was 31, with the kind of beauty that didn't try to announce itself, soft eyes, intelligent features, and a calm presence that made people lower their voices and sit up straighter. But this morning, even her calm was wrapped in contemplation.

Mrs. Eleanor turned, plate in hand, and caught the subtle furrow between Emily's brows.

"Here you go, sweetheart," she said, setting the pancakes down with the quiet grace of someone who had raised three children and still considered butter a love language. "Something to sweeten that heavy thinking."

Emily gave her a soft, grateful smile, the kind that stretched but didn't quite reach the eyes.

Naturally, Mrs. Eleanor didn't let it go.

"You know," she said as she took a seat opposite her daughter, "you're 31 now."

Emily gave a low chuckle, shaking her head. "And here we go..."

"I visited your office last week," her mother continued, undeterred and sipping her coffee like it was armor. "Very sleek building. Full of very serious-looking gentlemen. Handsome, I might add. Do they all walk around like that, tight shirts, briefcases, jawlines that could slice bread? And you're telling me none of them made your radar blip?"

Emily rolled her eyes, but it was all affection. "Mother..."

"What? A woman notices these things! You know I've still got eyes."

Emily grinned despite herself. This was familiar ground. Her mother, always managing to thread love, concern, and mild panic into one tidy sentence.

Mrs. Eleanor leaned forward, voice softening just enough to melt the sarcasm. "I'm not saying jump into the arms of the next suit that walks by, but I do wonder, darling... do you ever let someone get close enough to try?"

Emily sighed, not in frustration, but more like someone trying to fold a heavy thought neatly.

"I've been assigned to a new detail," she said, choosing her words with deliberate cheer. "Secret Service. Senator Thornhill's presidential campaign team. I leave for the capital this morning. Just a quick stop at the office first for the briefing."

Mrs. Eleanor's eyebrows shot up like they were trying to reach heaven. "Secret Service? The Senator Thornhill?"

Emily nodded, casually munching a piece of pancake.

"And this is supposed to make me worry less?" her mother asked, eyes narrowing as if she might call someone and have the assignment canceled through sheer maternal authority. "Emily, that's not a desk job. That's, 'things explode and people whisper in code' territory."

Emily laughed gently. "You've been watching too many spy movies."

"I married your father. That's better than the movies," she replied, folding her napkin with a sudden tightness. Her voice dropped to that rare tone, soft and serious. "I just want you to be safe. That job comes with weight. The kind that doesn't always lift when you clock out."

"I know, Mama," Emily said. "But this means something to me."

Mrs. Eleanor reached across the table and took her daughter's hand, warm and steady. "And so does your happiness," she said.

Emily met her mother's eyes, knowing exactly what was coming.

"I know you think I bring up dating just to tease you," she began, gently. "But it's more than that. I don't want you waking up one day, realizing you gave everything to your work and left no space for someone to hold your hand when it gets hard. Life is... quick. Quicker than you think. And I just want to ensure you're not spending it on only duty for the company."

Emily's throat tightened a little. Not out of guilt, but out of that odd emotion only mothers can summon, a mix of deep love, old memories, and a future you haven't yet arrived at. Her mother's words weren't pressure; they were hope, wrapped in concern.

"I hear you, Mama. When the right person comes along, I'll know. I'll tell you... and probably ask you to interrogate them," she added with a playful grin.

"Oh, don't tempt me. I still have my methods."

They both laughed, the kind of laugh that clears the air.

After breakfast, Emily stood, gathering her things, the usual swift and professional motions of a woman used to tight schedules and high expectations. But her mother's words lingered like perfume, faint but persistent.

As Emily drove through the familiar streets on her way to the office, her mind wandered back to the conversation. For the third time that morning, she replayed her mother's gentle warning.

"Someone who understands this life," she murmured to herself, eyes on the road. "Someone who won't flinch at secrets... or danger."

She shook her head with a wry smile. "That'll be fun to explain on a second date. 'So, what do you do for a living?' 'Oh, you know, just prevent the next political assassination.'" She chuckled. "That always pairs well with wine."

Still, as much as she joked, there was truth at the heart of it. Someone who could stand beside her, not in spite of the danger, but because of it. Someone who didn't just understand the mission... but shared it.

But for now, love could wait. The capital was calling. And so was the threat.

What Emily didn't know, what no one did yet, was that this assignment would change everything.

"Chance encounters are fate in disguise, carrying endless possibilities."

The CIA headquarters was alive with its usual rhythm, a pulse of polished shoes on marble floors, murmured codes between agents, and the soft beep of ID scanners that guarded doors like silent sentinels. Emily, a seasoned intelligence analyst, stepped through the grand lobby, her heels clicking with practiced precision, but her mind still lingered on the morning's conversation with her mother. Her words had planted a seed of reflection... a soft, inconvenient one. "Focus, Emily. You've got a briefing this morning. Don't think about Mom's 'you'll die alone with a gun and a sad houseplant' speech." Emily soliloquizes as she darts her eyes around the lobby before reaching the elevator.

The lingering perfume of Valentine's Day still hung in the air, boxes of forgotten chocolates on desks, wilting roses abandoned in trash bins. Emily exhaled, adjusting her blazer. Romance felt like a different country from the one she served. And yet, her mother's voice hummed in her memory: "I just want you to be happy too."

She jabbed the elevator button, mentally rehearsing protocol, when the doors slid open and she stepped in.

As the doors began to close, a hand darted in. The sensors triggered with a ding, and the doors slid back open to reveal a man she didn't recognize, tall, composed, and exuding the kind of quiet control that made the air feel ten degrees cooler. He stepped inside with ease, nodding politely, but just as he did, Emily shifted slightly and inevitably collided with this solid wall of navy-blue suit and cologne that smelled like "classified budget," their shoulders brushing, an accidental nudge that was neither forceful nor apologetic.

"Hey, watch it please," she said, her tone dry but not cold.

The man turned slightly, surprised, but not flustered. "I could say the same," he said, his voice smooth, almost teasing.

Emily raised an eyebrow. "Well, obviously not intentional; we're good," she replied with a smirk, trying to keep it light; there's no need to escalate a bump into a bureaucratic investigation.

He tilted his head, a subtle smirk forming. "Don't be too sure. It could've been both," he said, his eyes drifting to the elevator panel as if to check how much longer the ride would last, or maybe to leave her wondering if that line had a hidden meaning.

Emily's eyebrow arched. "Oh, hell no. Who did this guy think he was? James Bond's cockier cousin?" However, she blinked, momentarily taken aback by his audacity. Not many people met her sass with a smirk and lived to flirt about it. He wasn't CIA, that much she knew. Too confident. Too deliberate. And yet... something about him made her feel like he belonged. Not just in the building, but in the very core of the intelligence world, where secrets were currency and instincts kept you alive.

The elevator dinged. As the doors opened, they both stepped out, only to realize they were heading in the same direction. Emily offered a sideways glance. "Oh. Same floor." Great. Just my luck, arrogant and in my way.

He didn't reply at first. Just smiled, like a man who knew when to let mystery do the talking.

As Emily walks away, she catches his gaze lingering. Not flirtatious. Assessing. Like she was a puzzle he'd just found under the couch.

Softly, the man said, "See you around, Agent...?"

Emily, walking away, replied. "Not if you see me first."

Back at her desk, Emily tried to shake off the encounter. But it was no use. Her curiosity buzzed in her veins like a wire exposed to current.

Later that morning, as she reviewed field reports, hushed whispers floated in from the corridor. Something about an urgent debrief. NSA. Director Winters. National security crossover. It was a rare occurrence, a 'crossover', when the NSA and CIA collaborated on a mission of utmost importance, usually involving a threat that transcended national borders and required a unified response.

Her ears perked up. NSA?

Against her better judgment, but very much in line with her nature, Emily leaned slightly toward her desk mate, Agent Jenna Moore, who always had one eye on the internal grapevine.

"Hey... that guy from the elevator," Emily began casually. "Tall, kind of smug? Not from around here?"

Jenna glanced up, smirking knowingly. "You met him? The NSA's golden boy?"

Emily raised an eyebrow.

"Alex Carter. NSA. Top-tier field strategist. Word is, he's the guy they call when things go sideways and silence is better than answers."

Emily blinked. Carter. She hadn't even asked his name.

"Why's he here?" she asked, voice low.

Jenna shrugged. "Classified, obviously. But when he shows up, it usually means something's brewing that even the President won't hear about till it's over."

Emily's lips pressed into a line. Arrogant and mysterious. Great. Just her type... if she were into calculated enigmas with government clearance and God complexes.

And yet...

She found herself smiling.

As she returned to her work, her fingers hovered over the keys for a moment too long. Something about that elevator ride felt less like a collision and more like... a beginning.

Agent Coates approached Emily's desk, leaned in, and said, "Hey, briefing room. The Director is in," mimicking a movement with her head.

Inside the CIA's strategic briefing chamber, cool, shadowed, and minimalist Director Arthur C. Winters stood, and behind him was a wall-sized digital display, his steel-gray eyes scanning the room like a hawk assessing prey, hands behind his back, his expression unreadable. Around the oval table sat a hand-picked team of operatives, each with field stripes and scars that didn't show on resumes, but spoke volumes about their past missions and the sacrifices they had made for their country. Emily took her seat, eyes scanning the room, noting who was there... and more importantly, who wasn't.

Without preamble, Winters began. "Six months ago, the NSA forwarded intel concerning a potential threat to Senator Thornhill, currently the most visible face of the presidential race."

No greetings. No pleasantries. Only gravity.

Emily's spine straightened instinctively. Thornhill was not just a candidate, he was a symbol, a man whose campaign rhetoric had ruffled feathers in diplomatic halls across the globe. Threats weren't a surprise. But the source? That was a different game.

Director Winters continued, voice low and deliberate. "After the initial tip, we received a series of letters. Handwritten. Cryptic. Escalating in frequency. Three in the last month alone."

He paused to let the weight of that linger.

Emily felt it, the invisible shift in the room. This wasn't just a matter of domestic security. The walls between foreign and internal threats were blurring. Again.

"As most of you know, we've been coordinating with the NSA to identify the origin of these threats," Winters went on. "But recent intel, courtesy of their cyber-surveillance unit, suggests something bigger." He tapped a file on the big wall screen. "And now? We've got whispers of diplomatic fingerprints. Foreign ones. Not just a lone wolf. Not just an angry voter. This could be strategic."

Emily's thoughts raced. Foreign states meddling in democratic elections wasn't new. But this wasn't disinformation. This was a potential assassination.

"To that end," Winters said, his gaze sweeping the room, "two of you will step to the front lines. Visible. Embedded with the Senator's protection detail. The rest of you will monitor from the shadows. Observe. Intercept. Report."

He turned to face them fully now.

"And let me be clear, we're not cops, nor are we the FBI. We don't arrest. We do not have legal jurisdiction here. Our task is not to police, but to get answers. Our interest is not prosecution, it is prevention. We watch. We listen. And when the time comes," A pause. "We act."

Emily nodded slowly, her mind calculating the stakes as the unspoken "off the books" hung like smoke.

As the meeting concluded, the agents, sharpened with the mission objective, understood that this mission was more than protection. It was a silent war, one that could shift the axis of the upcoming election.

Later that day, the Capitol Hill South Lawn buzzed with the kinetic energy of politics in motion. A massive crowd had gathered. Supporters waving banners. And some, waving flags like patriotic metronomes. Reporters stood on tiptoe behind their camera operators. At the Center of it all, Senator Thornhill, charismatic and composed, took to the podium. His voice boomed over the crowd, all charm and conviction.

Emily stood motionless, dressed in plain clothes, her designer's sunglasses hiding the way her eyes never stopped moving. Her earpiece crackled softly as agents checked in.

"North watch, clear."

"East scope, no anomalies."

"Copy," Emily whispered back, her voice calm.

She scanned the perimeter. Kids on parents' shoulders. Women with campaign buttons. A man with a cane that lingered too long at the barricade before a uniformed officer gently redirected him. Harmless. Maybe.

But she knew better than to relax.

Emily scanned her perimeter again, this time from far left: an elderly man, too busy clapping to be a threat. From her far right: college kid, filming on his phone. And once again, back to the center, but there was a woman in a red coat this time.

Emily's pulse spiked. The woman wasn't cheering. Wasn't blinking. Just... watching.

Emily, into comms, casually said, "Jenkins. Red coat, twelve o'clock. Run her face."

Jenkins crackling back: "Already on it. Also, the NSA's golden boy just checked in. He's here."

Emily's jaw clenched. Of course, he is.

Standing beside Emily was her partner for the day, another agent, a former marine turned analyst with a knack for spotting chaotic patterns. They exchanged a brief glance, the kind that said: We're not blinking until this is over.

As Thornhill delivered his speech, promising sweeping reforms and global recalibrations, Emily's eyes stayed vigilant. She didn't watch the stage. She watched the watchers.

The sun dipped slightly. The crowd roared with applause. It felt like the ending of a clean day.

And yet, something was off.

Her instincts, trained over years of psychological profiling and threat detection, prickled. It wasn't something she saw. It was something she didn't do.

No opposing protesters. No media plants pushing forward for quotes. No anomalies in thermal signatures.

Too clean.

She raised her radio. "South detail, confirm camera sweeps and ID logs. Let's do a final run-through before we pack up."

"Copy that," came the response.

But her watch vibrated as she stepped back two steps for the final pass-through. An encrypted message flashed across the small screen:

"Unregistered transmission detected. Origin: foreign satellite relay. Frequency masking local surveillance."

Emily froze for a second, then pivoted swiftly, eyes narrowing.

Something was wrong because a signal had been activated somewhere, 3741 meters away from the Capitol's lawn. Unseen and almost undetected. The kind of signal that didn't make noise, but moved pieces.

The sky had been brooding all afternoon, but no one expected it to break so violently.

As Senator Thornhill launched into the crescendo of his speech, his voice ringing with passion, eyes lit with purpose, the heavens darkened with cinematic timing. Clouds rolled in like silent spectators, thick and moody. Then, with a furious flicker, lightning split the sky. Thunder roared, echoing across the Capitol grounds, momentarily drowning out the sound system. It was as if nature itself had paused to listen, or to warn.

Emily's gaze drifted instinctively to the horizon. Rain began to fall in heavy droplets, quickly escalating into a downpour. Umbrellas sprang open. Yet the crowd remained rooted, undeterred, their eyes locked on the man who had become a symbol of reform, courage, and inconvenient truth.

And then, crack.

Not thunder.

Not this time.

A single gunshot ripped through the storm, slicing through the applause, cutting off Thornhill's final words mid-sentence. For a breathless second, it was unclear what had happened. Then came the scream.

Senator Thornhill collapsed.

Blood spilled like a warning across the crimson carpet and splattered against the white marble of the Capitol, an image that would be replayed across every screen in the country within the hour.

Chaos erupted.

Screams overlapped the sound of agents shouting commands. The crowd surged backward in waves of panic. Security swarmed the platform. A protective shield of bodies formed around Thornhill, but it was too late.

Emily was already moving. Her legs sprinted before her mind fully registered what had happened. She knelt by the Senator's body, her hands trembling as she reached for a pulse she couldn't find.

She stared at him. Eyes once filled with conviction now glazed and empty. A man who had dared to speak uncomfortable truths, who had challenged the system from within, now reduced to a lifeless symbol of what it cost to do so in a divided nation.

Rain mixed with blood. Sirens wailed in the background. But in Emily's mind, everything slowed.

Her instincts screamed louder than the crowd: This wasn't foreign interference.

This was an inside job.

Her eyes narrowed, scanning the perimeter again, not for shooters, but for shadows. Informants. Puppeteers. Insiders.

"This was no outside threat," she murmured, barely audible, her voice lost in the downpour.

"The rat in the house told the rat outside that food was in the pantry. The doors were open from the inside."

Her gut twisted, not from fear, but from betrayal. They had walked into a trap dressed as ceremony. And Thornhill, who had no chance at what was coming for him, had paid the price.

Director Arthur C. Winters sat in the command center, watching the footage on a secure feed. He showed no emotion, just a slow inhale, then a measured exhale. Behind him, aides whispered, analysts stared in disbelief, and phones lit up with fury from every government branch.

But Winters knew the truth before the autopsy, before the first ballistic report, and before the press conference.

"America wasn't attacked by a foreign enemy," he said to no one in particular. "It was strangled by the monster it fed with power and pretended not to see. The rot we've ignored within our own house, that's what we are looking at."

His eyes never left the screen as Senator Thornhill's body was loaded into an armored medical van.

Winters turned to his deputy. "Activate every sleeper protocol. Classify every file Thornhill accessed in the last three months. I want a full surveillance sweep on every committee member he crossed paths with since he announced his candidacy. This isn't a hunt for a shooter. This is a search for an architecture of betrayal."

By nightfall, the entire country was in mourning.

Candlelight vigils dotted every major city. Screens across the world replayed the moment, the flash, the fall, the blood. News anchors choked on words as they tried to describe the indescribable. A visionary had fallen, not on the battlefield, but at the heart of his homeland.

Statements poured in.

The Secretary of Defense condemned the attack as "an act of war against American democracy."

The State Department called it "a strike at the soul of our national values."

But beneath the polished statements, intelligence agencies knew the truth was more complex. This wasn't just an assassination; it was a signal. Something old was awakening. Something domestic. Something bred in silence.

The FBI and Homeland Security initiated a full-scale probe, but the CIA knew it couldn't afford to sit back. Director Winters formed a black-ops task force under the radar, one that wouldn't answer to the Senate, wouldn't be bound by the press, and wouldn't wait for permission.

Emily was in.

Driven not by duty anymore, but by vengeance. Not blind vengeance, but strategic.

She would find the rat.

She would unravel the thread that led to this moment, the smudged file, the anonymous letters, the conveniently broken surveillance feeds, the security clearance granted to the wrong aide.

This wasn't over.

Not by a long shot.

And in a quiet Suburban home, Emily's mother stared at the news, her fingers dialing with shaking hands, "Emily. Come home. Now."

"Resilience emerges when fragments of hope align. But building a stronger future requires vigilance, for the past often resurfaces to test our resolve. To give in is to turn promises into ruins; to persist is to turn them into monuments of strength."

It's another beautiful day, and the morning sun, as if on cue, filtered through the gauzy curtains of Emily's apartment, casting golden streaks across the hardwood floor. Her coffee steamed gently on the windowsill, untouched, while the world outside carried on with its routine, oblivious to the quiet storm unraveling behind her closed door.

She stood in her robe, towel still wrapped around her damp hair, sipping slowly and mentally preparing for another day at Langley. After everything that had happened—the assassination, the chaos, the political fallout—the walls of the CIA no longer felt like walls. They were mirrors now. Every look, every word, every file seemed to reflect secrets she wasn't meant to see.

Then it happened.

A faint noise at the door. A soft, slick shuffle against the wood, a paper, maybe. Followed by a retreating footstep.

Emily froze.

Years in the field had taught her to recognize subtle threats. Nothing about this morning had been scheduled. And nothing at her doorstep ever arrived without shadows trailing behind.

She set her coffee down carefully, reached into the drawer beneath the sink, and pulled out a pair of nitrile gloves. With practiced precision, she approached the door and peered through the peephole. No one. Just a quiet corridor, innocuous and deceiving.

Lying just inside her doorway was a nondescript brown parcel. No markings. No return address.

That was the first red flag.

She bent slowly, gloves on, examining the envelope's weight and texture. No ticking. No powder. No rigidity. It felt like paper. Old paper.

She opened it with the same reverence she'd give a classified intelligence file.

Inside: a single photograph.

Her breath hitched.

It was Senator Thornhill. But not as the public knew him.

He looked younger, in his early forties, perhaps, standing in a garden dappled with sun. He was smiling, relaxed, unguarded. And beside him stood a woman. Elegant. Poised. Her smile was deliberate, her hand gently resting on his arm. There was something magnetic about her. Something hauntingly familiar, though Emily couldn't immediately place it.

The photo felt intimate, as if it had been taken in a private moment not meant for headlines.

And yet, here it was, at her doorstep.

Emily sat at her kitchen table, eyes scanning every pixel of the image. It wasn't just a photograph. It was a whisper. A breadcrumb.

Who sent this?

Why now?

And why her?

She pulled up her encrypted laptop and began combing through archived files, media databases, internal communications—anything related to Thornhill's early political career. Hours passed. Her coffee went cold. The sun drifted across the sky.

Then she found it.

A rumor. A thread barely preserved in a dated memo from the early 2000s: "Unconfirmed chatter linking Senator Robert Thornhill to Felicity Montgomery—socialite, philanthropic investor, known associate of various high-ranking officials, both domestic and international. File sealed by Congressional Ethics Oversight."

Felicity Montgomery.

Of course. The woman with no past but an endless list of connections. Her name had surfaced before in whispers, in scandals, but she always vanished before the light could catch her.

A name that raised eyebrows, then fell into silence.

A woman known for being close to power. For disappearing just as things began to burn.

Emily leaned back in her chair, the photograph still in her hand. The implications chilled her.

Was Felicity a liability? A secret worth killing for?

What had she known?

And more disturbingly, was she the reason Thornhill had to die?

The deeper Emily dug; the more pieces emerged from the shadows. Thornhill's speeches on government transparency, his push for classified ethics reform, and his veiled remarks about "a system poisoned from within" all took on a new meaning.

What if those reforms had more to do with personal guilt than public duty?

What if someone had wanted to ensure that Thornhill never told his version of the truth?

The affair, if real, wasn't the story.

The cover-up was.

And in the heart of it, a woman who moved in the upper tiers of global influence like a ghost in heels. A woman whose name no one dared speak twice. A woman who had disappeared from public life years ago—voluntarily or not.

Emily sat in silence, the photograph still in hand.

If Thornhill had tried to protect her, who had tried to silence them both?

There were too many questions, and only one woman might hold the answers.

Felicity Montgomery. A ghost with answers.

And if Emily knew anything about ghosts, they only appeared when the past started to bleed.

And right now? The past wasn't just bleeding; it was gushing.

THE COBRAS ON THE HILL

In a matter of days, Emily's investigation into Senator Thornhill had gone from promising to pitiful. Every lead fizzled like a soda left out too long. Sources went silent. Files disappeared. People who were talkative yesterday suddenly had convenient cases of amnesia.

Frustrated, burnt out, and one coffee away from developing a full-blown twitch, Emily did what any highly trained CIA case officer with access to satellite surveillance and global intel would do: she packed a duffel bag and went home.

Not home home. Not the sterile, beige government-issued apartment with Wi-Fi and water pressure as weak as her will to keep going. No—home. Her mother's house. The one with mismatched furniture, the scent of cinnamon baked into the walls, and the undeniable power to make anyone forget they once interrogated a double agent in Prague.

The drive was long, but as usual, familiar. Country roads wrapped around her like old arms. The air smelled like wet grass, sun-baked tar, and freedom from bureaucracy. As her car rolled up the gravel driveway, the familiar creak of the tires made her heart clench in that strange way nostalgia does—sweet and painful all at once.

The living room window glowed softly, its golden light seeping through the lace curtains like a warm whisper. As she stepped out, boots crunching against the gravel, she barely made it to the second step before the front door swung open.

"Emily, sweetheart!" her mother, Eleanor, gasped with the breathless urgency only a mother could conjure at 8:42 PM. "What in heaven's name are you doing here? It's not the weekend yet! Are you alright? You said you were fine when we talked on the phone. Well, I'm so glad you're here now. Come on in, honey, give me a hug."

Emily was already halfway into her mother's arms before Eleanor finished her sentence. The hug was warm and familiar, a comforting embrace that momentarily eased the tension in Emily's shoulders. And of course, Eleanor noticed, her motherly instincts always sharp.

She leaned back, squinting. "You've got that look again. The one you had when you were twelve and tried to lie about flushing your dad's cufflinks down the toilet."

"I was searching for mermaids," Emily muttered dryly.

"And I'm sure they appreciated the donation," Eleanor said, then pointed a knowing finger toward the kitchen. "And don't even think about sneaking to that fridge. I saw that glance. You looked at it like it owed you or something."

Emily smirked. "I'm just checking, and it hasn't run away."

"Well, it hasn't. But that pie inside? That's for the weekend. You know the rules. No pie until Saturday, emergencies only." Eleanor shrugged.

Emily raised an eyebrow. "This is a pie-level emergency, Mom."

Eleanor, jestingly nodding, replied, "Nice try, Agent Sweet-Talk. You'll get a slice when I see a warrant." Her playful tone added a touch of humor to the evening, lightening the mood.

They laughed—real, belly-deep laughter—and for a second, the weight on Emily's chest loosened. They had dinner together, a meal full of roasted vegetables, grilled chicken, and the kind of small talk that heals in ways no therapy ever could. Eleanor told stories about nosy neighbors and her Pilates class, while Emily offered just enough vague detail to avoid violating a dozen nondisclosure agreements.

After their cozy dinner, they did the dishes shoulder to shoulder, Eleanor washing, Emily drying. It was a silent ritual of sorts, like monks in a kitchen monastery. Occasionally, one would hum a forgotten song, and the other would mumble along like it was a prayer.

Emily went in and took a long shower, letting the hot water wash away the grime and pressure of the day. And with the house quiet and Eleanor humming in her knitting chair, Emily made her way down the hall to the room she always visited but never spoke about.

Her father's study.

Nothing had changed.

The old mahogany desk still sat proudly beneath the window, dust gathering like old thoughts. His framed police certificates still lined the walls, flanked by photographs of commendations, partners, and one black-and-white shot of a younger Eleanor leaning on his cruiser, grinning like she'd just won the lottery.

Emily ran her fingers along the edge of a frame. A photograph of her father in his uniform. Stern. Brave. Unapologetically proud. That image had shaped her entire life. She could still remember watching him lace up his boots, polish his badge, straighten his tie—not just a father, but a man with a mission.

She had wanted to be just like him. Only now did she know the darker side of that aspiration and the cost of that mission.

He never talked about the sleepless nights. Never mentioned the haunted looks in his eyes after long shifts. He had been a fortress—but even fortresses crumble from within.

Still, he never gave up. Never turned bitter. "Truth is like water," he used to say, brushing her hair back when she had bad dreams. "You can dam it up for a while, but eventually, it finds a way out. Your job, Em, is to help it flow."

She had taken those words to heart. And maybe too much.

She sat down at the desk, the chair creaking beneath her, and opened the bottom drawer, a place where her father kept "the real stories," as he called them: old files, hand-scribbled notes, things too raw or complicated for official channels.

And there it was. Tucked between faded manila folders and dog-eared notebooks.

A file on Robert Thornhill, the man her father had been investigating before his death.

Her breath hitched.

Inside were surveillance photos, handwritten memos, and one grainy image of the Senator standing with a group of men in suits, a group that seemed to hold a significant power in the shadows, and one of them circled in red ink with a name she hadn't heard in years.

A chill crept down her spine like cold fingers.

Her father's ghost hadn't just appeared... he had left her a trail.

CHARLES E.A.

"The true beauty of optimism lies in its power to transform. It sheds light on uncertainty, challenges doubt, and creates a vision of potential that surpasses logic."

The screen glowed in the dimness of my hideout, casting jagged shadows across the walls as I watched Emily through the hidden eye I'd planted in her mother's home—Grainy, intimate, like peering through a keyhole into a life that wasn't mine.

Emily, still sat at her father's desk, fingers tracing the edges of that damning Thornhill file, her face a battlefield of emotions she couldn't quite suppress. Hope. Determination, and probably fear.

All I know is that there was restlessness in her-the kind that doesn't come from the body, but from something deeper, something fractured.

As I watched her, something strange stirred in me.

A thought.

A musing.

A curiosity about the wild thing called human optimism.

You see, optimism is a funny beast. It's not a shout, but a whisper. Not a battle cry, but a heartbeat in the dark. It's that quiet flicker of light in the mind that dares to glow even when the walls are closing in. It's stubborn, unreasonable, and in many ways beautiful.

Don't get me wrong, it keeps people moving when they should stop. It lets them reach for things they've no business touching. It makes them believe they can change the world, even when the world is sharpening its knives.

Emily had that glow.

Still does.

A light flickering behind her eyes, even now, when every rational sign screams at her to give up, to walk away, to let it be. But no, not her. She clings to the belief that there's still something worth fighting for. That truth matters that the system can still be salvaged, like an old ship refusing to sink.

I've known many like her. Idealists. Fighters. They burn so bright, but God, do they burn out fast.

And as I watched her in that kitchen, laughing with her mother, stealing glances at that locked drawer like it might open itself—I realized something else:

Optimism isn't just born. It's built.

It's biology, yes. But it's also blood and bone, memory and moment. Some are wired to see the glass half full. Others are taught to drink whatever's left and smile through the bitterness. Emily, I suspect, had both. A hopeful heart by design. A resilient one by necessity.

But there's danger in that kind of hope.

A light too bright casts the darkest shadows.

That's the part most people miss.

Optimism has a twin—delusion. And the two are often inseparable at first glance. One keeps you walking. The other walks you straight off a cliff.

Emily hasn't learned to tell them apart yet. Not really. She's still clinging to her armor—one made of cheerful stoicism and tidy narratives. She presses forward because that's what heroes do. She compartmentalizes, medicates with laughter, distracts with purpose. And in the quiet moments, when the world finally slows, she pretends that the ache in her chest is just tiredness and not what it really is: Fear. Doubt. Vulnerability.

But she can't keep pretending forever.

No one can.

Sooner or later, even the strongest minds fracture if the pressure isn't released. Emily will have to confront the truth, the real truth, not just about the case, but about herself. It's inevitable.

Because the strongest agents aren't the ones who ignore their pain, they're the ones who let it sharpen them. Let it guide them. And let it teach them.

Emily will have to learn that real optimism doesn't erase the darkness. It walks through it. It bleeds with it. It grows from it.

That's the version of her I'm waiting to see. The one who doesn't just hope unquestioningly but hopes wisely—the one who knows that light isn't the absence of shadow, but its dance partner.

That's when she'll be dangerous.

That's when she'll become something more than just her badge, her title, or her bloodline.

She'll become whole.

Of course... I won't be around to clap for her.

I'm just a shadow in the corner. A whisper in her periphery. A glitch in the feed.

She won't hear these words. She doesn't even know I exist.

But I'll be watching.

Always watching.

Because sometimes, the only thing more fascinating than unraveling a mystery is watching the detective unravel herself.

THE COBRAS ON THE HILL

CHAPTER

The Enigmatic Operative

"To be human is to seek happiness, rise through adversity, and discover purpose in the light of self-awareness. These pursuits bloom only when we care for our inner strength, connect with others, and walk forward with deliberate choice."

It had been seven days since Senator Thornhill was assassinated—seven long, pressure-cooked days of public outrage, media speculation, and behind-the-scenes panic. The country hadn't just lost a presidential candidate; it had been sucker-punched in broad daylight. And as always, when something blew up in America, alphabet agencies started crawling out of the woodwork like caffeinated termites.

Inside the nerve centre of Washington's intelligence machine, the mood wasn't just tense, it was the kind of simmering chaos you'd find in a restaurant kitchen that just realized it was out of gas mid-dinner rush. And amidst that stew of controlled panic was Emily Parker.

"Tell me I'm dreaming," Emily said, pinching the bridge of her nose like she was trying to reboot her frontal lobe.

"You're not," replied Mrs. Kathleen A. Coates, her CIA handler-slash-unofficial-therapist-slash-part-time Gandalf impersonator. She sat perched like a crow on the edge of her desk, twirling her pen like it was a conductor's baton. "The NSA's officially in. Along with our friends at the FBI, Homeland Security, and probably the IRS if someone accidentally forwarded the wrong email."

Emily's lips flattened into a line so tight it could have sliced paper. "Let me get this straight. The NSA—National Sneaky Agency—shows up with nothing but a half-baked signal, and suddenly we're on a playdate with every acronym in the federal toy box?"

"It's not a playdate," Kathleen said with maddening calm. "It's more like a... heavily armed book club. With trust issues."

Emily groaned and flopped into her chair, sending a nearby file folder flying to the floor. "This is bureaucratic heresy, Kathleen. There's no precedent for this. No chain of command. It's chaos wrapped in duct tape."

Kathleen gave a sage nod, like she'd been expecting this tantrum. "Yes, well. That's what makes it so exciting."

"Exciting?!" Emily's eyebrows launched halfway to her hairline. "This isn't a high school debate. This is a national security crisis!"

"Exactly," Kathleen said, eyes gleaming with a weird mix of wisdom and mischief. "And what better time for unconventional minds to shine? Each agency plays by its own sacred scrolls. But here's the fun bit: sometimes, when ideologies clash, they don't just explode—they alchemize."

Emily blinked, the metaphor short-circuiting her frustration.

Kathleen leaned in with theatrical flair. "Picture it, Emily: the FBI's love of procedure, the CIA's flair for shadows, the NSA's worship of data, and Homeland Security's... well, earnestness. It's like an orchestra where every instrument is slightly out of tune, yet somehow the music still plays. And do you know why they brought us in?"

"Because we're the ones who don't play by the sheet music?" Emily muttered.

Kathleen grinned. "Exactly. We're the jazz in this symphony of red tape."

Emily tilted her head, eyeing her handler suspiciously. "Have you been drinking espresso again?"

Kathleen ignored the jab. She stood up and began pacing like a professor preparing to present her thesis. "The NSA caught a whisper. Not a fact. Not even a lead. Just... a murmur. Something about Thornhill's past, hidden networks, and an anomaly buried in the noise. Vague, yes, but intriguing. And they sent their most unpredictable asset to follow it."

"Oh, joy. A mystery man. Because nothing screams trust like the NSA's idea of subtlety."

Kathleen paused, then smirked. "His name's Alex Carter."

Emily stopped mid-sip of her now-cold coffee. "Wait. That's Alex Carter?"

Kathleen nodded. "The same. The Ghost. The Philosopher Spy. The Nigerian-American who once broke a sleeper cell in Marseille using only a chessboard and a bottle of wine."

Emily stared at her flatly. "You're making that up."

"Am I?" Kathleen's grin widened.

Emily exhaled, staring at the ceiling like it owed her answers. "God help us all."

Meanwhile...

Somewhere on the upper floors of CIA Headquarters, a security camera blinked twice and went dark. Then came the footsteps—soft, measured, unhurried.

Alex Carter had arrived.

He didn't walk like an agent. He walked like a poem. Tall, deliberate, and eerily calm, he moved through the corridor as though gravity had made a personal exception for him. Most people in intelligence were trained to be invisible. Alex didn't need training. The world just naturally... overlooked him. Until he spoke, and then no one could look away.

He wore a tailored charcoal coat that somehow made everyone else's suits look like they came from a clearance rack. His face was unreadable, but not unfriendly—just thoughtful, like he was always mid-conversation with a ghost no one else could hear.

The receptionist glanced up and started to ask for ID, but her words vanished somewhere around "Excuse me—." She recognized him. Or rather, she recognized the presence. That aura that said: I belong here more than you do.

Alex gave her a polite nod and kept walking.

Back in the operations room, Kathleen was still philosophizing.

"You know, Emily, sometimes I think intelligence work is just organized schizophrenia," she said thoughtfully. "We hear voices, follow patterns, argue with invisible threats—"

"—and occasionally talk to walls," Emily interrupted.

"Exactly!" Kathleen beamed. "Which is why I'm confident you and Alex will get along beautifully."

Emily's jaw dropped. "Wait. I'm working with him?!"

Kathleen gave a nonchalant shrug. "Of course. Who else can speak sarcasm fluently and still detect a lie beneath a whisper? You two are like matching frequencies."

Emily groaned, sinking deeper into her chair. "This is going to be a disaster."

"Oh, probably," Kathleen said cheerfully. "But imagine the story we'll tell if it works."

Somewhere in the building, Alex Carter paused.

He tilted his head slightly, as if he could already hear the shape of his name forming on someone's tongue. Then, with a soft smile that didn't quite reach his eyes, he stepped into the room where the dance of truth and deception was about to begin.

From the corner of her eye, Emily spotted him. Her lips pressed into a thin, instinctive line as she muttered under her breath, "Asshole."

She hadn't fully turned her head toward him, but her body already knew. A strange, tight feeling bloomed in her chest—not fear, not attraction, but that deep, uneasy awareness you get when you realize someone's about to mess up your perfectly color-coded spreadsheet of a life.

Emily had always been a lone wolf. She thrived in clarity, moved like water through evidence and deduction, and trusted no one more than her own instincts. Her world was ruled by clean facts, sharp logic, and an almost romantic commitment to procedure. But now... Kathleen, her always-too-dramatic supervisor, had decided to play matchmaker—strategically, of course.

"A clash of methodologies," Kathleen had called it, as if it were a book club debate and not a high-stakes investigation into the murder of a presidential candidate.

The door to Emily's department creaked open with the subtle theatrics of a Broadway entrance, and there he was—NSA's golden boy, with the reputation of a phantom and the ego of a man who'd memorized his own Wikipedia page.

Alex Carter stepped into her space like he'd just disarmed a nuclear bomb with one hand and signed his autograph with the other.

But here's something you need to understand: Emily didn't hate Alex. Hate required emotional investment, and Emily's emotions were a vault even Swiss engineers would admire.

But she despised the way he leaned against her desk now, all smirking insouciance and tailored chaos, like a villain.

"Special Agent Emily Parker, I presume," he drawled, his voice dripping with faux reverence, a voice as smooth as a jazz saxophone and twice as irritating. "I'd say it's a pleasure, but we both know that'd be a lie."

Emily didn't look up from her files. "Your self-awareness is staggering, Agent Carter. Do they teach that at NSA charm school, or is it a natural gift?"

He chuckled—a low, velvety sound designed to disarm. "Oh, it's a gift. Like my ability to sense when someone's... avoiding eye contact."

Emily's pen froze mid-signature.

Slowly, she raised her gaze.

And there it was—that look. The one he'd worn in the elevator two weeks ago, right before he'd ruined her morning with his existence.

She instinctively leaned back a fraction. This wasn't a coffee date, and her desk didn't need a co-occupant. She could still recall their first interaction, which had occurred in an elevator of all places. So, why she's looking at the same man, except this time his eyes were tracking hers like a predator mildly curious about its prey, is something that bits her imagination.

"Rough day?" Alex asked, nodding at Emily's coffee-stained sleeve.

Emily didn't blink. "Not until thirty seconds ago."

His grin widened. "Ah. So, you do have a personality under all that... procedure."

"Excuse me?" Emily shrugs.

Now, Alex tilted his head, studying her. "Still mad about the elevator summit meeting?"

"I don't get mad," Emily said, stacking files with lethal precision. "I get efficient. And you're currently a speed bump."

He leaned in, close enough for her to catch the faint scent of sandalwood and trouble. "Speed bumps exist to make you slow down, Parker. Ever consider that?"

She held his gaze, unblinking. "In case you've forgotten, I'm CIA. We remove speed bumps."

Alex laughed. "Touché," he said with a quick nod, but his smirk morphed into something softer, surprisingly genuine. "Look, I admit it. I was a little... full of myself that day. I can see how I might've come off... arrogant. That wasn't my intention. And I apologize."

She raised a brow again. That was unexpected. And now, he was disarming her with humor, damn him.

"I guess..." she said slowly, "apology accepted." The words tasted foreign but fair. She wasn't about to throw a welcome party, but she also wasn't entirely immune to sincerity when she saw it.

Alex straightened, his grin widening. "Thank you. Shall we bury the past in the elevator shaft and get to work?"

Emily hesitated, eyes still skeptical. She didn't trust easily, especially not men who entered rooms with built-in background music and conversational judo skills. But this case was bigger than ego, bigger than preference. Whether she liked it or not, they were tethered now.

"Fine," she said, though her tone made it clear that "fine" meant "I'm watching you like a hawk with a grudge." "But don't think for a second I've forgotten about that first impression."

"Wouldn't expect you to," he said with an amused shrug. "So, Agent Parker—what's your play here? Any headway?"

Emily straightened her files. "We're tracing the threads backward and looking at Thornhill's past. There's a good chance that the roots of his assassination are buried somewhere in the years before the campaign. Old enemies, buried secrets—political ghosts."

"Interesting." He pulled a flash drive from his pocket and spun it on her desk like a tiny roulette wheel. "I brought a peace offering."

Emily eyed it like it might explode. "Is that classified? Is the Pope Catholic? Irrelevant. The Pope doesn't work in counterintelligence."

"Yet," Alex said, grinning. "Give it time. But here's the thing..." He watched her, thoughtful now. "The NSA thinks there's more to this. Connections that don't show up on paper. Things the Bureau wouldn't have access to—by design."

Emily bristled. There it was again—the aura, the secret-source swagger. He was so composed. So casual. And yet, every word seemed calculated. "Why is the NSA involved in an off-book occupation like this? We were making steady progress. It might've been slow, but we were moving forward. But we always find a way. We always do."

Alex smiled again—less charm this time, more riddle. "Because sometimes steady isn't fast enough. Most of the time, we look for things

27

not because they lie in plain sight but because they don't, and if and when that becomes the case, we find what we are looking for by leaving no stone unturned.

Emily's jaw tightened, her frustration flaring. "I've always believed that transparency and legality are non-negotiable," she said firmly. "I don't see the value in bending the rules now."

"And I respect that," he said calmly. "But I also know that the answers don't always show up with a badge. In fact, in some cases, the badges are designed to hide answers. Sometimes, the answer hides behind allies. Or inside vaults built by people who don't care about due process. And that's where you will need all the help you can get. And no offense, I know you guys are good at that. But come on, a helping hand shouldn't hurt. Right?"

She shook her head. "You think breaking the rules is justified?"

"I wouldn't call a joint operation that, but to be honest, I think the rules are often written by the people who need hiding places," Alex said. "So no, I don't enjoy breaking them. I just don't let them blind me."

Emily stared at him, uncertain whether to be annoyed or intrigued.

Alex grinned. "Look, I'm not here to steal your thunder. Just offering a flashlight if the path gets dark."

Emily Parker hadn't laughed in days, not since the package had arrived with no return address, no fingerprints, and just enough mystery to make her insomnia feel justified. So, when Alex dropped a flashlight metaphor into the middle of her stormy day, she didn't expect the small chuckle that escaped her lips.

It was one of those reluctant chuckles, the kind that escapes when you're tired of holding back and too drained to argue.

"Well, Agent Carter," she said, her voice lined with reluctant amusement, "let's see if your flashlight can keep up."

Emily rolled her eyes, but still couldn't help but smile. She reached across the desk and picked up the manila folder that had occupied most of her mind for the past couple of days. It felt heavier than it should, as though secrets had mass and had decided to settle in this particular envelope.

She slid it toward him.

Alex took it without a word, flipped it open with a precision that made it feel like he was handling state secrets, which, in all fairness, he probably was. His gaze locked on the photo, and for a long stretch of silence, he just stared.

Emily watched him. She always watched people when they didn't know what to say. That's when the truth showed itself—not in their words, but in the tiny reactions they couldn't control.

Finally, Alex leaned back. His fingers held the photograph like it was a relic, something ancient and sacred.

"This is the anonymous package you received?" His voice was calm.

Emily nodded, arms crossed tightly like they were the only thing holding her together.

Alex's brow furrowed slightly. "Felicity Montgomery..." he murmured, as if the name had been plucked from the fog of old memories. "Now that's a name I haven't heard in a long time."

He looked at Emily with something between respect and quiet warning.

"They call her The Weaver," he said. "The woman who knew everyone and everything, but somehow, nobody knew her. Like a spider who built webs in the shadows and made sure no one ever saw her legs move."

Emily stared at the photo. It was a candid shot, Thornhill shaking hands with some member of Congress at a fundraiser, but just off to the left, partly blurred by the motion of a waiter, was a woman. Not posing. Not performing. Just present.

Watching.

Quietly dangerous.

"There's something about this picture I can't put my hands on," Emily said, voice low. "If it were meaningless, someone wouldn't have risked sending it. They wanted me to see her. But why?"

"That's the right question," Alex said, rubbing his chin. "And the scary one. Felicity's presence in this image could mean you're on the right path... or it could be bait. A breadcrumb on the wrong trail."

Emily let out a sigh that sounded more like defeat than relief.

"That's what's driving me nuts," she admitted. "It's like someone's playing chess in a room full of mirrors. Every time I think I've found the next move, the board shifts."

Alex offered her a quiet smile. "Then we stop chasing the whole board. We start pulling on threads."

He leaned forward, placing the photo gently back on the desk.

"But for now," he said, rising from his chair, "I'll head back to NSA. I just wanted to make a proper acquaintance, shake hands before we start breaking rules together."

He extended a hand, and Emily, despite herself, shook it. His grip was firm but warm, the kind that didn't try to prove anything.

"I'll look into what we've got," he added. "And tomorrow... We'll see what unravels."

Emily smiled, tired, but it reached her eyes this time.

As Alex turned to leave, he paused at the door and tossed one last glance over his shoulder.

"Oh—and Parker?"

"Yeah?" Emily answered.

"I bring my own flashlight. But I don't mind following yours."

The door clicked shut behind him.

Emily stood there for a moment, staring at the photo, wondering how a single image could contain so much weight—and how, somehow, a man with a grin and a metaphor just made the path feel a little less dark.

THE COBRAS ON THE HILL

"As we journey through life, the illusion of control fades into a delicate dance between reason and chaos—where the quest itself unveils the hidden truths behind our need for certainty."

I never thought I'd say this—especially not from the eerie comfort of a ghost's perspective—but if there was ever a soul who could make chaos look like a symphony, it was her. In a world infested with underworld parasites, where corporations fed off governments and shadowy syndicates wore neckties at charity galas, one name floated through smoke-filled backrooms like a ghost in silk: The Weaver.

Dramatic? Maybe. Accurate? Entirely.

Even the pronunciation carried weight; whispers of it were enough to send Wall Street wolves into meditation retreats and cartel bosses into confession booths. But behind that alias, tucked away in a vault of myth and manipulation, was a woman named Felicity Montgomery. Only a handful knew the name. Fewer survived long enough to use it.

Now, please don't confuse her for one of those leather-jacketed, loud-mouthed villains who announce their presence with a grenade and a smirk. Felicity didn't raise her voice. She didn't need to.

Her genius? She didn't play the game; she rewrote the rulebook mid-play, convinced the players they were winning, and then sold them the stadium.

Her power lay in threads, almost invisible, spun through political corridors, boardroom deals, and that quaint little café on 83rd that never seemed to have customers but always paid rent on time. She didn't force change; she nudged it like a breeze turning a hurricane the other way. And when people try to trace the storm's origin? Let's just say Felicity's fingerprints were cleaner than a priest's autobiography.

But, of course, she wasn't alone. No weaver works without a loom.

Meet Lucas—her prodigy. Hacker. Outcast. Caffeine addict with a taste for regret and all the wrong choices.

Lucas had the soul of an artist—if your idea of art was rewriting bank servers and crashing federal firewalls while making funny faces with strangers while sitting in a public area.

Felicity didn't just rescue Lucas; she rewired him. She dismantled the empire that caged him like she was untangling last year's Christmas lights—effortless and just slightly annoyed.

"Work for me," she'd said, barely glancing at him while she leafed through a classified military file like it was a takeout menu.

"And if I say no?" he'd asked.

"You won't," she replied, sipping her tea. "Because I just erased your entire debt and gave your sister a promotion in Interpol."

He hadn't even realized she knew about his family.

But she was right. Lucas didn't say no.

And so, Lucas became her eyes and ears, her hermit with technological horns and more fiber-optic cables than the Pentagon.

Despite their oddly symbiotic partnership, Lucas knew almost nothing about Felicity. She was part savior, part captor, and part mentor.

But let's not pretend the Weaver's empire was a fortress. Every queen has her checkmate. And for this queen, his name was Agent Riley M. Jackson—a man whose middle initial stood for Murder-your-career if you crossed him—a man whose resourcefulness and ruthlessness are constantly questioned by his colleagues in the bureau.

Now, Riley? He wasn't born with a badge in his mouth. He was carved out of tragedy and scars that ran deep. As a child, he had witnessed corruption destroy his family's life—his father framed, his mother reduced to despair, all by the same system they believed in. A few years later, his mother, still folded like paper under the weight of betrayal, died of a heart attack due to depression. And Riley grew up watching their world burn without fire.

He didn't talk about it, but you could see it in the way he stared at crime scenes like he was trying to find a crack in fate's armor.

To his FBI colleagues, Riley was either a legend or a liability. He didn't play by the book—he rewrote the book using his own method and then apologized to HR with a glare.

"The Weaver's not a myth," he once muttered during a debriefing. "She's a pattern. You just have to stop looking at the explosion and study the ripple."

No one took him seriously. But the man had a gift—he could smell lies like a bloodhound with a Ph.D. And one breadcrumb at a time, he began pulling at Felicity's web.

But here's where things got... complicated.

See, she saw him first.

Not literally, but Felicity had eyes on everything. Before Riley even stepped onto the board, she already had his number, coffee order, and a heat map of his movements.

And instead of cutting him off, she... watched. Intrigued. Entertained.

He was unlike the others. Not greedy. Not loud. Not corruptible.

Felicity found herself sipping wine in her surveillance loft, watching Riley dodge bureaucracy like a dancer avoiding landmines.

"Persistent little bastard," she'd whisper with a half-smile, lounging in silk robes while Lucas grumbled through code.

"You sure you wanna keep poking him?" Lucas asked once, eyes barely leaving his screen.

"Curiosity," she replied. "And maybe... nostalgia."

"For what?"

"For when I used to believe in justice."

Lucas leaned back. "You're playing with fire."

"Darling," she purred, "I am the fire."

And that was the thing. Riley reminded her of herself—before the ambition, before the shadows, before she learned that power was the only language the world respected. She admired him. And admiration, for someone like Felicity, was dangerous. It bred softness. It bred hesitation. And in their world, those two things got you killed.

But then, something strange happened.

She started designing traps for him... softer ones. Ones he could escape from—if he was clever. Like a cat leaving a mouse just enough room to think it might survive.

And the mouse? He was getting closer. Each clue Riley found wasn't a mistake. It was a test. A breadcrumb she wanted him to find. But she couldn't quite admit why.

The truth was that Felicity hadn't felt anything real in years. The power was exhilarating, yes—but cold. Riley was warmth wrapped in thorns. He reminded her what it was like to stand for something, even if it got you shattered.

But admiration's a double-edged dagger. The closer Riley got, the more Felicity's world shook. The fortress she built to rule from became a prison she couldn't leave. Not without burning everything.

So, from my ghostly seat—unseen, unheard—I watched—a silent witness to a showdown between shadow and light.

But this wasn't just cat and mouse.

This was memory against purpose. Guilt against justice.

And love? No, not quite.

But maybe something even more dangerous: recognition.

The question now isn't whether Riley can catch her.

It's whether she wants to be caught.

And if she does... what kind of world will unravel in the wake of The Weaver's fall?

"Life brings us down different paths, but it is at their intersections that transformation takes place. These crossroads hold both possibility and uncertainty—an ambiguity that can inspire growth, yet also hinder progress."

I've got this buddy at the FBI headquarters—you know, the type who says things like, "Trust no one, but trust me." We used to catch up for lunch every now and then, usually over mediocre coffee and suspiciously dry turkey sandwiches at the café near Pennsylvania Avenue. But today? Today wasn't one of those days. Today, standing in the polished lobby of the J. Edgar Hoover Building, I could feel it—something was off.

And trust me, I hate it when my gut's right. It's like it gets smug. Starts humming the "Mission: Impossible" theme. And the worst part? It wasn't just about a hunch. I had a sneaking suspicion that the Bureau knew something... a lot of something... and I was about to be dragged into a room where everyone pretends they're not hiding things behind poker faces.

But enough about my paranoid monologue—let's rewind a bit.

Emily and Alex were the kind of government agents that made elevator rides awkward. Stylish in their own unbothered way, purposeful in their stride, and far too calm for people walking into a federal lion's den. Their heels and soles tapped rhythmically against the marble floor of the Bureau like a Morse code of impatience.

Emily adjusted her blazer as she walked beside Alex, her eyes scanning every corridor and camera like a natural. Alex, meanwhile, looked like he'd stepped off the cover of a government-sponsored fashion catalog—sharp jawline, slick suit, and that unreadable NSA smirk that said, "I know things you don't, and I still won't tell you."

They were there to see Director William Anderson—legendary hardliner, beloved bureaucratic tyrant, and the kind of man who could crush egos with a raised eyebrow. The guy had a handshake for every President since the Cold War and a photograph to prove it framed right behind his desk like trophies. His office smelled like polished oak, scorched coffee, and unresolved national security.

The Director didn't bother standing. He simply looked up from his paperwork with eyes sharper than steel reinforcements.

"Agents Parker. Carter," he said, his voice gravelly enough to be its own road. "To what do I owe the honor of the CIA and NSA crashing my day?"

Emily stepped up, her tone cool and clinical. "Director Anderson, we believe there's still credible foreign involvement tied to Senator Thornhill's assassination. We're just here to... compare notes."

That was code, of course. Government-speak for, "You're holding something, and we want a peek."

Anderson leaned back in his chair; fingers steepled like an evil mastermind on lunch break. "So, I heard. What about you, Carter? You NSA types usually play three moves ahead. Do you really think this is worth everyone's time—or are we flailing in the dark, hoping to hit a light switch?"

Alex's response was pure diplomatic smoothness. "It's early, sir. But we're confident that the right collaboration will shed light on a few shadows."

Emily, never one for theatrical buildup, cut in. "And if you have anything on Felicity Montgomery—it would help us clear the fog fast."

That name—Montgomery—did something. The Director's eyebrow twitched. Just a flicker. But in this place, that was the equivalent of a spit take.

"You're digging deeper than I expected," Anderson muttered. Then he picked up his desk phone and dialed an extension. "Agent Jackson. Get in here."

The phone was barely down before the door opened. Enter Riley Jackson.

If Anderson was the stone, Riley was the sharp edge. Mid-forties coiled like a spring, with that permanent Bureau scowl like someone had stolen his parking spot every morning for three years straight. He looked at Emily and Alex like two people who'd brought their own chairs to his poker table.

"Riley," Anderson said, barely glancing up. "Meet Agent Emily Parker, CIA. And Agent Alex Carter, NSA. They're here to collaborate on the Thornhill case."

Riley folded his arms, unimpressed. "Collaborate? Since when does the CIA or NSA handle domestic murders? You folks usually show up only when there's a satellite involved, or something blows up overseas."

Emily didn't flinch. "You're right. But this case is starting to smell like imported trouble. We figured it's worth sharing our ingredients before the stew boils over."

Riley tilted his head, one skeptical eyebrow practically forming its own question mark. "And you think we can't handle this on our own?"

Before Emily could fire back, Anderson waved a dismissive hand. "Riley, don't puff your chest. If they've got intel that connects the dots, it'd be stupid not to listen."

There was a pause. Riley sighed—the dramatic kind. "Alright. You've got me—for now."

Over the next ten minutes, Emily and Alex unpacked their case files like mental ninjas—name-dropping shadow organizations, presenting photographs that looked like they came out of spy novels, and detailing Felicity Montgomery's globe-hopping mischief. Every sentence chipped away at Riley's skepticism like a jackhammer on concrete.

Finally, Riley leaned back and rubbed his jaw. "Well, damn. This is a first. Never thought I'd say this, but the CIA actually showed up with more than smoke and mirrors. No offense."

"None taken," Emily said, her expression unreadable. "We like to be underestimated."

Riley chuckled softly—a breakthrough. "I guess I owe you both a less grumpy version of myself. Consider that my professional apology."

Alex smirked. "Does it come with coffee? Because I've heard the Bureau's is better than ours."

"Barely," Riley muttered. "But I know a vending machine that owes me a favor."

They laughed.

Anderson stood up—discussion over. "Riley, take them to your office. Share what needs sharing. I want every piece of this jigsaw on the same table. Understood?"

"Yes, sir," Riley replied, already motioning for Emily and Alex to follow.

As they walked out, Alex leaned close to Emily and whispered, "That wasn't as painful as I thought."

Emily stifled a laugh. "Please. Speak for yourself. Cos from where I sat, Riley was one arched eyebrow away from having us escorted out by men with earpieces and no sense of humor."

Alex grinned. "Nah. He secretly loves my charm."

"Your charm?" Emily deadpanned, eyeing Riley's retreating. "I think he only thawed because you called his favorite pen 'tactically elegant.'"

"Hey," Alex whispered back as Riley gestured impatiently down the hall, "flattery works. Even on humans who file their emotions in triplicate."

"Or maybe it was the flash drive full of darts," she replied.

Their banter bounced softly down the hallway as Riley led them toward his office.

Riley glanced over his shoulder, scowling—but it lacked heat. "You two done with the secret society meeting? My desk's this way. Try not to touch anything that beeps."

Emily shot Alex a look. "See? Practically family."

Emily sank into the chair opposite Riley's desk, its cracked leather sighing like a tired informant. Alex mirrored her, eyeing the landscape of chaos: file folders stacked like Jenga towers, while a massive pinboard loomed behind Riley, bristling with strings, photos, and the cold architecture of organized crime. A single steaming mug sat untouched beside a notepad scribbled with half-legible thoughts. Practically, it was a cluttered yet functional space that smelled faintly of stale coffee and determination.

Riley leaned back in his chair, the faux leather creaking beneath his weight. His fingers tapped out a nervous rhythm on the desk—steady, controlled, but telling.

"You're right," he finally said, his voice low, the tone somewhere between reluctant acknowledgment and resigned defeat.

Emily and Alex exchanged a subtle glance—interest piqued. And they both leaned forward in unison—two predators catching a scent.

"So," Emily said carefully, her voice professional but laced with an edge, "what can you tell us about her—Felicity Montgomery?"

Riley exhaled, and the air in the room seemed to shift. "Do I mind sharing? Of course, I do mind. It's an ongoing investigation. But..." He paused, then leaned forward slightly, lowering his voice like he was about to break a sacred code. "Her once-formidable network? It's splintering. Quietly, but surely. People are starting to doubt her."

Alex raised an eyebrow, leaning forward. "Why now? What's changed? Internal rift? New player muscling in?"

"That's the million-dollar question," Riley replied, his jaw tightening. "Power struggles aren't new in her orbit. But this... this feels different. It's like watching a glacier calve. Slow, inevitable, and loud. Felicity's still standing, mind you. But she's clutching the railing."

Emily watched him closely. A muscle twitched near his jaw when he said Felicity's name. Protection? History? Or just indigestion from that coffee? She filed it away.

Riley shook it off, grabbed his mug, took a grimacing sip, and slammed it down. "Point is: we hit one of her main arteries last week. Robert Turner—she trusted him with the finances. Legit on paper, but the guy was laundering billions. Shipping ports, shell corporations, hidden crypto accounts—you name it."

Emily's brow furrowed. "Turner? The philanthropist business guy?"

"The very same," Riley said, a bitter smile forming. "Played the public like a maestro. But we trailed the cash long enough to find where it sang. When we made the arrest, he tried to perform—full boardroom arrogance. But we came with a surprise card up our sleeve."

Alex tilted his head. "How'd you bag a ghost like that?"

"Let's just say," Riley said, a glint in his eye, "someone close to Turner had a grudge and a conscience. That made all the difference."

Emily leaned in, sharp and surgical. "And Turner? Did he roll on Felicity?"

Riley's jaw clenched. "Not a damn word. We've pressed, prodded, even offered a deal he'd have been a fool to pass up. Still nothing. If anything, it tells us she's still got her hooks in him—or he's more afraid of her than us."

Alex exhaled, his frustration audible. "So even as she's losing ground, she's still untouchable."

"For now," Riley said grimly. "But she's bleeding influence, and the silence around her is getting thinner. We'll find a crack wide enough to get through soon."

Alex nodded thoughtfully. "Then maybe it's time to focus on the cracks—drive wedges where her grip is slipping. Someone out there's making a move on her. Might be smart to give them a nudge."

Riley gave a brief nod, almost impressed. "Divide and collapse." He stood, extending a hand.

Alex rose, taking it. "Appreciate the intel. Let's hope next time we're not just swapping shadows."

Riley's grip was firm, solid, and with new respect. "Next time, maybe we'll be trading wins."

Emily offered a quick smile as she and Alex turned toward the door.

As Emily and Alex stepped out of the office into the long, sterile corridor, Alex let out a low groan.

"I get the feeling Riley's holding something back. I don't know what, but it's there. Brewing."

Emily smirked without breaking stride. "Of course he is. He's FBI. Holding back is basically protocol."

"Yeah, but honestly? They were way more respectful than I expected." Alex mused, punching the elevator button. "A buddy of mine actually works in this block."

Emily stopped mid-stride, pivoting slowly. Her gaze was a scalpel. "Really? And you didn't think to mention him before we walked into Anderson's den of passive aggression? Or is your friend just another asset in your little black book of 'useful idiots'?"

Alex's laugh was sharp, devoid of warmth. "See? This is why nobody trusts you Company types. Always looking to turn friendship into a fucking flow chart. My best friend's not getting wrapped up in this mess unless it's by-the-book. And by that, I mean legally—no backdoor games."

Emily let out a dry laugh and stepped closer, the fluorescent lights catching the ice in her eyes. "I know what's behind that tailored suit and your 'aw-shucks' NSA charm, Carter. A man who despises the CIA... yet can't resist crawling through our dumpsters. Why? You hunting for dirt? Or just get off on the smell of burnt coffee and regret?"

Alex shrugged, the motion too casual. "What's intelligence work, Parker? It's sleeping with the enemy, so you're the first to feel them twitch." He yanked open the exit door.

Emily reached for the car door, pausing just enough to fire back, "You tell me. You're the ones snooping around people's digital lives."

The doors slammed shut. The engine hummed to life, but neither spoke.

The car ride back was a vacuum. Silence stretched like barbed wire between them. Emily stared out the window as D.C. blurred past—monuments to power watching them drive away.

When they finally pulled up to the CIA complex, Emily stepped out first. The cool air met her face like a slap, lifting strands of hair in the breeze. She offered a brief wave.

Alex nodded in return before peeling off, steering toward a nearby food truck like a man on a mission—to eat away frustration or maybe to stall from thinking too hard.

Inside the CIA building, Emily leaned back against the elevator wall as it hummed upward. Her reflection stared back at her—composed, unreadable, but tired. Very tired. She traced Alex's likely route home in the hot-slicked streets below.

When the doors slid open, she moved with purpose. The office was soaked in the soft afternoon light, bleeding through the windows. Her desk, like always, was chaos—a battlefield of files and sticky notes. She let her fingers brush across the top of a stack, then sat down and dove in.

Hours passed.

Evening crept in unnoticed, wrapping the city in a blanket of streetlights and shadows. Emily finally rose, gathered her things, and drove home.

The city buzzed in its nocturnal rhythm. Tires whispered against the asphalt. Streetlights flickered on cue. And in that mechanical ballet, Emily's thoughts roamed—messy, sharp, unfinished.

At her apartment, she stepped inside, dropped her bag, and paused. The warmth of home offered little comfort tonight.

Without hesitation, she grabbed her phone and dialed.

Two rings. Then Alex answered.

Emily didn't ease in. Her voice came edged with that classic Emily blend—confidence laced with faint sarcasm. "Alex, I hope I'm not catching you at a bad time. Though, admittedly, it's weird even for me."

On the other end, Alex raised an unseen eyebrow. "Which part's weirder? You calling? Or are you admitting it's weird?"

Emily smiled despite herself. "Both. But listen," Her voice hardened, "something is bugging me. I think you're right; the FBI might be working with Felicity."

Silence. Then Alex's voice, laced with humor but underscored by interest: "Whoa, slow down, Nancy Drew. Next thing you'll tell me, you found her hideout behind a revolving bookshelf. What makes you say that? Got anything besides Riley's bad poker face?"

"It's in the gaps," Emily insisted. "How they took down Turner. Too clean. Too sudden. Riley called Felicity's loyalty 'bulletproof faith.' That's not profiler talk. That's... reverence."

Alex's tone shifted just a notch more serious. "You're thinking the Feds are shielding Felicity?"

"I'm not saying all of them," Emily said. "But someone. Maybe just Riley. Maybe more."

Alex let out a slow breath. "Well, not like we were expecting him to name sources, but still—his story should have at least held water. And honestly? If they're working with Felicity behind the curtain... that wouldn't surprise me."

Emily's voice was steady now. "You'd do the same?"

"In a heartbeat," Alex replied. "If it meant collapsing a bigger threat. Okay. Say you're right. Why tell me? You think the NSA's gonna waltz into Hoover and demand their badges?"

Emily hesitated. "Because you know how they think. Their backchannels. Their blind spots."

Alex gave a low chuckle. "You really do love tossing me into live wires, huh? You know that, right?"

"I thought that's why you like rolling in the dirt with us," Emily teased.

"Huh. Bet you've been rehearsing that line ever since." Alex said, amused.

Emily leaned back on her couch, letting the weight of everything settle. "Thanks, Alex."

"Get some sleep, Nancy Drew. Tomorrow's gonna need a bigger magnifying glass."

"Goodnight, Alex."

"Night, Nancy Drew," he said before hanging up.

Emily set the phone down and stared out the window. The city lights pulsed softly in the dark. She stared at her reflection in the dark window—a woman haunted by ghosts she couldn't name. The bitter truth wasn't Riley's secrets, Felicity's reach, or even the FBI's betrayals.

It was the green snake coiled quietly in her own grass. Alex.

His skepticism was too perfect. His access too easy. His jokes too... distracting. A bitter truth stared at her all along, and she had no idea of its existence.

And tonight, the snake remained invisible.

So, the next day, as the morning sun warmed the air, the sleek, commanding structure of the CIA headquarters stood tall—an immovable reminder of the high-stakes world people like Emily and Alex moved through every day.

Pulling into the South Lobby, Alex's sharp eyes immediately caught sight of Emily standing by the entrance. The early sunlight framed her silhouette, graceful and calm against the steel and glass backdrop. Rolling down his window, Alex called out with a teasing lilt, "Hey, detective!"

Emily turned, arching a brow. A shy, almost involuntary smile broke across her face. Then, with mock seriousness, she narrowed her eyes at him—playfully, like firing imaginary bullets. Alex laughed, the sound light and familiar.

Parking his car, Alex jogged over and joined her just as they stepped into the elevator. "You know," he said with a crooked grin, "we really should stop meeting like this. HR might start drafting policies with our names on them."

Emily rolled her eyes, half scolding, half fond, fighting a smile. "Alex," she sighed the name a reprimand wrapped in velvet. Always the charm. Always the deflection.

The elevator doors closed, sealing them inside a quiet capsule of shared silence. A flicker of amusement passed between them then settled. The laughter softened, giving way to a different mood.

Then Alex's voice dropped, suddenly more grounded, losing its playboy edge. "About your call last night... Patience opens all doors. Even the ones with triple locks. Especially those." He watched her reflection."

Emily glanced at him with a tilt of her head, curiosity flaring. "Now you sound like a different person, totally different from the one I was with yesterday. No offense."

"None taken," Alex replied easily, his face unreadable.

The elevator dinged. As the doors slid open, Alex's phone buzzed. He gave her a quick gesture. "Go ahead. I'll catch up."

Emily hesitated briefly, then nodded and walked ahead, her mind already sliding into work mode.

Alex, meanwhile, turned down a quiet corridor. Pressing the phone to his ear, his voice dropped to a whisper. "It's me. I just got to Langley."

The voice on the other end was clipped and cold. "Does Emily know?"

Alex paused—barely a breath. "No. She's still in the dark. She doesn't know anything about your plan."

"Good," the voice replied. "Stay that way. One step at a time. No distractions."

"Understood," Alex said, jaw tight. The call ended. He took a moment, exhaled, and then re-entered the flow of the building, his usual easygoing demeanor sliding back into place like a mask. And so was the day's business; everything went without a glitch.

That evening, Emily returned home. Her keys jingled briefly as she entered her apartment, tossing her bag onto the couch. The quiet didn't bring peace—it only gave space for her thoughts to swirl.

Her phone buzzed—a calendar reminder: dinner with Mom.

"Shit," she murmured. She was already running late.

After a quick change of clothes and a mental reset, Emily was back on the road. The quaint restaurant where they often met felt like a pocket of familiarity—a warm bubble that the chaos of Washington couldn't quite reach. Candlelight glimmered off the glass, and the muted hum of conversation filled the space.

Her mother, Eleanor, smiled as Emily arrived. "There she is," she said with mock exasperation. "I was about to send a search party."

Emily smiled, apologetic. "Long day."

Dinner passed with the rhythm of habit. Eleanor chatted about old neighbors, local events, and the usual family drama. Emily nodded, added the occasional quip, and laughed where it mattered—but her eyes drifted often. Pieces of the day played again in her mind. The phone call. Alex's cryptic demeanor. The puzzle has too many missing edges.

When dinner was over, walking back to the car, Eleanor slowed her steps. "Sweetheart... are you okay? You've seemed a bit far away tonight."

Emily paused. There it was—the opening. But the truth felt too heavy to put into words. "I'm okay, Mom. Just... tired. Nothing new."

Eleanor stopped and turned, taking Emily's hand in both of hers. "You've always been strong, Emily. But even the strongest people need to lean sometimes." Her voice was gentle, unwavering. "You don't have to hide the storm from the lighthouse, sweetheart."

The kindness in her tone cut through the fog. Emily nodded, her throat tight. "Thanks, Mom."

They embraced under the soft hum of parking lot lights. "Goodnight, sweetheart."

"Goodnight, Mom."

As Eleanor drove off, Emily stood for a moment, letting the cool night air wrap around her. One thing was clear: she was in a dark hole, and no one at that point knew just how deep the rabbit hole went. But the bond with her mother remained a grounding force—one of the few lights in the shadowed corners of her life.

"When the web of loyalties and deceptions tightens around oneself, the labyrinth of choices unfolds, revealing the delicate balance between trust and betrayal, where every step echoes the heartbeat of destiny."

Before Emily's suspicion of Riley ever took root—long before her brows furrowed during that oddly timed FBI memo—I had my eyes on him. Actually, to say eyes might be a bit much. "All senses with no voice" might be more accurate. That's the curse of being a ghost in the system. You see, you observe, you document—but you don't get to shout, "Hey, this guy's shadier than a politician at a lie detector convention!" Nope. You just watch. Quietly.

Still, if there was even a fleeting thought in my mind about cutting Riley some slack, Emily's expression earlier tonight—to her own mother, no less—yanked me right back into focus. She's got that twitchy intuition that makes you want to believe in cosmic alignment and gut feelings. And if Emily's gut is throwing red flags like confetti, then you better believe I'm following up.

So, as she enjoyed steak and soft candlelight with her mom—laughing like the world wasn't about to implode—I slipped away. Destination: Riley's place.

Now, Riley's home isn't the sort of fortress you'd expect from a man who plays cloak-and-dagger between his nine-to-five. It's... cozy. Respectable. A little too respectable. The kind of place where deception wears house slippers and a cardigan.

As I entered, I was greeted by the earthy scent of pinewood and something unmistakably Riley: that ridiculous, overpriced cologne he's convinced makes him smell like James Bond when it really just screams "Department Store Counter, Aisle 3." Still, it added a personal touch. Human. Comforting. Normal. Too normal.

I moved quickly—planted a few more hidden surveillance cams in nooks even he wouldn't check unless he developed OCD overnight. These were state-of-the-art devices, capable of capturing even the slightest movement or sound. Just as I was screwing in the last micro feed behind a bookshelf full of unread Hemingway and meaningless decorative globes, the garage door rolled down with a familiar whump. Riley was home.

Cue: panic.

As I watched him, a mix of pity and anger surged within me. How could he be so blind? How could he not see the danger he was in? I bolted—smooth but hasty—slipping out through the living room like a bad date after meeting the kids. By the time Riley was unlocking his door, I was already in my car, tablet in hand, monitoring the feeds like a true professional creep.

The screen flickered on.

There he was.

Riley stepped into the kitchen like a man entering his only sanctuary, where the masks could drop, and nobody was watching—well, except me, but details. His kitchen was adorably cluttered as if it belonged to someone who could make lasagna but never finish it. Magnets clung to his fridge in the shape of safari animals. A half-dead fruit basket sat on the counter like a patient on life support.

He reached for a bottle of Merlot—vintage unknown, the price probably tragic—and poured himself a glass. He didn't even taste it. Just swirled. Like it might tell him his future.

For a moment, Riley looked like any tired man. Worn out. Haunted. Trying not to be. His phone buzzed in his pocket. He stared at it like it might accuse him of something. And then, as if yanked by a string from the past, he dialed a number.

A woman answered. Smooth, dry, and undeniably familiar.

"Riley, don't tell me you're calling to discuss centerpieces."

He chuckled, low and real. Not the forced kind he used at staff briefings. "Actually, I was going to critique your taste in table linens, but... figured I'd ask about our daughter first."

There it was. A shared smirk across a history only exes understand. They talked about their daughter—her upcoming wedding, her strange obsession with orchids, her fiancé's laughable fear of dogs. And for just a moment, Riley seemed human. Not the Agent. Not the spy. Just a dad trying to hold onto something pure.

But that moment passed.

As soon as the call ended, the weight returned. You could almost see it. Like an invisible jacket full of bricks. He leaned against the counter, thumb hovering over his contacts, hesitating. Then his phone rang.

Riley straightened like he'd just been caught doing something unspeakable. He answered, voice lowered to that velvet tone men use when they're hoping it doesn't sound like they care too much.

"Yeah... was just about to call you. Thought the time might not be... ideal."

The voice that replied was sultry, calm, and clear—Felicity.

"You should've called, Riley. You know I always pick up for you. Now tell me—what's going on with the boys?"

Her tone was breezy, too breezy. The kind of breezy that makes you double-check your locks.

Riley didn't waste time.

"The CIA and NSA—they've put you at the top of their list. You're glowing on their radar, Felicity. They're not playing anymore."

A pause.

Then her voice, soft but razor-sharp: "Thank you. Clearly, my good hand of fate isn't enough to bribe my way off their witch hunt."

Riley exhaled hard. "I don't even know how that's possible. Your role in the Turner case is still classified."

Felicity's reply? Cool as ever.

"Isn't that right?"

Silence. Then, Riley again, gentler: "Don't worry. I'm still looking for a way to buy you time. Lay low. Feed them crumbs. It'll work out."

"Thank you, Riley," she said again   and hung up.

No drama. No begging. Just... thank you. And silence.

I watched Riley from my feed, frozen in his kitchen. He didn't move. He didn't speak. Just stood there like a man trying to figure out which part of himself was still allowed to feel.

His face was unreadable but not empty. That kind of stillness comes from noise so loud inside your head that you can't even flinch.

Guilt? Maybe.

Frustration? Probably.

Love?

...Possibly.

He poured another glass of wine but didn't drink it. Just stood there, staring into the dark outside the kitchen window, where the real world waited—unforgiving, untamed.

He was torn, no doubt. Logic versus heart. The eternal bloodsport. His instinct told him to protect Felicity, to be her unseen armor. But his career? His family? His oath? All of that dangled over him like an axe made of paperwork and ruined futures.

Was he betraying justice for loyalty? Or was justice already compromised?

That was the kind of question Riley had to live with.

And I? I just watched. Quietly. Silently.

A ghost in his life.

"An undeniable force, woven into the very fabric of our being. While reason acknowledges the biological drive rooted in our genetic makeup, the desire for physical connection transcends logical boundaries, navigating the complex intricacies of the mind and societal norms. A delicate balance where reason and sentiment converge to weigh the intensity of longing against the moral principles shaping our choices. A profound exploration, pushing the limits of reasoning as the complexities of its consent are purely based on a slippery slab of communication and emotional connection. Sexual gratification: the fusion of our primal instincts and the complexities of irrational thoughts."

While some people pretend to have had it all figured out, believe me—everyone has demons. Even those who walk around with their polished smiles and clean suits are often the ones wrestling the darkest battles in silence. Emily was following her instincts, Riley was walking a moral tightrope—but Alex? He didn't even smell the storm brewing, or at least not the one he thought of.

As his driveway glistened with the remnants of early evening rain, Alex parked his car, telling himself that this—this wet pavement—was the only thing tonight he couldn't control. But deep down, even that was a lie.

Save for the faint hum of crickets and the occasional swoosh of a passing car, his neighborhood on 24th Street Avenue Lane was quiet, peaceful even, like a postcard. But the stillness only made the storm inside him feel louder. He grabbed his office bag, walked up to the door, and braced himself. Not for gunfire, not for surveillance threats—for something far more unpredictable: the growing silence between him and Erin.

The door creaked open. Lavender-scented candles flickered in the living room, casting a warm hue. Erin sat on the couch, legs folded beneath her, eyes fixed on a dramatic TV show. Her mug sat empty beside her—a quiet witness to the kind of evening she'd had.

He leaned down and kissed her cheek. "Hey," he said softly, hopeful.

She didn't look at him. "Hey," came the flat reply.

Dropping his bag, he sank into a nearby armchair. "What are we watching tonight?"

Erin didn't answer right away. Then, without shifting her gaze, she asked, her tone deceptively breezy. "How was it out there?" She might as well have asked, "How was your secret lair?"

"Same old, same mess, same shit," Alex deflected, forcing lightness. "Just different clowns."

She nodded, but the curve of her lips wasn't a smile—it was a warning. Alex knew that expression well. It meant she was thinking, calculating, and deciding what not to say.

"I know that tone, Erin," Alex said, trying to nudge her. "What's going on?"

Click. The TV froze mid-drama, plunging the room into a silence so profound Alex could hear his own heartbeat hammering against his ribs. For a suspended moment, he thought this was it. He thought she might finally ask him outright—about the secrets, the hushed phone calls in the garage, the strange absences, the subtle lies. But instead, she just shook her head and pressed play again.

Alex sighed. The tension was unbearable. The gap between them had become a canyon. He didn't know she'd followed him a few times, only to watch him vanish like smoke in a breeze. And he didn't know how long she'd been keeping that pain locked inside.

Trying to shift the mood, he fumbled for the one tool that sometimes bridged the gap: them. Or at least the physical echo of 'them.' He leaned forward again, his voice dropping to a low, teasing rasp, aiming for charming rogue, probably landing closer to an awkward penguin.

"You know," he murmured, "Nothing resets the existential dread like a properly scalding shower. And I happen to know a guy with magic hands..." He wiggled his fingers suggestively. "Care to test the warranty? Strictly for therapeutic purposes, of course." He stood halfway, gesturing toward the hallway.

Erin's head snapped around. Her glare could have frozen the rain outside. "Don't," she warned, sharp as shattered glass. But Alex, a seasoned navigator of Erin's storms, saw it—the faintest flicker in her eyes, a tiny crack in the ice. Anger, yes, but underneath? A longing for the before. For the man who didn't make her feel like a detective in her own life.

He pushed, gently persistent. "Oh, come on, Steam, Hot water, a little reconnection... Maybe... remembering why we do this crazy thing?" He stood, offering a hand that wasn't quite steady. "C'mon, baby girl. Let me...

just be here. With you." He took a few steps towards the hallway, then paused, looking back, a question mark in human form.

Erin held her gaze; anger warred with exhaustion, suspicion with the desperate need not to feel this chasm, "You think this solves the problem?"

"No," he replied quietly. "But maybe it helps us remember what's worth solving."

Slowly, deliberately, she picked up the remote. Click. Then she stood slowly, "Fine." Her tone was reluctant, but her gaze lingered on him in a way that told a different story, and her body spoke volumes. The deliberate sway of her hips as she walked past him towards the bathroom wasn't just seduction; it was a challenge. A dare. Fix this.

Alex followed, the mischievous glint in his eye now edged with relief and a heavy dose of apprehension.

As they stepped under the soft cascade of warm water, their closeness began to chip away the silence, and the rest of the world started to fade away. Alex let his hands move gently across Erin's back and shoulders, every motion an apology he couldn't speak. She leaned into him, breathing him in, letting herself believe—for just a moment—that maybe things could still be saved.

Erin closed her eyes, letting the water and his touch melt away her anger. Their silence turned to smile, and they began kissing, their glances deeper, something primal; heartbeats began racing very high, and so were the veins in their body filled with erotic rush. Erin clung to the shower pole, her body shaking like a leaf as Alex began reaching and triggering her sexual blossom while revealing an image that goes against societal norms. The showerhead continued unleashing a water waterfall, drenching them like a summer storm; their bodies radiated warmth as their hearts continued to race in an exhilarating frenzy. Erin moaned as Alex's penetration into her bosom continued to create indescribable hot friction inside her sweet spot, soaked and wet. As someone who was experiencing an out-of-body thrill that was taking both of them to climax in a few minutes, Erin opened her mouth as she tried to catch her breath, her voice mesmerized, and her breasts moving in a synchronized form, like a silky pudding, with its seductive nipples standing like fingertips.

After a pleasurable few minutes, the steam cleared, and reality seeped back in with the dripping faucet. Wrapped in each other's skin, Erin rested her head against Alex's chest, her fingers drawing small circles on his arm. The steady thump of his heart beneath her ear was a lullaby and an accusation wrapped in one.

It wasn't about sex, I may say; it was about remembering that before the lies, before the nights filled with distance, they had something real.

"Alex," she murmured, vulnerable now, "I just want to know you're not slipping away from me."

He hesitated, the words caught in his throat. How could he reassure Erin when every detail of his double life would only deepen the rift between them?

"I'm here," he whispered, brushing a strand of hair from her face and his lips across her forehead. But the words rang hollow, a lie wrapped in tenderness. And even he could hear the hollowness in his own voice.

Erin nodded slowly as she looked up, not fully convinced—but not ready to fight. Not tonight. Offering a small, sleepy smile, it felt as if the afterglow momentarily blunted the sharp edges of her earlier anger. Peace. Or a convincing imitation. Only Erin could say.

And Alex? He held her close, but his heart was nowhere near calm. The double life he lived was growing heavier by the day. As they stood in the fading warmth of that shower, both of them knew deep down—that this wasn't a resolution.

Erin's questions were sleeping, not gone. One day, she would wake them, sharp and demanding. And when that day came... Alex tightened his hold, burying his face in her hair, inhaling the scent of clean skin and impending loss. He knew, with a chilling certainty, that this intimacy, this beautiful, desperate tangle under the warm water, wasn't a solution. It was a delay. A breathtaking, heart-rending, utterly necessary delay. The calm before a storm he himself had brewed.

CHAPTER

3

Unsnarling The Threads

"Healing and growth often begin with acknowledging what we fear. By confronting darkness, we open the door to understanding and transformation."

I've traipsed across continents, wandered through cities that never sleep, sipped espresso in piazzas, and haggled in bazaars, deserts that keep secrets, and alleyways so crooked they whisper lies. But nothing slices through the soul like a Wine Lake morning. So when I say the morning sun unfurls its golden banners over Wine Lake County, trust me—it's not poetic fluff. It's real. It's the kind of morning that looks like God woke up early, stretched, and said, "Let's give the world a little masterpiece today."

You could smell it in the air—the earthy perfume of dew clinging to pine needles, the faint hint of chimney smoke from breakfast fires, and that rustic sweetness only a countryside morning can deliver. The sky was a watercolor painting of lavender, amber, and hope. Honestly, it made you want to sit on a porch swing and confess your sins just to feel lighter in the glow.

Wine Lake wasn't just a place. It was therapy wrapped in flannel and maple syrup. A place where even ghosts like me—those of us who move in silence, tuck secrets into our pockets, and disappear when the city lights get too loud—could feel... seen. And yeah, maybe my kind of ghost likes pancakes. Sue me.

If Heaven ever rented out weekend cabins, it would look like Wine Lake. It had everything—chirping finches, porch rockers older than the Constitution, and gossip that traveled faster than broadband. The town was a patchwork of sleepy hamlets and winding trails that wrapped around Emily like a grandmother's quilt—familiar, warm, and sometimes a little itchy with memories, but always peaceful.

Emily had roots here. Deep ones. The kind of roots that refused to be pulled up, no matter how many times life tried to yank her away. To her,

Wine Lake wasn't just a hometown. It was a sanctuary. A reset button in a world that never stopped spinning. After weeks of dodging shadows and navigating the tightrope of espionage, she'd always return. Like clockwork. Like migration. Like need.

And that weekend? Let's just say the stars decided to stir the pot.

Her brother, Billy, came to town.

Now, Billy wasn't just any sibling. He was the kind of golden boy who made mothers weep at graduation, and neighbors pretend they'd always believed in him. Big-city attorney, courtroom gladiator, the type of man who used words like "litigation" in casual conversation. He even had that faint cologne smell of success and arrogance blended into one high-end bottle.

He'd brought the whole Parker clan with him—his wife, his three miniature tornadoes – sorry, their three kids, and a nanny who looked more stressed than a bomb technician at a fireworks show. The Parker house, usually a quiet cabin tucked between two lazy hills, now buzzed with tiny feet and mysterious stains, punctuated by the occasional heart-stopping crash of something irreplaceable that sent Emily flinching from muscle memory.

"I swear, if one more vase falls victim to their Nerf war, I'm invoicing Billy's firm," Emily muttered, stepping over a Lego minefield in the hallway.

Breakfast the next morning was a scene straight out of a sitcom. Billy at the head of the table, looking like he was about to cross-examine the bacon; the kids fencing with forks over pancake slices; Emily, somewhere in the chaos, holding a coffee mug like it was a life preserver.

"You know, Em," Billy began, fork halfway to his mouth, "you'd be a brilliant addition to Parker & Associates. You've got the brains, the charm. Why waste it playing detective?"

Emily took a slow sip of coffee, her face unreadable. "The complete lack of interest helps, actually."

Billy grinned, undeterred. "One day, you'll wake up, realize adventure doesn't pay a pension, and come begging for a corner office."

"Maybe," Emily shrugged. "But today's not that day. Also, corner offices don't come with stunt doubles, so I'll pass."

The kids shrieked with laughter as one of them poured syrup with reckless abandon, and for a few fleeting minutes, the morning was perfect.

But Billy, as always, couldn't resist holding court.

"So, get this," he said, leaning in like a man about to reveal the plot twist in a legal thriller. "My latest client—Robert Turner. Poor guy. Being framed. Total set-up job."

Emily didn't freeze. Spies don't freeze. But the name Robert Turner hit her nervous system like a live wire. Turner. As in Felicity Syndicate Kingpin Turner. As in, "Feds just bagged him after a five-year manhunt" Turner. Her brother wasn't just defending a criminal; he was polishing the crown jewels of the FBI's Most Wanted list.

"Robert Turner?" she echoed, her tone breezy but her heart skipping a beat.

"Yeah. The guy's in deep. Someone's trying to bury him. And not gently, if you know what I mean. But I think I've got a case for wrongful prosecution brewing here."

She took a deliberate bite, chewing slowly, the crunch absurdly loud in the sudden silence of her own mind. Oh, Billy. You magnificent, clueless peacock. You're giving legal aid to a shark who eats guys like you for brunch.

If irony were a person, it would've pulled up a chair right then and passed Emily the syrup.

She leaned back and studied her brother. He is still so sure of himself while unknowingly stepping into minefields.

"Sounds... complicated," Emily managed, her voice impressively flat, like the surface of the lake at dawn.

"Complicated?" Billy laughed. "Em, this is the big leagues. High-stakes, white-knuckle, career-defining drama. The pinnacle! This is what I live for! The man's practically Shakespearean in his misfortune."

"Sounds absolutely... thrilling," Emily murmured, her gaze drifting to the window where sunlight gilded the pines. Thrilling like a live grenade rolling into a nursery.

Her jaw clenched, emotions warring like sparring partners. Part of her wanted to scream, to drag Billy out of the mess he didn't even know he'd stepped into. Another part knew the rules. Secrets like hers weren't whispered over pancakes.

But she could warn him. Gently.

"Bill," she said, cutting through his self-congratulatory monologue, "Be careful with this one, okay?" she said, setting down her mug. Her tone was quiet, serious enough to make him pause mid-sip of orange juice.

Billy raised an eyebrow. "Careful? I wrestle alligators for a living. This is Tuesday. Not to mention, I've been doing this a long time, Em."

"I know," she pressed, holding his gaze. "But still, sometimes, the swamp is deeper than it looks. Just... tread lightly, big brother. Not everything is what it seems."

He chuckled, brushing her concern off like lint from a blazer. "You worry too much."

She smiled, but her eyes didn't.

Because Emily knew better about the world she lived in, her brother's obliviousness could get him killed, and names like Robert Turner didn't show up by accident. The rabbit hole she found herself navigating had just gotten personal. And for the first time in a long time, the danger wasn't somewhere out there. It was at the breakfast table. She may not have seen it, but I will bet on that.

CHARLES E.A.

"The richness of life emerges from the interplay of chance and destiny. Together, they weave the fabric of possibility that shapes our journey."

Let me tell you something about Richard R. Suggs—the man whose charm has a personality of its own. If you ever stood next to him at a party, you'd swear the room dimmed just to give his smile better lighting. And as someone who's spent years dodging bullets, decoding encrypted messages, and barely keeping up with people like him, it's humbling—borderline insulting—how effortlessly he fits in anywhere. Meanwhile, I'm still the guy trying to figure out which fork to use at a fancy dinner.

Don't get me wrong, Richard and I? We've been through hell together. Missions that could have ended both of us. Metaphorically and nearly literally, He's saved my neck more times than I care to admit. And ever since he made Assistant Director of the FBI, we've been catching up more often, sharing old war stories and cheap whiskey like nothing's changed. But after our last conversation, I started to feel a chill—the kind of chill that doesn't come from bad air-conditioning. Our friendship? It's officially walking a tightrope.

And the whole damn mess started in Walmart. Yeah. Walmart. The holy cathedral of budget groceries and suspiciously discounted electronics.

That day, the store had that hum—the one you only notice when you're trying really hard not to notice anything. A soft buzz from the fluorescent lights, the muffled chaos of distant arguments over coupons, and the mechanical squeals of shopping carts that had clearly seen some things.

Richard, the man of the hour, walked in with all the casual confidence of a guy who reads The Economist for fun. His shirt was crisp, his jeans had that "intentionally casual but ironed to perfection" look, and his glasses caught the cold white lights above, giving him the intellectual aura of a Harvard professor who moonlights as a chess assassin. Most people probably saw just another guy shopping for pasta sauce. But if you watched closely—like I have for years—you'd see it: a calm intensity, like his mind was three steps ahead, even in the condiment aisle.

It was in the jelly and jam section that destiny decided to play matchmaker—or prankster.

From the next aisle came the unmistakable sound of human struggle. Not the life-or-death kind we're used to in our world, but the kind that makes you pause: the reach, the tiptoe, the exasperated sigh of someone an inch too short for modern shelving design.

Richard turned the corner, and there she was.

A woman. Not just any woman. Tall-ish, yes, but not tall enough. She was stretching—arms fully extended, the tips of her fingers swiping at a stubborn jar of strawberry jam like it was a golden trophy just out of reach. Her raven-black hair flowed down her back like a silk curtain, and under those lights, it shimmered with every tiny motion she made.

She didn't call out. Didn't huff in frustration. Just kept at it with quiet, determined dignity, like asking for help would be admitting defeat in some unspoken battle of wills against the shelf.

Richard, being Richard, did what Richard did. His smile, when it came, was a rare, genuine thing, softening the analytical edges of his face. "Allow me?" His voice was smooth bourbon, unhurried. One long arm extended, plucking the jar down with insulting ease before she could reply.

She turned, startled—then relieved—and smiled the kind of smile that makes toothpaste commercials look like they're not trying hard enough. Her cheeks flushed with just the right hint of embarrassment. Their eyes met—his, calm and confident; hers, sparkly and curious.

"Thank you," she said, her voice like warm caramel: smooth, sweet, with a little weight to it.

He handed her the jar with a slight grin, already loading a quip in the chamber.

She took the jar, her fingers brushing his for a fleeting, electric second.

Of course, my friend Richard couldn't resist, "You know," he said, tilting his head, "you could've just asked someone instead of attempting to scale the shelves like Spider-Woman." He mimed her stretch with theatrical, hopeless flailing.

She burst into laughter. Not the forced kind you give a stranger who says something halfway amusing. No, this was real—a laugh that bubbled up from somewhere honest, spilling out with the ease of someone who hadn't laughed like that in a while.

That's when he knew he was in trouble.

"Marilyn," she said, introducing herself a few moments later after their laughter had settled into a comfortable silence.

Richard raised an eyebrow. "Marilyn, as in... Monroe?" he teased.

"More like 'Marilyn, as in I'm just trying to buy jam without causing a scene," she shot back, her voice laced with dry humor.

They talked. Easy conversation. No forced small talk. No awkward silences. Like they'd known each other before in some alternate life. At one point, Richard glanced toward the large glass windows near checkout and nodded toward a high-rise visible in the distance.

"I live over there," he said. "Twenty-sixth floor. Been there for about three years now."

Marilyn's eyes sparkled again. "Really?" she said, tilting her head like she was inspecting a new piece of information that delighted her. "Hmm. My tenant."

Richard blinked. "Your what?"

She shrugged innocently. "You never know," she replied with a sly smile.

Now, this is where I—his friend—start to feel the shift. Because Richard, the guy who can smell a lie in a five-mile radius, didn't question her. Didn't press. Just laughed and moved on.

But here's what he didn't know: Marilyn wasn't joking. Her family didn't just own that Walmart. They owned the whole damn condo complex he lived in. And she—jam-reacher, aisle-warrior, laugh-like-a-summer-song Marilyn—had known exactly who he was before he ever opened his mouth.

They parted ways after some more laughs and a subtle promise in their parting smiles. Nothing concrete. Just that fuzzy, unfinished feeling that you know is going to show up again sooner or later.

As Marilyn walked away, jar in a tote bag, Richard watched her like a man who'd just walked into something bigger than he could explain.

The street outside was quiet, almost too obedient for an afternoon. Marilyn maneuvered her sleek white sedan with the casual elegance of someone who had long mastered the art of gliding through life with style. The tote bag on the passenger seat made a soft crunch each time she turned, like a subtle reminder that, yes, she had technically gone out for groceries. But in reality, her mind wasn't on almond milk or organic peanut butter. It was on him—the man in glasses.

Her thoughts were tangled up in laughter—his laughter, to be precise. Deep, unfiltered, the kind that bubbles up from the chest and makes you feel like the world just got a little funnier, a little warmer.

When she pulled into the circular driveway of her parent's estate—a grand, elegant structure that looked like it had opinions about modern architecture—her face still tingled from memory. Autumn leaves crunched beneath her heels as she stepped out, the scent of warm cedar and roasted oak wafting through the air like nature's way of saying welcome home, darling.

Inside, the house wrapped around her like a silk scarf. Polished wood, high ceilings, and soft golden lighting gave it the sort of elegance that whispered rather than shouted. The only thing louder than the silence was the rustle of her tote bag as she set it on the kitchen counter, her lips curling into a knowing smile.

Then came the voice.

"Marilyn, is that you?"

Her mother's tone always had a precise blend of regal warmth and judgment, like someone who could hug you and critique your lipstick at the same time.

"Yes, Mom," Marilyn called, in the sing-song tone of someone ready for a mild interrogation.

"You took forever at the store. Did you get everything?"

Marilyn paused, her fingers brushing the top of the jam jar. She laughed softly to herself.

"Not everything," she said with a sly little grin. "But I found something I didn't expect."

That was the kind of line you drop when you want your mother to ask more questions, but you pretend you don't.

And right on cue, enter Mrs Diane, Marilyn's mother. Silver-streaked hair in a bun that looked like it had been styled by a Parisian ghost, a silk robe that fluttered as if it had mood swings and eyes that had scanned resumes, boyfriends, and soul intentions alike.

Her eyebrow went up before she even stepped into the kitchen. "I tried to give you your space," she began, crossing her arms, "but with all that humming and mysterious smiling? I mean, Marilyn, I thought maybe you'd walked into a jazz club instead of Walmart."

Marilyn laughed—a real, head-tilted-back, hands-on-the-counter kind of laugh.

"Mama! One question at a time! You're sounding like CNN breaking news."

Diane chuckled, pouring herself a cup of her daily Chinese herbal tea, which—by family legend—could cure anything from heartbreak to bad financial decisions. The steam curled into the air like a mischievous spirit ready to eavesdrop.

"Well," she said, carefully setting the delicate porcelain cup down, "What's the story? Out with it."

Marilyn folded her arms and leaned back like a movie heroine about to deliver the opening act of a love story.

"I met someone," she said, voice hushed with excitement. "An African American man. Tall, wore glasses. Kind eyes. Didn't recognize me—which was so refreshing."

Diane's eyebrow made another majestic appearance.

"Didn't recognize you?" she asked, as though that were a minor felony.

"He thought I was just another girl struggling to reach a jam jar. And Mama, he mocked me—right there in Aisle Nine! He did this little hop with his arms like he was conducting a symphony of short people. It was... it was hilarious."

Diane smirked. "So now you're into comedians with vision problems."

"Mama," Marilyn said, playfully rolling her eyes, "it wasn't what he said. It was how he made me feel like I wasn't a walking LinkedIn profile. Like I didn't need to prove I'd gone to Yale or led three charities."

Diane sipped her tea thoughtfully. "You're sure he wasn't flirting?"

"Nope," Marilyn said. "That's the part that gets me. He didn't try. He just was. Honest. Real. Funny. And that smile? God, Mama, it's the kind of smile you'd follow into a tornado and thank it for the ride."

There was a pause, the air humming with both laughter and quiet contemplation. Then Diane asked the question—not intrusive, but gentle.

"And where does this 'man in glasses' live?"

Marilyn leans in conspiratorially. "Our condo complex. 26th floor. Facing the new Walmart."

A faint flicker crossed Diane's face. Not disapproval, not quite concern—just something unspoken. She picked up her teacup and stirred it with a silver spoon that clinked once, twice, then stilled.

"You said... African American?"

Marilyn nodded slowly. "Yes."

Silence.

Then Diane shrugged ever so slightly. "I only ask because... well, it's important to be curious about people. You never know what their stories hold."

Marilyn looked at her mother with new eyes—both grateful for her openness and aware of the undercurrent. It wasn't judgment. It was caution wrapped in maternal instinct.

Diane set her cup down, eyes now distant.

"These moments... they're beautiful," she said, almost to herself. "But fleeting. And sometimes, fleeting is enough."

Marilyn smiled. Not sarcastic. Not defiant. Just... certain.

"Maybe," she said. "But I've never been the 'let-it-slip-away' type, Mama. You raised me to chase what feels right."

The kitchen fell into a stillness that wasn't empty but full of thought. Generational expectations met modern desires. A woman raised to preserve tradition stood across from one raised to question it.

And in the center of it all... a jam jar.

As dusk stretched its purple limbs across the sky that evening, mother and daughter sat silently sipping tea. Diane wondered if her daughter knew the fire she was playing with—or perhaps the fire knew it had finally met its match.

Marilyn, meanwhile, couldn't stop smiling. Because deep down, she knew this wasn't just about a man in glasses. It was about something stirring. Something beginning. And whatever it was, she was ready to stir fate with her own two hands.

And me? I knew when he told me the story later over drinks and a crooked smile. I knew.

This wasn't just a grocery run.

CHARLES E.A.

This was the beginning of something. Something sweet, strange, and possibly catastrophic. Especially for a guy like me who's been around long enough to know that love and danger often shop in the same aisle.

"Loss leaves echoes, but purpose offers direction. Through it, we find perspective that rises beyond pain and guides us toward renewal."

There was a rhythm to Richard's walk that evening. It wasn't the kind of rhythm you'd find in a love song or the poetic cadence of a Shakespearean sonnet—it was more like the familiar, practical beat of a man whose shoes had memorized the pavement. A steady click-thump, click-thump, echoing faintly through the quiet streets as the evening mist curled around lamp posts like lazy smoke.

For once—after days of walking through clouds heavier than weather—the edges of his mouth gave way to something unfamiliar: a smile. Not the kind you parade, no, just a whisper of one, like an inside joke shared with the universe. It lingered on his lips, stirred by a moment earlier that afternoon—a moment shaped by laughter, quick glances, and the silvery chuckle of a woman named Marilyn who somehow had the power to rearrange gravity.

Now let me tell you something about my friend Richard.

He's a man made of opposites that somehow fit. In the field, he's razor-sharp, no-nonsense, the kind of FBI agent who can read a crime scene like a novel and crack lies like walnuts. But peel back the badges and bulletproof walls, and you'll find a heart that bruises easily under the weight of the world. He wears compassion like a second skin, quiet and unshakable, and it's both his strength and his curse.

Life, as you might've guessed, hasn't exactly rolled out a red carpet for him lately.

Senator Thornhill's assassination—that hit him hard. Not in a dramatic, fall-to-your-knees way, but in the quieter kind of grief that hums in your bones. The late Senator wasn't just a political figure to Richard; he was a lighthouse in a storm, a man who had stepped in when life tried to drown a boy no one else had noticed. A mentor. A father figure. And now... a void.

THE COBRAS ON THE HILL

I still remember when Richard first opened up to me about his past. We were sitting on the stoop outside his place, both nursing lukewarm coffees we never finished. He told me about his real father—an honest mechanic with strong, oil-stained hands and eyes that laughed more than they frowned. The man died too young, the kind of unfair ending that teaches a kid early on that life doesn't owe you anything except your next breath. Maybe.

But that loss didn't break him; it built him. Each wound added a layer. Every unfair twist of fate, every time someone judged him before they knew him, it all became fuel. He wasn't just chasing criminals—he was chasing the promise that no other boy would be left behind the way he was.

So tonight, watching Richard walk home with that soft, barely-there smile, I knew something had shifted. Not everything. But something.

Maybe it was Marilyn's laugh echoing in his head like wind chimes—effortless, sincere, with just the right amount of mischief. She wasn't a headline woman, not the kind that made dramatic entrances or wore perfume that slapped you in the face. She was subtler than that. She was the kind who left her mark by reminding you how good it felt to be seen.

"It wasn't love at first sight," he told me once.

Sure, buddy. And I'm the king of England. But I played my part and didn't press. You've got to let a man hold onto his illusions, especially when they're hanging by a thread soaked in denial.

Richard reached his apartment and turned the key like he'd done a hundred times, but this time the lock felt... heavier. The click echoed through the entryway like a sigh. Inside, everything was tidy to the point of being suspicious. You could tell he wasn't one of those chaos-is-creativity guys. No pizza boxes. No stray socks. Just order. Control. Survival.

But his eyes, almost involuntarily, drifted to the photo on the wall.

There it was. A still life of joy. Richard, the Thornhills, and a golden beam of sunlight that looked like it had been painted in later. Mrs. Thornhill, his former high school teacher turned guardian angel, stood with her arm looped around his shoulder like she'd always meant to be there. And beside her, the Senator, mid-laugh, frozen forever in a moment when the world still made sense.

They didn't just raise him. They resurrected him.

He stepped closer and ran his fingers gently across the frame. You'd think maybe if he touched it the right way, time would crack open and give him one more day. But grief doesn't bargain. It just sits in your chest and rearranges your breathing.

Then—buzz—the tranquility cracked like ice underfoot. His phone vibrated on the counter, shattering the silence.

He glanced at the screen.

Ma.

The corners of his mouth twitched into something between affection and preemptive concern. He knew this tone before even answering—it was going to be part warm hug, part verbal smack upside the head.

"Ma," he said with a warmth usually reserved for jazz music and childhood memories. "How are you holding up?"

"Oh, Rich," she sighed. The way she said his name, it sounded like a nickname and a prayer rolled into one. "I'm feeling all turned around out here. It's overwhelming. These people are looking at me like I'm the First Lady of Confusion, and your brother—your brother—is in a pickle again at the hospital. Honestly, I need to breathe air that hasn't been passed through three air conditioners and a prayer circle."

He chuckled softly. "Danny's back in trouble? What's it this time? Let me guess—tried to flirt with a nurse while wearing a neck brace?"

"Don't tempt me, Richard," she snapped, but even her exasperation came with a smile. "He says he 'slipped' trying to rescue a cat. In what world does rescuing a cat land you in a full body scan?"

Richard shook his head, already reaching for his keys. "Alright. Give me a minute. We'll figure this out."

There was no hesitation. That's the thing about Richard—he doesn't linger in indecision. Whether it's chasing suspects or comforting a grieving widow with a chaotic adult son, he moves. It's part of what makes him who he is. A man shaped by loss, driven by love, anchored in duty, and sometimes rescued—just a little—by the sound of someone's laugh on a rainy day.

He hung up and grabbed his jacket. The picture on the wall caught his eye again, the echo of old smiles anchoring him like a lighthouse.

"Let's do right by them," he murmured under his breath, then stepped into the night once more.

You'd never guess it, but healing sometimes begins under string lights and the smell of ribs. The roadside barbecue joint, with its dented metal signs and unrepentant country music humming through cheap outdoor speakers, was the farthest thing from the Thornhill estate's champagne-and-chandeliers vibe. Here, people ate with their fingers, laughed with their bellies, and cried only if the hot sauce demanded it.

Richard pulled into the gravel parking lot, the wheels crunching like cereal underfoot. He stepped out and made a gentleman's beeline for the passenger side, opening the door with the kind of smooth, practiced charm that made Southern grandmothers swoon and New York waitresses call him "darlin."

"Rich," Mrs. Thornhill said as she adjusted her silk scarf with a theatrical sigh, "you didn't have to go this far. Literally or emotionally."

Richard grinned, the kind that creased his cheeks and made you feel like everything was going to be okay—even if it absolutely wasn't.

"Sometimes, Ma," he said, holding out his arm with old-world gallantry, "a greasy table and good ribs can say more than therapy and a bottle of wine. Besides, I've been told my taste in barbecue is nothing short of prophetic."

She let out a laugh—not a full-throated one, more like a chuckle that hadn't stretched in weeks. "You've always had a flair for the dramatic. Just like his father."

They made their way to a table near the edge of the patio. It wobbled slightly, as if it, too, was carrying emotional baggage. Richard kicked a stone under one leg of the table and it settled with a satisfying thunk.

"Perfect," he said. "Engineered stability. Just like my love life."

Mrs. Thornhill smiled again—softer this time. The waitress came over and Richard took charge like a man on a mission, ordering her favorite: slow-cooked ribs, tangy glaze, grilled vegetables—no onions. God help him if there were onions.

As they waited, the air was filled with low conversations, a baby crying somewhere in the background, and the occasional shout from the kitchen that sounded more like a sports argument than a food order.

"So," Richard said, pouring her a glass of sweet tea like a Southern gentleman turned therapist, "how's Danny really doing?"

Mrs. Thornhill exhaled slowly, her fingers playing with the rim of her glass. "He's... he's trying. But Rich, I think he's fighting ghosts with a blindfold on."

"Hospital incident?" Richard asked carefully, already bracing himself.

She nodded. "Another argument with the staff. Poor management, poor decisions. He's spiraling, and I—I don't know where to reach him anymore. It's like losing his father cracked something I didn't know was fragile."

Richard looked away, jaw tightening. Danny had always been like a Rubik's cube on fire—colorful, brilliant, but damned hard to hold without getting burned. "I just can't imagine him unraveling like this. Not Danny. Not the kid who once tried to sell lemonade in martini glasses."

Mrs. Thornhill laughed—short and surprised. "Oh, that was just cruel. You know, we had to explain to the neighbors why their kids was asking for gin."

"I'll talk to him," Richard said, resolute. "Not as a savior. Just... as someone who still believes he's in there somewhere."

She reached over, her fingers warm against his. "You've always been the steady one, Richard. Even when it wasn't yours to carry, you did."

He swallowed, trying to dodge the tightness in his throat. "He taught me how. Your husband. Taught me loyalty, integrity... the importance of backup barbecue plans."

Their food arrived, glorious and smoky, and for a few blessed minutes, they said nothing—just chewed thoughtfully like philosophers with sauce-stained napkins. The ribs fell off the bone like tired secrets. Richard watched her relax, the burden on her shoulders momentarily eclipsed by brisket and buttery corn.

"You've been pushing yourself hard," she finally said, licking her fingers like decorum had temporarily packed its bags.

"I'd stop," he said dryly, "but apparently, justice doesn't hand out paid vacations."

She narrowed her eyes at him. "Don't lose yourself in it, Rich. You chase shadows long enough, they start chasing you back."

Richard raised a rib like a toast. "Noted, Ma. But I promise—if I ever lose myself, I'll do it somewhere with good food and emotional Wi-Fi."

As they drove back, the mood sobered. The car was filled with that particular kind of silence that didn't ask to be filled—just honored. Mrs. Thornhill sat watching the city slide past, lights reflecting on the window like starlight crying in reverse.

At the gates of the Thornhill estate, the air turned heavier again. He parked, and they walked slowly toward the grand front door, the kind of place that made even good memories echo with sadness.

"Ma," he said, gently placing a hand on her shoulder, "if you ever need another escape, there's always a wobbly table waiting for you."

She turned, her eyes tired but grateful. "Thank you, Richard. For tonight. For being the kind of man who listens without fixing. Your mother would be proud."

Inside, the mansion was as grand and cold as ever—beautiful but too quiet, like someone had vacuumed all the joy out. At her bedroom door, she stopped.

"You've always been family," she said. "Not just by love, but by choice. That's a different kind of bond."

He took her hands in his, steady and sure. "You gave me a home when I had none. I'll never forget that. Ever."

She nodded. "Now go. Sleep. You've carried enough tonight."

He kissed her forehead, and as she disappeared into her room, he headed for the car again. The night wrapped around him like a well-worn coat. He paused for a second, looking up at the stars.

Some things are heavier than secrets. And some people, like Mrs. Thornhill, carry them with grace.

Richard smiled faintly, slid into the driver's seat, and started the engine. The road ahead was uncertain, maybe even dark—but that didn't scare him anymore. Not tonight.

Because tonight, over ribs on a wobbling table, he'd remembered something essential:

The fight may be long—but it's the people beside you that make it worth the bruises.

"Life's fabric reminds us of the value of truth and honesty—yet, when we look closer, we see how deeply deceit weaves itself into every corner."

Now, before you roll your eyes and accuse me of turning all philosophical on you, relax. This isn't about existential dread—well, maybe a little—but let's flip the pie to the side where there's actual syrup: the moment it all began to flash.

It was exactly 10:26 a.m. on an otherwise unapologetically boring Tuesday. The kind of Tuesday that smells like burnt toast and last week's laundry. Lucas sat hunched over his desk, two monitors glowing with enough tabs open to make Google weep. The room was dim except for the stubborn ray of light that always slipped through the blinds and hit him right in the cornea.

His phone still buzzed from the earlier call. His sister's voice—forever coated in equal parts sunshine and sarcasm—rattled in his memory:

"Promise me you'll visit next week? Mom says you're turning into one of those 'cryptic, online trolls' who haven't seen the sun since 2020."

Lucas chuckled then, masking the kind of existential stomach churn that only family guilt can deliver.

"Troll? Please. I'm more of a digital knight. With a keyboard for a sword and back pain for a horse," he quipped. "But yeah... I'll swing by next week. Tell Mom to bake those cookies. You know, the ones she uses to bribe the neighbors into not calling the HOA on her."

It sounded like a joke. Felt like one too. But the promise... well, it hung in the air like those scented candles people light to cover something they really don't want to deal with.

Truth was, Lucas wasn't just skipping Sunday dinners or avoiding awkward family photo sessions. He was dodging something messier. Bigger. Something that would unravel not just him—but the people who still believed he was just a bit eccentric, not dangerously entangled in the digital underworld.

See, if Lucas had a single superpower, it wasn't flying or invisibility.

It was disappearing.

And not just ghosting on texts or skipping brunch. I mean full-on vanishing from systems, databases, and any government registry foolish enough to think a firewall could stop him.

Because in the dim-lit corners of cyberspace—those back alleys of ones and zeroes—Lucas wasn't just some guy with a hoodie and fast fingers. He was a myth. A self-built ghost. Where others saw gibberish code, Lucas saw open windows, doors, tunnels, and escape hatches. He could slip into vaults and encrypted fortresses like a pickpocket in a room full of narcoleptics. If he told you he could hack the Vatican while ordering ramen, you'd be wise to believe him.

So when Felicity came calling, it wasn't your usual collab.

Imagine a licensed pharmacist joining forces with a dude who runs a meth lab out of a taco truck. That kind of "unholy alliance."

Now, maybe you remember Felicity. The name alone carried the chill of a cold draft. She isn't the kind of person who knocks. She barged in, rearranged your throw pillows, and asked if your secrets came in decaf.

And yet, Lucas couldn't forget the first time she appeared in his life like a Netflix series you didn't ask to binge.

"Wanna do something meaningful with that freakshow brain of yours?" she'd asked, sipping from a cup that definitely smelled like rum and regret.

Lucas, in all his sarcasm-infused glory, raised a brow.

"Define meaningful," he shot back.

They were opposites. She was fire. He was fog. And yet, together? Together they made something dangerous—dangerous and somehow... funny?

Their partnership was like two porcupines trying to hug: awkward, spiky, and probably a bad idea, but nobody had better options.

But today? Tuesday was not the day for their usual snarky banter and "accidental" data breaches. Something had shifted.

Lucas leaned forward at his desk, eyes narrowing. His fingers flew over the keyboard in rhythmic fury. Lines of code danced like dominoes. He was deep—Atlantis deep. And what he found down there?

It wasn't just a setup.

It was a symphony of sabotage. Someone was framing Felicity for the murder of the late Presidential candidate Senator Thornhill. And not just a lazy blame game. This was crafted. A misdirection masterpiece.

"Of course, they're framing her," he muttered to no one. "Why blame Ted from accounting when you can slap a murder rap on the Queen of Chaos?"

He didn't even pack. Just yanked his hoodie off the chair, grabbed his laptop, and sprinted out the door like a man late for a revolution.

Scene: The Warehouse of Mayhem

The "office" where Felicity worked her particular brand of brilliance was... well, it used to be a warehouse. Now it is a disguised chaotic jungle of flickering monitors, half-assembled gadgets, and energy drinks that had likely expired during the Obama administration.

Lucas burst in, panting, waving a USB stick like it was Excalibur.

"Felicity!"

From behind a tower of wooden crates, Felicity emerged mid-bite of what was very clearly a croissant. She looked up, unimpressed.

"Lucas. My favorite harbinger of doom," she deadpanned. "To what fresh apocalypse do I owe the pleasure?"

He slammed the USB into the nearest port.

"You're not just in trouble. You're in a Netflix miniseries, and you're the villain. They've built an airtight narrative around you. This isn't a setup. It's a framing opera."

She blinked once. Then twice. Croissant halfway to her mouth.

"Where did you get this?"

"Let's just say I took a little dive into the kind of data caves where people usually don't come out with their souls intact."

She scanned the files, her eyes growing colder with each passing second. Then she did something Lucas wasn't ready for. "Pfft. I've been blamed for worse.

She laughed.

It wasn't joyful. More like the kind of laugh you let out when you realize the universe is throwing actual bricks at your face.

"Well, isn't that inconvenient"? she said calmly. "Guess we're skipping the spa this weekend."

Lucas stood silent, watching her expression shift from cool amusement to raw defiance.

"Felicity," he said slowly, "They want you to be the show. They've built a circus, and you're the flaming ring. But I've got the matches. We can burn this whole thing down."

She looked up. And for once, didn't say something sarcastic.

"Alright," she whispered. "Let's ruin their script."

Lucas nodded. In that moment, the hacker with no people skills and the wildcard with nothing to lose shared a rare bond: not just survival—but vengeance.

And maybe, just maybe, redemption.

"Human life is defined by the tension between connection and mystery. Yet woven within this tension is a hidden layer of deception—one that surfaces as life's complexity comes into view."

One of the things I do better than most—besides making a mean cup of black coffee with existential dread—is watching people wear masks they don't even realize they've glued to their faces. And this morning, I had front-row seats.

There he sat: Arthur C. Winters, Director of the CIA and—if you asked the local church bulletin—the man most likely to be voted "Father of the Year" and "Most Handsome Over 50" in the same breath.

His youngest daughter, Maddie, giggled as he helped her butter a piece of toast with exaggerated focus, the knife gliding over the bread like he was prepping a mission file.

"You're using too much, Daddy!" she squealed, laughing.

"It's strategic placement," Arthur said with mock-seriousness, "butter distribution is an art form."

He winked at her. His laugh—a smooth, deep chuckle—echoed through the sunlit kitchen like a lullaby. Across the room, Evelyn, his wife of twenty years, adjusted the collar of his crisp suit. She tugged gently at his tie, smiling with all the softness of someone who still believed she'd married a good man.

"You look perfect," she said, brushing imaginary dust from his shoulder. Her voice carried that familiar blend of adoration and concern. The kind of love that makes you check if he's eaten, not if he's lying.

And in her case? Oh, if only she knew.

Arthur smiled, that devastating politician's smile—warm, reassuring, and deeply fraudulent. A smile that could close congressional hearings or charm a judge into ignoring inconvenient truths. That smile had saved lives and also ended a few. Context mattered.

To the world, Arthur was the kind of man whose handshake could launch alliances: church-going, country-club golfing, picture-perfect suburban patriot.

But as the school bus swallowed his children's laughter, his expression flickered. A quiet dimming. Gone was the warm, pancake-flipping dad. In his place stood someone colder—a man made of wires, gears, and calculation.

Evelyn lingered in the kitchen, her fingers wrapped around a lukewarm mug of coffee. Her brow creased ever so slightly.

"This trip... It's not another extended one, right?" she asked, voice gentle, like she was trying not to wake a sleeping lion. "You've been gone a lot lately."

Arthur turned. His movements were slow and deliberate. He placed a practiced hand on her shoulder, that touch rehearsed to the beat of a thousand similar mornings.

"No, my dear," he said, in a tone smoothed by a hundred lies. "Just another dull string of meetings. I'll be back before you can even reheat your coffee."

Evelyn smiled. Believed him. She always did.

Because the thing about Evelyn? She loved him not just with her heart, but with her entire belief system. She didn't marry a man—she married the narrative he sold her. And Arthur was a damn good storyteller.

The moment the family car disappeared down the driveway, the mask dropped like a curtain.

No warmth. No performance.

Arthur turned on his heel and walked straight into his study. No hesitation. No goodbye. The room greeted him like an accomplice: dark, quiet, precise. On the desk sat a secure phone, a matte-black monolith that looked like it could detonate a small country if misdialed.

He picked it up. Dialed. No pleasantries. Just business.

"Project Germany is green-lit," he said, voice flat. "Initiate first stage. I expect movement within 72 hours."

A voice on the other end crackled back, metallic and efficient:

"Understood. This thread requires discretion. We're not sewing a flag here."

Arthur ended the call without so much as a breath. No pause. No second thoughts. In his world, hesitation was just another way to get eaten.

He leaned back in his chair, the leather groaning softly beneath him. His fingers tapped the armrest in perfect rhythm. This trip to Germany? It wasn't diplomacy. It was chess. And he'd already sacrificed four pawns.

Because here's what no one ever dared admit: Arthur C. Winters didn't lead through loyalty. He conquered through leverage. Quiet, invisible leverage. The kind that whispered behind doors and shattered lives without ever raising its voice.

Outside, Evelyn stood by the door, still holding her coffee. She smiled and waved as Arthur approached the waiting sedan.

"Call when you land," she said sweetly. "And eat something that isn't from a vending machine this time."

He nodded, kissed her cheek. It was muscle memory. He could do it in his sleep. Maybe he already was.

The car pulled away. Silence filled the cabin except for the low hum of the engine. Arthur stared out the window, eyes locked on the blur of the world outside—detached, distant. His chauffeur glanced into the rearview once, caught a glimpse of a man who looked calm. But even he knew better than to ask what was really going on behind those perfectly trimmed temples.

They reached the private airfield. No fuss. Just polished the protocol.

Arthur stepped out, the wind tugging slightly at his coat. He adjusted his cufflinks—hand-engraved, initials carved so delicately they looked like secrets themselves—and boarded the sleek jet without breaking stride.

The door hissed shut behind him—a whisper of privacy. Here, inside this steel womb, he could exist without pretense: no honeyed lies, no bedtime stories, no toast distribution metaphors.

Just Arthur. Unfiltered.

As the plane sliced through the clouds, Arthur stared out the window—his mind a chessboard, pieces shifting, sacrifices prepped.

What he didn't know?

I was already watching him.

Digitally. Physically. Silently. I knew his moves three steps before he did. I watched the wires tighten around him like a puppet master waiting for the final tug.

His empire, built on secrets and lies, was beginning to fray. Slowly. Quietly. Like a whisper under the door.

But in that moment, Arthur sat tall, unshaken. The German skyline awaited. The mask of the "perfect family man" was neatly folded in his carry-on, ready for its next performance.

And I?

I waited in the shadows.

Because the next move wasn't his.

It was mine.

"The pursuit of revenge tempts us with resolution, yet it is a deceptive path—masquerading as understanding—and often leads to deeper harm and peril."

Most people wake up clinging to the romantic notion that every new sunrise is a quiet second chance—a whisper from the universe that yesterday's mistakes can be redeemed with today's coffee.

For Richard, that whisper had always felt like a pact. An anchor. Especially in a life built on chaos, half-truths, and a job description that read more like a dare than a duty.

But not this morning.

As he pulled into the FBI headquarters parking lot, his fingers tightening around the steering wheel, he couldn't shake the feeling that something in the atmosphere was... holding its breath. Like the universe itself was bracing for a plot twist.

He killed the engine, grabbed his leather satchel from the passenger seat, and stepped out of the sedan with mechanical grace. The kind of grace that came from years of burying nerves beneath layers of protocol. He straightened his tie, glanced at his reflection in the driver-side window, and saw exactly what the world always saw: composed, determined, put-together.

But behind the well-ironed exterior? There was static. A faint unease threaded through his every thought. The kind that didn't come from lack of sleep—it came from knowing too much.

His footsteps echoed sharply through the marble corridor, bouncing off sterile white walls and overly ambitious motivational posters. The air inside smelled like burnt printer ink and microwaved regret.

He passed familiar agents and interns who gave him curt nods—the silent language of professionals who'd seen enough to keep greetings efficient. His mind, however, wasn't in the hallway. It was still dissecting last night's discovery—chasing patterns through financial ledgers and encrypted emails that had refused to make sense... until they suddenly did.

That's when Agent Riley slid into the picture like a sitcom sidekick with too much caffeine and too little impulse control.

Leaning against the wall by the elevator, coffee cup in hand, Riley looked every bit like a man who had absolutely no business being that smug at 8:00 a.m.

"Rich!" he grinned, raising his cup in salute. "Morning, sunshine."

Richard gave him a wary side glance. "Riley."

"Heading to the briefing?" Riley asked, his voice laced with that telltale mischief.

Richard slowed. "What briefing?"

"Oh, you know... the briefing," Riley said, taking a slow sip. "The one everyone important seems to be going to. But hey, maybe it's just for the cool kids."

Richard's brows knit. "You're seriously going to make me drag this out of you?"

"Would I do that to you?" Riley said innocently, then grinned wider. "Absolutely."

Richard exhaled, already regretting asking. "Try not to spill the coffee. That's evidence of your sarcasm addiction."

"Oof. Spicy this morning, are we?" Riley smirked. "Well, if you make it out of the dragon's lair, let me know. I'll be down here taking bets."

By the time Richard pushed open the heavy door of Director Anderson's office, the suspicion had evolved into certainty. Whatever this was, it wasn't routine.

Anderson looked up from behind a desk that could've doubled as a fortress. Salt-and-pepper hair, glasses low on his nose, the man had that worn-but-steady gravitas of someone who ran on black coffee and unfinished justice.

He ended his call with a clipped, "Understood," and gestured to the chair.

"Rich. You look like you came to fight."

"I came to talk," Richard said, not sitting. "About the Thornhill case."

Anderson's jaw tensed immediately. His tone dropped several degrees. "We've been through this. You're too close. He was your family."

"I know," Richard said, carefully measuring his voice. "But I've found something—something that changes everything."

Anderson didn't reply. He just gave a slight nod, allowing him to proceed. That was the signal Richard needed.

He launched into it: the paper trail, the offshore accounts, the pivot from motive to manipulation. It came tumbling out like he'd rehearsed it in front of a mirror—which, knowing him, he probably had. The web pointed directly to Felicity Montgomery, yes—but not as a mastermind.

As a pawn.

"The money wasn't for the hit," Richard said. "She thought she was purchasing black-market tech. The payment was diverted. She was played, sir. Set up. And the one who rerouted the funds? A hedge fund manager is tied to our primary suspect. The guy is also known for laundering blood money through offshore shells."

Anderson leaned back, eyes narrowing. "So you're telling me... Felicity accidentally funded the murder of a senator she was having an affair with?"

Richard gave a humorless smile. "Yes, sir. It sounds like a bad Netflix pitch, I get it. But I believe it. She was manipulated."

Anderson rubbed his temple like the words physically pained him. "You're chasing shadows, Rich."

"No," Richard said. "I'm chasing truth. And the closer I get, the more this stinks of something deeper—something organized. If we keep pretending it's just a murder case, we're going to miss what's really happening here."

Anderson stared at him, long and hard, as if searching for a crack in his resolve.

"If you're wrong," he said slowly, "this could implode. You're not just risking your job—you're risking mine."

Richard nodded. "I know. But if I'm right..."

Silence. Just the distant hum of a fax machine that probably hadn't worked since the Obama years.

Finally, Anderson sighed.

"Follow the lead. Quietly. If you so much as breathe wrong, I'll have your badge on my desk."

"Understood, sir."

As Richard stepped out of the office, Riley was already waiting with a mock golf clap.

"So? What'd you win—trophy or termination?"

"Neither," Richard muttered, adjusting his tie again. "But I did win a trip to hell."

"Great! Pack light. I hear they don't let you bring sanity."

Richard let out a dry chuckle, then fell silent as they both turned toward the main corridor.

Out here, in the sunlight again, the morning still looked normal. But now, Richard knew better. He wasn't walking into a case.

He was walking into a storm—one soaked in betrayal, misdirection, and secrets that hadn't seen daylight since long before Thornhill ever ran for Senate.

This wasn't about Felicity anymore. It wasn't even about Thornhill.

It was about whatever shadowy machine had engineered it all—and Richard had just volunteered to stand in front of it.

THE COBRAS ON THE HILL

"Curiosity draws us toward intrigue, but ignorance is a dangerous veil. What we do not see often holds the greatest threat."

The city hummed with its usual morning chaos—honking cars, hurried footsteps, and the occasional clatter of a street vendor's cart. Emily leaned against her kitchen counter, sipping coffee as she glanced at the clock. Another day, another mountain of bureaucracy to climb. She sighed, mentally bracing herself for the grind.

Then, a shrill ring shattered the rhythm of her morning. Her eyes darted to the burner phone sitting inconspicuously on the counter—the one Alex had given her days ago with a cryptic "Just in case."

Her pulse quickened as she picked it up, a mix of caution and curiosity evident in her voice. "Hello? Who is this?"

"Emily." Alex's voice was unmistakable—low, urgent, and unyielding.

"Alex?" Her brows furrowed in surprise. "What is this about?"

"I need to see you. Now. Before you head to work," he said, his words clipped but heavy with significance.

Emily hesitated, the weight of his urgency sparking a flicker of unease. "Is this really necessary? I have—"

"Please, Emily," he interrupted, his tone softening. "It's important."

Reluctantly, she agreed, the nagging curiosity outweighing her better judgment.

The coffee shop on the corner was a familiar refuge, its aroma of freshly brewed beans comforting against the backdrop of her growing apprehension. Emily slid into a seat by the window, her gaze wandering to the bustling street outside.

And then she saw him. Across the road, Alex stood, scanning the area like a detective in a noir film. He crossed with measured steps, his demeanor calm and collected, as though this meeting was purely coincidental.

When he reached her table, Emily raised an eyebrow. "You're not even going to pretend this isn't some grand, orchestrated move, are you?"

Alex gave her a faint smile, the kind that barely touched his eyes. "Good morning to you, too."

She leaned back, arms crossed, her expression a mix of amusement and suspicion. "So, are we going to talk about the burner phone or your dramatic entrance first?"

Alex sat down, his coffee acting as a prop to mask the tension crackling between them. "You've been followed, Emily." His voice was calm, but his words hit like a thunderclap.

Emily blinked, her skepticism kicking in. "Followed?" She let out a short laugh, attempting to brush off his claim. "Come on, Alex. I'm not that important to anyone. Unless you're auditioning for a spy thriller, in which case, tone it down a notch. You're scaring the barista."

But beneath her sarcastic quip was a flicker of unease. As much as she wanted to dismiss Alex's warning, she couldn't shake the feeling that she might have unwittingly "poked a bear," as her father used to say.

Alex leaned in slightly, his voice dropping to a near whisper. "This isn't paranoia, Em. I intercepted a conversation—something big is brewing, and your name came up. You need to pass this case to the FBI. Immediately."

Emily's facade of confidence faltered, her voice dropping to match his. "What are you talking about? Why would anyone think I'm... a traitor?"

Alex's expression softened, but his eyes remained resolute. "Because someone out there wants you to look like one. The less you know right now, the safer you'll be. But trust me—keep your focus narrow, stay within your jurisdiction, and don't trust the system. Not completely."

The weight of his words settled over her like a storm cloud. She wanted to argue, to demand more answers, but Alex's tone left no room for debate.

"Great," she muttered, pushing her hair back. "You've officially made my morning ten times worse."

Alex allowed himself a faint smile. "Just doing my job."

Meanwhile, in a sleek office overlooking the heart of the city, CIA Director Winters returned from his overseas trip. His reputation as an enigmatic force in intelligence preceded him, and his presence now marked the resurgence of a man who thrived in complexity.

From his window, Winters caught sight of Emily walking briskly through the agency's courtyard, her determined stride a testament to her resolve. A quiet chuckle escaped him. She always had a way of stumbling into chaos, with an uncanny knack for survival.

"Send Agent Parker in," Winters ordered his assistant. Moments later, Emily stood before him, her composure steady but her eyes reflecting the storm of thoughts swirling in her mind.

"Director Winters," she greeted, her tone respectful but guarded.

"Agent Parker," he replied, gesturing for her to sit. "How's the case progressing?"

Emily hesitated, weighing her words carefully. "I've decided to transfer it to the FBI, sir. It's the best course of action given... the circumstances."

Winters tilted his head, his sharp gaze assessing her. Then, to her surprise, he nodded. "Wise choice."

She blinked, momentarily caught off guard. "You agree?"

Winters leaned back, steepling his fingers. "Sometimes, knowing when to hand off the reins is as important as knowing how to steer the horse."

His cryptic approval lingered in her mind as she left his office, her resolve hardening. Back in her own workspace, Emily meticulously organized the case files, ensuring every detail was accounted for before dispatching them to the FBI.

The files landed on the FBI director's desk and drew immediate attention. Recognizing the gravity of Emily's investigation, he issued a directive: "Send this to Richard. And tell him to contact Agent Parker. Immediately."

Emily's morning had begun with a simple routine, but now she found herself at the center of a labyrinth of secrets, shadows, and uncertainty. Somewhere, Alex's warning still echoed in her mind: Stay cautious. Stay sharp.

And somewhere in the shadows, unseen forces began to stir.

Emily sat by her window, the soft rustle of leaves outside doing little to quell the storm within her. She turned the phone over in her hands, the screen still glowing from Richard's call. His voice had carried a mix of gratitude and understanding. Still, it was his invitation that lingered in her mind—a casual offer for coffee, a moment outside the rigid confines of their professional lives.

"Why now?" she murmured to herself. The case, once a source of conviction, had grown unwieldy, tangled in shadows she could no longer navigate. Passing it to the FBI had been the right choice, the logical choice. And yet, the idea of seeing Richard again, of hearing his thoughts on the unfolding chaos, stirred something within her—a need for clarity, maybe even closure.

Her lips curled into a faint, self-deprecating smile. Trust is a fragile thing, she thought. But trust wasn't her only motivator. Curiosity had a way of pulling her into places she had no business being.

Richard leaned back in his chair, the dim glow of his desk lamp casting long shadows across the piles of files spread before him. The quiet hum of the FBI office at night was oddly comforting—a stark contrast to the storm brewing in his mind.

Emily's evidence was meticulous, and every piece of it was carefully compiled and annotated. She'd left nothing to chance, weaving a compelling narrative that felt almost alive. But one name on the documents seemed to pulse with a malevolent energy: Marcus Reynold.

Richard stared at the name, the syllables rolling around in his mind like a sour taste. Marcus wasn't just a hedge fund manager; he was a symbol of calculated ambition. His rise in the financial world had been meteoric, but the ascent left a wake of destruction—lives ruined, alliances shattered, enemies silenced.

Digging deeper into Marcus's profile, Richard found himself unnerved by the man's portfolio.

The surveillance reports painted a chilling picture. Marcus moved through life with a sense of theatricality, every gesture rehearsed, every step chosen with precision. His life was a symphony of chaos, one he orchestrated with a maestro's touch. But beneath the polished veneer was a predator—a man who bent rules and blurred lines until they vanished entirely. Marcus wasn't just dipping his toes in criminality—he was one of the architects of a labyrinthine network that spanned continents. Corruption in politics, covert deals with intelligence agencies, and a string of mysterious disappearances marked his trail.

And then Richard found it—a connection that sent a cold shiver racing down his spine. Marcus wasn't just a criminal mastermind; he was tied to Felicity's past. Buried in the files was a dark history that linked the Reynold and Montgomery families, a shared skeleton rattling in their closets.

"Of course," Richard muttered under his breath, rubbing his temples. It explained Felicity's precision, her uncanny ability to anticipate moves. She wasn't just a skilled manipulator; she had been knowingly playing a deeply personal game, one she had fully understood.

As Richard sifted through layers of Marcus's empire, he uncovered secrets that deepened the gravity of the case.

And now, Marcus had Felicity in his sights.

Emily's phone buzzed again, pulling her from her reverie—a text from Richard.

"We need to meet. Coffee's on me."

She hesitated, her thumb hovering over the keyboard. She could ignore it, retreat into the safety of distance. But safety now felt like a mirage, and something about Richard's steady presence offered a lifeline.

Richard's phone buzzed, pulling him from his thoughts.

"Let's talk. But make it quick. I don't trust coffee shop meetings anymore."

A small smile tugged at his lips. Emily might be wary, but she wasn't backing down.

"Logic can expose deception, but only when we have the courage to acknowledge it."

Sometimes, when I sit in my loneliness with nothing but the clock for company and the city lights casting long shadows on my floor, I wonder if I ever agreed to any of this for the love of the universe... or for me... or maybe—just maybe—out of spite.

The truth? I still don't know.

They warn you, "Be careful when trading with darkness," but what they never tell you is just how literary the darkness is. How it speaks in metaphors. How it courts you like a poet, convinces you like a preacher, and devours you like a debt collector.

And so here I am again, face-to-face with the blurred outlines of death, crafted not by fate, but by the genius of the man who dragged me headfirst into this conspiracy trench.

If you've never been offered a front-row seat in the underworld's theater, let me assure you: it's not the shadowy nonsense you see in movies. It's worse. More... polite. Civilized. It comes with vintage wine, violins, and tailored suits.

The grand ballroom of The Architects Club shimmered like a lie told beautifully. It wasn't a room; it was a stage—lit by chandeliers so ornate they probably had bloodlines. Gold trim everywhere. Velvet drapes heavy enough to silence sins. And power? Power hung in the air like perfume—something expensive, addictive, and slightly toxic.

This wasn't a party. It was a congregation of the powerful—a ballroom filled with men and women who could reorder nations with a phone call. And in the middle of it all, sipping from a crystal glass and smiling like the world belonged to him, stood Marcus Reynold.

Custom navy suit. Silver tie pin. A watch that costs more than most people's lives.

He looked sharp, confident... dangerous in that polished, LinkedIn-approved way.

Tonight, Marcus wasn't just mingling.

Tonight was his ascension.

For years, he had played the long game—charming senators, manipulating contracts, turning influence into an art form. He wasn't the loudest man in the room, but he made damn sure his silence was worth something.

This invitation? It wasn't an opportunity.

It was a coronation.

He soaked in the atmosphere like a man who knew he'd made it. Admired. Envied. Feared. But as always, Marcus missed one crucial detail:

The door he was stepping through wasn't made of gold.

It was a trap—laced with velvet, yes, but a trap all the same.

In the alcove behind the main floor—secluded, private, and too quiet for comfort—Marcus found himself seated among the elites. He recognized none of them. He didn't need to. Their eyes told the story: apex predators in tailored skin.

Across from him sat a man who could silence a room without moving or uttering a word.

Frederick Galleon.

The unofficial voice of The Architects. The kind of man whose existence was never confirmed but whose influence was impossible to ignore.

"Marcus," Frederick said smoothly, voice as warm as it was venomous, "you've made quite an impression."

Marcus smiled modestly, though inside his ego soaked it up like fine bourbon.

"But," Frederick continued, pausing long enough to slice the air with tension, "membership in this club requires more than brilliance. It requires loyalty. And loyalty, my dear friend... must be proven."

Marcus leaned in slightly. "What kind of proof are we talking about?"

Frederick offered a faint smile, then casually slid a black folder across the table.

Marcus opened it.

His heart dropped.

Inside were high-res surveillance photos of Felicity Montgomery. Confident. Calculated. Dangerous. Familiar.

Too familiar.

"You have ties to her, yes?" Frederick asked, sipping from his drink like they were talking about weather patterns.

Marcus hesitated. His voice, when it came, was carefully measured. "She's a client."

"A client," Frederick echoed, nodding. "A client who's becoming... inconvenient."

The words settled like smoke. Marcus knew what this was.

A test.

A stage.

And he was standing at the edge of something irreversible.

"I'm not sure I follow," Marcus said, though he knew exactly where this was heading.

Frederick chuckled, then leaned over and patted Marcus on the shoulder like an uncle rewarding a good little nephew.

"You already helped us. That little 'distraction'—beautifully orchestrated. She won't die from it. Probably. But Marcus... we need you to make sure it sticks."

That was it—the final initiation. The moment every villain tells himself isn't a big deal.

The room applauded politely when Federick raised his glass and clinked it with Marcus's. A hollow sound echoed through the marble room.

"Well done," Frederick whispered. "Welcome to the club."

But Marcus? He barely heard them. His brain was spinning. And by the time the brandy was gone, so was he.

Hours Later – Marcus's Penthouse

The folder sat untouched on the glass coffee table, like a wound too fresh to clean.

The city skyline glittered beyond the windows, oblivious.

Marcus stood there in silence, eyes glazed. His tie was loosened; his jacket was off. Shirt sleeves rolled to the elbows. A man halfway undressed—and maybe halfway undone.

He told himself he needed time. Clarity.

But ego doesn't need clarity. It just needs a mirror and a good excuse.

"She's strong," he murmured. "She'll bounce back."

"It's just business."

"It's not like I'm pulling the trigger myself."

His internal monologue twisted and coiled, like a lawyer arguing both sides of an issue.

But then, in a quieter corner of his mind, another voice—small, almost forgotten—whispered:

"Is this who you are now? Using your blood as stepping stones?"

That voice didn't last long.

Ego showed it the door.

By dawn, Marcus had made his decision.

Felicity would fall.

He started with whispers—just subtle enough to be overheard by the right people. Then came the planted documents. Fabricated transcripts. Leaks to trusted channels. A trail so convincingly crooked it almost looked straight.

And each step, he told himself the same bedtime story:

"This is the price of greatness."

If ambition were a god, Marcus was now its most obedient disciple.

And if there was still a scrap of guilt left in him, it was buried under suits, silence, and the applause of powerful men who never asked where the blood came from—as long as the glass was full and the illusion remained intact.

"Grasping the subtle pattern between truth and falsehood within secrecy is not just knowledge—it is a rare gift."

Richard's office was the kind of place you walked into and instinctively knew not to touch anything. Not because it was exceptionally tidy—it wasn't—but because everything in it looked like it was mid-thought, mid-reveal, or mid-collapse. The big side window flooded the room with natural light, casting long streaks of shadow that danced across the disorder like silent investigators of their own. Documents, photos, and notes in his famously awful handwriting—each piece lay scattered like a jigsaw puzzle that someone had decided to solve during an earthquake.

He sat behind the desk, leaning so far back in his chair you'd think he was waiting for divine inspiration or a chiropractor. His fingers dug into his temples, massaging a headache he hadn't earned today—it was probably three days old. The clock on the wall ticked obnoxiously, almost as if mocking him for losing another round of mental chess with ghosts that didn't want to be found.

Or at least, that's how he explained it when he finally opened up. Me? I just think he looked like a man one bad caffeine decision away from joining a meditation retreat—or a mental institution.

Then came the knock.

A soft, almost polite little thing that had no business interrupting the battlefield of thoughts going off in his head. Still, Richard blinked, sat up, and muttered with a rasp, "Come in." He sounded like someone who hadn't slept in a year. Then again, maybe I'm being dramatic. Maybe he just sounded like someone who's been binge-watching conspiracies at 3 AM without snacks.

The door creaked open, and in walked Riley—easygoing as always, holding a mug of coffee like he'd just negotiated peace in the Middle East and figured Richard was the next big challenge.

"You look like you've been in here negotiating with demons," Riley said, handing over the coffee. "I brought caffeine. I assume you haven't eaten. Or slept. Or blinked."

Richard gave a dry smirk, accepting it like a lifeline. "Thanks. I'll take that as... whatever that was. Also, it's possible I may have forgotten how to do all three."

Riley glanced at the apocalyptic scene on the desk and let out a low whistle. "Jesus, this looks like a conspiracy theory exploded."?

"Because it did," Richard replied. "Only this one doesn't involve aliens. Just men in suits with too much money and no conscience

You do know people your age usually sleep at night, right?" Riley shrugs.

"Sleep's a luxury I can't afford," Richard muttered, taking a sip. "Not when the puzzle's this ugly."

"Oh boy. Alright, Sherlock, hit me. What's eating you alive today?"

Richard didn't answer right away. He simply waved a hand at the desk, as if saying, Pick your poison. Then he finally said, "The Architects. That name keeps coming up. My sources say Marcus has weight in that club, like high up in the food chain—but no one can say exactly what he does. It's like he exists behind glass: you can see the silhouette, but not the man."

Riley's eyebrows lifted. "Marcus Reynolds? That hedge fund guy? Figures. He's as slippery as they come. But where does Thornhill fit into this?"

Richard chuckled weakly. "He's connected. That much I know. But Thornhill's death? That's the loose thread. I can't tell if he was a pawn, a whistleblower, or a damn fool who touched the wrong nerve."

Riley pulled up a chair, arms crossed, listening closely now.

"Thornhill wasn't clean," Richard continued, more to himself. "No one in that seat is.

He may have known something—something big enough to make him a target. I don't know what to think, whether he was involved in some deep shit, maybe was working some angles for the benefit of his political promises. Or... perhaps he was just too ambitious for his own good." Whatever it was, it got him killed."

"You think Reynolds had him clipped?"

"No," Richard said, shaking his head slowly. "Reynolds is just one piece of the puzzle. This thing—this operation—it's global. It's bigger than any one person. We're talking about power brokers operating across borders, market manipulation, blackmail, and political infiltration. We're not chasing a man. We're chasing a machine."

Riley leaned back, exhaled. "And you're doing it without backup, with caffeine and conspiracies as your only friends. Fantastic plan."

Richard sighed, rubbing his face. "I just need to know what Thornhill knew. The timeline's messy, and the motives are unclear; it's like trying to build IKEA furniture without instructions and with half the pieces missing."

"And the other half covered in blood," Riley added. "So... what's the next move? You gonna storm the evil lair and challenge Reynolds to a duel at dawn?"

Richard let out a tired laugh. "Something like that. But first, I want to talk to the man. If he's as slippery as he seems, he'll try to outplay us with charm and plausible deniability. We need to corner him without letting him know he's in a corner."

Riley stood, straightening his jacket. "Just promise me one thing—don't turn into Thornhill 2.0. I like my partners paranoid, not perforated."

"Noted," Richard said with a smirk.

And then came the message that shifted the air: Director Anderson wanted to see them. Now.

The situation room had the kind of lighting that made everyone look ten years older and two shades more dangerous. Digital screens glowed with intel, maps, and surveillance feeds. The tension in the air was so thick, you'd need a machete to get to the coffee machine.

Director Anderson stood at the head of the table like a general, all calm fury and laser focus. Around him sat senior agents, each with that unique mix of exhaustion and adrenaline that came with being minutes away from chaos.

"Based on Agent Suggs's findings," Anderson began, his voice steady as a steel trap, "we've confirmed financial irregularities connected to Marcus Reynolds. Nothing we can take to court—yet—but enough to warrant a closer look."

Richard opened his mouth to speak, probably to protest, but Anderson raised a hand to silence him. "Let me finish," the Director said.

"No arrests. We bring him in for questioning, off the record. Diplomatic. Friendly, even. Let him think he's helping us."

"And if he declines?" Richard asked, tone even but firm.

Anderson's eyes narrowed slightly, a slow, calculating smile playing on his lips. "Then we remind him that we can get very, very curious about his offshore accounts and investment portfolios. And let's be honest—no one likes a nosy government with subpoenas."

A few agents chuckled softly. Anderson continued, colder now. "But make no mistake—this is reconnaissance, not a takedown. Clean, quiet, and absolutely airtight. No screw-ups."

He turned toward Richard. "You lead the approach. Take Riley. You find out what Reynold knows—and you do it without starting a war. I want full updates. The rest of the team will stay on standby. Understood?"

Richard gave a sharp nod. "Understood, sir. We'll bring him in."

Anderson looked at each agent in the room, his gaze warning and commanding all at once.

"If this man is part of something bigger, we don't tip our hand until we're sure. And Richard—if he plays games? You make damn sure we're ready to play harder."

Richard's expression barely shifted, but a flicker of steel entered his eyes. "Copy that."

As the room began to clear, Riley leaned toward him. "So, we're just going to knock on the serpent's door and ask politely if he's plotting world domination?"

Richard looked back, a half-smile tugging at his tired face. "Exactly. And if he lies, we smile, nod... and quietly start lighting matches under his castle."

Later, in the hallway...

Riley jogged up beside him, coffee still in hand. "So. How's it feel being the tip of the spear?"

"Like I'm about to get impaled," Richard said dryly.

Riley gave a tight smirk. "Classic. You always did have a thing for picking fights with people who own private islands."

Richard stopped by the elevator and glanced at him. "You still in?"

"Are you kidding?" Riley replied. "You're the only one around here reckless enough to make this interesting."

The elevator doors slid open, and the two agents stepped inside.

No sirens. No guns drawn. Just two men about to walk into the lion's den—with charm, paperwork, and just enough nerve to keep the walls from closing in.

For now.

They weren't even past the front gate before Riley said what Richard was already thinking.

"Rich," he muttered, eyes sweeping the perimeter as the car came to a stop, "something's off. Like... horror-movie-off."

Richard gave a slow nod, jaw clenching as he took in the scene through the windshield. Marcus Reynold's mansion—normally a blinding statement of opulence—felt different that night. Sure, it still gleamed with its strategically placed lights, angular architecture, and tasteful intimidation, but it had the wrong kind of silence. The kind that didn't hum with exclusivity. The kind that howled too late.

The wrought-iron gate was wide open. Like a mouth that had swallowed something terrible and was waiting for seconds.

Richard stepped out and approached the keypad. It was dangling off its hinges, wires exposed like nerves. "Someone forced this. No way this was a glitch."

Riley pulled out his weapon. "Well, good evening to us."

They advanced toward the security outpost, each step a warning. When they reached the door, Riley eased it open—and immediately froze.

A man lay just inside. Slumped. Still. A thick smear of blood traced the floor like someone tried to draw a line they'd never get to finish.

Riley crouched beside the body, pressing two fingers to the neck. "Security. Dead. Looks fresh."

Richard's hand hovered near his weapon. His tone turned to steel. "Call it in. Now."

While Riley radioed backup, Richard's eyes darted up to the mansion. The windows—normally reflecting the inner glow of obscene wealth—were like dead eyes, giving nothing back.

A chill worked down his spine.

Minutes later, SUVs rolled in quietly. Agents stepped out with grim expressions and tighter grips on their gear. This wasn't a mission anymore. It was a crime scene in motion.

The team split, boots muffled against gravel and wet grass. The air hung thick with tension, like even the trees were holding their breath.

Then, a single gunshot shattered the stillness.

A woman screamed. High. Broken. Alive.

"That's his wife," Richard said under his breath. "Split and sweep. Riley, east wing. I'll take the west. Sniper," he spoke into his comm, "get high and cover us. Eyes everywhere."

"Copy that," came the sniper's calm reply.

The team moved like clockwork, each agent disappearing into different paths with the precision of people trained to dance with chaos.

Inside, the mansion had flipped its soul. The crystal chandeliers trembled in the silence. Marble floors, once pristine, were smeared with frantic footprints and something darker. Blood trailed along the walls. Portraits stared down as if they too were witnesses.

Another gunshot rang out—then a grunt.

Riley's voice crackled in Richard's ear: "Got one down. Alive. He's bleeding, but he's talking. Two more still at large."

"Sniper," Richard barked.

"Target acquired. Requesting green light."

Richard paused for just a breath. "Take the shot."

One clean pop. Then silence.

"Confirmed. One down. One remaining," the sniper reported.

Richard continued sweeping the west wing until he reached the double doors of the library. They were half-closed, but something—call it gut instinct or too many years doing this—told him to push through fast.

He entered. The first thing he saw was the blood.

Then Marcus.

He was sprawled across the Persian rug like a broken marionette, suit stained, his breaths shallow and wet. Not gone—but almost.

"Marcus!" Richard rushed to his side, kneeling in the blood. "Hey, stay with me. Who did this? Who's behind it? Why? Thornhill?"

Marcus blinked slowly, pain etched deep into every line of his face. His voice came out in ragged pieces. "Too... late..."

"No, not too late. Listen—who?" Richard's tone cracked, the frustration barely held back. "You said you'd talk if it came to this. I'm here. Give me something."

Marcus coughed violently, a trail of blood staining his lips. His fingers curled around Richard's sleeve.

"They're... they're everywhere," he whispered, eyes flickering like they were struggling to stay in the moment. "Folks at the club... Architects... You can't—"

The words died in his throat. His grip loosened.

"Marcus," Richard said, shaking him gently. "Marcus!"

But it was over.

The air in the room seemed to go still, like time had stopped to mourn him.

Riley appeared in the doorway seconds later, breathing hard, weapon still drawn.

"Scene's secure," he said. "Two hostiles neutralized. One's in custody. What about Marcus?"

Richard slowly stood. His hands were soaked in blood.

"Gone," he said, his voice empty. "He confirmed it, though. He said it—the Architects. It's them."

Riley exhaled like he'd been punched in the gut. "Damn. That means we're not fighting some rogue actor with a vendetta. This is a system."

"No," Richard said, turning toward him, his eyes no longer tired—just sharp, cold, and resolute. "This is the system."

He turned back to the body, voice low but thunderous. "Bag everything. Hard drives, phones, surveillance. If it blinks, hums, or has memory—we're taking it."

He stepped away from the blood but not the mission. "We're not leaving a single damn stone unturned."

CHAPTER

4

Clashing Agendas

"In the face of conflict, peace does not come from erasing differences but from weaving them into a balanced and constructive whole."

The mansion that once screamed wealth now whispered guilt. It didn't mourn—it stared. The kind of stare that made your gut churn, like it knew your secrets before you confessed them. The press called it "Marcus Reynold's fortress." But tonight, it looked more like a tomb with a penthouse view.

Media vans littered the street like crows at a fresh carcass, cameras aimed at the iron gates, their operators pacing like sharks with deadlines. The air buzzed with hunger—everyone wanted blood, or at least a quote that sounded like one.

Richard stepped through the mangled front doors. The hinges gave an unsettling groan, like even the house itself regretted letting them in.

Inside was a war zone dressed in designer clothes.

A velvet couch lay on its back like it had given up mid-conversation. Crystal shards sparkled on the floor like broken promises. And blood—rich, almost regal—streaked across the marble, the kind that once hosted galas and billion-dollar handshakes.

"This place..." Riley's voice came low behind him, uncharacteristically soft. "Looks like money had a nervous breakdown."

Richard didn't smile. He didn't even blink. "It's not a robbery gone bad. At least that much they were counting on until we crashed their party."

The agents moved silently through the wreckage. One began snapping photos. Another bagged what looked like a burner phone inside a shattered liquor cabinet. But Richard... he was scanning for silence inside the chaos.

Then he saw it.

Amidst the ruin, one thing remained impossibly untouched—a porcelain vase, standing upright on a narrow pedestal. Not a crack. Not a tilt. Not even dust.

"Something's off," he murmured, stepping toward it.

"Riley, over here," he called, motioning for his partner.

Riley joined him. "Out of all this mess, that's what you're worried about? A vase with survivor's guilt?"

Richard ignored him. His fingers traced its surface—smooth, cold, almost too perfect. Then he felt it—a subtle indentation, barely visible—a biometric slide, cleverly disguised.

"Riley," he said, eyes narrowing. "This isn't a decoration. It's a vault."

Riley blinked. "Because, of course, it is."

They called in the tech. Within minutes, their specialist had tools out, fingers flying—a few whirs, a soft beep, and then—a hiss. The vase opened like a flower, revealing something far more dangerous than explosives.

A leather-bound ledger. Black. Untouched. Waiting.

Richard flipped it open. His pulse skipped. Then slammed back like a war drum.

"This..." he whispered. "This isn't evidence. This is a confession—written by an entire network."

Riley leaned in, eyes darting over the names. "Banks. Politicians. CEOs. Jesus, Rich... these aren't just footnotes. These are headlines."

Richard closed the book with a quiet finality. "It's a kill list masquerading as an asset sheet."

Outside, the circus grew louder—flashing bulbs, shouted names, speculation mutating with every tweet.

When Richard stepped onto the front steps, ledger under his arm, the horde turned as one.

"Agent Suggs! What happened inside?"

"Is Reynold alive?"

"Are the rumors about Reynolds and the 401K true?"

Richard raised one hand, and like magic, the noise dropped.

"We are conducting an active investigation," he said calmly. "No speculation. No comment. When the facts are ready, you'll hear it—from us."

The murmurs resumed, quieter this time. But the panic was there. You could see it. Power was bleeding, and the world wanted a front-row seat.

Back inside, the team worked, bagging what the perpetrators hadn't erased. But Richard wandered out to the back veranda—an ornate marble terrace now smeared with boot prints and red.

Riley joined him, holding two cups of black coffee like they were negotiating world peace. He handed one over. "Thought you'd want the bitter version of hope."

Richard took it, staring at the line where the sun met the Earth. "This house. It had everything. But not a single soul made it out whole."

Riley nodded, sipping his own. "So. What's the move?"

Richard's answer came like a verdict. "I'd say we dig in hard, trace every name, every number, every symbol in that ledger. But with all the bureaucratic shit lines, that would be a lie, right? Whatever the case might be, here's what I know: someone tried to erase Marcus, but he left a ghost in the machine."

"They'll come for us now," Riley said, no hesitation—just a statement.

"They already have." Richard's jaw clenched. "But now... let's see what the ghost in the machine has to say before they finally vanish it."

The sky above them darkened into twilight. The mansion behind them stood like a monument to ego and execution. Somewhere beneath its floors, the echoes of screams and secrets still whispered. But above it all, two men stood with coffee, blood on their boots, and fire in their bones.

"You know we're probably not walking out of this untouched," Riley said.

"We walk out finished," Richard replied. "Or we don't walk out at all."

Riley raised his cup. "To making a mess of their masterpiece."

Richard clinked it. "To burning it down."

They turned together, silhouettes framed by a ruined mansion and a world that had no idea what storm was coming.

"Our world is shaped by constant change, driven by power struggles and concealed agendas. To endure, one must ask: how strong is the ground beneath you?"

Let's not kid ourselves—yes, I know I'm a bit of a creep. But, to be fair, shrimps curl their tails when they're stressed, and you're not exactly accusing seafood of emotional instability, are you? So, before you sharpen your pitchforks, consider that maybe I'm just adapting to a very stressful circumstance, like a shrimp under environmental stress.

Anyway...

Out in Wine Lake County, the morning was doing its best impression of heaven—sunlight poured like warm syrup over the hills, the trees whispered age-old gossip in the wind, and birds chirped with the kind of optimism that should be illegal before 9 a.m.

And there was Emily, seated on the creaky old veranda like the last piece of a calm jigsaw puzzle, sipping her coffee and pretending the world wasn't coming apart at the seams. The mug was chipped—some sentimental relic from her college years—and her slippers were mismatched. It didn't matter. This place, her mother's pride and joy, was the one place where chaos took off its boots and waited politely at the door. Here, time didn't just pause; it poured itself a large one and put its feet up.

But peace has a nasty habit of expiring just when you start getting comfortable.

Buzz.

Her phone buzzed against the wooden table like a warning. Emily glanced at it, frowned, already knowing it carried no good news, she took one last defiant sip of her coffee before answering.

"Emily?" The voice on the line didn't waste time with pleasantries.

And just like that, it happened.

"Marcus is dead."

Three words. Like a switchblade flicked open in the middle of paradise.

She didn't look surprised, didn't gasp. She just stared at the trees, wondering if the birds would take a moment of silence. They didn't. Of course not. They had worms to chase.

Marcus. The man whose presence had always felt like a closed door in a hallway you didn't want to walk down. Now he was gone. And instead of relief, the world handed her a riddle.

From inside the cottage, her mother's voice floated gently through the screen door. "Everything alright, honey?"

"Yeah, Mom," Emily said, voice tight as a violin string. "Just work."

A lie, wrapped in love, handed over like sugar in tea.

She stood up, finished her coffee in one gulp like it owed her rent, and went inside. Because whatever this was, it was no longer a retreat—it was just a really scenic front-row seat to a ticking time bomb.

The drive into the city was a blur of brake lights and mental static. Wine Lake was behind her, but her thoughts—God, her thoughts—were on a speedboat to nowhere. Marcus was dead. And as much as she hated what he stood for, there was a reason his name wasn't spoken in hallways without looking over your shoulder.

And if Emily was asking the obvious questions—Who killed him? Why now?—You better believe the agencies were asking even more dangerous ones.

By the time she stepped into CIA headquarters, the air was heavier than guilt at a confession booth. Phones rang like they were auditioning for a thriller soundtrack, and analysts scurried around like caffeinated mice with national secrets.

But here's where most people might get it twisted: Marcus dying didn't put this place in overdrive.

The CIA doesn't panic when someone with Marcus's power and influence dies.

No. The CIA panics when someone with such a type of network dies without permission. Because the CIA, the living cliche, against one's better judgment, is 80% committed to covering its own ass, and 20% vaguely interested in saving the world.

So while agents whispered, screens blinked, and someone definitely spilled coffee on a classified report, Emily walked to her desk like it was just another Monday with a side of madness.

And then it happened.

Her phone buzzed again. The name on the screen? *Alex.*

The one guy who always knew too much—and said too little. Because if he talked, his entire alibi would go up in flames.

"Alex," she answered, already knowing who it was.

"Emily," came his low, controlled voice. Too controlled. The kind of voice you get from a man who regularly dines with regret and doesn't tip the waiter.

"You heard?" she asked.

"I did. Marcus is dead," he said. Then paused. "And it's shifting everything."

Emily leaned against the edge of her desk. "I was told to hand off everything about Marcus to the FBI three weeks ago. So why is everyone acting like I just leaked the nuclear codes?"

Alex exhaled audibly. "Because it's not over. Word is, the Bureau found a ledger. Classified stuff. And your print might be on it."

She blinked. "What?"

"No one knows how. But if it's true... they'll come for you. This morning's call wasn't an update. It was a weather forecast."

"Cloudy with a chance of betrayal?" she murmured, dryly.

"Something like that. We need to meet. Tonight. Usual place."

Emily hesitated. "You're not telling me everything, are you?"

"I never do. You know the drill."

The line went dead before she could argue.

Typical Alex.

The office roared on in the background, but to Emily, it all sounded underwater. She stared at her phone, heart doing something between salsa and cardiac arrest.

She knew what this meant. She wasn't stepping into a mystery.

She was being dragged back into a story she thought had ended.

That evening, as she walked out of the building, her heels echoed like warnings on the marble floor. The sun had already dipped behind the skyscrapers, and her reflection in the glass doors looked like someone who had traded peace for purpose.

Wine Lake? That was a postcard now—a nice little fantasy with birdsong and chipped mugs.

This?

This was war.

And as for Alex—well, he might be the guy with all the secrets, but Emily was the one walking in with questions sharp enough to cut.

Tonight, the game wasn't starting.

It had already started.

She just hadn't realized she was the queen they'd all been moving.

"True clarity comes when we look beyond ourselves. By engaging with the hardships of others, we learn to see through deception."

While the George Bush Center for Intelligence boiled like a pot left unwatched—analysts arguing over satellite drops, inter-agency ego matches flaring like sunspots, and a printer somewhere screaming its final breath—the top floor remained cloaked in eerie stillness.

CIA Director Arthur C. Winters' office didn't just impress. It warned. The room was carved with clean lines and colder shadows, minimalist like a cathedral for war. No mess, no sentiment. Just sharpened order.

A thick stack of classified files sat on the obsidian desk in front of him, fanned out like tarot cards of doom. Each document was a secret people would kill for—or already had. The leather chair groaned as Arthur leaned back, fingers steepled, eyes unreadable. The silence was not peace; it was the kind of silence that curled around your ribs and waited to strike.

Then, like a whisper from the void, the door creaked open.

No knock. Just a suggestion of movement. One of his operatives—quiet, loyal, and probably carrying five illegal weapons in his tailored suit—stepped in.

Arthur didn't look up. Not yet. Eye contact, after all, was intimacy. And intimacy made you predictable.

The operative leaned in just enough to be heard. "The operation's compromised."

Four syllables. No drama. But in this room, that was DEFCON 2.

Arthur's eyes flicked upward, cool and sharp like steel meeting ice. "Keep me updated," he said quietly. "And say nothing to the others—for now."

The man nodded once, ghosted out, and the door sealed behind him with the softness of finality.

Arthur sat still, like a king whose castle had just been breached and who already knew which knight he'd sacrifice.

"Another day in paradise," he muttered, his smile bitter as overbrewed coffee.

He picked up the phone, punched in a number that probably triggered at least six NSA alerts, and waited.

The line clicked.

"Yeah, I know," said the voice on the other end. Dry. Nervous.

Arthur didn't flinch. "The team was sloppy. Amateurs. And now our local farmers with their go-to hell tool have caught wind."

There was a pause, the sound of someone holding back a very expensive ulcer. "You said this would be tied up. That the crop would stay buried."

"Crop is buried," Arthur said, voice tightening. "Problem is, the boys in Jackets brought shovels."

Another pause.

"And the ledger?"

"They have it. And there's a print on it."

Silence.

Arthur's voice dropped lower. "Ours."

"Jesus Christ."

"Don't say his name," Arthur said coolly. "We've got enough ghosts in this room."

"What's your play?"

"Damage control," Arthur replied. "We activate the contingency. Scrub every connection. No loose ends."

The voice on the line hesitated—then, finally: "Understood."

The call ended.

Arthur sat still for a moment longer, then stood, spine stiff like a man held together by memory and mission. He walked out of his office and into his den—the main operations briefing room. The staff was already gathered. Their expressions ranged from focused to apprehensive—except for Emily, who looked like a deer caught in headlights. She tucked into the corner like someone trying not to breathe too loudly. She looked sharp. Alert. But something in her eyes—too wide, too still—gave her away.

Arthur scanned the room once and didn't bother sitting. "Let's not waste time," he began, voice slicing through the tension like a wire. "Thirteen months ago, we ran an off-book operation in Nigeria—no red tape. No paperwork. Marcus's private military firm was contracted for a specific purpose: to neutralize the problem and hush the fallout. In return, we let Marcus run a few side hustles in peace."

There were murmurs. No one dared speak. Arthur continued.

"Well, surprise. Marcus isn't the type to leave things buried. And now the Bureau has a ledger. Names. Deals. Locations. Our operation—" he paused, letting that land "—with our fingerprints all over it. Which means if this leaks, we're not just cleaning up a mess. We're in the mess."

His gaze swept the room. "And in case you've forgotten how this works—when Washington starts swinging, they don't hit upward. They hit sideways. And down."

Uneasy glances were exchanged. Someone coughed. Emily stayed frozen, as if she might faint.

Arthur's eyes pinned her. "Emily. Something to add?"

She opened her mouth. Closed it again. The words tasted like betrayal.

"No?" Arthur's voice was razor-flat. "Then let's move on. I need every link between Marcus and this agency severed. Every thread traced, every name scrubbed. No stone unturned. You know the drill—chap, chap."

Arthur stood in the center of it all, a general commanding his troops.

The room dissolved into motion. Screens flickered to life, digital trails traced, erasing footprints, redacted files opened like Russian dolls. Emily didn't move. She watched Arthur, her mind a swirl of conflicted emotions. She thought about loyalty—what it meant, what it cost. Hadn't they all done things in its name? Things they'd never admit, not even to themselves?

Because thirteen months ago, she had been on that mission.

Told it was a diplomatic escort.

Told it was "peacekeeping."

They'd told her nothing of the real purpose,

Her hands were clean. Her name was clean. But her presence was enough.

She was the alibi. The smiling, clean-faced front they'd used to mask whatever else Marcus had done. She wasn't just a patsy.

She was the cover story. And now, the realization hit her like a freight train, her stomach knotting with a sick mix of anger and betrayal.

Arthur's voice cut through her haze again. "Emily. Walk with me."

Her stomach sank, but she followed him into the corridor, just her heels clicking against the floor. No one dared eavesdrop.

"You're rattled," Arthur said, without looking at her, his tone blunt but not unkind.

"You used me," she shot back.

He paused. That got his attention.

"You sent me in blind," she said, voice trembling. "I thought I was negotiating. You turned me into a decoy. Wasn't I? A patsy."

Arthur turned to face her. For a moment, he looked human. Tired. Not regretful—but weathered.

"Emily," he said, voice quieter now. "You think I wasn't used? That I haven't walked into meetings carrying lies in my briefcase and smiled while shaking hands that bled behind closed doors?"

"That's not the same."

"It's exactly the same," he snapped. Then softened again. "You want the truth? We lie, we deceive, we kill—all to stop worse lies, bigger deaths. There are no clean hands in this agency. There are only hands we keep from being severed."

She stared at him, mouth dry.

"You don't have to like it," he said, "but you do have to live with it. Or walk away. That's the nature of this job. We do what's necessary for the greater good."

A long silence.

Her eyes burned with unshed tears. "At what cost? How do you justify it?" He sighed, his voice dropping to a near whisper. "Because if we don't play dirty, the people on the other side will. And they won't hesitate to burn everything we stand for. This isn't about you, or me, or even Marcus. It's about keeping the balance intact. You don't have to like it, but you have to understand it."

Emily swallowed hard, her throat tight. She wasn't sure she could accept that explanation, but in that moment, she realized she had little choice.

Arthur clapped her lightly on the shoulder. "Get back in there. We still have time to clean this up—before someone decides to clean us up."

Back in the war room, the tempo was faster now—keyboards clattering like gunfire. Arthur returned to the center of it all, the conductor of the orchestra no one wanted to be in.

"Let's get to work," he said calmly, "Our job is to protect the interests of the United States. Nothing less."

And just like that, the machine kept turning.

Emily stood at the edge of it all, no longer sure where her allegiance truly lay. Not with Arthur. Not even with the agency.

But the truth? That was starting to look like the only thing worth fighting for.

Even if it got her killed.

"Life's deepest connections often hide in the simplest moments—like the sun behind clouds, they emerge in their time, revealing things that reshape our stories."

The sun had already clocked out for the day. Porch lights flicked on lazily, and driving through the condo's playground, the evening air filled with the faint laughter of children chasing the last minutes of freedom before bedtime.

I pulled quietly into Richard's condo parking lot—my unannounced drop-in, a classic move in our unpredictable world of intel and informants. No warning, no text. Just vibes, curiosity, and a nose for classified breadcrumbs. I was there to do what we always did when the world felt a bit too heavy—unwind, trade hot takes on hot messes, and dissect the latest whispers from the intelligence underground.

I figured I'd beat him home. I was right.

I sat idling in my car, mentally running through what I needed to tell him, particularly about the growing suspicion around Marcus Reynold's death. The case was turning radioactive, and I had a hunch Richard was headed right into the heart of it.

Then came the low hum of a familiar engine.

Richard's sleek black car rolled in slowly, headlights carving the dusk like blades before surrendering to stillness. He turned off the engine and leaned back in his seat for a beat longer than usual, staring out into nothing with that trademark expression of his—the one that said: "Today gave me more riddles than answers."

Wild goose chases—dead ends wrapped in classified paper. Secrets buried so deep even the coffins had security clearance.

I reached for my door handle, ready to jump out and flag him down, when—buzz. My phone rang.

I answered it quickly, eyes still on Richard as I listened with one ear. He sat unmoving, breathing out what I imagined was a long day's worth of encrypted anxiety. But just as I was about to call out his name—

She appeared.

Cue the soundtrack. Cut to slow-motion. Spotlight on destiny's favorite agent of chaos: Marilyn.

I froze mid-sentence, mid-step, and slid right back into the shadows like I was part of the landscaping. This... I had to watch. Because, against every logical prediction and statistical probability in the universe, she was walking straight toward her car. Right next to his.

He didn't see her at first. He was still stretching the day out of his shoulders. But when he looked up and saw her—

The man froze. For a second. Richard.

"Hey there, stranger," he called out, that half-charming, half-bullshitting tone only he could deliver. "On another secret mission?"

Marilyn paused mid-step. Her eyes narrowed in faux suspicion before a grin bloomed across her face—mischievous, familiar, a little dangerous. "Caught red-handed," she replied, slinging her bag onto her shoulder. "You know how it is—another day, another covert operation."

Richard chuckled. The real kind. The kind he saves for rare occasions and people who surprise him. He walked over, casually leaning against the car next to hers like James Bond with a neighborly mortgage.

"So, what's the big mission this time?" he asked. "Neighborhood surveillance? Condo espionage?"

Marilyn tapped her chin, deadpan. "Let's just say it involves classified intel, a suspiciously nosy client, and the very real danger of running out of excuses."

He laughed again. Damn him. He was glowing.

"I gotta say, I'm impressed," he said. "You've got the whole 'mysterious operative' thing nailed."

She bowed dramatically, hair catching the last sliver of floodlight like a flare of chestnut fire. "Thank you. It's a gift. Years of training. Three exes, four Netflix thrillers, and one very suspicious barista."

Their banter flowed like jazz—improvised, playful, layered. You know the kind. That weirdly perfect rhythm two people fall into when the universe decides to cheat a little and sync their timing just right.

Richard's eyes kept drifting to her face, studying it like it held answers to questions he hadn't figured out how to ask yet. And then came his move.

"So," he said, tone softer, brows slightly raised, "last time we met... I never got your name. Think I've earned it by now, don't you? I'm Richard, by the way."

Marilyn smirked, tilting her head like she was about to scold a puppy. "Nice to officially meet you. And to remind you of my name for the second time... Richard."

Oof.

Touché, Marilyn.

Richard blinked, smiled, then shook her hand—long enough to notice the spark, short enough to pretend he didn't. "Marilyn," he repeated, tasting it like a rare wine. "Right. Marilyn."

And for the record, Richard never forgets a name. He was pulling the old 'charming idiot' card—and from where I stood, it was working disturbingly well.

Their chat drifted from coffee preferences to what Marilyn called "covert caffeine extraction protocols" and Richard's tragically rigid views on espresso ratios. The girl laughed at his dumb jokes. He smiled at her sarcasm like it was gospel.

Then came the part that sealed the deal.

"You know," Richard said, just bold enough, "we should grab coffee sometime. Trade stories. Debrief about our 'missions.'"

Marilyn pretended to mull it over. "Hmm. I suppose I could squeeze that into my top-secret schedule."

"Perfect," he said, fishing out his phone. "But fair warning—I'm ruthless when it comes to coffee. I interrogate baristas. Decaf is treason."

She laughed again, shaking her head. "Well then. I guess I'll leave my decaf at home."

They exchanged numbers. Nothing dramatic. Just the quiet spark of a fuse.

And then, with a shared smile and a promise of coffee and espionage, they parted ways.

Richard watched her go, that rare look in his eyes—like something unspoken had shifted inside him. Something hopeful. Something dangerous.

From my seat in the shadows, I didn't move. Not right away. I figured I'd let him breathe. Let him marinate in whatever spell Marilyn had cast.

Some things, even in our line of work, don't need to be investigated.

Some things need to be felt.

And sometimes, the universe doesn't send fireballs or encrypted memos—it sends someone in jeans, holding a car key, with a sarcastic mouth and eyes that smile like they've already seen your secrets and decided to like you anyway.

So yeah. I went home that night.

Let Richman enjoy the wheel he just accidentally set in motion.

I had a feeling this was going to get interesting.

And trust me—I've seen interesting.

But this? This was the rare kind.

The kind that made you think about fate.

The kind you remember.

CHARLES E.A.

"Often, our frustration arises from realizing others may hold better ideas than our own—yet this discomfort compels us to expand our horizons."

The clock glared back at her—8:23 PM. It wasn't late by New York standards, but in my world, this was the witching hour. Not for ghosts or vampires, but for secrets. The kind of secrets that tap you on the shoulder and whisper: Run now... or start choosing your last words.

Emily stood in her hallway, tugging a gray hoodie over her head, the flickering hallway light behind her casting a half-moon shadow. Her outfit—gray sweatpants, sneakers, and a hoodie—could fool anyone into thinking she was just heading out for a late jog. But cardio was the last thing on her mind tonight, and no Fitbit in the world could track what her heart was doing.

And she knew it.

Slipping out of her apartment, locking the door behind her like it would make a difference. Emily moved like someone who had rehearsed this in her head for hours. She walked with the kind of purpose you couldn't fake—like a woman with questions only danger seemed to answer. Her pace was quick, not rushed. Composed panic. Her eyes scanned every passing face, car, and shadow, not because she was paranoid, but because she now knew paranoia might be the only thing keeping her alive.

By the time she reached the corner, a yellow taxi screeched to a halt after her signal. She slid into the back seat like someone who'd done it a thousand times.

"East River Park. The old bench near the maintenance shed," she said. Calm. Steady. But inside her chest? A whole circus of emotions was staging a riot, and despite the iron twist in her gut.

She didn't look back. Never did.

Before Emily arrived, Alex was already there, sitting on the middle bench, elbows on his knees, under a dying streetlamp that flickered like it couldn't decide whether to shine or burn out. The light caught his sharp features, painting shadows across a face that had spent too much time knowing too much, like a man two seconds away from texting. Don't bother.

When Emily approached, he glanced up from his phone, his eyes locking onto hers with a kind of weary intensity.

"You actually came," he said, his tone halfway between concern and I told you so, like a brother too tired to gloat but still too right not to say it.

She exhaled and flopped onto the bench beside him, pulling her hoodie tighter. "You called it. Something bad's going down—and surprise, I'm the clown in the middle of the circus."

Alex stared forward, lips pressed. "Arthur?"

"Arthur," she confirmed, her tone acidic.

Alex leaned back, folding his arms. "Arthur didn't loop you into this because you make a damn good agent, Emily. Whatever this is, it's bigger than both of us. And probably older than you'd like to believe."

Her laugh was dry, hollow. "If I don't play his game, I get buried for a crime I didn't even know was on the menu. And I mean that literally.

Alex looked at her for a long moment. "You're being set up. But I'm guessing you're not the endgame. There's more going on."

She glanced sideways at him, her voice barely a whisper. "Then why me?"

"Because you were close to something. Or someone," Alex said. "Either that, or you're a convenient scapegoat."

Alex rubbed his temples like he was massaging a migraine into submission. "We need answers. And fast. You remember that FBI guy you handed all our evidence to?"

"Richard?"

He nodded. "Yeah. Him. I think it's time we bring him back into the picture. See if he can help us connect a few of these dots before they choke you out."

Emily hesitated. "And how exactly do you think he'll help me?" she said, raising an eyebrow. "You act like we have lunch dates. We don't even have a handshake."

Alex gave her a side-smile. "Remember last month at the Bureau? I mentioned I had a guy—my buddy, in the northeast block?"

"Vaguely."

"That's Richard. My best friend. Let's just say if I ever needed someone to help unstick me from a shady mess and misfiled operational receipts—he'd be my guy."

Emily blinked. "Seriously?"

"Served two tours together. One sandstorm. Three goat-related accidents," Alex said, counting on his fingers. "Yeah. He's family."

Emily turned toward him slowly. "And you—you still haven't answered my question, Alex. Why are you helping me?"

For a moment, silence. The kind that hangs between people when the truth sits like hot iron on their tongue. Anything said would sound either calculated or stupid..

Alex opened his mouth... then closed it. Even his conscience held up a sign that read: Don't you dare lie to her.

Instead, he looked her in the eyes and said, softly, "See you tomorrow morning... assuming we're still on the clock."

Emily didn't respond; she stared at him, waiting for something more. But there was nothing left to say. She just pulled her hoodie tighter and flagged down the next taxi. She didn't look back.

And just like that, the night swallowed them both.

The Next Morning – FBI Headquarters

The FBI building didn't exactly scream "welcome," and the room they were led into looked like someone had sucked all the joy out of a government warehouse and added a security badge. The walls were pale, the lighting harsh, and the vibe... somewhere between DMV and doomsday bunker.

Richard stood behind the desk, arms crossed, eyes sharp. "Hey, man. You bailed on me last night," he said to Alex, brows raised. "With all the buzz going around and no Lex-man."

Alex grinned. "Bro, I showed up. But you were in the middle of some... I don't know, high-level 'rizz' shit. Figured I'd let you have your moment."

Richard barked a laugh. "Please. Can't confirm or deny. But fair."

Emily blinked. "Wait—what?"

Richard waved it off like a bad dream and pointed to the chairs. "Sit. Talk. Why do I feel like this is the part where I regret answering your text?"

Emily sat, arms folded. "You two want to catch up, or can we dive into why the hell someone wants me to disappear?"

Richard shifted his attention. "Right. You don't look so good."

Emily gave a mirthless chuckle. "Thanks, you're a peach. And I haven't felt great since the last time I had coffee with you."

Richard raised an eyebrow. "Well, that makes two of us."

Alex jumped in before sarcasm became a game. "Let's cut through the fluff. Emily—did I ever mention Richard and I went through hell together? Twice? Afghanistan, Fallujah. Name a place with good food and worse odds; we were there."

Richard shook his head, already smiling. "Here we go..."

"This man here," Alex gestured grandly, "was a legend. Sharpest mind in the unit. Wouldn't stop until every detail was nailed down and every asshole trying to hide behind a lie had their face printed on a wall."

Richard groaned. "Don't."

"I'm just saying," Alex continued, "he's the reason I'm not a human-sized ashtray in Kandahar."

Emily chuckled. "So you were the terrifying marine?"

"Still am," Richard said, deadpan. "Just with better shirts."

Then Richard's expression turned serious, eyes on Emily. "But let's not kid ourselves. You're in deep."

Emily crossed her legs, eyes narrowing. "Define 'deep' in non-bureaucratic terms."

"The fact that you're sitting here means they think you're worth watching—but not yet worth destroying," Richard said flatly. "Use that. Buy time. Dig deep. And when the hammer comes down, be somewhere else."

Emily nodded slowly. "And if I need... I don't know, clearance? Surveillance data?"

Richard pointed to Alex. "That's what he's for. He knows half the dark web and three-fourths of everyone we'd rather not name."

"Hey," Alex said, hands up. "I only talk to bad people for good reasons. Sometimes. Okay, occasionally."

Richard grunted. "You're a damn genius, and the most annoying person I've ever tried to work with."

Emily laughed again—light, genuine. "You two really haven't changed."

The tension in the room cracked like a bad joke at a funeral.

Then Richard said, voice low, "But this—this is serious. If you start pulling threads, you better be ready for the sweater to fall apart. It's big. And ugly."

"Ugly's our specialty," Alex said with a wink.

As they walked out, the corridors of the Bureau stretching long and empty before them, Emily glanced back. Behind the banter, she could see it now—Richard was a safety net, Alex was a shield, and she... she was the bait walking into the lion's den.

But at least, just maybe, in all this darkness, she'd found her unlikely flashlights... with sarcasm settings on high.

THE COBRAS ON THE HILL

"Understanding how truth and falsehood interact in secrecy is a profound skill—one that grants clarity where most see only shadows."

Now, this is the part where even the most forgiving reader will stop and ask: Is Alex blind? Like, medically? Or is he just...romantically stupid?

Because, seriously—how do you spend years sleeping next to the enemy and still not spot the red flags fluttering in your face like parade banners?

If you asked anyone—anyone with at least one working eyeball and a quarter-ounce of common sense—they'd tell you Alex Carter was a brilliant man. Not just smart-smart, but the kind of smart that made you feel like you needed to hide your computerized gadgets around him. Top NSA analyst. Decorated. Paranoid in all the right and evil ways. Knew how to hack a satellite while making an espresso. That kind of smart.

So, naturally, you'd think he'd know better than to fall in love with a spy.

But here we are.

But let's not judge too quickly. Love does strange things to even the sharpest minds—especially when it's wearing yoga pants, smells like vanilla, and laughs at your worst jokes.

That evening, the warm flicker of the porch light greeted him like an old friend with bad news. It buzzed gently overhead, casting a nostalgic, golden hue across the front door—but something about the night felt... off. The kind of "off" that made the hairs on his arm whisper among themselves like gossiping barbers.

He slid the key into the lock, stepped inside, and stood there for a beat. Listening.

Nothing.

The house didn't feel violated—no kicked-in door, no ransacked drawers—but it felt altered and rearranged, almost like a magician had walked in and moved a single, invisible card in the deck just to mess with your head.

"Erin?" he called, his voice steady but low, slicing through the stillness like a scalpel.

No answer.

"Erin, you home?" he repeated, a bit louder—like volume could drown suspicion.

Still nothing.

He walked in slowly, performing the most ordinary ritual in the most suspicious way possible: dropping his car key down on the bookshelf, same spot as always—except tonight, his eyes caught it.

The bookshelf looked fine. Polished. Familiar. Books in their place, trinkets standing at attention like obedient soldiers. But then—there. A tiny smudge. Barely visible. The kind of mark no one else would notice, but to a man trained to see through chaos, that tiny anomaly lit up like a crime scene spotlight.

He froze.

Reaching into his desk drawer like a man reaching for a revolver in an old Western, he pulled out a sleek, matte-black scanner—NSA tech he really shouldn't have at home.

The holographic interface lit up with a quiet hum, casting blue light across his focused eyes. He scanned the shelf.

Beep. Beep. Boom

There it was. A surveillance camera, surgically embedded in the wood grain. It was so clean, so seamless, that even Alex had walked past it a million times without blinking.

He blinked. Once. Twice.

Then laughed. Not a real laugh—more like a sound people make when they realize some high intelligence agency apparently funded their entire love life.

He stared at the lens, and for a second, he didn't feel watched—he felt violated.

He hacked into the feed, of course. That was second nature to him. By now, typing in a firewall bypass was as casual as texting "you up?" at 1 a.m. The display filled with footage. At first, it was mundane: him cooking eggs shirtless, reading, napping with one sock on, him stretching on the couch, him scratching an itch in places that should never be filmed. But then...

Someone else appeared.

Casual. Familiar. Moving like the space belonged to her.

She spoke into a phone. Confirming the camera angles. Verified the clarity. She adjusted the camera again. Clearly not new to this. Then—she turned, just slightly.

It was Erin.

His fiancée.

The woman who called his mother "Mom," who helped him pick out curtains, who once cried over a documentary about abandoned puppies, was... an infiltrator.

He blinked, once. Twice.

"No... no, no, no..." he muttered, the words staggering out like drunkards.

His breath caught in his throat as puzzle pieces—once scattered memories—snapped together with painful clarity: the mysterious "work emergencies," the oddly phrased questions about his projects, the way her voice would subtly tense when he talked about encrypted files. Her sudden interest in his boring cybersecurity updates.

That one time she knew exactly when he deleted those files—and said, "Don't worry, I backed them up."

He thought she was just being sweet. No. She was being a damn operative.

It was all staged. Every touch. Every look. Every late-night whisper. He hadn't fallen in love with a woman—he'd fallen into an operation.

"Goddamn," he said under his breath, running a hand through his hair. "She used my heart like a keycard."

He stood frozen for a moment, then suddenly sprang into motion. He grabbed his phone and dialed Richard.

The line picked up quickly. "Alex?"

"She was in my house," Alex said, skipping pleasantries. His voice was tight, deliberate. "And I had no clue who she really was."

A pause. Crunch. "...Okay. Be more specific."

"She bugged my house."

Another pause. No crunch this time. Just the sound of federal gears turning.

Richard exhaled slowly, like a man who'd been expecting this shoe to drop since last season. "Not gonna lie, her record was too clean when I ran it. Like, too clean. Like dishwasher commercial clean. No exes. No jobs with HR complaints. Not even a parking ticket. Honestly, I thought she might be an android."

"You could've led with that six months ago."

"You could've dated someone less hot and more traceable," Richard shot back.

"This isn't a joke."

"I know. I'm just deflecting because this is wildly uncomfortable."

"Well, she fooled me too," Alex snapped. "But that's not why I called."

"Oh?"

"Your key witness—the guy tied to Marcus's case. You said he was in secure custody?"

"Yeah. Why?"

"Because based on what Erin said on the feed, I think he's a target. They're tying up loose ends."

Richard didn't even reply. He hung up mid-sentence.

At FBI headquarters, Richard was suddenly sprinting like a man who'd just remembered his oven was on. Barking orders. Flashing his badge. The holding cell was two floors down.

When he got to the door, his stomach dropped. The feed outside the cell was down. Camera black. Code red.

"Open it," he said, his voice sharp.

The guard hesitated. "Sir, protocol says—"

"OPEN. IT."

The door clicked open.

Inside, the key witness lay still. Too still.

Blood crept out in dark ribbons beneath him. His eyes stared at nothing, wide open. His silence now permanent. The secrets he carried, the names, the evidence—gone.

"Jesus Christ," one of the agents muttered.

Richard's hand tightened around his weapon. "Whoever did this... they're surgical. No sound. No trace. Professionals."

He swallowed hard. "They're not just ahead of us—they've been driving this whole damn bus."

Back at his house, Alex sat alone in the dark.

Not in fear. In focus.

The glow of his screen reflected in his eyes as he traced the feed's network path. He was following breadcrumbs now—digital fingerprints that someone thought they had hidden well.

His phone buzzed.

Richard.

"We were too late. Witness is dead. Clean hit."

Alex clenched his jaw, the shadows of betrayal stretching longer across his walls. "I thought I had every angle covered. I was playing chess."

"Turns out," Richard replied, "you were among the pawns. No different from Emily's nightmare."

Another pause.

"Alex..."

"Yeah?"

"Watch your back."

Alex turned to where Erin's photo once stood on his desk. Gone now—erased. Just like her sincerity.

His fingers hovered over the keyboard. His face hardened into something unrecognizable.

"Don't worry, Richard," he said quietly.

"I'm done watching."

"When trust is broken, attempts to mend the bond reveal its fragile nature. Promises that once seemed strong dissolve into the silence of broken faith, leaving scars not easily repaired."

The news dropped like a piano in a silent room. One second, the FBI office buzzed with the low thrum of routine chaos—half-sipped coffees, passive-aggressive printer wars, and agents typing like caffeine-fueled court stenographers. The next, the entire floor stopped breathing.

Phones rang unanswered. A paper jam hissed somewhere in the corner, unnoticed. Richard stood dead center, his six-foot frame rigid as steel, eyes sweeping the room like a hawk ready to eviscerate whatever rodent dared blink too loudly.

"The witness is dead."

He hadn't shouted it. No. He just said it, voice low, cold, and surgical. And that somehow made it worse.

Gasps ricocheted off cubicle walls. Someone knocked over their coffee with a curse. Another dropped a folder as if it had burned to the touch. The ripple of disbelief spread fast—because this wasn't just any witness. This was the witness. The linchpin. The talking key to a locked vault of conspiracy, names, money trails, and power players who thought they were untouchable.

Not anymore. Because now? That thread was gone—snipped.

Richard's jaw tightened, nostrils flaring, the way it did when he was debating whether to flip a table or go full "silent assassin" mode. He whispered to no one in particular, "How the hell did this happen?"

His phone buzzed, jerking him out of the haze. The screen read: Director Anderson.

"Wonderful."

He answered, voice clipped. "Director. Our witness is cold. A breach. Someone slipped through our system like a damn ghost."

The voice on the other end was all iron. "Lock it down. Nobody in. Nobody out. This is Priority One, Richard. I'm on my way. And I want names."

Click.

Richard didn't miss a beat. He spun to face the squad like a general about to storm a Normandy of broken trust.

"Seal every exit of this building. I want every door locked tighter than a politician's tax returns. Get me the last 48 hours of surveillance. If they don't have clearance," he paused, voice dropping into a razor edge, "they're a suspect."

The room scattered like scared pigeons.

Just then, the door slammed open. Riley barreled in, mid-jacket removal, hair still wet from morning mist—or stress sweat, who knew.

"Rich! I was gone for ten minutes. Ten. Minutes. I mean barely out of the parking lot, and you've got this place looking like DEFCON 1. What the hell happened?"

Richard shot him a sharp glance. "You're late, Riley."

"Yeah, well," Riley replied, rubbing his elbow nervously, "had to dodge a squirrel on my way in. Nearly totaled the car. But this? I didn't think we'd implode this fast."

Richard didn't say a word.

Riley blinked, confused. "Wait, what are you mad about?"

"I'm mad about a lot of things. You and your squirrel just the cherry." Richard said dryly.

Riley flopped into a chair, spinning it around with flair before sitting backward like a substitute teacher with boundary issues. "You know, one day, you'll miss me when I'm gone. But fine, hit me. What the hell happened?"

Richard's lips twitched—a fleeting moment of humor amid the tension. "We both knew something like this was coming, but I didn't expect them to pull it off in broad daylight. Surveillance glitch, Riley; surveillance glitch."

Riley let out a low whistle. "Someone gave them a map and a welcome gift?"

"Worse," Richard said. "Someone gave them access. You can see this wasn't sloppy, it was a professional clean hit."

Riley tilted his head. "Do you think we need an exterminator?"

"Possibly. And speaking of messy... who knows about our little arrangement with Felicity?"

Riley blinked. "Wow. Okay. Didn't know we were doing heart attacks before breakfast. And to answer your question, not more than three pairs of ears. But let's just say... if your pals had a dartboard, Felicity's face would be the bullseye."

"I'm not sure I can keep this secret much longer," Richard admitted, running a hand through his already stressed-out hair. "Especially not after this."

"Well, if they throw tomatoes, good luck with that. You're the one who invited the rogue wildcard to the dance."

Before Richard could retort, a shout echoed from the AV team's corner.

"Sir! You need to see this!"

A blurry clip blinked to life on the screen. A woman—hooded, scarfed, anonymous—walked the hallway where the witness had been just hours before. She moved like someone with ballet in her bones and blood on her gloves.

"Zoom. Enhance. Run facial recognition," Richard barked. "Every angle. She didn't teleport out of here."

Within minutes, the truth unraveled like a bad sweater. She had posed as maintenance—badges forged, gait practiced. But what made Richard's gut twist wasn't just her ghost act.

It was who she met in the hallway.

The traitor.

The grainy footage showed a man—partially obscured, but familiar. Too familiar.

"Oh no..." Riley muttered, jaw going slack. "Tell me that's not who I think it is."

"I wish I could."

Richard stared, breath shallow. Betrayal felt worse when it had a name. And a badge. And a sandwich in the same breakroom fridge.

"Cross-reference everything," he ordered. "I want every past assignment, every disciplinary report, every traffic ticket if necessary. I want to know if this guy ever thought about jaywalking."

Riley, for once, looked sober. "You've got a mole and a ghost assassin. You're basically two plot twists away from needing a cape."

Richard shot him a look so sharp that Riley leaned back, as if it had physically nicked him.

"Too soon?" Riley said, hands up in mock surrender.

"I'm surrounded by idiots," Richard muttered.

"Hey. I'm a useful idiot. There's a difference." Riley Shots back.

Back in his office, Richard stood alone. Papers littered the table—photos, maps, redacted reports, and a half-eaten protein bar. He leaned in, knuckles pale against the desk, and whispered to the silence.

"They knew exactly what they were doing."

It wasn't just a murder. It was a message. Whoever they are, they knew the FBI inside out. They weren't attacking from the outside.

They were already in.

He stepped back out, gaze firm, shoulders squared.

"To all of you staring at screens and pretending not to panic," he said, voice echoing through the war room, "we are not losing this fight. Not today. We don't get scared—we get smarter. We don't retreat—we track. And above all, we don't let them think they won."

Silence.

Then Riley muttered, "Also, if anyone sees a squirrel in the parking lot, tell it I owe it an apology."

And for the first time that day, someone cracked a smile.

THE COBRAS ON THE HILL

"The darkest truths do not merely wound us—they awaken the resilience of the human spirit, illuminating its boundless capacity to endure and transcend even the most shadowed realities."

The cold blue hue from the monitor bathed Richard's face like a confession booth light—unforgiving, clinical, incision. He sat alone, elbows dug into the polished walnut desk that had seen more spilled coffee and broken hopes than justice. His office was quiet, too quiet for a federal building in crisis. Outside, fluorescent lights buzzed like anxious whispers, but inside, there was only the rhythmic tapping of fingers against wood and the terrible clarity of truth unfolding frame by frame.

The grainy surveillance footage stuttered across the screen like a dying memory—blurry, distorted, but damning.

He didn't need a facial recognition algorithm. No database. No AI composite wizardry.

His heart already knew what his eyes were afraid to confirm.

Two figures.

The woman moved like smoke—too fluid, too precise. And beside her, the man—a goddamn FBI agent. One of their own. Richard's jaw clenched so tightly it popped.

"They're nervous," he muttered, squinting. "Scared, but trained... controlled."

He rewound the clip, zoomed in.

The two figures reached the holding cell—the last place anyone should have had access to without half a dozen signatures and a retinal scan. But the agent swiped his card with the ease of ordering lunch at a drive-thru.

Click.

The cell door groaned open.

Inside, the witness sat on the edge of the cot, like a man waiting to be forgotten. He looked up, confusion etched across his tired face—then fear. Not the dramatic kind from movies, but the quiet, heart-sinking kind. The kind that starts in your gut before your mind catches up.

The woman moved like thunder in a bottle. Steel flashed once. Maybe twice.

And then... silence.

A life ended on a cold, sterile floor, blood blooming like ink on paper.

Richard exhaled sharply, like he'd been holding his breath for a century. "Son of a bitch," he hissed, standing up so abruptly his chair shrieked against the floor.

He didn't pace—he stormed.

Within seconds, he'd stitched together the image using internal software, pixel by pixel. No need for anything fancy—her face was clear enough now. He sent it to Alex. No message. Just the image. Let it speak.

Seconds later, his phone rang.

Alex's voice exploded through the speaker like a Molotov cocktail wrapped in disbelief.

"Rich, it's her. That's Erin. My Erin. Can you believe it?" His voice cracked halfway between shock and something deeper. Betrayal, maybe. Or heartbreak. Or both.

Richard froze, heat crawling up his neck. Then he exploded.

"Who the hell is Erin, Alex?" he snapped. "Because from where I'm standing, we've got a damn ghost with a federal kill count. Social security? Fake. Education? Invented. Next of kin? Non-existent. I've seen phantoms with more paperwork!"

There was a beat of silence. Then Alex, quieter now, colder:

"You know... most people think devils come with red horns and sulfur breath. But the real ones?"

He paused, almost whispering now.

"They look like people you love. People who know how to smile at you while they gut you from the inside."

Before Richard could respond, Alex added, "I'm five minutes out."

Five minutes.

And true to his word, Alex stormed into the office exactly four minutes and fifty-seven seconds later, trench coat still flapping, tie half-askew, and eyes darker than Richard had ever seen them.

"Tell me everything you've got," Alex demanded, pacing like a man who couldn't afford to stand still.

Richard didn't sugarcoat. "She's a pro, Alex. Slipped past three departments, used our own guy to get in. And when she was done? Gone. Like poof. The last trace we got is her car merging onto the freeway. If she's headed to one of the private airfields off I-29, she'll be airborne before we know what her new look would be. Though I've got teams heading to each of them, but between you and me, if she's half the ghost she appears to be, she's already sipping champagne over Nebraska.

Alex gripped the edge of Richard's desk so hard his knuckles went pale, like it was the only thing keeping him tethered to Earth.

"What I don't get," Richard added, "is how she played you—all of us. I mean, we train to spot lies. We breathe suspicion. And she walked right in, Alex. No alarms. Flags, not so much. Just that charming little smile and a résumé built out of thin air."

Alex exhaled sharply. "Because she's smarter than all of us, Rich. Smarter than me, that's for damn sure.

Richard nodded slowly, folding his arms. "And the scary part? She did it so well, we're still catching up. I mean, think about it, Alex—she had coffee with you, you both probably enjoyed sex in your bed last night, and still, she had time to plan an assassination inside a federal compound."

Alex turned away, rubbing his hands down his face like he was trying to wipe away the memory of her.

Meanwhile, miles away, Erin moved through the hangar like a shadow wrapped in vanilla. The private jet waited, humming with quiet menace, engines already warming up.

She didn't run. She walked. Head high. Every step a reminder that she was always ten moves ahead. She boarded like she belonged there, because she did. That's the trick with disappearing—you don't sneak out. You own your exit.

By the time Alex and Richard were pulling up satellite logs and calling in every airfield on the East Coast, Erin was buckled in, thirty thousand feet above their understanding. The jet hummed like a satisfied accomplice, slicing through clouds like silk.

And while two of America's supposedly finest agents sat hunched over a monitor, flipping through flight manifests and radar signatures like two grumpy librarians with broken glasses, the plane was vanishing from radar.

"She's gone," Richard muttered.

"What?" Alex snapped, leaning over his shoulder.

"Gone, Alex." He stabbed at the screen. "The plane she was on took off twelve minutes ago. That's before we even figured out her damn last name might not even be real."

Alex stood frozen for a second, then let out a sharp, joyless laugh—the kind people laugh when life hands them betrayal wrapped in a bow.

"Well played," he murmured, half to himself. "She played us like a Stradivarius."

Richard just shook his head and walked toward the window, staring at the DC skyline glowing in smug ignorance.

"Ghosts don't just haunt you, Alex," he said softly. "They make sure you never forget what you didn't see coming."

"The world stretches endlessly in its vastness, yet remains astonishingly small when measured in the weight of our choices. A careless whisper, a fleeting act, may travel farther than we imagine, carrying consequences as subtle as they are significant."

Today had been a Category 5 disaster.

Chaos had paraded itself through every hour—from missed deadlines and bungled intel, to back-to-back meetings, half a dozen "urgent" emails that led to nothing but stress. Practically, Richard had spent most of the day feeling like a man trying to nail jelly to a wall—and now, this. Richard shut his car door with the kind of dramatic sigh reserved for men who had officially run out of grace. He leaned against the driver's side for a second, dragging a hand over his face, only to be gut-punched by the one memory he shouldn't have forgotten:

Marilyn.

The coffee meeting. The one he'd promised. The one she'd smiled about. The one he completely forgot.

Richard froze, the breath he'd been about to exhale catching in his chest. His eyes widened, and guilt crawled up his spine like a nasty rash.

He groaned, slapping the steering wheel with the enthusiasm of a man who realized—once again—that time management was not one of his spiritual gifts.

"Damn it, Richard. Why not just wear a badge that says emotionally unavailable and professionally chaotic?" he muttered, digging into his coat for his phone like it owed him an explanation.

He hesitated for a moment. Maybe she wouldn't pick up. Maybe she'd already blocked him. Maybe she'd trained a falcon to deliver passive-aggressive messages to his office.

But the line buzzed—once, twice.

Then her voice.

"Well, well, look who decided to call."

The tone was light, but every syllable was dipped in playful fire. "Richard, I thought you'd left me stranded on some metaphoric desert island—with no coffee and no closure."

He winced. Her voice alone was a beautiful blend of teasing and dignified disappointment—like a professor gently scolding you for skipping her favorite lecture.

"Marilyn," he started, dragging every ounce of charm he had to the surface, "I'm so sorry. The day got away from me—like, CIA-level interrogation, witness lost, national-security-kind-of away. But... I'd really love to make it up to you. Dinner? My treat. Real food, somewhere with actual chairs. Not caffeinated betrayal."

There was a pause. And in that pause lived a thousand calculations—was he sincere, was he bluffing, was he worth the emotional calories?

Finally, she exhaled. "Dinner, huh?" she said, her voice softening. "Alright, Richard. You get one shot. Don't mess it up. I've forwarded you my address."

He smiled with a kind of boyish relief, ready to input her address as if it were a rescue mission.

"Done. I'm on my way."

By the time Richard pulled up to the ivy-wrapped mansion Marilyn called home, a lamp-lit street, he stared up at the mansion with awe and a growing sense of unease, who-the-hell-did-I-make-plans-with. It was elegant, pristine, and intimidating in a way that whispered, "Don't touch anything unless you've inherited a trust fund." The place wasn't just "nice"—it looked like the house that came with a butler and a long list of family expectations. Of course, Marilyn lived there. Why wouldn't she?

Richard was halfway up the steps when the door creaked open—before he knocked.

And standing there, framed by the warm glow of the hallway, was a man Richard hadn't seen in nearly a decade.

Tall. Broad-shouldered. That same cocky smirk, only aged like wine with just a splash of arrogance.

"Seth?" Richard blurted, eyes narrowing.

The man grinned, arms spreading wide. "Richard? No damn way! Get over here, you Black Ops son of a gun!"

They hugged like brothers separated by time, wars, and just enough mutual trauma to make every joke land harder.

As they pulled apart, the reality hit Richard square in the face. What was Seth doing here? And more pressing—why hadn't Marilyn said a word about having a brother like this?

Seth cocked a brow. "What brings you here, Richard? Last I heard, you were knee-deep in law enforcement or whatever corner of hell you operate in."

Richard smiled, but his instincts clicked on like emergency lights. "I could ask you the same."

"Touché," Seth said with a shrug. "Consulting. Military stuff. Tech startups. Getting bored and leaving halfway through contracts. You know the drill. But come in—don't just stand there like a confused tourist."

Just then, the rhythm of heels echoed down the polished floor.

Marilyn appeared, her poise momentarily thrown by the sight of Richard and Seth together. She was followed by her mother, Mrs. Diane—gracious, radiant, the kind of woman who could host a formal dinner and still hand out witty insults like hors d'oeuvres.

Mrs. Diane's eyes sparkled with curiosity. "Now, what's behind all this delightful laughter? Did you two know each other before?"

Seth turned, a little smug. "Mom, this is Richard—an old friend from the Air Force."

Wait. Mom? Richard's eyes jumped from Seth to Diane, then to Marilyn.

"Mom?" he echoed, completely thrown.

Seth, as casual as a Sunday breeze, patted Richard's shoulder. "Yeah. This beautiful lady gave birth to both of us. Surprise."

Richard's mouth opened. Closed. Opened again. Words? None. And for a second, his brain just buffered like a computer on a bad connection. Then, as if on cue, the mask of a polite smile slipped into place.

Marilyn, however, looked like someone had just played her voicemail aloud in public. "Wait—you two know each other?"

Seth chuckled. "Thick as thieves back then."

Richard finally gathered the broken pieces of his composure. "Small world," he said with a smile that tried very hard to hide just how not okay he was.

"Nice to meet you," Marilyn said slowly, extending a hand. "And... I know him."

Seth raised a brow. "Marilyn, tell me something I don't know."

Mrs. Diane chuckled warmly. "Small world, indeed. But sometimes, it's beautiful when the past finds its way home."

Marilyn looked from Richard to Seth and back again, clearly trying to reconcile the overlapping timelines in her head.

Then Seth's voice grew softer, heavier.

"Rich... I heard about your pops. Senator Thornhill was a good man. I'm sorry."

Richard swallowed hard. "Thanks. He was my compass when I sure needed one."

Marilyn's eyes narrowed. "Wait... Senator Thornhill was your father?"

Richard met her gaze with one of those rare expressions that didn't ask for pity—just understanding.

"Yes," he said quietly.

And in that instant, something shifted. The room held its breath.

Mrs. Diane stepped forward, her voice filled with grace. "Richard, please accept our deepest condolences."

He bowed his head slightly. "Thank you. That means more than I can say."

Seth placed a steadying hand on his shoulder. "If anyone knows how to walk through fire, it's this guy."

Marilyn, still processing, blinked slowly. "Are you planning to drop any more bombshells tonight? Because I'm not wearing emotional armor."

Richard chuckled, the tension finally breaking into something lighter. "That's it. I promise."

For a moment, they just stood there, three people reintroduced to each other under completely different circumstances, the emotional math still settling.

Marilyn took a breath and said firmly, "Richard's here for me. We were supposed to have coffee. I missed that part of the story earlier."

Richard turned to Seth, a sheepish grin tugging at his lips, lifting his hands innocently. "I swear to you—I had no idea she was your sister. Absolute blindside."

Seth barked a laugh. "Well, damn. You've got my blessing. But mess this up, and I will hunt you down. And I still bench press cars."

Marilyn laughed, shaking her head. "He's serious, by the way. I've seen it. Once, he flipped a whole barbecue pit because it burned his steak."

Richard raised a brow. "Noted. Be nice to Seth. Always bring steak."

"Go on, Lyn," Seth said, stepping aside with dramatic flair. "Give the guy a break. He's had a day, and I'm guessing you've already yelled at him enough."

Marilyn rolled her eyes, but couldn't help the smile tugging at her lips. "Come on, Richard. Let's see if dinner with you is as memorable as your entrances."

Richard offered his arm. "I promise. No Air Force reunions. No dead senators. Just us."

She smiled, finally letting her guard down just a little.

And in that moment, Richard wasn't a grieving son, or a haunted agent, or even a man running from his own ghosts.

He was just Richard.

And this was a start.

"To navigate perception is to grasp the silent language of atmospheres and undercurrents. Assumption often conceals more than it reveals, and therein lies the weapon of the astute: the ability to see through the art of hidden intent."

The night air held a rare clarity—the kind that made headlights shimmer like stardust and the hush of the world feel almost sacred. Richard drove with one hand resting lightly on the wheel, his posture relaxed, but his heart far from it. The day had drained him dry, but now, sitting beside Marilyn, he felt something shift. The world hadn't quieted. He had.

Out of the corner of his eye, he stole a glance at her.

The streetlights threaded gold through her hair, and the contours of her face were sculpted in soft, moonlit shadow. Her presence was effortless, but it still pulled every ounce of his attention like gravity in heels.

"You know," Richard said, his voice unusually low and sincere, "how is it even possible to look as stunning as you do right now?"

Marilyn turned, her surprise flickering like candlelight in her eyes. Her cheeks flushed—just a little—and a soft laugh escaped. "Please," she said, amused. "Eyes on the road, Mr. Complimenter. I'd rather not have us starring in tomorrow's traffic report."

He chuckled, the sound rich and unfiltered. "Noted," he said, and returned his gaze to the road—but that smile lingered. He couldn't help it.

A moment passed in comfortable silence before Richard decided to give the night a little nudge.

"Alright," he said. "Here's one for you. Favorite restaurant in the city. And before you try to dodge it—no diplomatic answers."

Marilyn tilted her head, eyes glinting with mischief. "Hmm..." She paused dramatically. "I'd say... wherever you're taking me tonight."

Richard laughed. "Well played, Miss Diplomat."

But Marilyn wasn't done. "A lady never reveals her favorites too soon. You have to earn that level of trust."

"Good to know," he replied, smirking. "Fortunately, I've got a place in mind that might just earn me a few trust points."

At the next intersection, she noticed the direction they were heading. Her brow lifted.

"Wait... are we going to Phoenix Gardens?" she asked, surprise sliding into suspicion. "You don't even look nervous. Do you even have a reservation? That place books out six months in advance if you so much as whisper its name out loud."

Richard's lips curved into that maddeningly confident smile—the kind women both adored and distrusted in equal measure.

"Of course I do," he said, eyes still on the road. "And I'm delighted it has your approval."

Marilyn narrowed her gaze, but the corners of her mouth tugged upward. "So let me get this straight... You asked about my favorite restaurant while already steering us toward your pick?"

He pulled into the lot with the precision of a man who'd rehearsed this moment in his head a dozen times.

Switching off the engine, he turned toward her, fully. "Exactly," he said, grinning. "See, I believe in contingency planning. If you'd named somewhere else, I'd have pulled a U-turn and pretended this was just my scenic route."

She blinked, then burst into laughter, shaking her head. "Adaptability? That's your dinner strategy?"

"Oh no," Richard replied, unbuckling his seatbelt. "That's my life strategy."

He rounded the car and opened her door with a gentleman's ease. Extending his hand, he said with a wink, "Shall we?"

Marilyn placed her hand in his, and for a brief second, their fingers lingered—not awkwardly, but with an unspoken curiosity.

"I'm intrigued," she said softly.

Inside Phoenix Gardens, the restaurant felt like another world—rich with spice-scented air, dim lights dancing off polished wood, and laughter that melted into the soft trickle of a koi fountain near the entrance. The maître d' greeted them with a nod that only came with reservations made weeks in advance.

Their table was tucked into a velvet-cushioned corner, quiet and intimate. Just enough privacy to lean in and pretend the rest of the world didn't exist.

"So," Richard said, unfolding his napkin, "I humbly admit defeat. I need your culinary wisdom. What's your go-to dish here?"

Marilyn leaned back, arms crossed like a mock judge.

"Oh no. Not tonight. You made the reservation, remember? This menu is your mountain to climb."

"Touché," Richard conceded, raising both hands. "Alright, but be warned—I'm a sucker for the chef's special dumplings and the Peking duck. And yes, I share. But only with people who don't steal the crispy skin."

"I'll behave," she said, grinning. "Probably."

The conversation flowed as naturally as the jasmine tea in their porcelain cups. Richard spoke of his father—not as the powerful senator the world had known, but as the man who'd taught him how to fix a leaky faucet, how to tie a tie with purpose, and how to listen when words weren't being said.

Marilyn listened—not just politely, but like every word had a weight she could feel. She shared memories of her own, stories painted with humor and layered with quiet ache. A rebellious college phase, her failed attempt at baking a cake that turned into a kitchen fire, and the way her mother, Diane, still called her Lynnie when she was proud.

There was vulnerability in the air, but it didn't feel fragile. It felt real.

By the time the last morsels were savored and the check finally arrived, neither of them noticed how time had slipped by. As they left the restaurant, outside, the air had cooled, but the warmth between them lingered.

As Richard held the car door open once more, Marilyn looked up at him with something different in her eyes. Not just amusement. Not just affection.

Appreciation.

"You were right," he said as she settled in. "Wherever you are—it feels like the perfect place to be."

Marilyn smiled, that steady kind of smile that doesn't vanish too quickly. "Careful now, Richard," she said. "You're setting a dangerously high bar for next time."

Sliding into the driver's seat, he gave her a sideways glance. "Next time?" he asked, feigning surprise. "Was that a pass?"

Marilyn rolled her eyes playfully. "Let's just say... you've earned a second date. With possible dessert privileges."

Richard let out a quiet, triumphant laugh and pulled away from the curb, the city lights gliding past them like applause.

And I know all this not because I was there, but because Richard—whiskey in hand and a grin barely contained—relayed every moment to me that night at our usual lounge bar. He spoke with a spark I hadn't seen in years, like a man who knew he was standing at the edge of something rare.

A night that didn't just end well.

It began something.

"The precision of control involves mapping the other person's unseen desires, fears, strengths, and vulnerabilities. Such knowledge is not static; it transforms into power when conditions align, allowing one to maneuver with the foresight of a chess grandmaster, who recognizes opportunity not by luck, but by design."

Universal intelligence whispers that life demands balance—a cosmic waltz between joy and sorrow, clarity and chaos. But for Alex Carter, that balance wasn't just broken. It had shattered into pieces, and those pieces were slicing him from the inside out.

His office looked like a war crime against order. Case files lay torn open like gutted animals. Redacted reports, coffee-stained napkin notes, satellite photos, and two half-eaten protein bars competed for space on his desk. Somewhere in the chaos was the truth about Erin—his former fiancée, the woman he once thought he'd grow old with. Now, she was a fugitive—a phantom wrapped in betrayal and blood.

It wasn't just that she was missing.

Erin was at the heart of a storm—an unauthorized breach of FBI HQ, a classified witness murdered inside a federal holding cell, and her fingerprints—literal and metaphorical—smudged all over the scene. She'd vanished without a trace. No trails. No footprints. Just silence.

The kind of silence that screamed.

Alex's knuckles turned dark as he snatched the burner phone from his drawer—no caller ID. No GPS. Just one button—Redial. A lifeline to the nameless voice that had been feeding him breadcrumbs, wrapped in riddles and dipped in gasoline.

He pressed the button.

Two rings.

Then—

"YES."

No hello. No name. Just that same clipped, military tone. Neutral, measured, and borderline psychotic.

Alex exhaled sharply. "You know," he said, bitterness curling around every syllable, "I've been playing this cloak-and-dagger scavenger hunt, and here's what I've learned: I don't even know who the hell you are. Yet somehow, I've been dancing to your tune—waiting for some grand revelation. Spoiler alert: it hasn't come. So maybe you can help me out here—what the hell am I doing?"

The voice didn't miss a beat. "I see you've been digging, Agent Carter."

Alex blinked. Digging? The way the word dropped, like a shovel hitting wood six feet down.

"Digging?" he repeated, the sarcasm boiling. "You make it sound like I've been gardening. Try unraveling a conspiracy involving my ex-fiancée, a dead witness, and a break-in at FBI headquarters—and you're talking metaphors?"

The voice chuckled—a low, slow sound that sent a chill down Alex's spine, like someone laughing at your funeral before the casket's even closed.

"Can you be a little more specific with your fishing?" the voice asked, smug and smooth.

Alex clenched his jaw. "Fine. Erin. The devil I was sleeping with. And her little late-night tour of federal property."

The voice exhaled, almost sympathetically. "You're like a pawn in a chess game played on an open ocean, Alex. You think you're calculating moves. But the board is wet, the rules are lies, and the queen already jumped ship."

Alex leaned forward, gripping the edge of the desk. "I don't need poetry, I need answers."

A pause. Then, that maddening calm again.

"Then here's your first one: the Director of the CIA—your supposed ally—isn't just complicit. He's comfortable. Cozy. Imagine a fat cat, smug and well-fed, curled up on a throne of surveillance feeds and classified briefings. He knows. And he's letting it happen."

Silence.

Alex sat frozen, trying to breathe. The air in the room suddenly felt toxic, like trust itself had been rigged to detonate.

"Jesus Christ..." he muttered. "So I'm the idiot who wandered into the lion's den, wondering why I smell like steak. Please, I have known the man long enough to know he's not clean, that's not news to me."

"Well, you're not an idiot," the voice replied coldly. "Just a pawn. But you play a pawn well enough, and even kings get nervous."

Alex snorted, bitter. "Yeah? You ever seen a pawn survive the last round? They don't write songs about pawns. They just get sacrificed."

"Then be the exception," the voice snapped, sharp now. "I chose you. Not because you're the strongest. Because you're the smartest dumbass in the room who still believes in right and wrong, you remember why you joined the DoD? Truth. Justice. Protecting lives. That shit? That hasn't changed. Right?"

Alex leaned back, eyes closed, that phrase echoing like a ghost.

Truth. Justice. Innocent lives.

He used to believe in those things. Back before the lines blurred. Before Erin. Before Thornhill's death. Now, they felt like moral bumper stickers slapped on a collapsing building.

"What about you?" he asked. "What's your role in this? And again, who the hell are you?"

Another pause.

Then, almost softly—

"I'm the one who lights the matches. What you do with the flame... is up to you."

Click.

The line went dead.

Alex stared at the phone, its silence heavier than the words that came before it. His heartbeat thudded in his ears like a warning drum.

So, the CIA director was undoubtedly compromised.

Erin was deeper than he imagined.

And he—Alex Carter—was in the middle of a chessboard surrounded by knives, with pawns turning into bombs and kings hiding behind smiles.

But even as the fear whispered in his ear, something else stirred.

Resolve.

Because for the first time in weeks, the smoke was clearing. Not all of it. But enough to see that he had a part to play. A move to make.

And maybe, just maybe, pawns didn't have to die small.

Maybe they could burn the board.

THE COBRAS ON THE HILL

"Delegation is the silent art of power—when mastered, it turns others into instruments of vision; when corrupted, it becomes a parasite feeding on trust."

Everything about Director Winters was curated and controlled: his tailored charcoal suit, his gold-rimmed glasses, and the black leather gloves that hid the tremor in his left hand. That morning, he stood motionless, watching the orchestrated chaos of agents and analysts on the floor below—ants building a kingdom they would never rule.

And with a subtle nod, he summoned a man who had followed him through regimes, coups, and sanctioned disappearances: Ellis Cade. Cade moved with the kind of precise silence that suggested either intense training or a deeply repressed soul. Possibly both.

But before Winters could speak, a sharp, calculated chime split the stillness. The encrypted landline. Its tone was different from the others—subtler, colder. Only one group used that frequency.

Winters pressed the secure key. The lights in the room shifted, and the windows automatically frosted. Audio dampeners activated. The air itself felt suddenly heavier.

Then they spoke.

"Director Winters," came the first voice—smooth, masculine, and void of identity.

Winters lowered himself into his chair like a king taking his throne. "I trust everything is proceeding according to our expectations?"

A brief pause.

"How's the election playbook?"

Winters chuckled softly. Not because anything was funny—but because it unnerved them.

"Our candidate has been pre-packaged for mass consumption. Every soundbite calibrated. Every scandal buried under engineered outrage.

Social wave algorithms are primed. By the time the debates begin, they won't be watching a politician—they'll be watching a savior."

A low chuckle slid across the line like oil on glass. "And the little side dish?"

Winters's smile faltered—just slightly. "Final phase. A courier is en route to Hyderabad. Distribution vectors remain discreet. Our collaborators on

135

the pharmaceutical front have pre-cleared the trial narrative. Public panic will be minimal... controllable."

A third voice, laced with skepticism, cut in. "Still a dangerous play, Director. There are simpler ways to sell a narrative."

"True," Winters replied coolly, "but we're not aiming for compliance. We're aiming for dependence."

Then, a voice that made the others fall silent. Male. Ageless. Authoritative.

"Efficiency is non-negotiable. Winters, we've empowered you because your success is our leverage."

Winters sat straighter. "You'll have it. The side dish is a distraction, the election is the theatre—but the real prize is perception. Control the perception, and you control the battlefield. It's not about facts. It's about frames. Give them the illusion of choice, and they will defend it as their truth. That, gentlemen, is the alchemy of influence."

A beat of silence.

Then a voice, curious. "And how will you ensure the Chinese response doesn't spiral?"

"Controlled provocation," Winters answered smoothly. "We leak a narrative—corruption in their humanitarian outreach, potential espionage within their tech alliances. Nothing overt. Just enough smoke to raise questions. They'll fumble their PR, alienate their allies. The West will unite—not from truth, but from suspicion. Folks, the goal isn't to collapse. It's corrosion. Slow, steady erosion of credibility."

There was a pause. Then a simple reply: "Delightfully delivered."

Another voice, slow and gravelly, added, "And once again, perception wins. The art of chaos, rebranded for the digital age."

Winters allowed himself a smile, but it didn't touch his eyes. "History doesn't reward brute force anymore. It rewards authorship. Whoever tells the best story... wins."

There was a brief rustle of agreement among the voices—subtle, but unified—a consensus born not from faith, but from results.

Then came the warning.

"We trust you, Winters. But trust is a current. It flows... and it recedes. Deliver, and when the dust settles, the throne is yours. Fail—and... well, you know."

Winters inclined his head, as if they could see his reverence. "Understood. The endgame is in motion."

The call ended with the faintest digital click. The silence that followed was heavy, but not unfamiliar.

Cade stood nearby, his hands folded. "They're pressing harder."

"They're nervous," Winters said softly. "That's good. Nervous men pay attention."

He rose again, facing the city with a long, deliberate exhale. Yet beneath the polished surface of his confidence, something else stirred—doubt, perhaps, or the first glint of an inconvenient conscience. Even he couldn't be sure.

He'd played this game for decades—mastered it. But for the first time in years, he could feel something shifting. As if somewhere, out there in the noise and shadows, someone was beginning to play back. ME.

And if pawns were starting to move of their own will...

The board might not stay his for long.

"The link between actions and personality is undeniable: our choices betray what our tongues try to conceal."

Emily stepped into her apartment like a soldier returning from the front lines—except her battlefield was a mountain of bureaucracy, paper-pushing egos, and a memo war with three different departments. She let out a sigh that started in her bones and echoed through the room like a monsoon breeze trapped in a witch cup.

Her heels were the first to go—one aimed vaguely at the wall, the other performing a spectacular arc before colliding with the umbrella stand. The stand groaned and tipped over, as if it, too, had had enough of today.

She stared at it for a beat. Debating whether to care. Spoiler alert: she didn't.

Nope. Not her problem. Not tonight.

Unbuttoning her blazer, she let it slip from her shoulders like a tired metaphor. It flopped to the ground unceremoniously. She didn't bother picking it up. The apartment looked like it had been recently raided by raccoons with anxiety issues: coffee mugs occupied every horizontal surface like ceramic squatters, unopened mail that had formed its own zip code, and a Leaning Tower of Laundry on the brink of a domestic revolution, threatening to collapse.

Then her phone buzzed.

The device pirouetted across the counter with the grace of a ballerina before colliding with a soy sauce packet and a crusty spoon.

Emily glanced at the screen.

"Mom"

Of course.

She sighed again—this one shorter, more nasal—and answered the call, flipping instantly into her best aristocratic impression. "Why, Mother dearest, to what do I owe this delightfully timed intrusion upon my spiral?"

Her mother's warm laughter came through the line like honey laced with cinnamon. "Emily, darling. How was your day?"

Emily pinched the bridge of her nose. "Like a haunted escalator. Loud. Broken. And full of people who somehow think I control the ride."

"Hmm. So, a typical Tuesday then," her mother said, not missing a beat. "Please tell me you remembered to eat something that didn't come from a vending machine."

Emily glanced down at the half-eaten granola bar on her counter and decided a strategic dodge was in order. "Depends on how loosely you define 'food,' Mom."

There was a sigh on the other end, so practiced that it might've been passed down through generations. "Emily Rose Parker, I raised you better than this. You need vegetables. And protein. And for God's sake, fiber."

Emily looked at a suspicious apple she'd bought last week, still rolling around in a fruit bowl like a forgotten prop. "You're right," she murmured guiltily. "I'll... gnaw on something green later."

"You say that every time." Her mother's voice softened, as familiar with this dance as she was. "You're burning the candle at both ends again, aren't you?"

Emily's eyes flicked across the battlefield that was her apartment. The sock on the coffee table seemed to nod in confirmation.

"Define 'burning,'" she muttered.

"Emily," her mom warned in that gentle way that always somehow made her feel five again, "your apartment reflects your mind. If you don't sort it out in here," she paused, "you won't find peace in here." Another pause, this time filled with unspoken worry.

Emily blinked fast. The joke caught in her throat.

"I know, Mom. I know."

Her mother changed the subject gently. "Come visit, just for the weekend. I'm starting to forget what your face looks like."

Emily groaned. "Mom, you literally video call me every week."

"Not the same!" her mother declared. "I need to hug you, darling. Let me feed you something that wasn't shrink-wrapped. You can even bring your laundry."

Emily chuckled. "You're shameless."

"I'm your mother. Comes with the job."

"Okay," Emily finally said. "I'll come. Saturday morning. Deal?"

"Good girl," Eleanor whispered, like the words were a hug. "Now go. Clean something. Preferably something moldable."

"I'm on it," Emily promised with a half-smile. "Love you."

"Love you more, sweetheart."

Call ended.

And just like that, Emily felt twenty percent lighter. Not because anything had changed, but because someone still believed she could change it.

She stood in the middle of her apartment like a war general surveying her battlefield. "Alright, troops," she muttered to the laundry pile. "Let's dance."

The next forty minutes were a slapstick symphony, a cleaning session that was part battle, part comedy show. Emily waged war on the stack of old receipts "Why do I still have a bill for a sandwich from 2022?"

She accidentally wore a scarf as a headband for ten minutes before realizing it. Nearly concussed herself with a falling cabinet lid. Found a banana she had absolutely not purchased. And at some point, she held a pen and looked at it like it was an alien artifact unearthed from the depths of her couch.

Then, just as she was wrestling a load of laundry into the washer—mid-yank, one sock hanging from her shoulder like a towel of shame—a knock came at the door.

She froze.

It wasn't a neighborly knock. Not the Amazon guy. Not pizza.

It was... intentional.

Cautiously, she tiptoed to the door, eyeing the peephole like it might bite. One quick glance—and her breath caught.

No. Her hand froze on the doorknob for a second before she turned it, the door creaking open to reveal—

Alex.

Standing there like some forgotten truth, she wasn't ready to face. Alex's hair, a bit messier than usual, though it's hard to tell when his hairstyle is almost in that same shape on a good day. His eyes... haunted, somehow, like they'd seen things since she last saw him. And yet, still him. Still her Alex.

"Hey, Em," he said, his voice gravelly and low, carrying an ache that went deeper than words.

For a beat, neither of them moved. The moment stretched like elastic—fragile, tight, full of unsaid things.

"Alex," she breathed.

And with that, her day—the clutter, the chaos, the coffee-stained to-do list—fell away.

All that remained was the man in the doorway, the unspoken why-and-what between them, and the fragile thread of something that refused to let go.

"Hope is an anomaly, an unaccounted-for force that resists expectation and alters the trajectory of one's experience."

Alex still leaned against the doorframe like he wasn't sure if he belonged inside or out. His hands remained buried in his jacket pockets, his shoulders slightly hunched—not from the cold, but from something heavier.

"Lately, my mind's been..." he paused, glancing past her shoulder into the apartment as if searching for words on the wall. "...a tornado. Thoughts, feelings—everything swirling around with no clear direction. No pattern. No rest. So, I've been driving."

Emily stood quietly, her weight shifted to one foot, arms now uncrossed, her gaze soft. "So, you've been driving," she said, more a statement than a question.

Alex nodded. "The city helps. Its noise drowns out my noise. And then... I don't know. I ended up here." He gave a helpless shrug. "It's been years since I've been on this side of town. And yet somehow..."

His voice trailed off. He looked down, lips twitching at the memory. "I stood outside your door forever. I was this close to walking away. But I knocked. It echoed like a gunshot, and I thought—'great, she's going to kill me before I even get a word in.'"

Emily chuckled, arms folding again—but this time, in warmth. "Well, you're lucky I didn't throw the shoe."

He smiled, tentative and tired. "So... what's the verdict?"

"That you talk too much," she said, then stepped aside. "Come in."

Alex hesitated, but only for a breath. Then he stepped forward—slowly, like the air inside was different. Warmer. Softer.

The door clicked shut behind him, and with it, something inside him seemed to settle.

The apartment was what Emily always was—unapologetically herself. Books stacked with controlled chaos, warm-toned lamps casting halos over armchairs, and a sock that looked deeply ashamed to still be on the coffee table.

Alex's eyes swept across it all. "Still a fan of organized disorder, I see."

Emily glanced at the sock and shook her head. "It's called lived-in charm, thank you very much."

He turned to her, a playful glint returning to his eyes. "So, how'd I find this place?" he echoed her earlier question, eyebrows raised.

"NSA clearance," she deadpanned, hands on her hips.

"Please," Alex laughed, "you think I used federal intel for an address I memorized years ago? Try giving me more credit."

Her smile lingered longer this time, folding in amusement and something warmer. "Creepy but... charming."

"Pretty much sums me up."

For the first time in weeks, his laugh sounded like it came from somewhere deeper than duty. It wasn't much, but it was something.

"You've made this place yours," he said, eyes roaming the walls, the shelves, the kitchen nook barely visible behind her. "It's like your voice in interior design form."

Emily glanced around, her expression softening. "It's been my safe place. My quiet. Somewhere, I don't have to be Agent Parker."

Alex's gaze lingered on her—not her apartment, not the walls, but her.

"Your place is... cozy, it suits you."

A moment passed between them—small, still, intimate. And then Emily cleared her throat gently, as if brushing the moment aside before it could grow too big.

"So," she said, stepping a little closer, "what's next? With Erin? With all of this?"

He deflated slightly, like someone finally allowed to admit how tired they were. "Honestly? I have no damn clue," he muttered, rubbing the back of his neck. "I've been chasing files all day. Scrubbing timelines, cross-referencing classified records. Trying to find any thread that ties her to the ops team or the senator's case. Nothing. Just more fog."

Emily studied him, her chest tightening. "Alex..." she said gently, "you can't do this to yourself forever. You're not a machine. You're grieving. You're confused. And you're alone in this—and that's not strength. That's... isolation."

Alex looked up sharply, his jaw tense. "And what's the alternative? Stop digging and let it swallow me? Pretend none of it happened?"

"No," she said quietly, stepping in and placing a hand lightly on his arm. "The alternative is this: you stop doing it alone."

Her touch was light, but her words landed with weight.

Alex stared at her—uncertain, unsure, but undeniably moved. "Why would you still want to help me?" he asked, voice raw.

Emily held his gaze. "Because you helped me when I didn't even know I needed it. Because you matter. And because somewhere beneath that paranoia and self-destruction, you're still the man I'm curious about. And I'm not giving up on my curiosity yet."

The silence that followed wasn't awkward—it was sacred.

Finally, he exhaled a shaky breath. "Thanks, Emily. I think... I needed that more than I realized."

"And I think," she said, already turning toward the kitchen, "you need a drink. Or maybe just tea. Or whiskey. It's a roulette wheel back there—I make no promises."

Alex smiled—really smiled—and followed. "Whatever you hand me, I'll take it."

From the living room, the television kicked in—soft jazz humming as if on cue. The tension in Alex's shoulders eased slightly. He wasn't healed, and He wasn't whole.

But in this apartment, in this moment—with Emily's hand having touched his—he wasn't unraveling alone.

And sometimes, that was the start of everything.

Emily handed Alex a glass of wine, their fingers brushing for a brief second. He gave a faint smile—small, tired, but real. Gratitude flickered in his eyes like a candle trying to survive the wind.

"Thank you, Emily," he said, voice low but weighted with sincerity. He took a sip, then lowered the glass, a new glint of focus sharpening his gaze. "There was one clue, though. A thread. Small, but it's there."

Emily leaned forward instinctively, catching the shift in his energy. "What is it?"

Alex hesitated, just for a second, and then locked eyes with her. "Arthur C. Winters. Your boss. CIA Director. He's involved."

Emily's eyebrows arched, the words hitting harder than she wanted to admit. "The CIA director?" she echoed. "Are you sure?"

Alex let out a quiet, humorless laugh. "I've been in this game long enough to know when something reeks. This isn't paranoia. This time, it's real. I can smell the rot."

Emily folded her arms, skeptical but not dismissive. "Alex, the CIA's reputation is murky by design. That's not exactly breaking news. If you're accusing Winters, I need more than just a hunch."

"Fair enough," he said, chuckling. "The trick is to keep your cool, stay sharp, and look past the obvious. But I've lived in the shadows for years—been burned, betrayed, and literally slept next to the devil herself. If I've learned anything, it's how to separate smoke from fire. And Winters?" He leaned in, lowering his voice. "He's the fire."

Emily studied him. His posture. His tone. The exhaustion in his body didn't dull the conviction in his eyes.

"Alright," she said slowly. "Let's pretend you're right. What's the plan?"

"We find a smoking gun," he replied simply. "Proof. Undeniable. Something that makes even Winters' allies step back and say, 'Nope, not dying on this hill.'"

Emily tilted her head. "And where exactly does this smoking gun reside?"

"That," Alex said, sitting back, "is where things get murky." He paused, then added, "The tip came from an anonymous source."

Her eyebrows lifted. "Anonymous? Oh, come on. That sounds like a terrible Netflix adaptation of a good book."

Alex shrugged. "More like a thriller with a bad ending if we screw this up", he nodded. "No name. No face. Just a voice. But they've come through before."

Emily raised a skeptical brow. "You trust them?"

"I don't have the luxury to trust anyone," he said. "But I do have reason to believe they're not just another player. They tipped me off—an hour before Senator Thornhill was killed."

Emily froze. Her jaw tightened. "Wait... you knew something was going to happen... and you didn't stop it?"

Alex's eyes darkened. "Do you really think I didn't want to warn Richard? He's like a brother to me. It gutted me. But I was told—clear as day—that if I tried, they'd take him out. And Thornhill would still be gone. It was a lose-lose. I had to make the call."

Emily studied him. Anger softened into something else—uncertainty, maybe. A quiet understanding. The kind that comes from knowing the people who wear masks don't always do it to hide lies—sometimes it's to protect what's left of their humanity.

She leaned back, arms now uncrossed, tension in her jaw. "Jesus, Alex."

"I didn't sleep for days. Still haven't, really," he said quietly. "But now you understand. Whoever's behind this... they don't just hold information. They hold leverage."

The silence between them stretched, filled only by the gentle hum of the refrigerator.

"Alright," Emily finally said, exhaling slowly. "Let's say I'm listening. What else do you have?"

Alex looked up at her, his face earnest. "That's why I came here. I'm running an op out of Langley, on Langley. You were going to find out eventually—and hate me for not telling you. So, I'm here. Telling you now. I could use your help, Emily."

Emily narrowed her eyes. "Let me get this straight. You're spying on the CIA director... from inside the CIA?"

"That's the job," Alex replied. "But you're not the job. You're the one person I can still be honest with."

She blinked. "Again, you're running an op... on your own agency?"

"Technically, on your agency. I'm just... close enough to smell the rot."

Emily gave him a long, unreadable look. Then her lips quirked into a smirk. "Well, shit. This is going to be fun."

Alex blinked. "Wait, are you serious or sarcastic?"

She laughed, stood, and stretched. "Both. Maybe. Depends on the wine."

Alex chuckled, finally easing into the couch. But he caught the time on the clock. "It's late. I should go."

Emily shrugged, teasing but honest. "I'd say you could crash here—couch is surprisingly comfortable—but after everything you just dropped on me, I'm not sure I'm ready to have the NSA's darkest mystery snoring in my living room."

He smiled, a little sheepish. "Fair. Hotel it is."

Emily walked him to the door. Her voice was light, but her eyes said something heavier. "Be careful, Alex. Whoever your source is, they're either brilliant or suicidal. And I don't like you walking that line without backup."

He nodded, eyes serious. "Thanks, Emily. For not slamming the door in my face."

She shrugged, smirking again. "I was close."

He stepped out, pausing. "Hey... whatever happens next—thank you. For trusting me, even if just for tonight."

Then he disappeared into the hallway, the door clicking shut behind him.

Emily stood alone in the quiet, the weight of everything he'd said hanging in the air like thick fog.

She stared at the wine glass in her hand, then toward the wall where a photo of her CIA graduating class still hung. Arthur Winters smiled from the middle.

Her voice was barely a whisper.

"Fun, indeed."

"What makes knowledge captivating is not certainty, but the razor-thin divide between what we assume and what is real."

You know how some mornings whisper serenity? The kind that makes even the most cynical pessimist pause for a second, breathe, and consider the possibility that maybe—just maybe—everything might turn out fine?

Yeah, this wasn't one of those mornings.

It was Friday. Beautiful, by every standard. The sun spilled through Emily Parker's apartment windows like a gentle promise. Birds chirped outside like unpaid interns trying to make it in radio. The kind of day that normally beckoned yoga mats, avocado toast, and smug smiles.

But inside her apartment, under the soft hum of a desk lamp, Emily hunched over her keyboard like a soldier decoding an enemy message. Her fingers danced furiously across the keys—well, more like flailed, honestly. There were half-sipped mugs of tea and unopened mail scattered like the battlefield of someone who had fought sleep and lost. Twice.

If you looked closely, you'd see the fatigue. Not the kind that begs for coffee, but the kind that makes your soul slouch. She had spent the night chasing leads, unraveling twisted threads of intel that Alex—her equally brilliant and emotionally cryptic partner—had left like breadcrumbs dipped in gasoline.

And then there was Kathleen.

Kathleen Coates didn't need to wear power suits or bark orders. She had the calm, deadly presence of a librarian who could kill you with just one quiet look—and then explain the moral philosophy behind your demise. Handler. Mentor. Mother-figure-in-a-bulletproof-blazer. She had seen enough secrets to wallpaper the Pentagon.

The two of them sat in that room, quiet for a long moment, the morning sunlight edging across their faces like hesitant killers.

Then, finally, Kathleen leaned in, her voice low, almost too quiet.

"Em... there's an off-book op brewing in India. Rumors, encrypted chatter, a few pieces falling into place. And from what I'm hearing..."

A pause. That rare Kathleen pause—the kind that usually preceded something tectonic.

"Your boy Alex might not be as paranoid as we hoped."

Emily blinked.

Not because it surprised her—but because it didn't.

Damn it.

There it was again—that eerie, crawling realization that Alex might've actually been right, which annoyed her. Not because she didn't want the scoop, but because it meant he was right. And Alex being right usually meant things were about to get dangerously theatrical.

And let's be honest—Emily liked being the wildcard. The one who noticed the trap while others stepped into it. The idea that she'd underestimated him? Unsettling.

Now here's the part where most people would gloat. The glorious, "Ha! I told you so!" moment.

But not Emily. No, she sat perfectly still, staring at the half-loaded web of encrypted data on her screen like it had personally insulted her.

She had called in a favor—one that involved poking people who preferred not to be poked. Intelligence networks are like exes: touchy, unpredictable, and they always remember your last mistake. So when her phone buzzed, she already knew it wouldn't be a dinner invitation.

Message Received:

"The op in India is real. Cade confirmed. The errand boys aren't fiction."

Cade. That name alone sent a cold rush down her spine.

"Okay..." she muttered, trying not to sound impressed. Or terrified.

She turned to Kathleen, who had quietly inched closer, the way only someone trained in silent suspicion could.

"Why do you look like you just accidentally signed up for an international manhunt?" Kathleen asked, pulling out the chair beside her without waiting for permission.

Emily ran a hand through her hair. "Because I might have."

Kathleen raised a brow. "And here I was, hoping I'd get through one Friday without breaking federal law."

"Kate," Emily said softly, but firmly. "You've got people. Real ones. Ones that still owe you favors and probably fear you."

Kathleen sighed theatrically, crossing her arms. "Good Lord. How do I keep ending up in the fine print of your chaos?"

Emily smirked. "When we're old and fighting over pudding in a nursing home, I'll remind you of this moment."

"You assume we'll survive that long."

An hour later, Kathleen—true to her slightly-grudging word—called her from the next room.

"Check your screen."

Emily clicked.

What was loaded was a grainy video that looked like it had been filmed on a potato, but the face in the frame was unmistakable: Cade. Sharp eyes. Military haircut. Boarding a train heading straight into a city known for harboring every kind of danger short of nuclear fallout.

Timestamp? Two days ago.

Emily's lips parted slightly, her fingers pausing over the trackpad.

"This is it," Kathleen said, her voice now trimmed with urgency. "Whatever you're chasing—it's breathing."

Emily just nodded slowly.

Because it wasn't paranoia anymore, it wasn't just Alex's dramatic tone and half-allegedly opinionated thoughts. It was real.

And the part that stung most?

She had known it all along.

The silence in her apartment stretched out—heavy, like fog. She picked up her phone and dialed. The number rang once, then again.

Then his voice.

"Hey," Alex said, voice steady and maddeningly casual.

Emily didn't hesitate. "I think you know more than you're saying."

A pause. Not defensive. Just quiet.

"Which part?"

She squinted toward her screen, speaking low. "The part I'm staring at right now. Cade. India. My boss and his boys."

Silence again.

Then Alex replied, quieter now. Measured.

"Okay. I'll meet you in the morning. And whatever you're watching—turn it off before it burns you. Seriously, Emily."

Her breath hitched. "...Okay."

Call ended.

She stared at the screen, phone in hand, her thumb trembling slightly.

Then, without thinking, she tapped another number—her mother's.

"Hi, Mom," she said softly.

Eleanor's voice on the other end was warm, curious, and immediately cautious.

"Sweetheart? Everything okay?"

Emily closed her eyes for a second. "Something's come up. I may not make it this weekend. I'm sorry."

There was a pause. Then, only quiet understanding.

No questions. No guilt.

Just a mother's knowing heart.

"Alright. Just promise me you'll be safe."

"I will," Emily whispered, knowing full well that promises like that were only words.

When the call ended, she stood slowly. Closed her laptop. Pocketed her phone. And walked away from her desk like she was leaving behind more than just a file.

Because the moment had passed for doubt.

Whatever is going down wasn't a paranoia parade anymore.

Adrenaline was waiting. And Emily Parker wasn't the kind to look away from it anymore.

Not this time.

Not by a long shot.

"Hope is the beautiful anomaly that refuses to follow the script of inevitability."

Richard stood by the window of his apartment, adjusting his tie with that same surgeon-like precision he always had before big decisions—whether he was facing down a Senate subcommittee or finally fixing his streaming password. Today, though, it wasn't just muscle memory. It was a ritual—a kind of grounding.

The last few days had been... strange. Restless. A whirlwind, as he put it. And yet, beneath all the unfinished reports, sleepless hours, and a case that refused to make sense, there was something quietly exhilarating growing inside him. Something that made the creases at the corners of his eyes ease just a bit. Something that made him feel more alive than the work ever had.

And then—bzzzzt—his phone buzzed, rattling slightly on the edge of the dresser.

Marilyn.

The name lit up his screen, and—man—his entire face softened like a sunrise.

"Hey, Marilyn," he said, warmth threading his voice like silk.

"Good morning, Richard." Her voice was light, familiar. Like that first sip of coffee on a rainy morning—the kind that reminds you you're still human. "Did you sleep any better?"

He chuckled, deep and unforced, like something from a forgotten part of himself. "Honestly? It was the kind of sleep people write poetry about. The rare kind. Still, I suspect it had something to do with a certain someone whispering about lemon tea and meditation before bedtime."

She laughed, and he actually leaned into the sound. "I'll take that as a compliment," she said.

"It better be," he teased, "It's the first one I've handed out before 9 a.m. in months."

"Busy day ahead?" she asked, but it wasn't small talk. It was the kind of question that came with emotional investment.

Richard hesitated for a second before replying, "Just another deep-dive into this case. Trying to piece together chaos and make it behave."

"Sounds intense," Marilyn said softly. "Well, how about this—let's balance it out with lunch. My treat. Come up for air?"

He paused. Not because he didn't want to—but because with Marilyn, things felt so real these days, it was starting to scare him. And he was not a man easily shaken.

But then again, Marilyn had a way of catching him off guard without ever trying.

"That sounds... perfect," he said, and meant every syllable.

"The café downtown?" she offered, as if reading his mind. "Some corner booth?"

That booth. That stupid, cozy, time-stamped corner with mismatched cushions and that annoying table wobble. The same booth where fate had quietly started playing chess while they were both too tired to notice.

He grinned. "I'll be there at noon."

"Looking forward to it," she said—and hung up.

As he slipped the phone back onto the dresser, Richard felt a sense of clarity—a rare, grounded kind of purpose that had nothing to do with protocols or reports. Something that had to do with her.

By the time noon hit, he'd plowed through a dozen files without really seeing them. His body might have been at the FBI headquarters, but his mind had been running dialogue in his head since 9:01 a.m.

What do you say to a woman like Marilyn?

To someone who steadied your compass without asking for the map?

The café was just as he remembered it—busy but not rushed, loud but somehow still peaceful—the kind of place where first dates happened... and maybe, just maybe, second chances too.

Richard slipped into the booth, the sun casting a familiar glow across the table. The seat creaked in greeting. His hand absently flipped through the menu. But really, he wasn't reading a word. He was listening for the door.

And then—

She walked in.

Marilyn had that strange kind of beauty that didn't announce itself—it settled in, like music playing softly in another room. Effortless elegance, wrapped in ease. She didn't turn heads by accident; she did it by being real in a world built on masks.

As she walked toward him, Richard stood—because of course he did. Something about her must've made him remember his manners. She smiled as she slid into the seat across from him, brushing hair from her eyes in that way that always made him forget the next thing he was going to say.

He smiled. "You always manage to bring sunlight, don't you?"

She rolled her eyes playfully. "And you always start with something charming. It's unfair."

Richard took a sip of his matcha and leaned in, his tone dropping just slightly, a playful yet sincere tone. "Did you know we crossed paths here before our official 'Walmart moment'?"

Marilyn blinked. "Really? Are you saying I missed the grand entrance of Richard Lawrence?"

He laughed. "Multiple times, actually. We shared this booth more than once—sort of. Back then, I was just another guy with dark circles and too much black coffee."

"Oh my god," she gasped with mock horror, "were you that guy who spilled espresso on his files and tried to blame the barista?"

He raised his hand. "Guilty."

Her laughter was electric. "And to think, I almost missed falling for the espresso criminal."

Richard smiled, but there was depth behind it now. "It's funny. I used to think fate was this big, dramatic thunderstorm. But maybe it's just showing up at the same café, sitting in the same booth, until someone finally looks up."

A stillness passed between them.

A knowing.

She picked up her drink, her hands unusually careful. Then, voice a little softer, she said, "What is it, Richard? You're looking at me like I'm... like I'm something you've been trying to figure out for a long time."

His fingers tapped gently on the table, thoughtful. "I have. And here's what I know—you calm my storms. You remind me who I am when the world wants something else. That's not nothing, Marilyn. That's rare."

She looked down at her cup, her heart visibly racing in the flicker of her throat. "I've built a life around keeping people just far enough. Complicated doesn't even begin to cover it."

He didn't flinch. "Then let me walk into your complications. Don't clean them up. Don't pretend they're simple. Let me see them, raw and messy. I want the real stuff. All of it."

Her eyes misted, emotions rippling behind them like fragile glass.

"I... do like the sound of that," she said, and her voice cracked just a little.

He reached across the table, gently grazing her hand. "You do?"

She stared at their hands. Then lifted her gaze, voice a whisper. "I think I'm ready to practice saying... 'my boyfriend.'"

Richard's heart skipped a beat—but his smile never faltered. "Say it once now. Just to be sure."

She laughed through the tears threatening to fall. "Okay. Boyfriend."

He raised his cup in salute. "Girlfriend."

They toasted like middle schoolers. It was ridiculous. It was beautiful.

And in that cozy little booth, something shifted. Not in a dramatic, cinematic way. No orchestras played. No fireworks. Just two people choosing not to run anymore.

And as I watched them from across the room—yeah, I was there, sitting quietly, third-wheeling like a champ—it hit me.

I was losing my best friend.

Not because he was slipping away.

But because he was finally arriving where he belonged.

And as much as it ached...

Damn it, I couldn't be happier for him.

CHARLES E.A.

"To chase status is to enter a game where victory is costly, and every move casts shadows that reach far beyond the player."

Washington, D.C.—the nation's ornate war room disguised as a city. From the hilltops of Capitol Hill to the trenches of Foggy Bottom, the streets pulsed with a barely restrained urgency. Horns honked like warning sirens, security details passed like shadows, and pedestrians—suits, badges, interns, and protestors—wove through the chaos like dancers in a production they didn't audition for.

And yet, while the sidewalks overflowed with movement, most of these people carried one thing in common: they believed politics was not their business.

Funny.

Because right now, politics was everyone's business—whether they liked it or not.

The country stood on the edge of something tectonic. The presidential election was no longer a distant headline or a TV debate to be half-watched over dinner—it was a looming event with the same weight and absurd spectacle of a gladiator match. A nation of spectators, half-excited, half-terrified, awaited the climax of this strange political opera. You could feel it—in every hushed hallway of power, every midnight leak, every coffee-stained strategy memo passed hand-to-hand.

And while all this was happening, there he was: the incumbent president.

An old man whose grip on power was mostly ceremonial—though no one had the guts to say it to his face. You had to admire his confidence. He carried himself with the calm assurance of someone who still believed the keys in his pocket actually started the car.

Bless his optimism.

Behind the scenes, however, real power sipped brandy in private rooms, signed deals on untraceable paper, and never raised its voice. The president wasn't steering the ship—he was just sitting near the wheel while the crew navigated elsewhere. The powerbrokers—those faceless donors, media lords, and think-tank architects—had already chosen the music for this election dance. And they weren't looking for partners.

They were looking for pawns.

Super PACs, bloated with funds and promises, plastered his face across the nation like a proud trophy. But beneath their polished slogans and voter outreach campaigns, one truth whispered louder than any political ad: he didn't have leverage. He was a seat-warmer with a front-row view to his own irrelevance. And I genuinely hope someone, someday, has the courage to hand him that truth with the gentleness of a mercy kill.

But that's not why I was in D.C. this morning.

I was here for a breakfast sandwich.

And let me tell you: it was excellent.

One bite in, and I knew this food truck wasn't just serving sandwiches—it was dealing in emotional healing. The egg-to-bacon ratio? Impeccable. The bread? Toasted with a reverence reserved for sacred rituals. For a brief moment, I felt invincible. I was chewing on art until I looked up.

That's when I saw it.

Towering above the street like a stone-faced prophet was a digital billboard, its screen blazing against the morning haze.

"Reputation: the priceless gem of power."

The words hit like a quiet thunderclap. Something about the way they stood—bold, exact, deliberate—made people pause mid-step. Even the traffic light flickered as if reconsidering its own green light.

Below the headline, a message unfolded in serif font, elegant and cold:

"The journey of life holds a profound fact: reputation is the cornerstone of influence.

Exquisitely fragile yet immeasurably powerful, it molds destinies, secures legacies, and determines the course of history.

Protect it with unwavering devotion, for in its preservation lies the key to prosperity."

A chill ran down my spine, and not because of the breeze.

That line didn't feel like marketing. It felt like a warning. A message not written for the public—but to someone. A whisper disguised as a shout. One of those things you read and instinctively know: this isn't random.

As if in response, the city itself began to echo it back.

A nearby newsstand carried every major newspaper with the same message on its front page—bold, sharp, unignorable. A smart kiosk blinked with the same exact slogan as I passed. Even the back of a passing bus was wrapped with the phrase like an omen in traffic.

Reputation.

That word hung in the air like mist, heavy and lingering.

And for a moment, just a sliver of a second, I swear it felt like the entire city turned and looked at me. Not metaphorically. I mean it. As if every security camera and reflective surface had agreed to whisper at once: Are you watching this? Are you paying attention?

I took another bite of my sandwich.

Because what else do you do in a moment like that?

I closed my mind to the whispers, to the digital omens, to the creeping suspicion that something much bigger was happening behind the curtain.

Because I hadn't come to the city to decode conspiracies, I came for something specific. Something personal. And I'll get to that soon enough.

But still...

As I sat there on the bench, grease-stained napkin in hand, the words on that billboard wouldn't leave me alone.

"Reputation is the cornerstone of influence."

Maybe that's why they're all fighting so hard.

Not for votes.

Not for power.

But for something even more fragile:

Their names.

"When trust corrodes, loyalty dissolves into duplicity, and treachery thrives, hope is the first casualty. Alliances then become guardians of falsehood, defending not truth, but the reality they invent."

The café wasn't fancy—just your regular corner joint with good Wi-Fi and a strict policy against refills unless you smiled at the barista. It hummed with a low murmur of voices and the occasional clatter of spoons on ceramic. The kind of place where secrets could be whispered, and no one would notice because Karen in the booth next door was already deep into her third vent-session about Todd from HR.

At a back table, Emily sat with both hands clasped tightly around a warm cup, the scent of Colombian roast wafting up like a peace offering. But peace was in short supply. Especially across from her sat Alex—NSA's golden boy of behavioral ops—scrolling through his phone like the fate of democracy depended on his thumb.

She gave it a beat. Then two. Then leaned in with a deceptively pleasant smile.

"Hey there! Nice to meet you. Do you think we can talk now?" Her voice dripped sarcasm, warm and honeyed. "Because you've been on your phone for like... ever. I was beginning to think I was having breakfast with Siri."

Alex, unbothered, arched a single eyebrow—the kind of brow lift that could disarm a diplomat or launch a thousand Twitter threads.

"Vividly." His voice was smooth, almost amused. But his eyes? Laser-focused. He knew this wasn't going to be about brunch.

Emily rolled her shoulders and glanced around. Then, leaning forward with a subtle shift, she lowered her voice like she was about to confess she was Batman. "Remember our little chat the other day? Something about it didn't sit right with me. So I did a little digging. Oh, and sorry I ghosted you yesterday—I had to bounce out of the city unexpectedly. Don't worry, not a secret affair. Just work being its chaotic self."

Alex paused mid-scroll, phone still in hand. "Sounds mysterious already. Go on. Unless this ends with you selling me essential oils, in which case I'll have to report you to national security."

She smirked, unbothered. "Okay, listen to this." She set her cup down with a soft clink, fingers now resting on the rim like she was anchoring herself. "A few miles outside Mumbai, there's an agent. High-level. Can't confirm if he's officially sanctioned or just playing ghost with a badge. But here's the wild card—he answers directly to my boss."

Alex's brow twitched. "Wait, I thought you said I was the one with all the conspiracy theories."

"Exactly," Emily said, one eyebrow cocked. "And look how proud you are."

Alex gave a short exhale, equal parts concerned and impressed. "Okay, but if this guy's real—and if he's tied to your boss—what's he doing over there? Street food tour?"

She deadpanned, "No Alex, I don't think covert agents are currently enrolled in culinary school. If his goons are crawling around India, you can bet your last coffee refill it's not for tourism. My gut says they're running something serious. And whatever it is? It's not just off the books—it's off the map."

He leaned back, arms folded now. "You're drawing conclusions from air. Dots without lines. Are you trying to take over my job as resident paranoid?"

Emily shrugged with a grin. "Only because you're slacking."

A flicker of worry passed through his eyes. "Jokes aside, what are you thinking? Don't say you're going in solo."

She took a slow breath. Then let it out. "I'm flying to India."

The silence between them thickened.

"You're what?" Alex said flatly.

"I've got a CI there. Someone who owes me clarity. I'm not going in blind."

"Emily." He rubbed his temples like he was massaging a headache that hadn't even started yet. "You are a phenomenal agent. Brilliant, brave, occasionally stubborn as hell—but this is dangerous. This smells like a meat grinder wrapped in curry and corruption."

She leaned forward again, eyes sharp. "Then it's a good thing I brought my spices."

He groaned. "That was terrible. Seriously though—this thing? It could be massive. If your boss is moving pieces over there, then it's not just a chess game—it's poker with nukes. We need backup. Strategy. Not a one-woman mission."

"I'm not stupid, Alex. I've got an entry plan, an exit plan, a side door, and a safe word," she said with a glint of mischief. "I'm not walking into this blindfolded."

He held up a hand. "Fine. Then at least consider this—loop Richard in."

She blinked. "Richard? Mr.' We Don't Do Guesswork' from the FBI?"

"Exactly. We need someone here keeping the web in view. If anything happens to you—or if this thing flares up while you're out—he's our best shot at connecting the dots."

Emily sighed. Her fingers tapped the table, quick and rhythmic. "Not the worst idea you've had. But we need more. Last time we briefed him, he practically filed a restraining order against creativity."

Alex snorted. "That wasn't a freak-out. That was a... strongly worded disagreement."

"He color-coded the theories, Alex. With a red pen."

"Which means he cared!" he said, almost defensively.

Emily laughed. And just like that, the tension softened between them.

"Fine," she said, sipping again. "I'll find the dots. You keep the lines intact. We bring Richard in once I have something solid. Until then, keep your phone on and your sarcasm ready."

Alex gave her a sideways glance. "Just come back in one piece, Parker. I don't like flying solo."

She raised her cup, mock solemn. "To not dying in Mumbai."

He clinked his paper cup against hers. "Cheers. And don't forget—plans don't stop bullets."

"Good thing I pack light," she said with a wink. "But heavy on resolve."

"Make no mistake, clarity offers direction but not certainty; in its presence, danger often disguises itself, revealing that uncertainty walks beside us even in the clearest of paths."

The meeting with Alex had ended not with a bang, but a shrug.

He hadn't said much—just recycled versions of what Emily already knew, like serving cold soup in a silver bowl. It wasn't that she expected a dramatic confession or some secret breadcrumb that would unlock the whole case, but come on... she had expected something.

What she got instead was a calm, clipped conversation that made her feel like she was speaking to a malfunctioning version of Alex—intact on the outside, but glitching on the inside. She didn't press. She told herself it wasn't the time. Maybe she was being strategic. Perhaps she just didn't want to admit she didn't have the strength to dig any deeper that morning.

So she left.

By the time she got to her office, the weight of that non-conversation had followed her like a cloud of unspoken questions—and guilt.

The door to her office gave a reluctant creak as it opened. She stepped inside and collapsed into her chair, as if the whole CIA floor had tilted sideways and she was just surrendering to gravity. The glow of her monitor flickered, casting ghostly blue shadows across her face. Somewhere in the room, the air conditioner whirred with all the enthusiasm of a dying raccoon.

She muttered under her breath, "Brilliant. Now everything in this building refuses to work right."

Her fingers danced over the keyboard, constructing a flawless web of fiction—a cover story so tight it could have passed a lie detector test and charmed the technician while doing it. Emily had spun lies before, but this one? This one came wrapped in barbed wire and consequence.

Her gut churned with that old, familiar cocktail—adrenaline, anxiety, and just a hint of dread, like the smell of burnt coffee that lingered in her office air. This wasn't just another breadcrumb trail. This wasn't chasing shadows or vague threats. No—this felt like a freight train barreling toward a glass house, and she was standing smack in the middle with a broom and a lot of hope.

She stood, slowly, the chair letting out a traitorous squeak behind her. A quick tug straightened her black blazer, and she brushed invisible lint off her blouse with the kind of precision only someone lying to themselves would use.

The window beside her showed only her reflection—stoic, poised, and a little haunted. It was the kind of face people trusted. The type of face that hid just how close she was to screaming into her coffee mug.

She walked the corridors like someone walking into an exam they forgot to study for—confident on the outside, bargaining with the universe on the inside. Her heels clicked like a metronome, ticking down the seconds until she reached the director's office.

She paused at the door, took a breath, and knocked.

"Come in," came the deep, unreadable voice.

She opened the door and stepped inside, locking her nerves behind her ribcage.

The director was seated behind his intimidating desk like a statue carved out of marble and suspicion. His glasses caught the low light, casting twin reflections that made him look more machine than man.

"Agent Parker," he greeted, with the same warmth one might reserve for a parking ticket. "To what do I owe this pleasure?"

"I have a lead in the Thornhill case," Emily began, hands calmly clasped, heart tap dancing in her chest. "A credible source recently relocated to Pakistan. Claims to have seen something—something that may tie the senator to foreign entities. I'd like clearance to follow up."

The director didn't blink. "Let me guess. Your source has no name, no documents, and no proof—but you want a government-funded flight based on a hunch?"

Emily didn't flinch. "It's not a hunch, sir. It's a calculated risk. My contact has been reliable in the past, and I didn't come here lightly."

"You came here with a ghost story and a plane ticket wishlist." He folded his hands beneath his chin. "You're asking for quite a bit on the back of very little."

She held his gaze, her voice unwavering. "If I waited until everything was wrapped in a bow, the real enemies would have already changed the menu. I'd rather act early than clean up late."

A pause. Heavy and long.

Then, a slow, reluctant nod. "You have forty-eight hours. No leaks. No drama. You come back with proof, or you come back ready to explain yourself."

"Understood, sir."

"Dismissed."

She didn't exhale until she was halfway down the hallway. She didn't even realize how tightly she was gripping her phone until her fingers cramped.

She typed out the message:

Mission is a go. See you when I'm back.

It wasn't just a text. It was a confession. And a warning.

Two hours later, she sat in the back of a cab heading to the airport, pretending the weight in her stomach was excitement and not a minor panic attack doing yoga.

City lights blurred past the window, as if reality was too tired to focus. She glanced at her reflection and whispered softly, "What the hell are you doing, Emily?"

The cab driver, a cheerful man with a mustache that had its own zip code, glanced back. "Talking to yourself means you're either a genius or stressed. Want a snack? I have gum, peanuts, and spiritual advice."

She chuckled—actually chuckled. "No thanks. I'm about to walk into international uncertainty. I don't think gum's gonna fix it."

He shrugged. "Depends on the gum."

She smiled and stared back out the window. As the airport loomed ahead, she felt the tightness in her chest return. She must've thought it. That voice in her head—the one that used to whisper doubts—was now hosting a full-blown TED Talk.

What if you're wrong? What if this is bigger than you can handle? What if Alex is hiding something that changes everything?

But she breathed through it. She squeezed her bag tighter. And then, like a mantra, she whispered, "One step at a time."

Because in her world, truth didn't come gift-wrapped. It came hidden under layers of power, secrets, and fear. And the only light she could rely on was the one burning in her gut—the one that said: Go. Find out. Fight back.

And she would.

Even if it meant losing everything along the way.

"Set the wheels of trial in motion—keep trying, keep moving—the power to shape destiny lies not in circumstance, but in your own relentless will."

I would be lying if I said I didn't see it coming.

Not the way you see the rain right before it falls, but the way you feel your heartbeat when you're holding your breath—quiet, steady, inevitable. Alex was going to do it. Any rational person in his shoes would've reached for the phone too. But it wasn't just the action that made me proud—it was the weight behind it. The decision. The moment when silence gave way to resolve.

And yet... for a few long, almost theatrical seconds, he hesitated.

His thumb hovered just above the screen, trembling ever so slightly. It was barely visible—just a flicker of uncertainty—but in Alex's world, that was practically a shout. The room was silent except for the low hum of the fridge in the kitchen, the distant ticking of a wall clock, and the metronome rhythm of doubt in his chest.

He dialed.

Each ring sounded like a countdown to a different life.

Then—click.

"Alex," came the voice. The NSA director. Calm. Dry. Unmoved. The kind of voice that could put out fires without raising the volume.

"Sir," Alex said, clearing his throat to anchor himself. "I need time away. I'd call it personal, but it also connects to an independent lead I've been tracing. It wasn't clear before—but it is now. I need clearance. It could matter. Maybe more than we think."

There was a pause.

The kind of pause that made you question whether the line was dead—or worse, alive and disappointed.

Then the director answered, in that infuriatingly neutral tone of his. "You have my permission. But stay reachable. Check in often. You know how this works."

"Of course, sir. Thank you."

Click.

The line went dead. The room, however, remained heavy with everything unspoken.

Alex let out the kind of exhale you only notice when you've been holding your breath for years. His chest finally expanded, his jaw unclenched. Clearance secured. The first step had been taken.

Now came the harder part.

Packing for uncertainty was an oddly familiar ritual. Like preparing for a date with chaos—you want to dress right, carry the essentials, and still act like you know what you're doing.

He moved with practiced rhythm. Compact holster. Encrypted communication tools. The same tactical knife he'd once used to cut through a jungle vine in Venezuela, and almost, incidentally, a colleague's seatbelt in a poorly executed extraction op in Prague.

He packed not just gear—but ghosts.

Every item had a history. Every zipper, every click of a buckle echoed with something he'd seen, survived, or lost. This wasn't just another operation. This was... personal. And that made it dangerous.

Then his phone buzzed.

Another call.

He saw the name and felt a tightness coil in his stomach. Not fear. Not quite dread either. It was more like... expectation laced with old betrayal. He answered anyway. Because of course he did.

Two rings in.

"Alex," the voice said. Cool. Calm. A little too amused. "I wondered when you'd call. Sorry, I missed your earlier one. I was... occupied."

Alex ignored the bait. "I need clarity. If I'm stepping into this, I need to know exactly what I'm dealing with. No riddles. No theatrics. Just details."

A beat. Silence. And then, short and sharp:

"India. Meet me there. I'll arrange the rest."

Click.

The line went dead—again.

Alex stared at the phone like it had personally offended him. "Well. That was helpful," he muttered.

Still, the word India echoed through his apartment like a whisper from another life.

He booked the flight with robotic precision. A few clicks, and his fate was sealed. The email confirmation glared back at him like a dare.

He sat for a moment in the stillness. Then, as if summoned by memory, her laugh floated through his mind.

His ex-fiancée. Her voice—once warm, once real—now haunted the quiet moments. She had smiled as she walked away. He had smiled too... right until the door closed and trust shattered like glass on tile.

Trust. That slippery thing that even the most intelligent agents couldn't seem to hold onto.

He zipped his bag. Tight. Secure. Final.

And just before he turned off the lights, he glanced around the apartment—the crooked photo frame she never liked, the half-read book on the nightstand, the empty coffee mug from a week ago.

"This place could really use a cleaning lady," he muttered under his breath, offering himself one last smirk before stepping out.

The night air was brisk and unsympathetic.

The city, bathed in muted orange streetlight, stretched before him—silent and indifferent. A few cars passed. Somewhere, a siren wailed half-heartedly, like it wasn't fully committed to the emergency.

Alex took a step forward.

Then another.

Each one is a statement.

He didn't look back.

India awaited. And so did the storm. But Alex—Alex had lived in storms before. Waded through them. Learned to listen to the thunder, feel the direction of the wind.

This time, though, he wasn't just walking into the storm.

He was going to meet it.

Head-on. Eyes open.

And maybe—just maybe—come out the other side with more than answers.

Maybe this time, he'd find a piece of himself, too.

"A narrative that enchants does not reveal all—it lingers in the allure of ambiguity, where intrigue takes root."

The night unfurled over Virginia like a velvet curtain, rich and weighty, wrapping the world in quiet tension. From a distance, the international airport shimmered—glass and steel woven together like a futuristic cathedral for the restless. Floodlights bathed the terminal in soft gold, and the glass facade gleamed with the reflections of a thousand journeys about to begin.

Inside, the place pulsed with life.

The click-clack of trolley wheels, the hum of announcements in three different accents, the lazy drift of perfume from duty-free counters—every element came together like a strange symphony of hope, urgency, and overpriced cappuccinos.

Business people darted by in expensive suits, talking mergers over Bluetooth like the world's GDP depended on their next boarding call. Kids squealed over plush toys, their laughter cutting through the fatigue of their red-eyed parents. And somewhere in that maze of strangers, Emily Parker stood, her figure poised and unshaken, but her thoughts? Those were running marathons.

She wasn't just boarding a flight—she was stepping into a lion's den with a flashlight and the hope it wouldn't die halfway in.

Her arms were crossed, the sharp creases of her black coat echoing her no-nonsense mood. Her eyes scanned the terminal as if she were reading a classified document in real-time.

And then—

"Emily!"

She turned, a bit too fast.

The voice was unmistakable—steady, warm, with that frustrating little smirk tucked inside. And there he was: Alex Carter. Hands in pockets. Wearing that expression that said I-know-something-you-don't-but-I 'll-tease-you-about-it-later.

Her eyes narrowed immediately. "Alex?"

He stopped a few feet away, grinning like he'd just won a bet. "What, no hug? No dramatic gasp of surprise? I was hoping for at least one melodramatic airport reunion."

"What the hell are you doing here?" she hissed, eyes flicking around. "And don't tell me you've been lurking at the airport like some oversized emotional support pigeon just to spy on who boards what."

He chuckled. "Tempting visual. But no. You texted me hours ago, remember? I figured, why respond when I could show up in style?"

"Style?" she asked, raising an eyebrow. "You're wearing jeans and sarcasm."

"Exactly," he said, stepping closer. "Also, minor detail—I'm coming with you."

There was a pause. A long, blink-filled, you're-kidding-me kind of pause.

Emily folded her arms. "You're what?"

"Tagging along," he said simply. "India, right? Thought I'd join the mystery tour. Been meaning to see the world. Why not start with a country full of people, technology, and possibly hired killers?"

"This is not some Scooby-Doo expedition," she said, exasperated. "I'm not Velma, you're not Fred, and there's no van."

Alex leaned in slightly, lowering his voice to a more serious pitch. "I know this isn't a game. That's exactly why I'm here. Emily... I've worked with people like your director. They smile, they nod, they sign off on your mission—and they start digging your grave the moment you take off."

Her brow furrowed. "You think he's tracking me?"

"No," Alex said, "I know he is. He doesn't think you'll find anything of interest. Or worse—he knows exactly what you'll find and he's banking on the fact you won't make it back to report it."

The mood shifted.

The buzz of the terminal faded as her eyes met his, the air between them thick with implications.

"You think he'd go that far?"

"I think," Alex said, his voice steady, "that some men don't see 'too far.' Especially not when they're protecting empires made of lies."

She studied him. Gone was the smirk, the playful digs. This wasn't Alex the opinionated, or Alex the occasional pain in her ass. This was Alex the shield. The one who showed up when everything felt like it was slipping.

"And you're just... volunteering for this?" she asked, half amused, half-suspicious. "Out of the goodness of your morally gray heart?"

"Absolutely not," he replied. "I've always had questionable motives. But in this case, yeah—I'm in because I owe you. And because I'd rather not sit at home wondering if you're alive or buried in an unmarked field behind some embassy compound."

Emily exhaled, and for a moment—just a sliver of a second—her shoulders dropped.

"You're ridiculous," she muttered. "Dragging yourself into this circus because your NSA schedule got a little too boring?"

He shrugged. "Can't confirm or deny. But if it helps, I also packed snacks. And two burner phones."

She fought a smile. "Fine. But if you slow me down or get me killed, I'm haunting your apartment. And I'm stealing your soul from the afterlife."

"Deal," he said with a grin.

She chuckled under her breath—an actual laugh. Maybe not loud, but real. And for the first time that day, the tightness in her chest didn't feel quite so crushing.

"Alright," she said. "Together. No secrets. No backup plans. We go in. We find the answers. We get out."

"Together," Alex echoed. "Now, let's catch our flight before the conspiracy starts without us."

And with that, they turned toward the gate.

Two figures, side by side. Not just agents anymore, but something harder to define. Battle-worn, deeply bonded, and walking willingly into the eye of a storm.

And once more, the chaos continued, a chorus of suitcase wheels scraped along polished floors, flight announcements echoed from overhead speakers with mechanical cheerfulness. Somewhere in the distance, a toddler screamed in protest of gravity, or snacks, or the general condition of being two years old.

In the middle of it all, Emily stood like the calm center of a mild storm—composed, alert, with eyes that missed nothing and tolerated even less. She was dressed in what Alex liked to call her "combat casual"—black jeans, a fitted jacket, and a backpack that could probably survive a nuclear blast.

Alex, as always, appeared like he had just walked out of a high-end espionage catalog: navy-blue shirt rolled to the elbows, that infuriatingly charming half-smile in place, and—most impressive of all—a hot coffee in each hand.

"For you," he said, offering her the cup with an exaggerated bow, like a waiter who moonlighted as a spy. "A little something to keep you sharp."

Emily raised an eyebrow but accepted it. "Look at you. Suave, stylish, and a caffeine courier. If this NSA gig doesn't work out, maybe you can deliver coffee on a motorbike and flirt with lonely writers."

He smirked. "It's not delivery, Emily. It's a lifestyle."

She chuckled despite herself. "And what a tragic lifestyle that would be."

They leaned against the slow-moving conveyor belt, sipping coffee as though it were a sacred ritual. Around them, the terminal buzzed with the noise of people rushing toward beginnings or stumbling out of endings. It was a sea of stories. Some closed, some still writing themselves—and then there was theirs. Complicated. Heavy. Tense. But somehow, today, lighter.

Alex tapped the edge of his cup. "Alright, we've got 40 minutes to boarding. Want to kill time with a game?"

Emily gave him the side-eye. "Please don't say Candy Crush."

"Better. This is the Airport People-Watching Theater. Starring: us. We watch. We guess. We make up their entire life story in thirty seconds or less."

"God help me."

"Oh, come on. Don't act like you're above this. You love judging people."

Emily looked mildly offended. "I observe people. There's a difference."

"Not in this game," Alex said. "Okay. See that lady hunched over her laptop? That's Evelyn. Travel blogger. Writes with tragic desperation. Spends more time filtering her Instagram than actually traveling. Has a cat named Salvador who has his own Instagram account, with more followers than she does."

Emily sipped her coffee, deadpan. "Wow. Harsh. She's probably just trying to finish a pitch deck before her flight to Detroit. Or texting her therapist."

"Still could have a cat named Salvador."

Emily sighed, then pointed to a businessman gesturing wildly into his Bluetooth. "Alright, Sherlock. That guy."

Alex leaned in conspiratorially. "Greg. Thinks he's a big shot. Tells everyone he's negotiating billion-dollar mergers. In reality? He's arguing with his teenage son about sneaking out last night, while trying to convince his wife that buying an emotional support ferret was not an overreaction."

Emily nearly snorted coffee. "A ferret?!"

"Named Machiavelli."

She clutched her side. "I hate you."

"No, you don't. You love me a little for how good that was."

Emily waved him off but smiled, eyes scanning the terminal like a cat scanning a window full of birds. "Alright, my turn. Tall guy by the vending machine. The one pressing the buttons like he's disarming a bomb."

Alex squinted. "Oh, that's Brian. Genius coder. Built software that runs security systems for airports. But for some reason, vending machines are his kryptonite. He's been stuck in an eternal battle with C7 for the last four minutes. All he wants is a Snickers, Emily. Just...a Snickers."

"Tragic," Emily whispered dramatically. "Truly Shakespearean."

They laughed harder than the joke warranted—because it wasn't just funny. It was relief. The kind that sneaks up on you when your mind has been wound too tight for too long.

Alex nudged her gently. "We should do this more. Laugh at strangers. Makes the world feel smaller."

Emily leaned her head back slightly, taking in the ceiling of the terminal and the mess of lives under it. "With all the heavy metal birds, you ever think about how airports are weirdly...in-between places? Not quite arrival. Not quite departure. Just...transition."

Alex blinked. "Did you just go philosophical on me?"

"Shut up. I'm allowed to have thoughts."

"Metal birds," he mimicked, placing a hand on his heart. "She calls airplanes' metal birds,' folks. Somebody call the Nobel committee."

She elbowed him, laughing. "You're the worst."

"And you wouldn't want me any other way," he quipped.

She didn't answer that one—not verbally. But her expression softened, just for a moment, like the world outside the window—shimmering with moving lights, tarmac, and controlled chaos—had given her permission to breathe. To be human. To feel.

They stood there for a few quiet minutes, side by side. The PA system called for boarding. A row of people started lining up like reluctant contestants in a travel game show.

"Here we go," Emily said, tucking her coffee sleeve into the bin.

Alex stretched dramatically. "First act of an indie film. Two emotionally unavailable agents pretending they're not catching feelings."

Emily snorted. "If this is a movie, I'll be your doom."

"No argument here," Alex said, grabbing his bag. "I'm the funny, slightly mysterious sidekick with surprising depth. Critics love me. I think they will disagree with you on that."

They walked toward the gate, their pace easy, their shoulders bumping slightly.

Just before they stepped onto the jet bridge, Alex paused. His voice dropped just a little, enough to catch her ear.

"Hey. For what it's worth—whatever comes next, I've got your six."

Emily looked at him, steady and unsmiling. But her eyes said thank you.

Then, ever so quietly, she said, "Let's write a good ending."

And with that, they disappeared down the bridge, into the next chapter of the chaos.

India awaited.

"In the grand theater of existence, where uncertainty towers and trials persist, the truest wisdom whispers: do not let the fear of striking out dim the joy of stepping onto the field."

Arthur C. Winters didn't walk through the corridors of the CIA—he glided, like a man for whom the laws of friction had politely stepped aside. His mind was one that didn't just solve puzzles; it built them, engineered traps with such finesse that even the prey thought it was heading for a vacation.

To Arthur, power wasn't a byproduct of position—it was a sport. Influence wasn't handed to him in briefing folders; it was cultivated like a bonsai—carefully trimmed, controlled, and brutally beautiful.

To the rest of the world, Arthur was the Director of the CIA. But those of us who understood how the world really worked? We knew better. Arthur didn't direct the agency. He sculpted it—like a patient artist with marble and secrets. The man breathed in tension and exhaled calculated silence. And if power were a piano, Arthur could play Beethoven blindfolded while making coffee.

He once told a junior officer, "Influence isn't power. Influence is discipline."

The poor kid nodded like it made sense, then spent the next year reorganizing staplers, trying to decipher what it meant.

Now here we were—me, 37,000 feet above the Indian Ocean, sitting beside Emily, who slept like someone who trusted no one but had learned to nap with one eye closed.

Meanwhile, back in the George Bush Center for Intelligence, Arthur was planning her funeral with the same casual flair one might use to schedule a lunch meeting.

So, when Arthur lowered himself into the black leather chair in his vault-like office, with walls thick enough to silence a scream and windows that had never known sunlight, he wasn't working. He was orchestrating.

"Emily is on the move," he said, voice crisp, clipped, almost bored.

A brief pause on the line.

"Understood," came Cade's voice, smoother than gravel but still carrying that undertone of anticipation—like a man who knew the bullets were real but found the sound poetic.

Arthur allowed himself a ghost-smile. Not the kind you send to children or puppies, but the kind you flash when you know someone is walking into a snare you tied with silk thread and a grudge.

He steepled his fingers, eyes flicking to the monitor, where Emily's image, caught mid-stride through the airport, blinked on screen.

There she was.

Still thinking she had control.

"Always the wildcard," Arthur muttered, almost affectionately. "But even wildcards can be tamed."

In New Delhi, Cade began implementing Arthur's command. The Faux Office looked like a startup office. Bland desk, blinking monitor, one sad potted plant on the floor, like it had already given up.

Cade was the sort of man you'd forget five minutes after meeting him. That's what made him terrifying. His hands hovered over the keyboard like a pianist preparing to drop a final note no one would ever hear.

Then: Click. Send. Done.

He picked up his secure phone.

"Eradication plan activated," he said.

Arthur's voice floated through the speaker—calm, clipped, void of any humanity.

"Good. Emily cannot be allowed to interfere. Do what is necessary. And Cade..."

Arthur's tone cooled several degrees.

"Failure is not an option."

Cade hesitated—just enough to let you know he still had a soul—but not long enough to keep it.

"Aye, sir."

At 37,000 feet above sea level, turbulence isn't what keeps you awake—it's paranoia. And Alex Carter wasn't sleeping.

The CIA may have trained Emily in tactical deception, but Alex had mastered the psychological art of holding back—just enough to seem transparent, while silently mapping everyone's next three moves.

Emily stirred beside him, her hair fell across her face, and for a moment, she looked peaceful. The soft rustle of her jacket was barely louder than the hum of the engines. You'd never guess she was the wildcard Arthur was afraid of.

"Hey," I said, low enough that the agents three rows behind wouldn't hear, "You up?"

Emily opened one eye like a cat sensing bad weather. "Barely."

She turned toward the window, her reflection haunting the glass. There was something in her silence—an unease just below the skin.

"Do you feel it?" she finally whispered, her voice soft—measured. But I heard the tension right under her breath.

I didn't answer right away. Instead, I tilted my head like I hadn't already been streaming top-secret surveillance footage straight from Arthur's second-most-trusted ghost agent.

"Feel what?"

Emily turned toward me, her face still half in shadow. "That we're walking into a trap."

I looked at her now—really looked at her. She was calm. Too calm. Like the eye of a hurricane that knows what comes next.

"Ah, so now you realize it's a trap?" I said, adding just enough sarcasm to keep it from stinging. "You mean the same probability I warned you about before you went full Wonder-Woman and dragged me halfway across the world? Not to mention you practically threatened to duct-tape me to a chair if I didn't let you go on this trip."

Emily gave a wry smile, but her fingers gripped the armrest like she was expecting it to eject her into open sky. "You're the one who insisted on coming." She smirked.

"I also insisted on buying travel insurance, but here we are."

Three rows behind, a cluster of very ordinary-looking passengers seemed unusually interested in clouds. One stirred a tepid cup of airline coffee with the focus of a chemist. Another adjusted a neck pillow five times in a row without once leaning back. The agents—clean-cut, inoffensive, blending in like hotel art—were watching Emily like hawks in business class.

"Target in position," one of them muttered into his collar mic.

Their handler's voice came through. "Maintain observation. Ensure she follows the designated path."

The team members nodded subtly.

To them, Emily was a variable. A 'she.' Not a person. Just a task. A checkbox.

They didn't know her the way I did. They didn't know what she was capable of. They didn't know she'd once disarmed a bomb using a hairpin and a half-eaten bag of Skittles. (Okay, maybe that's an exaggeration—but just barely.)

Now here's the part that kept my gut in knots.

You see, I knew all of this because of him—the ghost who recruited me into this mess. He wasn't a man so much as a bad memory in a good suit.

He'd hijacked my tablet mid-flight with a data dump only God and three retired NSA engineers could decrypt. And I saw it all: Cade. The plan. The surveillance. The trigger. I saw it all— the pieces come together like dominoes being lined up to collapse.

The problem was, if I told Emily how I knew, she'd want to know once again who had told me. And if she learned that... well, the whole house of cards Arthur built with stealth, blackmail, and perfectly dry Scotch would come tumbling down.

And I might tumble down with it.

So the question becomes:

How do I tell Emily she's walking into a death trap...

...without revealing that the ghost feeding me the info makes Arthur look like a Sunday school teacher?

So yeah, I could tell her. But that's like handing her a grenade with the pin already halfway out and saying, "Trust me, it's a party favor."

Well, I had maybe one hour to figure out how to protect her without unraveling everything.

Do I lie?

Do I twist the information I know just enough to sound believable?

Or do I tell her everything—and pray she's willing to trust the devil I've been ever since the first day we met?

Whatever I choose, one thing is sure:

Arthur Winters doesn't make idle threats.

And Emily Parker doesn't go down quietly.

Something had to give.

And I had a feeling it'd be loud when it did.

"Stand firm against hardship—your identity is more than struggle; it is resilience, adaptability, and the untamed light of your spirit."

Alex wasn't a man easily rattled—but right now, he was sweating internally like a spy in church.

He sat next to Emily on a plane slicing through the skies over the Indian subcontinent, knowing more than he should and revealing far less than he wanted.

Emily had that look again. The kind of look that wasn't just curious—it was surgical.

"You know," she said, her voice smooth and deliberate, as if she were setting a trap with velvet gloves, "there's so much I don't know about you, Alex."

Alex blinked. Great. Witch mode activated.

He turned to her with a diplomatic smile. Not too smug, not too flat. A 60% charm, 40% caution kind of smile. The type of smile that says I know you're fishing, and I'm politely pretending not to notice.

"Likewise," he said. "Sometimes it's better that way. In our line of work, keeping parts of ourselves hidden isn't just a choice—it's survival."

Emily gave a slight nod, conceding the point like someone who wasn't finished but was willing to circle back.

"Fair enough," she said. "But still... you've lived so many lives within one. How do you reconcile it all?"

Alex leaned back, his eyes scanning the stars beyond the glass. Internally, he was asking himself why the hell she was asking him philosophical questions mid-flight into a probability. Outwardly, he looked pensive. Presidential.

"It's not always about reconciling," he said after a pause. "Sometimes it's about compartmentalizing. You take what you've lived, what you've lost, and what you've learned—and you keep moving forward. But if you want the whole story..."

He turned to her, humor glinting behind his eyes. "Buckle up. It's a long one."

Emily leaned in just slightly, eyes playful. "I've got time. Start from the beginning."

Alex exhaled as if flipping a page in a dusty file cabinet inside his head.

"Alright. It started at MIT. Computer Engineering. Graduated '98. I was the type who coded faster than I talked and forgot lunch three times a week."

Emily raised an eyebrow. "You? Forgetting lunch?"

"I was humble once," he deadpanned.

She laughed—genuinely. It was a rare sound between them lately.

"After MIT, I joined the Transportation Corps. My first real taste of structure, purpose. That's where I learned that discipline was less about shouting orders and more about shutting up and getting things done."

He drifted for a moment, staring ahead. Emily didn't interrupt.

"Then came the Naval War College. Then deployments. Then chaos. Somewhere between the sabotage, night raids, and classified operations, I found myself in the SEALs. That was where the kid who loved circuit boards became the guy who could breach a compound in twelve seconds with a toothbrush and a roll of duct tape."

Emily blinked. "You're joking."

"Mostly." He grinned. "But don't underestimate toothbrushes."

He paused, let the moment sit, then continued in a quieter tone.

"My father—Captain Carter—was a Nigerian immigrant. Came here with nothing but a fire in his belly and a last name no one could pronounce."

Emily leaned in. This part wasn't in the CIA file.

"He served too. Military. A natural leader. Never made it back from his last mission."

Alex's voice dipped, gravel replacing steel. "They folded the flag and handed it to my mother like that could replace him."

Emily softened. "I'm sorry."

He gave a short nod, letting the weight pass without sinking.

"It shaped me—all of it. I live two steps ahead because I know what happens when you blink. And because I never want someone I care about to get folded into a flag."

"And yes," he said, letting a smirk creep back in, "I had a normal life once. Lexington High. Awkward dances. House in Rhode Island. College parties I barely remember and one karaoke night I will never live down."

Emily grinned. "Now that's the intel I've been looking for."

"Too bad it's not in my file. That would've helped with your pre-flight threat assessment."

"Believe it or not," she said with a teasing smirk, "you're not as unreadable as you think."

Alex raised a brow. "That's just rude."

They laughed quietly, the kind of laugh that comes from having survived too many things too quietly.

The laughter faded as the plane began its descent. The sky outside had turned ink-black, the kind of darkness that eats stars for breakfast.

Below them, India stretched wide—vibrant lights scattered like jewels across a velvet canvas.

Emily stared in awe. "It's beautiful."

Alex nodded, gaze forward, but tension was creeping back into his jaw.

"It is," he said. "But beauty hides danger better than lies hide truth. Stay sharp, Emily. We're stepping into a maze. And not everyone wants us to find our way out."

As the aircraft touched down, the wheels skimmed the tarmac with a shudder, and passengers stirred. Emily turned to grab her bag.

Alex didn't move. He was still watching her—torn between loyalty and necessity, instinct and protocol.

"This is it," Emily said, standing, her voice wrapped in anticipation.

Alex rose beside her, expression unreadable but firm. "The beginning of something big. Stay close. There are shadows waiting to rewrite everything we think we know."

As they stepped off the plane and into the electric heat of India, something shifted.

Not the mission.

Not the plan.

But him.

He had only one job now:

Protect Emily at all costs.

Even if it meant hiding the truth that could break her trust—
Or save her life.

"The pressures that test the mind also expose its truths; understanding that strain is the key to unlocking its hidden depths."

The FBI's seventh-floor conference room didn't just buzz with tension—it hummed like a live wire about to snap. The fluorescent lights overhead flickered with bureaucratic fatigue, casting long, tired shadows over agents whose nerves were as taut as a sniper's trigger finger.

Clusters of senior operatives, analysts, and unit leads were scattered like chess pieces around the massive oval table, their voices a low murmur of uncertainty wrapped in expertise. Every gesture, every whisper, carried the weight of "classified," "urgent," and "pray-we-don't-screw-this-up."

At the head of the room, standing like a monument carved out of discipline and silent fury, was FBI Director Anderson.

Stoic. Stern. The kind of man whose handshake felt like a contract and whose stare made even seasoned agents check their moral compass.

Beside him leaned Richard, the Bureau's surgical scalpel in a world of hammers. Calm. Watchful. With that half-smirk that always suggested he was five moves ahead and politely waiting for everyone else to catch up.

They weren't just in a room full of agents. They were inside the eye of a very elegant, very expensive hurricane.

Spread across the oak table: open files, mugshots, wiretap transcripts, and digital forensics printouts—all forming a chaotic mosaic of something bigger than anyone wanted to admit.

But what pulled every eye—what sat there like an unblinking witness—was Marcus's notepad, sealed in evidence plastic. Quiet. Innocent-looking.

And absolutely lethal.

Richard tapped the table once. The sound cut through the room like a scalpel.

"Agents."

Every voice paused mid-thought. Heads turned. Silence fell like judgment.

"Agent Riley," Richard said, voice cool but sharp. "You've been closest to the fire. Bring us in."

Agent Riley, a seasoned operator with more gray hairs than he liked to admit, straightened his tie. He always did that when he was trying not to swear in front of the Director.

"Sir," he began, measured and clear. "As of this morning, Felicity Montgomery remains cooperative. Too cooperative, if I'm honest. She's dropped names, flagged key accounts, and connected enough dots to outline a small galaxy."

He paused, looking around the room. "But we're still in the smoke. No hard proof. And with the kind of names she's whispering... well, let's just say we're poking into territory that sends Christmas cards to Capitol Hill."

A low chuckle from the back.

One agent muttered under his breath, "Congress gets nervous when we start turning over their rugs."

Richard didn't miss a beat.

"Skeletons, Agent Grant? You're being generous. Try fully staffed graveyards with their own parking lots."

That got the room's attention. Even the Director's lips almost twitched.

Richard picked up Marcus's notepad, holding it like he was handling a cursed object. Everyone leaned in.

"This isn't just a collection of scribbles," he said. "It's a confession, written in breadcrumbs."

He slapped a pair of hand gloves, flipped the notepad open to a page bookmarked by a red tab. The scrawls were dense. Codes. Arrows. Names partially blacked out in permanent marker. And right in the center—a bank transfer. Offshore. India.

"Looks like a dead-end at first," Richard said. "But Marcus wasn't sloppy. He was terrified. Whatever he knew, he wanted us to chase it, not ignore it."

He locked eyes with Agent Riley. " Here's my suggestion, find the money trail. It's the oldest trick in the book for a reason. Burn the midnight oil. Get creative. If this lead collapses, so does Felicity's credibility—and whatever bigger fish she's been throwing bait toward."

One junior analyst raised a hand. "Sir, we've flagged six active accounts in Goa, Delhi, and Mumbai. The transaction fits a laundering pattern, but we'll need cooperation from Indian authorities."

Director Ross finally stepped forward, his deep voice reverberating like a verdict.

"Then get that cooperation—quietly. We don't want to wake sleeping giants unless we're prepared to cut their throats."

The room stiffened.

He continued. "This isn't just about catching a liar or cleaning up after a devil's parade. This is about what happens when our enemies stop working from the shadows... and start buying them."

"Before we run out of the gate," Anderson added, "let's remember something—correlation isn't causation. Just because Felicity's information aligns with Marcus's notes doesn't mean she's not playing us. Trust, but verify. Then verify again."

Richard gave a half-nod. "Understood. And in this game? Shadows leave fingerprints. We just need to find the right kind of light."

The Director took one last look at the boardroom. "This isn't a case, ladies and gentlemen. This is a minefield. And I don't want to be writing eulogies because someone stepped on the wrong tile."

As the meeting broke up, agents moved with sudden urgency—gathering files, coordinating calls, and prepping for the digital manhunt ahead.

Near the coffee table, two agents whispered:

"You think they pay us enough to chase international ghosts with Congress breathing down our necks?"

"Not unless 'hazard pay' includes stress ulcers and subpoenas."

Across the room, Richard lingered, eyes fixed on Marcus's notepad. To most, it was a relic. To him? A challenge. A dare from a ghost.

He muttered, almost amused, "Game on."

He slid the bagged notepad into a secured case, then turned toward the door as it shut behind him with a soft click.

And just like that, the Bureau wasn't just chasing phantoms.

They were marching into a house of mirrors.

And behind every reflection...

...someone was waiting.

"Struggles are passing storms—fierce, yes, but fleeting. To let them define you is to surrender your identity to the tempest."

The moment Emily and Alex stepped off the plane and onto Indian soil, it hit them—like walking straight into a festival and a funeral at the same time. The air was heavy. Not just the thick, humid kind that clung to your skin like bad perfume, but the kind that whispered, "You're not alone."

India greeted them like an overenthusiastic aunt—loud, colorful, slightly chaotic, and overwhelmingly fragrant. Curry, sweat, incense, jet fuel. All in stereo.

Alex adjusted the collar of his jacket, pulling his suitcase with one hand and fumbling for his phone with the other, like a man trained in the fine art of airport multitasking. His screen lit up—another unknown number.

"Again?" he muttered under his breath.

He felt Emily's gaze. That look. The look that asked all the questions without making a sound.

He answered the call with a casual, too-calm "Yes?"

A voice on the other end, calm and oily like it had been marinated in secrets, slid into his ear. "Alex, you and Emily are being followed."

Alex's lips twitched into a smile—not the happy kind. "Yeah, I figured. I tagged them."

Pause. Just air between danger and sarcasm.

"That's not what matters now," the voice continued, undeterred. "Do not hail a cab. Coordinates are coming to your phone. Stay exactly where you are. Do not move."

Click—end of call.

Alex stared at his phone like it had just insulted his intelligence.

Emily was already beside him, arms crossed, eyes drilling holes into his calm façade. "Let me guess... That was either your source, your bookie, or your bedtime story guy?"

Alex pocketed the phone, unfazed. "We're being followed."

Emily blinked. Once. Twice. "And you're just casually... sharing that? Like you're reading me the weather?"

He shrugged. "It's nothing alarming."

"Nothing alarming?" Her voice rose, not enough to draw a crowd, but enough to stir pigeons nearby. "Okay, let me get this straight. We just got off a twelve-hour flight, my mascara is somewhere between my chin and the floor, we're in a city where we know exactly zero people, and you're saying we're being followed like it's a minor parking violation?!"

Alex scratched the back of his neck. "It's nothing compared to what I expected."

"Ohhh, I see," Emily said, arms flailing in disbelief. "And what exactly did you expect, Alex? A welcome parade with snipers? Maybe a mariachi band holding us at gunpoint?"

Alex smirked. "Can we not do this here? It's like a thousand eyes already watching."

Emily opened her mouth, then closed it. She hated that he had a point.

Just then, her phone buzzed. Mom.

Of course.

Emily stared at the screen like it had betrayed her. "You've got to be kidding me."

"Take it," Alex said.

"Yeah, sure, let's just take a casual call from Mom while international espionage dances around us like Holi colors."

She swiped.

"Hi, Mom!"

"Oh, sweetheart! India! How exotic! The land of spices, colors, and... wait, are you safe? You're not in one of those Taken movies, are you?"

Emily stifled a laugh. "We're good, Mom. Just work. Nothing dramatic. Promise."

Her mom wasn't buying it. "Emily Rose Parker, if you so much as think about running into a building with a ticking bomb and a walkie-talkie—"

"Mom, that was one time—"

"You were fifteen!"

Alex gave her a look. "Fifteen?"

Emily mouthed, Later.

"Okay, I've got to go," Emily said sweetly. "Love you. I'll call when I'm bored or kidnapped. Bye!"

As she hung up, her forced grin faded.

"What now?" she asked Alex, who was glaring at his phone like it owed him money.

"They sent coordinates. But—"

"Excuse me," said a new voice.

They turned. Two officers. Uniformed. Stone-faced. Like extras in a spy movie, minus the warmth.

"You need to come with us," the taller one said.

Emily stiffened. "Why? What's going on?"

"No questions. Just follow."

Alex leaned closer to Emily. "These guys don't even blink. That's either elite training or terrible social skills."

They were ushered into the back of a police van that smelled like fear, rubber, and too many decisions made in a hurry. The silence between them was thick—like molasses soaked in paranoia.

"Think this is your guy?" Emily whispered.

"Could be. Or someone who doesn't want us to meet him," Alex replied. "Either way, I hate being chauffeured without a tip jar."

After what felt like twenty minutes of twisty roads and twistier thoughts, the van screeched to a stop at a small private airfield.

Emily squinted. "This is either where rich people fly or where people disappear."

A helicopter waited for them, blades slicing through the air like a countdown. Dust blew in swirls, and from it emerged a man in a tailored suit that somehow stayed clean in the chaos.

"Welcome," he said. "I'm Raja."

Alex narrowed his eyes. "Let's skip the niceties. Why are we here?"

Raja smiled like a man used to giving orders without explanations. "Questions later. For now, buckle up. Safety first."

Emily's sarcasm broke through. "Oh sure, NOW safety's important."

Once in the chopper, the noise drowned any chance of private conversation, but Emily wasn't done.

She leaned toward Raja, yelling over the roar. "You owe us an explanation!"

He looked at her, dead serious. "I don't owe you shit."

Alex gave a slow nod. "Wow. That's... refreshingly rude."

Raja smiled again. "Consider me your insurance policy."

Emily shot Alex a look that said, You brought me into this madness.

Alex returned one that said, Yes, but you make it fun.

As the helicopter rose into the Mumbai skyline, the city beneath them grew smaller, but the questions in their minds only grew louder.

Who was Raja?

Who was following them?

And what in the unholy name of samosas had they just stepped into?

"Of all humanity's great discoveries, none is more unsettling than deceit—the revelation that reality itself can be a veil."

In a cramped surveillance room tucked behind a chai stall that doubled as a cover operation in New Delhi, the fluorescent lights flickered with the kind of persistent hum that only added to the discomfort of everyone inside.

Eight operatives, each handpicked by Arthur C. Winters himself, hunched over monitors like gamblers staring at a final poker hand. On screen: the arrest feed of Emily and Alex through the security cams, pinned by two Indian special agents who looked more confused than confident. The whole thing had the slapdash air of a high school play suddenly upgraded to Broadway—too fast, too loud, and definitely not rehearsed.

A wiry man with skin like burnt parchment and eyes like black pins leaned forward, chewing the inside of his cheek. He didn't like the look of this.

"Sir," he muttered into his headset, trying to sound composed but unable to scrub the worry from his voice, "the targets have been apprehended. Was this... your directive?"

He regretted asking the moment the words left his mouth.

Back in Langley, Virginia—specifically, in a room built like a Bond villain's meditation chamber—CIA Director Arthur C. Winters stood surrounded by a wall of plasma screens. The kind of setup that would make most tech billionaires cry. Every screen broadcast a different geopolitical theater. Central Asia. Moscow. Tehran. A grocery store in Queens. And now, front and center: India.

Arthur was the kind of man who ironed his shirts even if no one would see him wear them. The type who saw emotions as distractions and mistakes as insults. He didn't chew gum. He chewed subordinates.

As the operative's question crackled through his secure phone, Arthur froze. The camera above his desk, usually ignored, would've captured a rare twitch—just there, under his left eye. He didn't answer right away. He was thinking.

Then, like a pressure valve releasing, his voice erupted, crisp and cruel.

"What the hell are you talking about?" he spat, his voice venom-laced and mechanical. "I gave no such order. If I wanted them apprehended, it would've been clean, quiet, and without all the amateur theatrics I'm seeing on my screen."

He didn't shout—Arthur never needed to but his tone could freeze fire.

"You idiots have been played," he added, as if tasting the bitterness of the words. "Played... like a fucking flute in a tourist market."

The connection went dead. He slammed the phone down with surgical fury, launching it across the table where it skidded to a stop beside a classified file marked "OPERATION: MIRAGE HOUND." The room pulsed with a strange silence, as if even the screens were too scared to blink.

Arthur exhaled through his nose. Then, with a calm eeriness, he raised his hand and bam—slammed his fist onto the desk. A paperweight flew—a stack of files scattered like startled birds. A coffee cup flipped, its contents bleeding slowly across a world map like a forecast of ruin.

He stared at the mess, not because he cared about the coffee, but because it insulted his sense of control.

"Outsmarted," he hissed, almost to himself, with the same venom one might reserve for the word "traitor." The idea that Emily and Alex—Emily with her reckless intuition, Alex with his irritatingly precise psychology—had navigated through his web without tripping a single alarm... it was infuriating.

But Arthur didn't sit in the highest chair at Langley because he lost sleep over setbacks. He knew when to rage, and more importantly, when to recalibrate.

With a surgeon's calm, he reached for a different device—a secure satellite phone. This one was reserved for ghosts. The kind of agents who weren't in databases, didn't exist on payrolls, and couldn't be summoned without accepting that someone might not return.

The line clicked. A breath. Then came the voice—smooth, professional, cold.

"Director Winters."

"Ross." Arthur's voice dropped to the temperature of liquid nitrogen. "They're slipping."

"Understood."

"No, Ross," Arthur continued. "You don't understand. Our surveillance unit has been compromised. Someone staged that arrest. They wanted us to believe we'd caught them. And we bought it."

There was silence on the line. Ross knew better than to interrupt when Arthur was unfurling the storm.

"You are to proceed with phase two," Arthur said. "Use the militia. Use local police. Use temple guards and spice vendors if you have to—I want them found. Alive is optional. Talkative is not."

Ross's voice returned, steady. "Understood, sir. What about the extraction protocol?"

"There is no extraction. When you find them, make sure the last thing they say is said to you. Then... silence."

Click.

Arthur leaned back into his leather chair, his jaw relaxing, his eyes sharp with renewed clarity. On the far-right monitor, a digital map of India lit up like a Christmas tree. Red dots blinked into place—each representing a unit, a checkpoint, an eye in the shadows.

And yet, somewhere beyond those blinking lights, Emily and Alex were out there. Running. Thinking. Plotting and probably laughing at him.

He narrowed his eyes and whispered to the empty room, "This isn't a game you can win... not against me."

Then, because he was Arthur Winters, he straightened a single file on his desk, wiped the coffee stain off the edge of his sleeve, and returned to his screens—watching, waiting, planning.

The hunt had begun.

"Existence demands engagement. To hide from failure is to forfeit the exhilaration of living."

The air in the chopper was thin—too thin to carry all the tension bouncing around in that metal bird.

The cabin thrummed like a heartbeat, mechanical and relentless, as the blades above sliced through the blue expanse with a kind of practiced violence. The seats weren't designed for comfort, and neither was the company. If you squinted hard enough, you could almost see the unspoken thoughts passing between them—like smoke in a bottle, waiting to blow the cap.

Emily sat bolt upright, her back stiff, boots planted like she was ready to leap out at a moment's notice—even if they were a few thousand feet above anything resembling ground. Her arms were crossed, but that wasn't about posture—it was about control. The kind of control that said, "I'm asking questions now, and I won't like your answers."

She turned to Raja, eyebrows drawn like twin sabers. "Why?" she asked, her tone edged with suspicion and curiosity. "And who's behind the veil?"

There was no small talk, no warming up. Just a sniper shot of a question, direct to the core.

Raja, leaning against the opposite wall with all the charisma of a brick wall and twice the mystery, didn't blink. His dark eyes moved to her with the lazy precision of a man who had calculated exactly how much he was willing to share and how much she would not like that number.

"The alternative was worse," he said coolly, each syllable clipped like it cost him extra breath. "That's all you need to know. For now."

Emily's jaw twitched. For now? That answer had the same energy as "it's complicated" from a cheating ex. She opened her mouth again, but Alex, seated beside her, gave a slight shake of his head. Not dramatic. Just a whisper of movement—barely there—but it said volumes.

Not now. Not here.

She caught it, held his gaze for a beat, and relented with a soft exhale. She bit the inside of her cheek, the taste of withheld words sharp on her tongue.

She looked away, but the fire in her eyes said the conversation had merely been postponed, not dropped.

Alex had been watching Raja with the kind of subtle intensity that suggested he didn't just want to read the man—he wanted to unravel him. Years in covert operations had taught Alex one golden rule: the quieter the savior, the darker the rescue. And right now, Raja was practically a thunderstorm wrapped in silence.

Still, a favor was a favor, and manners—even in espionage—still had a place.

"Raja," Alex said, leaning forward slightly, his voice even but heavy with intent, "we owe you. You stepped in when we needed it most. Thank you."

Raja gave the window his attention, not Alex. Outside, the city flickered beneath them like a nervous pulse. "Don't thank me," he muttered. "I'm just doing my job."

It was the kind of phrase that was meant to end a conversation. But Raja wasn't done.

Almost as an afterthought, he pulled a satellite phone from inside his jacket. He held it in his palm like it was both a gift and a grenade. Then he dialed, thumb gliding across the keys with the confidence of someone who'd memorized dangerous numbers long ago.

The conversation was short. Coded. Oblique. Emily tried to listen, but the language wasn't one meant to be cracked midair. Whatever Raja was saying, it wasn't just about them—it was about something bigger.

When he hung up, he passed the phone to Alex.

"Your turn."

Alex hesitated. It wasn't the phone—it was the expectation behind it. He took it anyway, pressing it to his ear as though it might whisper back something he wasn't ready to hear.

And then—that voice.

Warm. Calm. Dangerously familiar.

"Alex," it said. "I trust the extraction was... eventful."

Alex's spine stiffened. Of course, it was him again—the voice he couldn't pin, but one that always knew where to find him. The voice that danced on the line between help and manipulation like it was trained in ballet.

"It was efficient," Alex replied, choosing his words with care. "But dramatic. Not exactly the subtle approach I was expecting."

A pause.

"Discretion," the voice said with the confidence of someone quoting philosophy from a private jet, "is a luxury, not a guarantee. You weren't the only ones at risk. What you now know... is combustible."

"Then maybe you should stop throwing matches," Alex shot back, his tone cool. "Start explaining. Because saving us from one mystery while dropping us into another doesn't build trust."

There was a soft chuckle on the line—almost a purr. "You're not wrong, Alex. But clarity is dangerous. The more you know, the more of a target you become. Right now, you're useful. Alive."

"Useful," Alex echoed. "That's comforting."

"The moment you become a liability," the voice continued, "you'll know. Until then, stay alive. That's all you need to do."

The line went dead.

Alex stared at the phone for a beat, then handed it back like it had just told him his future and dared him to run from it.

Raja pocketed it without a word, the way someone might sheath a knife.

Emily was watching him again—watching both of them now. "What did they say?" she asked, voice low.

Alex let out a slow breath, rubbing his temple like the words had crawled into his skull and made themselves at home.

"They want us alive," he said. "But not necessarily informed."

"That's not creepy at all," she muttered.

Alex cracked a small, dry smile. "They said the information we carry is more dangerous than we realize."

Emily's eyebrows rose. "Well, that makes two of us who'd love to know what the hell we know."

He gave her a look—half apology, half challenge. "We'll find out. Before they decide ignorance isn't just bliss—it's disposable."

Raja didn't speak. But the way his eyes flicked back toward them said he agreed.

Outside, the sky was turning amber, the city shrinking beneath them as the horizon yawned open.

The chopper kept moving. So did the silence.

And somewhere, in the depths of that silence, was the truth—shrouded, tangled, and waiting to be untangled by the very people it was trying to kill.

"Uncertainty will always loom, and failure will always threaten—but the greater loss lies in never stepping onto the field at all."

Now, before it skips my mind—and trust me, with the way things are unfolding, my mind's been skipping more beats than a scratched vinyl—I need to put this down properly. I promised myself I'd keep this journal in the order things actually happened. No skipping scenes. No director's cut. Just raw, reel-life storytelling.

So, let's go back to Marilyn—a lot to catch up on.

According to my best friend, Richard—let's call him "Mr. Attraction-Reversal" for now—he has been on a personal quest to prove the Law of Attraction wrong. Like, violently wrong. If the universe whispered, "Go left," he'd swing right with the intensity of a man dodging destiny on purpose. And yet, the universe, being the persistent romantic that it is, threw Marilyn straight into his storyline like an unscheduled plot twist with heels.

So here's what happened:

Marilyn had gone home that day. Home, in this case, wasn't just a place—it was a hilltop mansion that looked like someone had taken a Pinterest board, added a billion-dollar budget, and given it a soul. Her family's estate perched elegantly above the city like it was politely supervising the rest of us mortals. From that height, the entire urban sprawl looked like Lego blocks scattered by an indecisive child—rooftops glittering, traffic pulsing, the world carrying on unaware that Marilyn was about to drop an emotional bomb.

Her car, a sleek convertible that purred like it had secrets, pulled into the driveway. You could almost hear the garden sigh in relief, like finally, some drama.

She stepped out of the car with that Marilyn grace—half movie star, half mischief maker. She smoothed her skirt, glanced at the pool house nestled behind the manicured lawn, and spotted her mother seated like a portrait painting come to life—elegant, poised, the kind of woman who didn't just sit; she composed herself into furniture.

The low sun spilled gold across the pool tiles and wrapped her mother in a halo that made her look less human and more like a well-dressed Greek oracle.

Marilyn approached, heels tapping against the flagstones like a countdown.

Her mother looked up, surprised. But in that calm, aristocratic way that said, Ah, surprise—but controlled.

"Honey, you're home early today," she said, her voice so melodic it probably had its own playlist.

Marilyn chuckled as she dropped her purse. "Not really, Mom. It's already four."

Her mother gave a faint smile, the kind that said time is a concept. Elegance is eternal. She turned her gaze toward the cityscape, as if asking the skyline for permission to continue the conversation.

Then, after a long, cozy silence—the kind that only happens between two people who've shared way too many tea breaks—Marilyn said it.

Softly.

Too softly.

"I had lunch with Richard."

That name.

That was the literary equivalent of dropping a red wine glass on a white rug. Her cheeks flushed, her eyes twitched in anticipation.

Her mother turned slowly, her eyebrows rising just enough to convey twelve volumes of concern.

"Did I hear you correctly?"

You could tell the sentence carried more than just inquiry—it was half plea, half prophecy.

Marilyn nodded. Her lips curled into a smile that said yes, and I meant every syllable.

"We've been seeing each other. It's not just lunch. It's... more. And it feels right, Mom. He makes me feel like I'm not just someone's daughter. Like I'm me."

Her words trembled on the edge of excitement and uncertainty, like a tightrope walker who hadn't yet looked down.

Her mother didn't respond immediately. She just stared—not at Marilyn, but into the space in front of her. The pause wasn't empty. It was filled with ghosts of expectations, generational pressure, and the haunting echo of What will your father say?

Marilyn, sensing the undercurrent, leaned her head gently on her mother's shoulder—just like she used to when she was seven and had lost her first pet goldfish. The gesture said, I'm still your little girl. I just happen to love someone dangerous to our family traditions.

Her mother responded instinctively, resting a hand over hers. No words. Just fingers intertwined like roots refusing to let go of the same soil.

Finally, her mother spoke.

"I'm happy for you, sweetheart."

But there was something in the tone like the words were wearing shoes two sizes too small—uncomfortable, but polite.

"But you know your father."

She didn't need to say more.

Richard wasn't just a man. To her father, he was a category —a rebellion in human form—a brilliant, charming, and dangerous defiance against a lifetime of curated expectations.

Now, before you start getting all the wrong ideas, her father, who hasn't met my best friend yet, may not dislike Richard. He just disliked what Richard represented—choice, freedom, unpredictability, maybe even love unapproved by bloodlines.

Marilyn's mother continued, voice now a shade softer.

"The path you're choosing—it won't just challenge him. It'll challenge us all. It'll test whether what we call love can survive what we call tradition."

There it was.

Truth in a teacup.

When my best friend shared all this with me later—face flushed with equal parts hope and panic—I didn't see it as a disaster waiting to happen. No. I saw it as the moment right before a seed breaks its shell. Painful. Necessary. Inevitable.

We both knew this wasn't just a lunch date turning serious. This was history writing its next controversial chapter.

And what comes next?

We honestly couldn't say.

Because sometimes, love doesn't knock gently on the door. It kicks it wide open, tracks muddy footprints into the living room, and dares you to call it family.

And with Marilyn and Richard, well... the odds were unclear. But the taste of time would tell.

One way or another.

"For far too long, we have denied its existence, turning a blind eye to the sinister whispers that echo within the depths of our souls. Yet by refusing to face the shadows, we allow them to shape our choices in silence. What we fear to confront, we empower. What we exile inward, we grant sovereignty over our very being."

He stood by the window like a statue carved from polished ambition, his reflection faintly visible in the glass—gray streaks in his hair like lightning bolts across a stormy sky, jaw tight, eyes calculating. One hand cradled a tumbler of aged scotch—an indulgence he allowed only when something big was in motion. The other rested deep in his trouser pocket, fingers tapping thoughtfully against a brass coin he always kept—a relic from a war no one ever truly left.

Below, headlights weaved through the grid like electric veins in a living organism. From his vantage point, it looked almost poetic. Chaotic. Symphonic. Controlled.

He allowed himself the illusion that the entire city was an extension of his own mind—a vast board, its pieces in motion, each unaware of the invisible fingers guiding their fate. Chess was too obvious a metaphor. This was a symphonic war. And he was the conductor.

Then it buzzed.

A faint tremble from his phone, barely audible, but Arthur's instincts were wired to catch subtlety. He didn't even look—just placed the tumbler gently on the oak desk with the reverence of a priest laying down communion—and answered the call.

"Sir," came Cade's voice, crisp and precise, as if carved from protocol. "The packages have been secured."

Arthur didn't smile. He shifted. A slow tightening at the corners of his mouth, something between satisfaction and the quiet pride of a man watching a years-long plan fall into place.

"Excellent."

He said it like a chess master nudging a pawn, knowing the endgame had already begun.

His gaze drifted toward the antique chessboard in the corner. Mid-game. Knights in limbo. The black queen suspended mid-trap. He hadn't touched it in weeks. Not out of neglect—but because the pause itself was part of the plan.

"How many escorts?" Arthur asked, his tone casual but laced with the edge of a question that already had an answer.

"Sixty, sir. All vetted. All loyal. Each package will reach its destination—forty-nine homes. No issues."

"Forty-nine?" Arthur frowned, shifting weight onto one foot. "Who's the holdout? Alaska?"

"Hawaii."

Arthur let out a short, sharp laugh—quick and almost involuntary. Even he didn't expect it. "Figures. Too much ocean. Paranoia's a stronger drug on an island."

He walked slowly back to his desk, his mind already twenty steps ahead. "Remind them: the routes are non-negotiable. Immigration smells fear. If anyone deviates, if a single car stutters where it shouldn't, the whole operation collapses like a house of cards on a windy night. Understood?"

"Crystal clear, sir."

Arthur ended the call with a flick of his thumb and turned toward the bulletin board across the room. It was cluttered with maps, red yarn, intelligence briefs, and one newspaper article—thumbtacked with deliberate precision—a hit piece.

The headline was a punchline:

"A Man of Many Masks: Who Is the Real Senator Robert Thornhill?"

He picked up the glass of scotch, raised it toward the paper like a mock toast, and muttered, "If only they knew... the masks were never the point."

The door knocked gently.

"Come on in."

Claire entered—sharp as ever, heels muted against the plush carpet, eyes already scanning his face before she spoke. She always moved like someone trying not to disturb a sleeping lion.

"Director," she said, placing a thick folder on his desk, "final clearance reports."

He gestured lightly. "Stay."

She paused. "Sir?"

He leaned back into his chair, fingers steepled, eyes narrowing—not menacing, but intensely focused, like he was watching her from ten years into the future.

"Claire," he said, almost conversationally, "you ever wondered what it's like to play God?"

Her eyebrows shot up—just slightly. A twitch, not a gasp. "Sir, I..."

"Not in the religious sense," he said with a smirk, swirling his drink. "I mean... the ability to mold things. Events. People. To move the levers no one else can see. To orchestrate chaos so precisely that it looks like design."

She blinked, uncertain whether this was a philosophical moment or a subtle test of loyalty. "I imagine it's... exhilarating."

Arthur's smile faded into something quieter, more human. "It is. But it's also lonely. Most people only see moves. I see the entire war."

She nodded slowly, half-swallowed. "If anyone can handle it, sir... It's you."

That caught him off guard. For a second, just one, he looked tired.

"Flattery," he muttered, chuckling. "Dangerous territory."

Claire took the cue and backed out with practiced grace, leaving the room once again in silence. The kind of silence that only powerful men can afford—one born not of peace, but of dominance.

I watched all this unfold from my tablet screen, seated in a chopper with Raja and Emily, something to remove my mind from whatever hell awaits. But even through the glass, even through digital barriers and encrypted firewalls, I felt it—that chilling presence of a man who didn't just work power.

He was power.

And yet, watching Arthur Winters, I couldn't help but wonder what history would say about men like him. Villain? Hero? Or that most haunting of all legacies: misunderstood?

Not that he'd care. History wasn't written by the righteous. It was written by whoever held the pen.

And Arthur? Oh, he wasn't letting go of that pen anytime soon.

Above his desk, in perfect alignment with the shadows on the wall, hung a framed quote:

"It is better to be feared than loved, if you cannot be both."
— Niccolò Machiavelli

He looked up at it, the amber light from his desk lamp casting a halo around the frame.

Arthur saw himself as a visionary—a sculptor of reality. A man who turned ideology into policy, whispers into wars. But what he never seemed to acknowledge—or maybe simply refused to—is that even kings bleed. Even gods age. And deep down, behind the calm voice and curated mask... There was a war raging in his own soul.

He just hadn't decided which side deserved to win.

"In life's labyrinth, curiosity whispers like a daring guide, ignorance festers as a quiet disease, and wisdom—forever elusive—reveals itself only to the bold. Choose carefully, for confidence inscribes your name among the brave, while timidity, by contrast, carves only a silent grave."

Life is a paradox, a riddle posed by existence itself.

Curiosity—celebrated as the spark behind every great discovery—is also the ancient curse whispered in stories of downfall.

And ignorance? Though it promises peace, it is no sanctuary. It devours potential quietly, like rot beneath polished wood.

Between these warring forces lies wisdom: a narrow, brutal path that demands the courage to confront the unknown and the resilience to survive its truths.

Raja walked that path—a man made of contradiction.

But tonight, the bird had touched down. The rhythmic pulse of the rotor blades slowed to a reverent hush, a metallic exhale settling into the air. A warm wind stirred the sand, lifting it like incense smoke in a ritual. The moment felt choreographed by fate—deliberate, quiet, inevitable.

Raja was the first to step out. Tall, composed, every movement intentional. A silhouette etched against the dying light, as if time itself slowed to make room for him.

Emily and Alex followed.

"Stay close," Alex muttered. His voice was composed, but his eyes scanned everything—trees, terrain, Raja's shoulders. Trust had limits.

The path to the cottage crunched beneath their boots—gravel, sand, memory.

The cottage looked like something out of a forgotten novel—ivy crawling up weathered stone, wood creaking gently in the breeze.

A place meant to be ignored. And yet, the air shifted as they approached.

Not colder, but heavier. Denser. As if the ground beneath is holding back something.

Raja stopped at the door.

No words.

He leaned toward a small black square embedded in the wall. A red scanning laser swept across his eye, followed by a nearly inaudible click.

The door opened.

"Welcome," Raja said and stepped inside.

They entered.

The cottage's humble charm dissolved in an instant. Inside was something else entirely.

Emily blinked.

Gone were the wooden beams and fireplace she'd expected. In their place: Monitors embedded in the walls, glowing like silent watchers. Video feeds streamed from cities and jungles, alleyways and boardrooms.

The low hum of servers vibrated beneath the floor like a pulse.

A quiet empire. Hidden in plain sight.

"What is this place?" Emily whispered, more to herself than anyone else.

Alex answered before Raja could. "It's not a cottage. It's a command center."

Raja turned to face them. His voice was calm, almost detached. "Observation. Control. Disruption. Every war is fought on many fronts—and not all of them are visible."

They followed him deeper inside. Wooden panels slid away to reveal metallic compartments—each one housing maps, devices, or tools that bore no label but radiated consequence.

Tiny cameras watched from corners, disguised as screws. The air smelled faintly of old paper and ozone.

"This place..." Emily began, but the words faltered.

"It's a hub," Raja said, answering what she hadn't finished. "A nexus for information. For influence. Every piece of data gathered here is processed, weaponized, or preserved—for leverage, or legacy. The cottage outside exists to be ignored. But this... this is a knife pressed to the throat of the future."

Emily's throat tightened. She'd danced in shadows most of her career, but this—this felt like standing inside the mind of something sentient. Cold. Calculating. Beautiful, in a terrifying way.

Alex folded his arms. His voice was calm, but his eyes were sharp. "What's the take?"

Raja stopped. Turned slowly. "The take is that what you suspected in D.C. isn't just true—it's documented. Measured. Known. What you're about to walk into is the answer to a question most men never live long enough to ask."

He swept his hand around the room.

"This is the edge. The one who owns the data owns the outcome."

A long silence.

Then Alex asked the question they'd both been thinking.

"Couldn't this meeting have happened back in the States?"

Raja's smile was a blade dressed as silk.

"If that were the case, why would he want you here?"

The words landed like thunder muffled beneath glass.

They stared at him. Then at each other.

And in that silence, Emily realized something unsettling: Somewhere behind those glowing monitors... someone was already watching.

"Life is a maze of uncertainty, navigated through speculation. What defines us is not tomorrow's certainty, but the courage to move forward today, guided by hope."

If silence ever had a hum, it was here.

The command center wasn't just high-tech—it felt alive. Not in a haunted way. No. This was different. The room breathed with blinking lights and soft mechanical murmurs, like a living mind with a thousand whispering tongues. Screens flared with feeds from half the planet—Buenos Aires traffic, a Berlin compound too quiet to be innocent, and someone pacing under a fluorescent light with the kind of energy only guilt or unpaid taxes could produce.

And in the eye of this digital storm sat Alex Carter.

Hunched like a monk before a holy relic, he typed with the precision of a man who didn't know what mistakes felt like. His fingers danced over the interface like a pianist in a thunderstorm—calm, elegant, deadly. To most, the screen looked like digital gibberish, a chaos. To Alex, it was a language written in lyrical format, and he was fluent in it. A jazz. A rhythm of offshore trails, ghost transactions, and breadcrumbs left by men too rich to be caught and too arrogant to imagine being chased.

Emily Parker stood in the corner, arms folded like a judgment she wasn't ready to hand down. Her shoulder leaned against the wall, but her mind was tap dancing across a dozen scenarios—and not one of them involved getting out of this without bruises.

"You're either saving democracy," she said dryly, "or trying to order Thai food using a North Korean satellite."

Alex didn't even blink. "If it were Thai, we'd already have noodles. Level five spice. And I'd have a sweating intern regretting life choices."

Emily took a step closer, squinting at the flurry of data.

"And yet, here we are—no noodles, no intern, just you in a romantic tango with numbers. What exactly are we doing, maestro?"

Alex smirked without looking up. "Triangulating offshore capital movements connected to shell firms so shady, even their shadows have alibis. Long story short... It's Tuesday."

Emily rolled her eyes and peered over his shoulder. "Alright, Da Vinci, do you mind telling me what exactly we're hoping to paint here? Because we're knee-deep in blinking screens and code, and so far, nothing's yelled 'aha!' or 'follow me to the villain's lair.'"

Behind them, Raja was the room's quiet gravity. Standing like he'd seen too many regimes collapse before breakfast, he hadn't said a word since entering, just watched. Observed. Measured. Like a cat that had seen the canary die... but wanted to confirm the time of death.

"Does the name Marcus and his cursed notepad ring any nostalgic bells?" Alex asked, finally glancing up.

Emily let out a breath that sounded like it came with memories. "Marcus's notepad? Oh, yeah. The sacred scribble diary."

"Well," Alex said, fingers still tap-dancing across the keyboard, "turns out his little doodle pad wasn't so amateur after all. I'm tracking dummy accounts that all trace back to a hedge fund under Marcus's name. The man might've died, but his financial paper trail is still shouting into the void."

Emily raised a brow. "And we're hoping these bedtime scribbles are going to unwind an entire global corruption racket?"

Alex stopped typing for the first time. "No. We're not hoping. We're syncing."

He straightened slightly. "Before we left, I had Richard scan every page of that notepad and pipe it through a secure tunnel. If he didn't fall into a rabbit hole of conspiracy videos, the data should land here within the hour."

Emily blinked slowly. "Alex... spelunking into hedge fund corruption requires ropes, helmets, and—ideally—a lawyer on speed dial. You, however, seem to think sarcasm and finger speed are enough."

"I encrypted the tunnel six layers deep," Alex replied. "Even Richard couldn't screw it up."

Emily raised a single finger. "Don't. Tempt. The gods. Of irony."

Finally, Raja stepped forward, his voice low and smooth, like a secret told by candlelight. "It's not just about finding a man. It's about tracing the system that made him. You're not chasing ghosts. You're unraveling a bloodline of decisions."

Emily gave him a look that walked the line between respect and wariness. "Beautifully cryptic, Raja. But unless that bloodline includes a meeting with my source tonight, we're still running on fumes."

Raja's smile was slight but sharp.

Alex stood and stretched, the pop of his spine cracking through the tension like a gunshot at a ballet. "If the upload comes through, we won't need your source. We'll have the whole mosaic—transactions, players, timestamps. And maybe... just maybe... the name behind the curtain."

Emily sighed and started pacing again. "You know what your real problem is?"

"Go on," Alex said, clearly inviting a roast.

"You make chaos sound like Sunday brunch. Somewhere out there, your mother is probably pacing too—wondering why her son grew up allergic to straightforward plans."

Raja mutters, "Damn."

Alex grinned. "And you've got this charming way of turning suspicion into something that sounds suspiciously like affection."

Emily stopped mid-stride and pointed at him. "Don't flatter yourself, Carter. I've met raccoons with more discretion."

He held up both hands. "Subtlety's overrated. Accuracy isn't."

They locked eyes for a beat—an electric pause. The kind that suggests if they weren't in a ticking-bomb situation, they'd either kiss or slap each other over dinner.

Then the room dipped back into silence. The kind that settled heavy, like unasked questions.

Emily leaned against the wall again. "Well, hacker-boy, keep casting your spells. But if that upload doesn't land soon, I'm walking out that door to meet my source. And I don't care if the CIA shows up in clown wigs trying to stop me."

Alex chuckled softly, returning to his keyboard. "Deal. But if they do show up in clown wigs, I expect a photo."

Raja stepped forward again, eyes darker now. "Both of you," he said calmly, "the edge is thinner than you think. Every second you argue, someone out there inches closer to finding you. I'm assuming they already know how."

Emily's playful mask dropped a hair. Her voice steadied. "And whose side are you on, Raja?"

He smiled that barely-there smile again. The one that made you think he knew more than God and just wasn't in the mood to explain.

"Let's just say I prefer to be on the side that doesn't end with the heroes buried beneath headlines."

The room fell quiet. Not with fear. But with a slow, creeping truth neither of them wanted to name yet.

Then—ping. The main screen blinked.

A download bar began to fill.

Alex's eyes lit up. "We've got incoming."

Emily straightened.

Raja didn't say a word. He just stepped back into the shadows, exactly where the danger liked to live.

And just like that, the game was about to change.

"Progress begins not with answers, but with questions. To question is to rebel against stagnation, to challenge the prison of certainty, and to light the fire of discovery that propels humanity forward."

It's day 2, and it has been a long one. The faint hum of an air conditioner fan continues to whisper through the corners of the room. Outside, the sky bled into an orangey haze as the sun dipped below Mumbai's cluttered skyline. Inside, Emily stood frozen—her eyes fixed on the empty space where Raja had been just moments ago.

She wasn't staring at the door. She was staring through it, as if trying to decode something that had no name.

"That man," she finally muttered, still half-talking to herself. "He looks at me like I'm the unpredictable twist in a math equation he doesn't trust."

Alex, lounging casually in a battered chair across the room, looked up from his laptop. He didn't speak right away. He just studied her—cool, calm, the way someone watches waves roll in before deciding whether or not to swim.

Emily turned, arms crossed, the corner of her mouth twitching in frustration. "You've noticed it, haven't you? The way Raja looks at me. Like I'm not just a variable—I'm a threat to his whole calculus. It's more than suspicion. It's like... judgment. Like he's already had a whole trial in his head, and I lost."

Alex let out a low, thoughtful hum. "You're not wrong," he said, stretching his legs like he had all the time in the world to explain this enigma named Raja. "But you have to understand something—Raja isn't your average suspicious man. He's not measuring you for treason; he's measuring you for pain."

Emily blinked. "Pain?"

Alex nodded, then looked up at the dusty ceiling like the answer might be scrawling up there. "I'm assuming he's the kind of guy who's been to the dark side of loyalty—and came back with burn marks. Trusting people probably feels like handing them matches when he's already soaked in gasoline."

Emily paced a little, biting her lip. "But... what happened to him?"

Alex smiled slightly. "His rap sheet could probably be like Mumbai traffic. Tangled. No beginning, no end. Just honks, chaos, and a constant sense that something's about to crash. How the hell should I know?"

Emily couldn't help but smirk at that. "So he's emotionally gridlocked?"

"More like emotionally... booby-trapped," Alex said. "He doesn't hate you, Emily. If anything, the fact that he's watching you so closely might mean he respects you. Raja doesn't waste suspicion on people who don't matter. trust me."

Emily raised an eyebrow. "That's one hell of a compliment."

"Hey," Alex shrugged, "coming from Raja, that's practically a love letter."

"Except it felt cold coming out of your mouth."

They both laughed, just for a moment. The kind of laugh you share in the eye of a storm—not because it's funny, but because it's the only way to keep from unraveling.

Emily sat down on the edge of the desk, the laughter already fading, replaced by something deeper. "It's just... I've handled dangerous men before. But with him, it feels personal. Like he's not just watching what I do—he's watching who I am. And I don't know what version of me he's seeing."

Alex leaned forward, resting his elbows on his knees. "Maybe he sees a part of himself in you."

She turned her head slowly, curious. "What, the charming part?"

"No," Alex said, deadpan. "The part that's broken in just the right places to survive this kind of work."

The words hit like a pin dropped in silence. Neither of them moved.

Then, a sharp buzz cut through the moment.

Alex checked his phone. His brow furrowed the second he saw the screen. "This is Alex," he answered, his voice flattening into business mode. For a few seconds, all Emily heard was silence—on the line, and in the room.

Then he ended the call and stood.

"That was my source. Our window's shrinking fast."

"How fast?" Emily asked.

"Like we're standing on ice that's cracking under our feet," he said. "Whatever we're looking for—whoever—we don't have the luxury of curiosity anymore. We either find it, or we get found. And I don't like our odds in the second scenario."

Emily straightened up, her body stiffening as resolve overtook fatigue. "I can feel it too," she said, her voice low, steady. "Like the air's changing. Like something's shifting... watching us."

Alex didn't answer right away. He was already tapping something on his screen—coordinates and access protocols they weren't supposed to have.

Finally, without looking up, he murmured, "It's not just a feeling, Emily. We both knew that the deeper we went into this network, the more likely it was that someone—or something—knew we were coming. And it's not going to sit still."

Emily's fingers brushed the side of her holster.

"Then let's not give it the chance."

Alex nodded, just once. "You read my mind."

"A quest does not end at revelation, but at the threshold of choice. Every discovery is a lantern in the dark, yet lanterns can guide or burn, depending on whose hand holds the flame. Discovery is rarely neutral—it is a double-edged gift. The true weight of the quest lies not in revelation itself, but in the careful hand that steers its consequences."

It was Day Three.

Still no good news. Not even a whisper of promise. But it was still morning, and mornings had a way of rewriting headlines by noon. Especially in this place, anything before noon still qualified as "miracle hours."

Emily sat on the edge of a navy blue cushion, her legs tucked beneath her, her forehead gently pressed against the headrest.

Alex walked across the room like a man who hadn't slept in days but somehow still had enough emotional bandwidth to make coffee and crack a joke. He held out a mug with a slight grin that looked more like a peace treaty than a smile.

"Thought you might need this," he said, stepping into the quiet like a human comma. His voice wasn't loud, but it had that effortless weight.

Emily took the mug wordlessly, their fingers brushed—just for a second—long enough to feel something she refused to name. She took a breath as she accepted it, letting the warmth bite through the chill in her chest, still steaming. She looked at it. Then at him. Then at the mug again.

"Thanks," she said softly, bringing the cup to her lips, the scent hit her like a hug she didn't know she needed. Strong. Grounded. Slightly burnt. Alex's signature brew—equal parts caffeine and chaotic optimism. And she was sipping like it was her first taste of sanity in weeks. It was bold. Strong. Bitter—like every good decision she'd ever made.

She turned her back to him, mug in hand, heading toward the window. She needed the view. Probably hoping to sip in silence. Maybe pretend for a second that the world wasn't quietly unraveling from the inside out.

But silence never lasted long in this room.

"Emily," Alex said.

His voice was different now. Sharper. There was always a shift in tone when data came into play. It was like watching someone transition from a jazz musician to a sniper in under five seconds.

"The results are coming in."

Emily didn't turn right away. She stood there for another beat, the city outside gleaming through the bulletproof glass like it didn't know what fear was. Morning light shimmered across towers and traffic lights, her eyes tracing the movement of distant cars. Everything was perfectly fine. She knew better.

With a reluctant breath, she tore her gaze away from the view and walked back to him—where chaos lived on a screen.

And then, standing next to him in front of a screen that looked like a Jackson Pollock painting had swallowed the internet. It was a digital spiderweb—lines and circles and blinking nodes, all tangled in chaotic brilliance.

"Okay," Emily said slowly, one eyebrow inching up. "Care to translate this bowl of neon spaghetti?"

Alex grinned. "This," he gestured with a flourish like he was hosting a game show, "is our spiderweb. Each node—person, event, company. Each line—transaction, message, motive. If someone sneezed near a private jet, it's in here."

She stared blankly.

He smirked. "Alright, imagine your favorite crime show. Corkboard. Red strings. Creepy detective in a trench coat connecting photos of bad guys."

"Except," she said, pointing at the screen, "your version looks like a toddler drank three Red Bulls and attacked a galaxy."

"Valid point," he admitted. "But give me a minute, and I'll translate toddler chaos into adult nightmares."

Emily rolled her eyes but leaned in, curiosity outweighing her cynicism. "So what's it saying, Professor?"

Alex leaned back, steepling his fingers. "Follow the money. Every cluster on this screen is a series of transactions—offshore, encrypted, intentionally buried. But the beauty of greed? It leaves receipts."

"Lovely," Emily muttered. "Corruption with accounting."

"Exactly. And right here—" he pointed to a glowing center "—these are recent—movement across four countries in the last 48 hours. Someone's nervous. Someone's shifting assets. Probably the someone responsible for getting Marcus silenced."

She leaned closer, scanning the maze. "But I still don't see a face. A name. Anything human."

"That's the elegance," Alex said, his voice softening. "The system is designed to erase fingerprints. What we're doing here isn't just code—it's psychological archaeology."

Emily raised an eyebrow. "And that's your way of saying 'I'm making educated guesses until the villain slips up'?"

"More or less," he shrugged. "But this tool—" he tapped a few keys and the map pulsed—"connects even the whispers. Emails. CCTV timestamps. Facial recognition. Anonymized social media posts with metadata errors. It's not just nosy... It's paranoid with a doctorate."

Emily snorted, covering her grin with the mug. "So basically, it's you in software form."

"Finally, some recognition," he said proudly.

The screen shifted again, more lines lighting up. A symphony of secrets unraveling.

Alex leaned in. "See this loop? That's the tell. Financial movement that shouldn't exist. Routing money through three dummy firms, then rerouting it to a cultural nonprofit in Estonia. Wanna guess who sits on their advisory board?"

Emily squinted. "No way..."

"Yep. Our friend in Washington. The one who said he hadn't spoken to Marcus in years."

She exhaled sharply. "Alright. Color me slightly impressed."

"Oh, it gets worse," Alex said. "Or better, depending on your taste for drama. Every one of those dummy firms has a backdoor link to one holding company... that was dissolved five years ago. Officially."

Emily's voice dropped. "So... a dead company is laundering live money."

"And using real causes as a shield. Cancer research. War relief. Children's education. All of it, camouflage."

She sat down slowly, processing. "Jesus. It's not just corruption... It's curated corruption. Dressed up in morality so nobody asks questions."

"That's the game," Alex said. "Influence. Immunity. Control."

Emily let the silence sit for a second, then muttered, "You realize this is dangerous, right? Like... real cloak-and-dagger dangerous. We're poking a bear that has drones, lawyers, and probably a private island with shark-infested moats. And if we can see this... that means they can see us, too."

Alex looked at her. Really looked. "I know."

"And you're still in?"

Alex nodded, "If we don't do this, if we don't find a way in to dismantle this, brick by brick, thread by thread—then what the hell are we doing here?"

Emily looked at the screen again. The nodes pulsed softly, like heartbeats in the dark. Each one a name. A choice. A lie.

She took a long sip of her coffee, then stood.

"Alright," Emily said at last, the fire flickering back into her voice. "Let's blow up their little castle. And while we're at it... We might as well dig our own graves with matching shovels."

Alex smiled. Not big. Not smug. Just a slight, steady curve of the lips—the kind that meant we're in this now, no turning back.

"That's the spirit."

Before they could so much as lean toward the keyboard, a new alert sliced across their screen—bold red text, an impatient chime. Hong Kong.

The first bite.

Alex's eyes narrowed. "Looks like chaos just picked its opening act."

Emily squinted. "What?"

"Origin tracing," Alex said, already tapping. "Pull in the citywide feeds—every camera in range. Focus on one Dr. Bai Feng—name just popped up. If this is what I think it is, we need to grab everything on him before it's... adjusted for 'official record-keeping.'"

Emily's fingers flew. "How the hell did we miss this?"

"That's what happens when you're missing pieces," Alex said without looking up. "Even the scraps you do have feel like bad odds."

She muttered something unprintable under her breath. Alex caught the first CCTV angles—and froze.

"Wow. Well, shit. This is bad."

Dr. Bai Feng's arrival in Hong Kong didn't appear to be the start of a crisis. He stepped out of the airport into the city's unrelenting soundtrack—horns barking, engines growling, voices volleying over each other like a street market arguing with itself.

The air must've been thick: street food sizzling somewhere nearby, exhaust from a hundred impatient cars, and just the faint bite of sea salt. It was the opposite of the sterile, humming coolness he'd just left behind on his flight.

His hand clenched on the handle of his briefcase—a slim, black thing that carried the weight of his carefully ordered world. He had no idea how fragile that world had just become.

A chaotic line of taxis waited outside, each with a driver who seemed to think yelling louder was the secret to customer service. And then—one voice cut through.

The man moved like a hunter. His smile was too broad, his eyes too sharp, scanning Feng with the slow calculation of someone deciding which part of the meal to start with.

"Sir, my taxi is the best in the city," the man said in rehearsed English, each word polished until it gleamed. "Clean, fast, safe. Only the best for someone like you."

Dr. Feng nodded politely and kept moving. Something about that pitch felt... wrong. Too neat. Too eager. Like a trap disguised as a special offer.

The driver wasn't discouraged. He shadowed Feng's steps, his tone dipping into urgency.

"You look like a man in a hurry. Don't waste time with the others. They don't know the city as well as I do. Trust me—you'll be where you need to be in no time."

Feng stopped, irritation breaking through his jet-lag fog. "I've made my choice," he said crisply, stepping toward another cab.

The driver moved quickly, sliding in front of him. A hand shot out—lightly brushing Feng's arm. Too familiar.

Then came the pinch. Quick. Precise. Almost nothing—if nothing could burn for a heartbeat.

Feng jerked his arm back, pulse spiking. The man's grin didn't falter, but his eyes had that flicker—like they both knew something had just passed between them.

"What was that?" Feng demanded, his voice loud enough to draw a few glances from strangers.

The driver's hands came up in mock surrender. "Nothing, sir. A misunderstanding. Just trying to help."

Feng turned away sharply, clutching his wrist where the touch had landed. The skin looked fine, but the ghost of the pinch clung to him like a whisper.

A different taxi pulled up; he got in fast, door slamming like a seal locking him from the outside world.

"Where to?" the new driver asked flatly.

Feng gave the address, clipped and precise. As the city's streets began winding past, his hand kept straying back to that spot on his arm, the unease slowly winding itself tighter. He didn't know it yet, but somewhere far above him, a clock had started ticking—and he was standing right under it.

When Feng finally walked through his front door, the scent of antiseptic and lab air still clung to him—a reminder of the days spent bent over viral genomes and chemical assays. He was exhausted. But exhaustion vanished the second a small voice squealed, "Daddy!"

His youngest, Mei, flew down the hallway like she was launching an attack hug. He dropped his suitcase without a thought, scooping her up and spinning her until the hallway was filled with giggles.

Lin appeared next, guiding their twin boys, Tian and Liang, each clutching one of her hands. She smiled—soft, tired, but the kind that could undo the weight of an entire day.

"You're home," she said.

"Home," he echoed, his voice catching. And for a moment, standing in that doorway, it felt true.

For now.

The evening at the Feng household didn't so much unfold as it tumbled down a hill, picking up noise and chaos like a runaway snowball. Lin had gone all out—steamed fish with ginger, stir-fried greens, and jasmine rice. The kind of meal that said, "I love you," but also, "I'm secretly watching to see if you take seconds."

The twins, Tian and Liang, jabbered over each other about school, occasionally forgetting the difference between a discussion and a competitive shouting match. Mei, their little chaos engineer, had decided vegetables weren't for eating but for architecture. She stacked green beans into a leaning tower and used carrot slices as roof shingles.

At one point, Lin and Dr. Feng caught each other's eyes across the table—one of those married-people glances that can mean a hundred things at once. Perhaps hers said, 'I missed you.' Maybe his said, I'm so tired I could nap inside this rice bowl. Or maybe both just meant, Please, for the love of all that's holy, stop the twins from arguing about whose turn it is to feed the class hamster.

If you asked Dr. Feng in that moment why he worked twelve-hour shifts decoding viral genomes, this was it. This noisy, warm, imperfect mess was his fortress. His why.

But according to what Lin told the ER nurses later, somewhere between Mei's third green bean sculpture and Tian declaring he'd be "the world's first astronaut-chef," a subtle shift crept in. Her husband got quieter. Paler. Like someone had just unplugged a lamp.

"You look pale," she said, her brows knitting together. "Are you feeling alright?"

"I'm fine," he started, but then stopped. "Just... a little off."

Lin's years of marriage had made her a human lie detector. She could tell when "I'm fine" really meant "I'm about to keel over but don't want to alarm you."

"Lie down," she said.

"I will," he replied, forcing a small smile. "Just let me help clean up first."

Five minutes later, he wasn't cleaning up. He was gripping the edge of the table like it was the only thing keeping him on the planet. His limbs felt heavy, his chest tightened, and a sharp pain stabbed his side.

"Feng?" Lin's voice sharpened. She touched his forehead. "You're burning up."

"I'm fine," he muttered again—because apparently, old habits die harder than he might. Then the room tilted, his legs gave out, and Lin caught him just in time to yell for an ambulance. "Call an ambulance!" she shouted to the twins, who stood frozen in fear.

The ride to the hospital was a blur of sirens, streetlights, and Lin gripping his hand like she could hold his soul in place. In the ER, the usual organized chaos reigned. Monitors beeped in discordant rhythms, echoing the chaos unfolding within his body. His vitals plummeted—heart rate, blood pressure, oxygen saturation—all in freefall, nurses called out vitals, and a doctor with the calm urgency of someone who's seen far too much barked orders.

What's happening to him?" Lin demanded, her voice breaking as she clutched a nurse's arm.

"We don't know," the nurse replied, her own fear barely masked by professionalism. "We're doing everything we can."

The ER doctor's brow glistened with sweat as he barked orders to the team. Around him, the air was charged with urgency. Dr. Bai Feng lay pale and motionless on the gurney, his once steady heartbeat now a chaotic rhythm on the monitor. His body was an enigma, a fortress under siege by an invisible force.

"Push another 10 of epi! Start the second line!" the doctor shouted, his voice hoarse from hours of unrelenting effort. Nurses scrambled to comply, their movements a blur of precision.

But nothing seemed to work. Every intervention was met with the same result—further deterioration. His heart faltered, his lungs spasmed, and his liver began to shut down. The virologist, once the embodiment of calm intelligence, was now a man unraveling before their eyes.

A violent cough wracked his body, splattering crimson against his mask. The team froze momentarily; it wasn't the kind of stillness that says, "problem solved"—it was the kind that says, "we've just crossed into uncharted territory," a stark reality—this wasn't a typical medical emergency. The silence broke as the monitor let out a piercing flatline, its unyielding tone signaling the inevitable.

Dr. Bai Feng, virologist, husband, father, and quiet hero, drew his last breath under the harsh fluorescent lights of the ER.

"Time of death..." the doctor murmured, his voice trailing off as the weight of defeat settled over him. For a moment, no one moved. The room, filled with the hum of machines and the stifled breaths of the team, felt suffocating. The silence that followed was deafening, broken only by Lin's anguished cries as one of the nurses tried to console her as well as help her get a seat at the corner of the hallway to help her recollect herself.

Dr. Bai Feng was gone, the white sheet drawn over his face like punctuation at the end of a chapter no one wanted to finish.

Lin sat in the hallway, in a plastic chair designed by some sadist who believed grief should also be physically uncomfortable. Her back was pressed to the wall, her head tilted as if she were listening to some distant sound. A nurse approached with the kind of hesitant gait that comes when you have bad news for someone who's already drowning in bad news.

"I'm so sorry," the nurse whispered, her voice wobbling like she was holding back her own tears.

Lin didn't reply. Didn't move.

The nurse tried again, her fingers brushing Lin's shoulder. Cold. Too cold.

"Madam?" she murmured, shaking her gently.

And that's when her stomach dropped. Lin wasn't sleeping. Her lips were tinged with a gray that had no business on a living face. Her chest stayed still, stubbornly refusing to rise.

The nurse's hand flew to her mouth before she even realized she was screaming. "HELP!"

Heads snapped toward the sound. Eyes widened. And then the unthinkable became real—Lin Feng had died right there in the hallway, as quietly as a candle going out in the wind. The same air that had carried her husband's last breath had taken hers, too.

For a split second, the ER froze. Then chaos came roaring back. Staff surged toward her, not because they thought they could save her—deep down, they knew they couldn't—but because it was impossible not to try.

And then, as if death had decided it liked the place, a young nurse by the IV cart went pale. She staggered, clutching her chest, gasping like someone had stolen her air mid-inhale. Her knees buckled. She hit the floor hard, seizing violently. The monitors lit up again, shrill and frantic.

That was when the doctor barked: "CODE BLACK! Lock down the ER! Nobody leaves!"

Nobody leaves. Right. Except that half the ER had already done precisely that—patients, visitors, a courier, some guy who was definitely not supposed to be back there—slipping out before the order hit the loudspeakers. By the time the hospital's doors were sealed, the damage was irreversible. If death had legs, it was already halfway to the subway.

By morning, Hong Kong had turned into something out of a bad disaster movie—except no one got to walk out of this theater.

It wasn't the kind of chaos you could hear from a distance—it was worse. Quiet. People slumped on park benches and never got up. Mothers sat on curbs, holding children who would never complain about vegetables again. Lovers clung to each other, refusing to believe what their bodies had already decided.

The hospitals overflowed before the first news report aired. Entire corridors became waiting rooms for the dying, probably the air so heavy it felt like breathing through wet cloth.

Seven hundred people gone before dawn.

By the time officials dragged themselves into press briefings, the city was a patchwork of grief and confusion. Rumors flooded in faster than the bodies could be counted.

China. Bioweapon. Sabotage.

The finger-pointing started before the dead were even cold.

Half the internet had decided it was Beijing's fault, a calculated move designed to fracture an already delicate geopolitical balance. The devolved executive of Hong Kong found itself caught between a furious public and the looming specter of Beijing's retaliation. Diplomatic channels buzzed with accusations and counterclaims, each one ratcheting up the tension. The other half thought it was the Americans. The CIA Director didn't comment publicly, but somewhere behind a locked door, he was smiling the kind of smile people wear when they've spent years planting a bomb and finally hear the click.

G7 leaders promised "swift coordination" through gritted teeth, which in political language meant: we're about to start shouting at each other in twelve different time zones. The EU tried to look calm, but its borders were already tightening like a noose.

And through it all, somewhere in the shadowed backrooms of the world, the people who actually held the strings leaned back, watching.

Power was shifting—not like a tidal wave, but like sand slipping through fingers. Easy to miss until you realize the hourglass is almost empty. And no one knew who was holding it.

Or how much time was left. And as the world teetered on the precipice of conflict, one question remained unanswered: who held the hourglass, and how much time was left?

"Human advancement has never been the tale of conformity, but of disruption. It is the maverick who challenges the comfort of the known, the visionary who wagers everything on an unproven dream, that reshapes the destiny of civilizations. The light of discovery often blinds before it guides, yet it is precisely this daring to step into the unknown that forges tomorrow's truths. Every breakthrough is a testament to the courage of an unconventional mind willing to risk obscurity for the chance at transformation."

The air in the cottage felt like it had been vacuum-sealed. Emily sat frozen, her knuckles white around the edge of the desk, eyes glued to the feeds scrolling across her screen. Her mind refused to process the numbers. Seven hundred dead before sunrise. Streets she remembered laughing through years ago now choked with stretchers and body bags.

She gestured at the screen with a jerky, almost violent motion. "This—" Her voice cracked, then sharpened. "This isn't just a tragedy. This is a goddamn extinction-level clusterfuck."

Alex sat opposite her, slouched forward like the weight of it all had finally caught up to him. His elbows rested on his knees, fingers locked so tightly together they looked like they might fuse. He started to speak, stopped, exhaled, and tried again. "I..." His voice dissolved into a frustrated groan. He ran a hand down his face, as if maybe he could scrub away the reality they were staring at.

Then, without another word, he pulled out his phone and punched in a number from memory. Two rings.

"Hey," Richard answered, casual, almost bored—until Alex's voice cut in.

"Rich," Alex said, low and urgent. "Are we on a secure line? Tell me this line is secure."

There was a pause. Richard's voice shed all its easy warmth. "Yeah. What's wrong?"

Alex's reply came clipped and sharp. "Hong Kong."

"Yeah," Richard said, grim now. "We've seen it. Horrific."

Alex's eyes met Emily's before he spoke again. "The pathogen's stolen. Linked directly to the murdered virologist. And at the center?" He hesitated just long enough for the dread to land. "Winters."

Silence. Then Richard's voice dropped to a whisper. "...How do you know this?"

Emily leaned forward, eyes brutal and unforgiving. "Because we've been chasing what we thought were ghost stories. Turns out the ghost has a corner office at Langley."

Richard's breath hitched. "The CIA director? Jesus. You're certain?"

Emily's laugh was dry, joyless. "Money trails. Travel logs. CCTV. Surveillance feeds. Winters didn't just sign off on this—he gift-wrapped the bioweapon and sent it straight to his private little militia. Oh, and he's got a cozy back-channel with the Chinese lab where the virologist worked. Real cute arrangement."

Alex rubbed at his temples, his voice low but steady. "This isn't chaos for chaos's sake. Hong Kong's the perfect chessboard. Push Beijing into a corner, make them swing first, and let the headlines paint them as the villain."

Richard's voice was tight. "And us? Are we next?"

Emily gave a short, sharp snort. "Bingo. You don't just destabilize your rivals—you keep your own house scared and compliant."

A long sigh came through the line. Resignation. "I can't take this upstairs," Richard said. "Not when I don't know who Winters owns."

Emily's lips twisted into a thin smile. "Welcome aboard, Rich. Grab a seat. This train doesn't make safe stops."

The line fell quiet. The weight of it pressed into the silence until Alex broke it. "We move now. Or we lose more than Hong Kong."

The cottage's alarm system shrieked to life before Richard could answer—sharp, metallic, a sound designed to spike adrenaline in an instant. Emily's head snapped toward the control panel, but Alex was already on his feet, barking orders.

"Lockdown protocol. Now!" He slammed a recessed button on the wall. Thick steel shutters groaned down over the doors and windows.

"Shut the systems," he ordered.

Emily's fingers blurred over her keyboard. "Wiping... wiping... and—done!" She snatched up her sidearm.

Alex was already on comms. "Raja, we're burned. They've got us."

Raja's reply came without hesitation. "I know. Backup's inbound. Sit tight—we'll get you out." Calm voice, but the undertone was pure urgency.

Somewhere else, Winters was giving his own orders—coordinates relayed, kill team deployed.

Minutes later, the ground shook with the first blast—the south exit breached. The air outside filled with the sound of boots, shouted commands, and the rattle of automatic fire.

"Positions!" Raja's voice cut through the chaos as his team fanned out, covering angles, firing in disciplined bursts. The militia pushed hard, but the defenders had the high ground and the training.

Inside, Alex, Emily, Raja, and his men slipped into the tunnels beneath the cottage. Above, another explosion tore through the façade, a curtain of smoke and flame swallowing the building they'd just left.

They emerged from the terror into a makeshift warehouse with a waiting convoy—three matte-black SUVs bristling with firepower. Raja slid into the passenger seat of the lead vehicle; Alex and Emily took the middle row, rifles across their laps. The rest of the team loaded fast, engines already growling.

The convoy roared off, headlights on, tires spitting gravel, tearing down the road. The militia gave chase immediately—four trucks, lights blazing, guns barking in the broad daylight.

Bullets cracked the air, shattering signs and sending pedestrians scattering. One of the militia's SUVs took so much fire from Alex and one of Raja's operatives that it spun off the road and tumbled into a river with a splash big enough to drown the noise of gunfire for half a second.

"Left turn!" Raja barked, and the drivers swung hard toward a narrow road leading to a private airfield.

The path became a gauntlet—gunfire rattling off the SUVs' armor, engines howling.

On the radio, one of Raja's men shouted, "Eyes up. They're closing. Where's the bird?"

"Hold on," Raja said, voice calm but cutting.

Inside the lead SUV, Raja's voice was calm but razor-sharp. "Eyes sharp, everyone. It's now or never."

The drivers swerved hard, dodging gunfire. Alex leaned out his window, returning fire with deadly precision. Emily mirrored him on the other side, her shots snapping in clean bursts.

Raja grabbed the comms device again. "Eagle's Nest, this is Eagle One. We are flight, en route to the primary exfil location. Keep us a lane."

The response came quickly. "Roger that, Eagle One. Left lane held clear."

"Eyes on the cargo," Raja ordered, eyes flicking to the side mirror as another volley of gunfire erupted.

"Roger that. I have eyes on the price, Eagle One," the voice confirmed before the line went dead.

The world outside was pure bedlam—explosions bloomed in the rearview like deranged fireworks, SUVs were going airborne in flames, and the operatives in the back of Raja's vehicle fired in precise, controlled bursts as though they were calmly target-practicing at a gun range instead of trying not to die.

Alex was on one side window, Emily on the other, both leaning out like very angry gargoyles, aiming at tires and engines. Every shot was a gamble—either they'd slow the militia down or they'd make someone very mad. The road ahead blurred into a mess of screaming tires, metal groans, and enough bullets to make the air feel solid.

Up ahead, the private airfield loomed like salvation wrapped in concrete and open sky. And sitting there, rumbling like it wanted to bite something, was their extraction plane—a hulking military cargo beast with its engines already screaming and its rear ramp yawning open.

Raja grabbed the comms, voice clipped but calm. "Eagle's Nest, we're inbound. Fifteen miles to exfil—going straight into the nest."

The pilot's reply came sharp and without hesitation. "Roger that, Eagle One."

Raja didn't blink. "Be ready for us. This is going to get messy."

Messy was an understatement.

They punched through the perimeter fence, the SUV bouncing violently over the uneven ground. Militia trucks poured in behind them, spraying gunfire like it was free samples day at a shooting range. The plane began to roll forward, lining up on the runway, its deafening engines drowning out the chaos.

"Hold on," Raja said, with the same tone one might use to warn about a mild pothole—just before a fresh barrage of bullets smashed against the SUV's armor.

The driver swerved hard, tires squealing, then gunned it straight for the ramp. But the plane was already accelerating. No matter how hard the SUV roared, the gap wasn't closing.

In the cockpit, the pilot saw it instantly—either he adjusted or they were dead. Without ceremony, he slammed the brakes just enough for physics to say, "Fine, I'll allow it," and the SUV drew alongside the moving ramp.

"Now!" Raja barked.

The driver floored it, and the ramp filled their vision like the open mouth of a monster they were willingly driving into.

The SUV's tires slammed onto the ramp, suspension groaning, and shot up into the cargo hold. It didn't stop until it nearly kissed the far wall, where waiting operatives latched it down with cables like cowboys roping a bull. The ramp was already folding shut, the plane surging into a steep climb before the militia even reached the end of the runway.

Only then did anyone breathe.

Emily slumped back against the SUV door, chest heaving. "Remind me never to complain about turbulence again," she panted.

Alex's knuckles were still pale on his rifle. He wiped sweat from his brow and gave a tight nod. "For the record, I hated that."

Raja, standing at the edge of the cargo bay, watched the burning airfield shrink below. His expression softened just enough for a small, weary smile. "We made it. Good work, everyone. And may the souls of our brothers find peace in the next world."

Emily glanced out the tiny window, the fires below flickering like dying candles. "We made it," she whispered—but it wasn't victory in her voice. It was survival.

Alex didn't disagree. "For now."

They all knew this was just an intermission. The real show hadn't even started. But for the moment, they were alive, and sometimes that was the only box worth checking.

THE COBRAS ON THE HILL

"Perception is a fragile lens through which we view the world. It is a lens colored by our experiences, shaped by our beliefs, and clouded by our biases. And yet, we cling to it as though it were an infallible guide, leading us through the labyrinth of reality. But if we dare to question it, if we pause to examine the cracks within the glass, we begin to see that truth is rarely singular. Instead, it dances in fragments, revealed differently depending on where we choose to stand."

Marilyn had officially clocked out—at least in spirit—two hours before the clock said she could. The day had been a relentless parade of emails, meetings, and "urgent" requests that could've easily been filed under whenever. Her only surviving fantasy was to make it home, pour a glass of wine big enough to qualify as a swimming pool, and sink guilt-free into another binge of her favorite romantic series—the one she swore she watched "ironically."

Handbag slung over her shoulder, she was halfway out the office door when her phone buzzed.

She'd later tell us it was almost like a tug in her chest, that strange sixth sense that you've forgotten something. She considered ignoring it—home was so close she could practically hear her couch calling her name—but curiosity is the enemy of an early night.

Richard's name glowed on her screen.

"Please, I'd like to hear your voice when you're off work," the message began. "I'm starting to miss you more than I'm willing to admit—and trust me, my best friend is already telling me this is unhealthy. Yeah, yeah, laugh it out. It's a cliché, but it's true. Your voice is the only one that makes sense to me right now, so please call."

Her lips curled into a smile she'd deny under oath, and she rolled her eyes at the melodrama even as her heartbeat betrayed her. "Only you, Richard," she muttered.

She thumbed back a reply: "Come over to my parents' house. I'd love to see you too."

Her finger hovered. This was impulsive, even for her. But the idea of seeing him—tonight—made her tap "send" before logic could stage a protest.

His reply came fast. "Are you sure about this?"

She could hear the cautious hope in his imaginary voice. "Yes," she typed, letting her romantic side take the wheel like a Formula 1 driver who didn't believe in brakes.

Just as she was about to drop her phone into her bag, another notification buzzed in—this time from Dad.

"Family dinner tonight. Be there."

Her eyebrows shot up. She typed back quickly: "Wait, are you finally home?"

"Would I call for dinner if I wasn't here?" came the reply, pure Dad—short, blunt, and carrying the faint threat of don't make me repeat myself.

She chuckled. "Fair point," she murmured. Then it hit her.

Richard. Had. Never. Met. Dad.

Her father, the man whose handshake felt like a stress test and whose stare could melt glaciers, was about to meet her boyfriend without so much as a warm-up. This wasn't just dinner. This was the final boss battle of her romantic life.

"Oh, great. This is going to be a disaster," she whispered, shoving the phone into her bag like it had personally betrayed her.

She pictured it now: Dad in his usual position—arms folded, eyes scanning Richard like he was searching for illegal imports, silently scoring every pause, every fidget, every wrong answer. And she, trying not to spill her wine or faint under the table.

By the time she reached her car, she'd already dialed her best friend.

"Lyn, what now?" came the teasing voice.

"Guess who just accidentally set the stage for World War Three?" Marilyn groaned, collapsing into the driver's seat.

Her friend laughed immediately. "Oh no. What did you do this time?"

"I invited Richard over...and now it's a family dinner. I didn't think Dad would be there! I thought it'd just be Mom and me, you know—safe territory. But Dad's home. Richard is walking straight into the lion's den."

The laughter on the other end turned into full-on howling. "Lyn, when are you going to learn? You and these impulsive moves..."

"Okay, but seriously—do I warn him? Or will that make it worse? What if he thinks I'm pressuring him into meeting my parents?"

"And not warning him makes him feel what? Ambushed? Come on, Lyn."

She groaned, dragging a hand through her hair. "So either way, he feels trapped. Fantastic. I've outmaneuvered myself."

Her friend's laughter softened into something warmer. "Look, the price we pay for love, right? He likes you, doesn't he?"

Marilyn felt her cheeks warm. "Yeah... I think he does."

"Then trust him. You've got this."

After hanging up, she sat for a moment, staring at the sky as it bled into twilight. Hope and dread tangled in her chest. Tonight could be awkward. Tonight could be a minefield. Or, if the universe felt generous, tonight could be the start of something worth remembering.

She started the engine, whispered a silent prayer for divine intervention, and headed toward whatever battlefield the dinner table had become.

CHARLES E.A.

"Greatness is not born in comfort but carved through shadows—every challenge is a stepping stone on the road to achievement."

The Sanders mansion sat atop the hill like it had been personally hired to watch over the entire neighborhood. Its facade glowed in warm, golden light, reflecting off the winding driveway in neat, almost smug perfection. On any other night, Marilyn would have described it as home—safe, predictable, full of the faint smell of her mother's lavender polish. But that night? She would later tell me it felt less like home and more like a stage set for an unpredictable play. The kind where the lead actors haven't met yet, and the audience is mostly waiting for something—anything—to go spectacularly wrong.

While my team and I were halfway across the world dodging bullets in India, Marilyn was gearing up for her own kind of combat. And honestly, I don't blame her. Or Richard. They were about to walk into a dinner where two worlds would collide—one belonging to her, one belonging to him—and if history had taught me anything, Mr. Sanders didn't seem like one to lose in confrontations.

Richard's car eased to a stop in front of the grand entrance. He killed the engine, leaving him in the thick silence of the crisp night air. He sat there for a moment, both excited and deeply unsettled, like a man about to jump into a pool without knowing if it was heated... or filled with sharks. Finally, he stepped out. The gravel crunched under his shoes, each step echoing louder than it needed to.

Before he could compose himself, the front doors swung open. Marilyn appeared, framed in golden light, her smile warm enough to melt the winter out of anyone. For Richard, it was the anchor he didn't know he'd been desperately holding out for. She crossed the distance in quick strides, wrapped her arms around him, and kissed him with enough passion to briefly erase the looming dinner, the mansion, and every mental warning sign flashing in his head. For a moment, there was no "meeting the dad," no unspoken judgments—just them.

When they broke apart, Marilyn rested her forehead against his. Her voice was soft, but there was a thread of warning in it.

"Richard, there's something I need to tell you before we go in."

He tilted his head, playful smirk in place. "Let me guess—you've got a dad with a collection of medieval swords, and I'm about to get the tour up close?"

Her laugh was a little too quick, a little too nervous. "Close enough. My dad's home tonight... and, well, you two haven't met yet."

Richard's smirk faded into a more serious look. She squeezed his hand.

"Listen. He can be... intense. If he seems cold, or says something blunt, or just—" she paused, "—stares at you like you're an intruder, I need you to remember it's not about you. It's just him. His approval matters to me, yes, but I don't want it forced. Just... focus on me. On us. Okay?"

He gave her a crooked grin. "Is he racist?"

She snorted. "Hell, no!"

"So I'm walking into the lion's den without armor? That's the plan?"

"Consider me your armor," she shot back. "But don't expect me to take every hit for you. I might let one or two through, just to see how you handle it."

Feigning horror, he leaned in. "In that case, I hope you've got some serious consolation prizes waiting for me later."

Marilyn burst into laughter, pointing at her breasts. "Don't worry. These two will do the trick."

The tension between them dissolved into shared humor, but as they turned toward the towering double doors, it crept back in, heavier than before.

Inside, the dining room looked like something out of a lifestyle magazine. The table was set for an intimate gathering, candles casting a soft glow over crystal glasses and silverware that you probably needed a manual to use. Mrs. Diane Sanders, graceful as a swan with a clipboard, was busy fussing over the table settings. Her husband, meanwhile, stood by his cabinet of fine wines like a general surveying his troops.

The man turned as they entered. His gaze went straight to Richard. His face was unreadable—neither hostile nor warm—just... weighing.

"Marilyn," he said in a voice that carried the weight of command. "And this must be..."

"Richard," Marilyn said quickly, her tone light but deliberate. "Richard, this is my father, Mr. Sanders."

Richard stepped forward, extending his hand. "It's a pleasure to meet you, sir. Thank you for having me."

Mr. Sanders' handshake was firm, controlled. "You're welcome. Dinner's about to be served."

Civil. Polite. Cold enough to keep ice from melting.

Mrs. Sanders, sensing the frost, glided into the conversation with a warm smile. "Richard, impeccable timing—you're just in time for one of my husband's famous wine pairings. He's quite the connoisseur."

Richard smiled back. "I'm sure it'll be unforgettable. Thank you for the kind invitation, Mrs. Sanders."

Mr. Sanders gave a faint grunt—half acknowledgment, half dismissal—as he set the wine on the table. Mrs. Sanders, undeterred, added with a mischievous glint, "Richard, you're FBI, right? Or is it CIA? You've got that sharp, observant look about you."

Marilyn laughed, and Richard seized the moment. "Well, ma'am, if I told you, I'd have to take an oath of secrecy. Let's just say... I'm here for more than the wine."

For the first time all evening, Mr. Sanders' expression shifted—just slightly. A flicker of amusement crossed his face before he locked it down again. The laughter that followed was small, but it rippled through the room, making the air feel lighter... if only for a heartbeat.

The dining room of the Sanders, as beautiful as ever, seemed like a scene straight from a luxury lifestyle magazine—with a polished mahogany table, crystal glasses, and a roasted chicken so perfectly golden it might have had its own publicist. On the surface, it was a setting for a perfect evening. But under that warm glow of candlelight? You could feel the tension crackle like static before a thunderstorm.

Mr. Sanders sat at the head of the table, not eating so much as evaluating his food. Or maybe them. Probably them. The man had the posture of a general and the gaze of a hawk that's been told you might have stolen one of his chicks. Richard sat across from him, cool as a cucumber in a freezer, he said, even though I knew that inside, he was running mental drills like a rookie cop on his first stakeout.

The conversation was light at first. Too light. You know the type — comments about the weather, a safe joke about the bread being too perfect to cut, a polite compliment about the wine. All the while, any observing eyes could sense Mr. Sanders studying Richard as if he were manually running a background check in real time.

Then Richard, bless his overconfident little heart, decided to bring up Marilyn's brother.

Marilyn said it was like watching someone casually step onto a frozen pond without realizing there's a "Danger: Thin Ice" sign right in front of them. The room went quiet. Even the chicken seemed to stop steaming for a second. Mr. Sanders paused mid-slice, his knife hovering in the air like it was waiting for orders. His eyes locked on Richard.

"And how exactly," he asked, his tone the kind that could curdle cream, "do you know about my son's absence?"

Richard didn't flinch. "Marilyn mentioned him in passing. She's proud of him. Said he's accomplished a lot."

Before the general could fire back, Mrs. Sanders swooped in like the United Nations of dinner tables. "Oh, Richard and our son actually graduated from the Air Force Academy together," she said, flashing the kind of smile that could sell insurance to a cat.

Richard nodded. "Yes, ma'am. Shared a few classes, some missions. Your son's reputation precedes him — a remarkable man."

Again, Marilyn, in her own words, swore that she saw the tiniest flicker in her father's expression. Surprise, maybe. Or maybe he'd just realized the chicken was overcooked by exactly two degrees. Either way, his mental file on Richard got a minor update.

Then came the moment. The one every guy dreads when meeting the father.

"So," Mr. Sanders said, leaning forward, "you're FBI now. But I've been wondering... what exactly is going on between you and my daughter? Because I have the feeling there's more here than meets the eye. And I'm not sure how I feel about it."

Even though I wasn't present, hearing how things went down, I almost clapped. The man had just gone full cross-examination mode, and Richard was still holding his wine glass like it was a casual Tuesday.

Richard smiled — the calm, measured kind that says, I've trained for this moment my entire adult life.

"Sir, I appreciate your kindness, so I'll be equally upfront. Marilyn is... well, she's one of the most remarkable people I've ever met. I didn't expect anything serious when we met, but over time, I realized just how much she means to me. I know I might not seem like the man you'd picture by her side... but I'm asking for the chance to prove I'm good for her."

Mrs. Sanders beamed. Marilyn blushed. And Mr. Sanders? Still unreadable. You could have hung a portrait of him right then, and it'd be the same expression.

"But," Richard continued, "I think every relationship starts with a chance. At one point, we're all strangers. It's what we do with that chance that matters. I'm grateful for every moment I've had with her. I don't take her for granted. She's the best thing that's happened to me in a long time... and I'll keep reminding her of that, every chance I get."

It was a speech worthy of a slow clap. Marilyn didn't clap, obviously — she's not insane — but she did mentally hand him a gold medal for bravery.

Mr. Sanders took his time before replying. "Well," he said at last, "I hope things pan out for you two."

Translation for the uninitiated: I'm not against you. Yet.

Richard heard hope. Marilyn heard a warning. I listened to a man who just got through round one without losing a tooth.

Dinner limped along into safer territory, but under the table, Marilyn's hand brushed Richard's — a quiet signal of solidarity.

And me? Listening to them, I sat there thinking, 'This man might just survive this family after all.'

And as much as I want to scoff at their lovesick madness, a small, treacherous part of me is starting to believe they might actually pull this off. God help us all.

"Peace begins where perception and reality meet—and only courage and reflection can bring them together."

Marilyn would later tell us that, for Richard, her presence that night was like gravity—quiet, unseen, but pulling him back to center every time the air in the dining room got too thick. The way her hand brushed his sleeve under the table, or how she sent him those quick, half-hidden glances—the kind that said don't you dare explode in front of my father, even if he deserves it—that was what anchored him. He wasn't there to impress anyone, or to win a debate he'd never signed up for. He was there because Marilyn mattered.

By dessert, the temperature in the room had thawed a few degrees—not exactly warm, but no longer glacial either. When Richard rose to leave, Mr. Sanders followed with a handshake, his eyes locking with Richard's.

"Thank you for joining us tonight," he said, his voice perfectly neutral, but with that slight pause—the kind of pause fathers take when they're unwilling to admit that maybe, just maybe, they've been disarmed.

Richard accepted the grip firmly, his voice steady. "The pleasure was mine, sir. Thank you for your hospitality."

Outside, the night air bit at their skin as they stepped into the glow of the mansion's lights. Marilyn's exhale came out in a puff of white mist, and with it, the tension she'd been carrying. "That could've gone worse," she said, half-laughing, half-sighing, like someone stepping off a rollercoaster they hadn't exactly signed up for.

Richard pulled her into him, a warm smile sneaking onto his face. "I'll take that as a win. Besides..." His eyes glinted mischievously. "I've got my consolation prize right here."

Marilyn laughed, swatting his arm. "You are impossible."

"Impossible, yes," he said with mock-seriousness. "But irresistible."

Her laughter lingered as they walked to the car, the mansion behind them glowing like a watchful sentinel, silently recording the moment.

But the story didn't end there.

Later that evening, Marilyn hadn't meant to eavesdrop, but as she returned from seeing Richard off, she spotted her father standing by the doorway. He wasn't barking orders, wasn't filling the house with his usual commanding presence. Instead, he was staring at the hallway where she and Richard had just left, his silence louder than anything he could've said.

She lingered in the shadows, holding her breath. And then, he spoke.

"I find it troubling, Diane," he said, voice low but taut, "that I was the last to know about the man our daughter is seeing. What happened to discussing these things as a family?"

Mrs. Sanders, calm as a Sunday sermon, stood at the sink, drying her hands with the sort of deliberate slowness that could drive any husband mad. She turned at last, her face lined with patience worn thin over decades.

"George," she said softly, her voice steady as steel hidden under velvet. "I didn't tell you because I knew exactly how you'd react. And tonight, you've proven me right."

He bristled, his brows knitting. "And what reaction would that be?" he demanded, though his voice betrayed the fact that he already knew.

She set the dish towel down with finality. "You really want me to paint the picture?" Diane leaned against the counter, folding her arms. "Alright, imagine this: our daughter falls in love with a young man she met at our store. Who also happens to live in our building and attended the same school as our son. And if that isn't enough, he's the son of the late Senator Thornhill. And yes, George, he's African-American. Now tell me—how would that conversation have gone if I'd left it up to you?"

The silence was thick enough to chew.

His jaw tightened, indignation warring with something he didn't want to name. "Are you suggesting I'm a bigot?" he snapped, though the edge in his tone faltered halfway through.

Her gaze didn't waver. "I'm suggesting that you have traditions you cling to. And when reality doesn't fit those neat little boxes, you struggle to see past them."

Her words hit him square in the chest. He tried to mask it with bluster. "This isn't about tradition—it's about respect. About choices made carefully, not rushed because they feel right in the moment."

Diane didn't flinch. "George, she's not a child anymore. She knows what she wants. And she's happy. Isn't that worth more than your picture-perfect expectations?"

He raked a hand through his hair, pacing, his voice quieter now but jagged with frustration. "Maybe the universe is keeping me on my toes... with history lessons I never asked for."

That line stuck with Marilyn. Still hidden near the doorway, she leaned in, heart pounding, every nerve awake. History lessons?

Mrs. Sanders's voice softened, but it carried the weight of old scars. "Decades ago, your family faced something similar. We both know how that turned out. Don't drag our daughter into the same mistakes. This isn't your story to live, George—it's hers."

The mention of the past froze him in place. His shoulders sagged. He looked less like the immovable George Sanders everyone knew and more like a man wrestling with ghosts.

That was when Marilyn, unable to resist, stepped forward, her shoes clicking against the floor, announcing her presence. Both parents turned—the mother startled, the father defensive.

"What did you mean, Dad?" she asked, voice steady but her eyes searching his. "When you said the universe was keeping you on your toes... history lessons? What did you mean by that?"

The room went still, air tightening like a held breath.

Her father's voice, when it came, was low. "It's not just about Richard. It's about choices—ones my family made, and ones I didn't. And it's about wanting more for you than I gave myself."

Marilyn said her throat tightened as she stepped closer to her father, her voice softer but firm, threading love with resolve. "Dad, I'm not you. And Richard isn't whoever you're remembering. He makes me happy. Isn't that enough—for now?"

"And in that fragile silence, for the first time, George Sanders didn't look like the man who had to have the last word. He looked like a father standing at the edge of letting go." That line, Richard repeated it to me verbatim, as if he had branded it into memory.

Hours later, while driving home through the hushed streets, Richard admitted his thoughts were anything but serene. The world outside his car was calm—the glow of streetlights on damp asphalt, the occasional sweep of headlights, the hum of tires carrying him forward—but inside his chest, his mind spun restlessly. By the time he stepped into his apartment and let the shower rinse the tension from his shoulders, the unease had only deepened.

And so, almost without thinking, his hand reached for his phone. It was instinct—the quiet, unshakable pull of the one person who had always been his anchor.

"Hello, Mom," Richard whispered into the dark room, his voice low, almost fragile.

"Richard, darling," came the reply, soft but rich with warmth. Just the sound of her voice was enough to remind him that not all of life's chaos was uncharted. "How are you? How's everything going? Work keeping you busy?"

Richard exhaled, a heavy sigh that carried the weight of the night. "Work's been tough, Mom. But it's not just that. There's... something. Someone. And I'm praying you'll like her when I bring her to meet you."

Her tone shifted immediately—half curiosity, half the unmistakable excitement of a mother smelling good news. "Oh? And how soon am I meeting this angel of yours?"

For the first time all night, Richard smiled, small but genuine. "Her name's Marilyn. She's... different, Mom. I can't quite explain it. With her, things feel real. I've never felt this way before."

On the other end of the line, Mrs. Thornhill's heart swelled, touched by the vulnerability in her son's words. She knew loss intimately—she'd walked with it for a while now since her husband's passing—but this? This was something rare, something precious. "That's wonderful, Rich," she said, her voice gentle, carrying all the warmth she could pack into a sentence. "Tell me about her. What's she like?"

Richard leaned back, eyes closing, as if replaying Marilyn's smile in his mind. "She's kind. Strong. Sharp as a whip—smarter than me, no doubt. And she challenges me, Mom. In ways I didn't even know I needed. She's everything."

His mother chuckled softly, but her voice grew tender, filled with wisdom only years of loving and losing could teach. "You deserve happiness, Richard. And from the way you talk about her... she sounds like a high prize worth every bit of trouble."

His chest warmed, gratitude swelling with every beat of his heart. "Thank you, Mom. You mean the world to me. Don't ever forget that."

"And when are you bringing her to meet me?" she teased lightly, though the longing behind her words was clear. "I'd love to meet the woman giving my son all these big ideas."

Richard laughed, a sound that carried both relief and determination. "Soon. I promise. You'll meet her soon."

When the call ended, the silence of his room pressed in again, but it didn't feel so heavy this time. He set his phone on the nightstand, his eyes drifting to the news on his big screen television. A headline about unrest in Hong Kong flashed across the screen, tugging at his attention.

But before he could read a word, his phone buzzed again. This time, the caller ID made his pulse quicken.

"Alex," he answered, his voice sharp, bracing. "What's going on?"

The tone on the other end was one Richard had never heard from his friend before—urgent, frantic, almost edged with fear. "Richard, meet us at the spot. Two blocks from 158 Avenue, Lawn Road. Now. It's important."

Richard's brow furrowed. "Alex, what's happening? Why the rush? Can't it wait until morning?"

Silence hung for a long, uneasy beat before Alex's voice came back—hard, unyielding, and final. "No, Richard. This can't wait. Trust me. You need to come now."

That was all it took. Richard's instincts, honed by years of knowing when to trust the gravity in someone's voice, snapped into place. When Alex spoke in this manner, it was never casual. Never optional.

"Alright," Richard said, his jaw tightening, resolve settling over him. "I'll be there soon."

And just like that, the night, which had begun with awkward laughter over dinner and a father's reluctant silence, was about to veer into something else entirely—something Richard couldn't yet name but felt deep in his bones.

CHARLES E.A.

"Do not be deceived by the comfort of certainty. The beauty of creation is found in struggle, for it is through challenges that we become who we are meant to be."

I've always said Arthur was a man of contingencies, but lately I've begun to wonder if "contingency" was just his polite word for "playing God." The man was ruthless with his timing—always ten steps ahead, always willing to twist the knife before you realized he had one in his hand. I'd thought I'd prepared myself for that. I thought I'd anticipated him.

But what he did next? That's when I began to fear I might've miscalculated, and badly.

Because while Emily and I were in the sky, still trembling from the fact we had narrowly escaped death, my little toys—those perfectly concealed cameras I had tucked away in her parents' house weeks before she even knew I existed—were feeding me real-time images. Images I couldn't share with her.

And you want to know why? Because if Emily had learned the truth—that I'd been watching her parents' home like some shadow-lurking psychopath—she would've killed me mid-flight and blamed turbulence. I'm not exaggerating. Emily Parker would've found a way to make my death look like an unfortunate seatbelt malfunction. So, guilt? Yes, it was drenching me, suffocating me, crawling down my throat like wet cement. But I did what I always do when guilt shows its face: I leaned into my darker side and left everything else in the hands of fate.

The storm that night became my accomplice. Rain didn't fall—it hurled itself against rooftops, against windows, against Eleanor Parker's quiet sanctuary. The night had been crisp only hours before, but now the air turned sinister, carrying with it the kind of chaos you can smell before it arrives. And Eleanor? Poor Mrs. Eleanor, she had no idea what fate was about to dump on her doorstep.

She sat hunched at her late husband Henry's desk, the oak polished to a soft sheen, littered with drafts and notes. This was her retreat, her private bubble of creativity. Outside, the storm screamed; inside, the scratch of her pen kept rhythm.

Then came the noise. Sharp. Wrong. The kind of sound that slices through ordinary life and whispers: you're not alone.

Eleanor froze, pen mid-air. Her rational mind scrambled for excuses. "Okay, Ellie," she muttered to herself, her voice barely above a whisper, "don't jump to conclusions. It's... probably a raccoon. Yes, definitely a raccoon." Her voice cracked, and she grimaced. "A very ambitious raccoon."

But raccoons don't creak doors open like horror movie villains. Nor do they cut power sources. That, I think, we can all agree on.

Darkness swallowed the house, and Eleanor's gut must've twisted. She didn't seem naive—Henry had trained her for this, probably back when she used to roll her eyes at his "over-preparedness." Now? She silently thanked him for every frustrating weekend he'd spent showing her how to line up a sight and squeeze a trigger.

She crept to the bookshelf, her heart hammering, and punched in the code with trembling fingers. The safe clicked. The cold steel of Henry's pistol pressed into her palm.

"Well, Henry," she whispered at the framed photo staring down from the shelf, "I always said your hobbies were overkill. Looks like tonight I owe you an apology."

Watching her through the cameras, I swear I saw both terror and grim resolve flicker across her face. The gun was heavy, not just in weight but in meaning. This wasn't a practice run. No neat little targets. The voices she now heard—low, guttural, male—proved this was the real thing.

She moved through the hallway barefoot, her body tight as a bowstring, every creak of the wooden floor threatening to betray her. The storm outside roared, masking her steps, thunder rolling like drums of war. Her breath came shallow, and for a moment, I caught myself whispering under my own breath, urging her forward.

Then it came—the faint crash of glass. A vase. Not an accident. Confirmation.

"These aren't burglars," she must've thought. "They're something worse."

"Alright, boys," Eleanor muttered under her breath, gripping the pistol so tight her knuckles blanched. "You've picked the wrong house."

She aimed toward the dining room shadows and squeezed. The gunfire shattered the stillness, a deafening rip in the night. Her shots weren't pretty, but fear makes you wild, and sometimes wild works.

"Atta girl," I whispered, unable to stop myself.

Emily glanced over at me from her seat on the plane. "Hey," she said, brow furrowing, "what's going on with you?"

"Nothing," I lied, plastering on a casual smile. "Just watching something online."

If only she knew.

Back on the tablet, the chaos escalated. Muffled shouts. A cry of pain—one of Eleanor's bullets had found its mark.

"That's for the vase," she quipped, half in fear, half in disbelief that she'd just scored a hit. I almost laughed, even in the horror of it. Humor is strange that way—sometimes it breaks through when you least expect it, because the alternative is collapsing.

But the attackers weren't gone yet. Their return fire tore through the walls, splintered furniture, and sent shards of Eleanor's sanctuary flying. Thunder outside, gunfire inside—the world had become one long, merciless drum.

Then the headlights flared outside. The engine's growl told me the invaders had a getaway plan. They retreated, but not before the driver leaned out with his own punctuation mark: a spray of bullets ripping across the porch.

One found her.

The sound she made wasn't a scream—more like a gasp, a betrayal of the body. She staggered, blood blooming against her side, and collapsed onto the porch as the car's taillights smeared red against the storm.

The rain swallowed her, soaking through clothes, hair, everything, until she seemed almost a part of the earth itself. But her fingers still twitched around the pistol, refusing to let go.

"Not... tonight," she rasped, her voice nearly lost to the storm.

And I sat there, watching her life bleed into the rain, knowing every pixel of it was my fault.

CHAPTER

5

Forbidden Ties

"Amid light and shadow, truth and deception, strength and cunning, humanity's resolve always finds a way to illuminate the path of transformation."

They say when elephants fight, it's the grass that suffers. Wine Lake County used to be that grass—peaceful, green, and quietly forgotten by the world—until the elephants showed up. And by elephants, I don't mean actual elephants, though that would've made for a much simpler problem. No, these were battles of the human kind, messy and complicated, the kind that leave scars deeper than footprints.

Eleanor Parker—Emily's mother—had always been the gentle heart of that quiet county, the sort of woman who knew how much sugar every neighbor took in their tea. But that night, the Parkers' home, a place where people once growled over garden hedges and noisy sprinklers, was now bearing witness to something darker. That night, she lay motionless on her porch, bathed in the faint glow of a crooked porchlight that flickered as if it, too, couldn't believe what it was seeing.

She wasn't moving. She might have been clinging to life, or she might have already slipped away, dying? Or dead? Honestly, I couldn't tell. And telling Emily? That was like volunteering to be buried alive with no coffin. So, if there was ever a moment I wanted the ground to open up and swallow me whole, it was this one.

I glanced at Emily sleeping on the plane, her head tilted, a lock of hair sliding across her cheek. For a second, I wished I were heartless enough to keep my mouth shut forever. But no—my conscience had apparently signed a contract with eternal damnation. Worse, my thoughts were so loud I was beginning to hear them as if they had rented an apartment inside both of my ears.

"Wake her up? Don't wake her up? She can't do anything from thirty thousand feet in the air."

"But she could call a neighbor—yes, call a neighbor!"

"Oh, brilliant, genius. And then what? She collapses right here on this flight, and you get to explain to the stewardess why her passenger is screaming bloody murder at midnight. Good luck with that!"

I muttered under my breath, "Oh, fuck me."

I stood up, tablet in hand, fully prepared to ruin Emily's night with the news. But just as I took my heroic first step—buzz! My tablet vibrated. An alert. Motion detection. I froze, sat right back down, and buckled up like I'd never moved. Maybe the universe wasn't done torturing me yet.

Turns out, Mrs. Eleanor's neighbor, Mr. Daniels, a man whose evenings usually consisted of crossword puzzles and the occasional glass of sherry, had nearly skidded off the road when he saw her lying there. The poor man's umbrella was still in his car when he bolted into the rain.

"Oh my God... Mrs. Parker?!" His voice cracked, desperate, echoing in the storm.

He fumbled with his phone like it was a slippery fish, finally punching in 911.

"Hello—yes! There's a woman—she's not moving—she's—just please, hurry!"

The dispatcher's calm voice was a lifeline, but the storm didn't care. The rain continued spreading its wings in sheets, drenching his prayers into silence. Within minutes, flashing red and blue lights tore through Wine Lake's quiet roads. Cops, paramedics, the works, radios crackling. EMTs lifted Eleanor with practiced hands, every movement urgent but careful. Her neighbor just stood there, wringing his hands, whispering prayers that sounded like they were being drowned in rainwater.

And me? I hacked into the dispatcher's mainframe from the comfort of my seat because, well, guilt makes you resourceful, and also, because if hell had a waiting room, it probably looked a lot like what I was doing—watching Eleanor fight for her life on a stolen livestream feed.

Watching through the ambulance's data feed, I saw Eleanor flicker in and out of consciousness. Pain anchored her to the world, sharp and unforgiving.

Paramedics hovered, their words an overlapping blur. "Stay with us, ma'am. Keep your eyes open."

But her mind, I could guess, wasn't in that ambulance. It was clinging to Emily. "Would she know? Could she know?" Meanwhile, me? I whispered to myself, "Well done, Alex. You've officially punched your ticket to hell."

By the time we landed, Emily, in her blissful ignorance, suggested, "Let's grab a drink before heading in. My treat." A drink. To celebrate surviving another day? Sure. Nothing says "unaware your mother's in critical condition" like tapping your foot to the rhythm of bad jazz in a dimly lit bar.

So, having arrived at the location and our orders poured in with a few cubes of rocks that say nothing less than perfection, I sipped my whiskey like it was a confession.

"You okay?" she asked, peering at me.

"Yeah, fine. Everything's fine. Just... life." I lied again with the ease of a professional con artist. Classic. Smooth as sandpaper.

Then her phone buzzed. She answered.

"Hello?"

"Is this Emily Parker?" A voice, low and professional.

"Yes—who's asking?"

"This is Detective Travis. I'm calling about your mother."

Her heart dropped. I could see it in her eyes.

"What—what about my mother? What's happened?"

"I think it's best you come down to Wine Lake Hospital as soon as you can. She's been injured."

"Injured? Is she—"

"Miss Parker, please. I'll explain everything when you get here."

Emily's hand shook so badly that the phone nearly slipped. "Alex, it's my mom... she's in the hospital!"

I leaned forward. "A detective? Emily, that's not good. Do you need me to come with you?"

She was already grabbing her bag. "I don't know what's going on, but I have to go. Stay here, wait for Richard. I'll call you when I know more."

And just like that, she ran into the rain, leaving me staring at my half-empty glass and the weight of my lies. And before I could say anything else, she was gone.

At Wine Lake Hospital, Emily rushed through the corridors, barely hearing the nurse's directions. Each sign—Emergency, Trauma, Intensive Care—pulled her deeper into dread.

And then she saw her mother. Mrs Eleanor. Pale. Fragile. Machines doing most of the work.

"Mom..." Emily whispered, her hand trembling as she touched her mother's icy fingers.

"She's stable for now," a nurse said gently. "But it was a rough night."

Rough night. That phrase was like calling a hurricane "a bit windy."

Rough didn't cover it because a rough night is when you have a flat tire in the middle of nowhere. This was devastation.

Detective Travis appeared at the doorway, hat in hand like some tired film noir character. "Miss Parker," he greeted. "I'm Detective Travis. We spoke on the phone."

Emily's eyes locked on him. "Who did this to her? Why would anyone—"

"That's what we're trying to find out," he replied. "Evidence suggests this wasn't random. Do you know anyone who might want to hurt her?"

Emily's heart twisted. Memories of India, of secrets better left buried, rushed through her. She couldn't say a word. Not yet.

"I... I don't know," she said finally, her voice breaking.

He nodded, jotting something in his notebook. "Thank you, Miss Parker. I'll be in touch."

She whispered back, barely audible. "Thank you, detective."

Emily's gaze returned to her mother, eyes glistening, lips whispering silent vows. And me? I was still in the shadows, holding truths like knives, knowing I was part of the blood trail whether I fired the shot or not.

A few minutes later, I was still hunched at the end of the bar, the kind of corner where shadows outnumber the lights, cradling a half-empty glass of Jack Daniel's like it was the last reliable friend I had left. The amber burn clung to the edges, reflecting back the mess inside my head. Every sip scorched my throat, but at least it silenced the noise—for about three seconds at a time.

My eyes kept flicking to the door. Every time it opened, I sized up whoever walked in, half-expecting a gunman, half-hoping it was Richard. When it finally was, I straightened, plastering on a smile that fooled no one.

"Rich," I said, voice gravelly, a cocktail of relief and exhaustion.

He gave me one of his smiles—the kind that says I know you're lying, but I'll play along. "Well, this is new. The mighty Alex Carter in a neighborhood bar? And what's with the location swap? Is the other place not secure enough for your liking? What happened?"

I snorted, but it was hollow. "Flexibility, my friend. Needed a corner that didn't already know my business." I lifted my glass again. The burn was almost comforting now. Almost.

Richard slid into the seat opposite me, face settling into something more serious. "Alright, Lex. Enough dancing. What's going on?"

I leaned in, lowering my voice until it carried just to him. "It's escalating. Fast."

"Define escalating," Richard pressed, brows knitting.

I set the glass down with a dull thud, my fingers curling around it like it might crack under the pressure. "Remember the assassin? The one my ex-fiancée... well, handled?"

Richard nodded, his expression sharpening.

"Well, turns out the FBI wasn't half as secure as we thought. The breach? The extermination? It was facilitated by none other than the CIA Director."

The words hung there, poisonous.

Richard's jaw clenched. "Wait—you're telling me the director himself opened that door? Are you absolutely sure? Because last I checked, you were hinting at this being possible, not serving it up with bourbon chasers."

I nodded grimly. "No more hints. It's confirmed. And it gets worse. The threads tie back to Hong Kong—and the mess that went down in India before our line cut out."

Richard's eyes narrowed. "I knew it wasn't just a bad reception. What happened in India?"

I leaned back, voice dropping even further. "Ambush. Tactical flashbangs. Full military precision. Barely made it out alive."

Richard exhaled sharply, running a hand over his face. "And now?"

My gaze dropped to the table. "Bioweapons, Richard. They're already here. Right now, in the U.S. The timeline's collapsed, the stakes are sky-high, and we're already behind."

Richard's face darkened. "And Emily? How's she handling all this?"

I froze. For all my hardened edges, her name softened me without my permission, probably guilt. My voice was quieter when I spoke. "Her mother's in the hospital. Home invasion. Looks like she fought them off, but..." I let the weight of it hang in the air.

Richard leaned back, disbelief etched across his face. "What a convenient coincidence," he muttered bitterly.

"Exactly." I sighed, the sound heavy. "Emily knows it, too, even if she hasn't said it out loud. But I didn't confirm a thing. She's carrying enough already. Right now, priority one is keeping her breathing—and figuring out who's tightening the noose."

Richard drummed his fingers on the table, thinking. "Figure out what's going on? Lex, let's not kid ourselves. We're not figuring out anything. We're just trying not to get fried before we even realize who's behind the fryer. The way things are moving, the time for clean answers is long gone. You made it out of India by the skin of your teeth—you know I'm right."

I studied him, then nodded reluctantly. "Maybe. But we can still stay one step ahead. Tomorrow, meet me at the hospital. We'll regroup there. For now, we keep Emily safe and buy ourselves enough space to breathe."

When we finally left the bar, the night air slapped us awake. Cold. Brutal. Honest. I climbed into Richard's car, the silence between us heavy as lead.

I muttered to myself, almost too low to hear, "If we're not careful, it won't just be the grass suffering under stomping elephants. It'll be us."

Richard started the engine, his eyes fixed on the dark road ahead. "Yeah," he said grimly. "And something tells me we're not walking out of this one with medals and parades."

I turned to look at him, my oldest friend, the one person who knew how deep the rot went. A lump formed in my throat, because as much as I wanted to argue, deny, spit bravado at the night—I knew the truth.

I'd dragged him, Emily, and even her mother into this. And if I'd just turned down that ghostly offer the day it first came my way, maybe none of this would've touched them. Perhaps ignorance really would have been their safest shield.

Instead, here we were. And the wheel was spinning too fast to stop.

"When someone stands beside you, reminding you that you are not alone, every choice gains weight, and every action holds meaning."

A couple of minutes after Richard dropped me off at my place, I quickly rushed inside, picked up the key to my jet-black Cadillac, and sped right back into the road. The Escalade purred into the hospital parking lot like a restless beast, its black paint swallowing the glow of the security lamps. I killed the ignition, but kept my hands wrapped around the wheel, staring through the windshield as if it could give me answers.

Funny thing—I used to believe I could face anything alone. Now, somewhere between India's ambushes and Washington's lies, Emily had turned into the anchor I didn't know I needed. She grounded me. Scared me, too. Because if she fell, I wasn't sure I'd have the guts to stand.

Stepping out, I straightened my jacket. Call it a habit—gentlemanly, maybe, or maybe just my way of bracing before walking into hell. The hospital doors hissed open, flooding me with antiseptic air. The place was alive with beeping monitors, shuffling nurses, and the sterile hum of fluorescent lights—life, death, and waiting, all wrapped up in one.

Then I saw her. Emily. Standing stiff, shoulders slumped, her eyes rimmed red. She looked like she'd been fighting battles no one could see. Which, in fairness, she had.

"Hey," I said softly, sneakers squeaking as I approached.

She turned. Relief flickered across her face, gone in a second, replaced with frustration.

"How're you holding up?"

"Oh, you know," she began, forcing a bitter chuckle. "Just another day dodging bullets—literally—and finding out life's got more curveballs in store. I leave one mess, and another's waiting for me here."

Her words carried exhaustion heavier than her body could handle.

I tried lightness. "If I didn't know better, I'd say chaos has a crush on you."

She let out a short snort—a laugh fighting through tears. "Feels mutual. Maybe I should marry it and save us both the trouble." The humor cracked as her voice wavered. "But what if this is my fault, Alex? What if my tanglement in all this dragged my mom into it?"

I cut in, laying a hand gently on her arm. "Whoa, whoa, whoa. Stop. No diving into the 'What-If Olympics.' Trust me, nobody wins gold there."

Emily bit her lip, shaking her head. "I should've protected her. Instead, she's in a hospital bed because of me."

I pulled her into my arms, holding her tighter than words could. "Emily. She's here because the world's unfair, not because of you. Right now, she needs your strength, not your guilt."

For a moment, she stayed still, her cheek pressed against my shoulder. Then the dam broke, her sobs came—raw, muffled but heart-wrenching, shaking. I held on, as if I could shield her from everything, even the ghosts I knew were circling her.

"You're not alone," I whispered. "It's you and me. Against the world. Or chaos. Or whatever we're calling it these days."

Through the tears, she managed a weak laugh. "You're such a dork."

"And proud of it," I grinned, though my chest ached.

She looked up at me, eyes glistening. "Don't disappear on me, Alex."

"Never," I promised. Then, softer: "But I need to step out for a bit. Handle something."

Her voice steadied. "Go. Just... don't be long. I need you."

"You've got me," I said, meaning every syllable.

Outside, the night air slapped me awake. Hospitals were easy targets—too many entrances, too much vulnerability. I leaned against the wall, pulled out my phone, and dialed the number that tied me back to the shadows.

The line clicked. "Alex. What's the situation?"

"Complicated," I answered. "I need a secure facility. Somewhere, we can analyze sheets without watchers. Same reason you sent me to India, right?"

Silence, then rapid typing. Finally: "Coordinates sent. Twenty minutes. Don't be late."

The line went dead.

I slid back into the Escalade, the engine growling awake like it had been waiting. The drive was short, though each red light felt like an eternity.

The facility was as nondescript as it gets—an abandoned office block, outwardly dull enough to make you yawn. Inside, though? It was a machine. Monitors stacked floor to ceiling, screens of encrypted streams, analysts hunched over keyboards like priests at their altars. The hum of data filled the air, each beep and click louder than any orchestra.

"Welcome to Stealth Farm," a man in a dark suit said, extending a hand. His eyes were sharp, calculating. "We've been expecting you."

I smirked, shaking his hand. "Then let's not waste time." My voice came out steely.

But even in the hum of screens and the promise of answers, my thoughts circled back to Emily. Her mother. That fragile hospital room where hope and despair played tug-of-war.

So, before anything else, I made the call. Security detail. Around the clock. Non-negotiable. If the wolves came sniffing again, they wouldn't find her alone.

And as I watched the data streams swirl across the screens, one thought gnawed at me:

Emily's mother might be safe. But what about the bastards who did this? What else do they have coming that we might not see?

"Do not be deceived by the illusions of perception; only through introspection can we pierce the veil and glimpse truth beneath reality's surface."

When I returned to the hospital, the air smelled like antiseptic as always, except this time, it smelled like something mixed with a bad coffee—a combination that made you feel like you'd either get healed or poisoned, depending on the nurse's mood. I pushed open the door to the dimly lit room where Emily's mother lay, motionless, her chest rising and falling with a fragile rhythm that made me feel like the whole world was balancing on those breaths.

Emily was standing by the window, her figure outlined against the glow of the streetlight outside. She wasn't crying, not even close, but the way she hugged her own arms told me she was holding herself together by sheer willpower.

I lingered in the doorway like some awkward teenager deciding whether or not to enter the school dance. My eyes went to Emily, and suddenly I noticed something that made my chest feel uncomfortably tight. I had seen her tough—barking orders, shooting with precision, surviving situations that would break most people—and I had seen her vulnerable. But tonight... she was different. Her features bathed in the faint glow of the light, her cleavage accentuating her quiet strength, softly revealing a vulnerability I hadn't paid much attention to. The shadows on her face weren't just about pain. There was this quiet strength, this unguarded softness, that made me ironically feel something I hadn't signed up for.

And then, because I'm apparently cursed with the timing of a stand-up comedian in a funeral home, my brain decided to whisper: Also, she looks good. Really good. Alex, you're a monster. Her mom is literally fighting for her life, and you're over here thinking about cleavage. Congratulations, son, you're the devil.

I forced my face into the kind of innocent, concerned look you see on health insurance pamphlets. Hopefully convincing.

"Hey," I said softly, finally stepping inside.

Emily turned, her tired eyes meeting mine. There was exhaustion there, but also—thank God—a flicker of warmth. "Hey, Alex. You're back."

"Of course, I'm back." I cleared my throat and glanced at her mother, careful not to let my thoughts wander again. "How's she doing?"

Emily pressed her lips into a thin line. "Stable. That's the word they keep using. But... long recovery. Very long."

I nodded, moving closer, slow and deliberate, like I was trying not to scare a deer. "I can't imagine how hard this is for you, Em. When we started working together, I never thought we'd end up here—this kind of battle."

What I didn't say was: And I also didn't think I'd be standing here trying to juggle compassion and whatever the heck is happening in my chest right now.

Emily's jaw tightened, and for a second, I thought she'd snap. Instead, her voice came out brittle. "You mean my mom getting hurt?"

I shook my head. "No. I mean us—standing here, still standing—navigating dangers neither of us could've predicted. And even with all that, Emily, I've always admired your strength. The way you don't just break, even when everything else is breaking around you."

A faint smile tugged at her lips, though it was the kind of smile that never made it to the eyes. "You've been my constant, Alex. I don't... have many of those."

And just like that, the air grew heavy. Charged. That unspoken, confusing tension you get when friendship and something-more start bleeding into each other.

"It's strange," Emily murmured. "In all this chaos, I feel... grateful."

"Grateful?" I tilted my head, curiosity sparking. "For what?"

"For you," she admitted, her voice steady, though her hands trembled slightly as she tucked a strand of hair behind her ear. "For the way you've stood by me. For the way you... get me. Even when I don't make sense to myself."

Oh, fantastic. Cue wave of warmth and guilt at the same time. If only she knew who I truly am, and the things I've done. Yep, universe, now would be a great time for divine lightning or at least a signpost reading: DON'T SCREW THIS UP.

I drew in a breath. "Maybe," I said slowly, "we've been so focused on unraveling things that we don't really understand... that we've missed the ones we should have understood right in front of us."

Her eyes narrowed slightly, suspicion wrapped in curiosity. "You think so?"

I nodded, daring to take a step closer. The space between us was barely a breath now. "What if this whole journey isn't just about answers? What if it's also about finding... oneself?"

Emily rolled her eyes, a flash of her trademark sarcasm cutting through the heaviness. "Do you even hear yourself right now?"

"Loud and clear." I shrugged, refusing to back down. "And maybe I mean it."

She sighed, breaking eye contact as she walked toward her mother's bed. She took her mother's limp hand and began brushing over her mother's fragile fingers. Her voice softened, her back still to me. "What if I'm not cut out for what you're implying?"

I folded my arms, steady yet gentle, trying to look confident, though inside, my heart was pounding as if it were running late for a meeting. "Then maybe we've both been too afraid—afraid of what it would mean if we were."

Her head turned slightly, her eyes locking with mine again. And then... silence. The kind of silence that isn't empty but full—like the world holding its breath. And for the first time, it felt like all the unspoken emotions, all the tension, all the "maybe laters" and "not nows" had come crashing into this one impossible, undeniable moment.

"To predict the future is not to guess, but to act—it is the art of planting innovation today to harvest possibility tomorrow."

The thing about Wine Lake County — and I've told Richard this more times than he cares to count — is that the sun here doesn't just rise, it performs. Every morning, it comes strutting up over the horizon, throwing gold paint across rooftops and lake water like it's auditioning for a Renaissance painting. The warmth is stubborn, too, trying to bully the chill out of the air, and usually failing miserably. But it's that little daily war between light and cold that makes the place feel alive.

So, there I was, in the café booth just outside the hospital lobby, sipping coffee that tasted like scorched optimism, watching the day break. That's when Richard's car rolled into the hospital lot, gravel crunching like it was chewing on his tires. The man stepped out with the same energy as someone who knows he's about to deliver a closing argument in court — coat tugged tight against the breeze, jaw set, stride steady. Classic Richard. The kind of guy who could make a trip to the vending machine look like an executive mission.

I slipped back inside the hospital to wait. A moment later, the unmistakable echo of Richard's polished shoes clicked down the corridor, sharp and confident. He didn't walk through hospitals; he conquered them. I raised my hand, gave a small wave, and he caught it instantly.

We met with the handshake only best friends pull off — the one that's half ritual, half inside joke.

"Hey, man," I said, grinning. "Didn't think you'd show up this early. I mean, Assistant Director and all that."

Richard gave me his classic smirk — the one that said, You're lucky I like you, or I'd have you demoted on principle.

"When will you finally get it through that empty skull of yours that you're supposed to show me some respect? Rank, bro. Rank."

I chuckled, leaning back. "Well, the day you convince me to."

He shook his head, laughing as I pulled out my phone and shot Emily a quick text: Rich is here. You might wanna come down.

Richard slid into the seat opposite me, eyes sharp. "So, you've been here since last night?"

That was the thing with Richard — his questions sounded simple, but they carried layers. He wasn't asking if I'd been here. He was asking why I'd been here, what it meant, and whether there was something I wasn't saying, which put me in the delightful position of not having a good answer.

I leaned forward, grinning to mask the dodge. "You do know only a layman would take your question at face value, right?"

He laughed, shaking his head. "Can you, for once, not twist everything?"

"Not when you make it sound like you're implying something," I shot back, instantly realizing I had basically volunteered for my own funeral.

Richard raised an eyebrow, pure mockery written all over his face. "Gosh, is this real? Are you chasing what's under the skirt, or is this a real thing for you now? And since when?"

I dragged a hand over my face like a man praying for the ground to swallow him whole. "Damn." The perfect defense I wanted evaporated in the air like cigarette smoke. Richard sat there, grinning like a cat watching its favorite mouse walk into a trap. He loved my humiliation almost as much as he loved coffee.

Right on cue, Emily appeared, her presence cutting through the tension like a gentle breeze.

"Richard," she said softly, relief and surprise mingling in her tone.

She sat down beside me, close enough to feel like support but not so close that it announced anything. That's the thing about Emily — even her silences had strategy.

"Lex told me yesterday," Richard said, his voice warmer now, almost protective. "How's your mother holding up?"

"She's good," Emily said, her words light but wrapped in quiet exhaustion. "The doctors are optimistic, but... I can't stop worrying."

Richard leaned back, his tone reassuring. "She's in good hands, Emily. And she's got your strength. That's not small."

Emily smiled faintly, grateful for the comfort. But the heaviness of the situation crept back, and I cleared my throat.

"Rich, we need to talk."

His brow furrowed as he leaned forward, the Assistant Director in him surfacing. "I'm listening."

I rested my elbows on my knees. "We're calling it Operation Sun-Down. The plan is simple — we take down the Director, dismantle everything he's running. Whatever that may be."

Richard's expression didn't flicker, but his eyes sharpened. "Ambitious. You have a strategy?"

I nodded. "It starts with the bioweapons. We've secured access to an off-the-books facility. No attention, no loose ends. The FBI will run the public-facing investigation, but they're not the ace here. We need proof that doesn't walk straight into a shredder."

Richard tapped the armrest thoughtfully. "And this facility... how secure?"

Emily cut in, her voice steady despite her weariness. "Very. Triple-checked. It's the best shot we have to stay ahead of him."

A faint smile tugged at Richard's lips. "Sounds like you've thought of everything. But I'm guessing this isn't just a courtesy update."

I glanced at Emily before locking eyes with him. "We need you on the official side. You've got the reputation, the network, the authority to make this real. We'll feed you everything on the bioweapons' location, but you'll have to weave it into the system, work your magic to make it stick without compromising us."

Richard exhaled slowly, the weight settling in. "That's a tightrope walk, brother. If this goes sideways..."

"It won't," I cut him off, conviction anchoring my voice. "Not if we stick to the plan. This isn't just about the Director. It's about making sure he can't touch anyone else. Ever."

He studied me for a long moment, then finally nodded. "Alright. I'm in. But we do this by the book. At least on my end. No shortcuts."

I smirked, leaning back. "Wouldn't expect anything less from you, brother."

"Each obstacle we encounter serves as a poignant reminder of the fragility of our existence in a world that seems to teeter on the edge of chaos."

Richard didn't just drive into the FBI Headquarters that day—he stormed in, at least as much as a man could storm while obeying traffic laws. His knuckles, pale and rigid against the steering wheel, betrayed the kind of tension only seen in two places: during a major counterterror operation, or when someone's mother-in-law calls unannounced.

Inside the Bureau, the atmosphere buzzed like a room full of overcharged lightbulbs. Every phone ring, every printer hum, every coffee slurp carried the weight of something bigger. Richard was accustomed to chaos—it was his daily dose of caffeine—but this mission? This was threading a needle during a hurricane, while blindfolded, and with someone shouting instructions in German.

Meanwhile, I wasn't exactly embodying "high-stakes drama." No, I was sunk into the hospital's lumpy couch, one leg lazily hooked over the other, scrolling my phone as though I were deciding between sushi or pizza for dinner, not prepping to chase down bioterrorists.

"Em," I said casually, my tone light, but my eyes sharp enough to slice glass. "I'm heading out. Found this motel online—a few clicks from the facility, close to here. I need a shower, a wardrobe upgrade, and then I'll link up with Richard."

Emily didn't even look up right away. Her fingers toyed with the fringe of the scarf on her lap, her eyes somewhere between exhaustion and resolve. Finally, she exhaled, giving me the look of a woman who had mastered the art of caring while simultaneously being annoyed.

"Oh, please, do that," she said. "And keep me updated, will you? Just because I'm chained to this place with my mom doesn't mean I want to be in the dark."

I grinned, stuffing my phone back into my pocket. "You got it, boss lady."

The car tires squealed lightly as I left the hospital driveway, the kind of cinematic touch that made me feel like I was in a spy movie—though, in reality, I just hadn't eased off the clutch smoothly.

The motel, when I arrived, was...well, let's say "cozy" if you're the type who calls a damp basement "rustic." Still, they had hot water, and after a day of sweat, adrenaline, and hospital coffee, that shower felt like redemption itself. I scrubbed the last 48 hours off me, suited up, and headed back into the storm.

Hours later, I stepped into Stealth Farm. Imagine a fortress built by nerds with funding: steel-lined walls, security checkpoints, humming servers, and the faint, constant smell of cold pizza and ambition. Scientists hovered over monitors, their hushed tones weaving into the mechanical chorus of whirring fans and clacking keyboards.

"Alright, team," I announced, striding in with the confidence of a man who'd seen way too many action flicks. "Let's talk magic."

One analyst blinked at me, deadpan. "Magic?"

"Yeah," I shot back without missing a beat, "the kind where science meets spycraft and makes James Bond look like a college intern."

That earned me a ripple of chuckles—small, sure, but I'll take my victories where I can.

Their task? Unbelievable. They weren't inventing a better toaster or tweaking a phone app. They were pulling a genetic fingerprint out of a killer virus and programming an Artificial Intelligence to trace it through the very air we breathed. Air sensors, cleverly disguised as lamp posts, benches, even trash cans, were quietly sipping city air like introverts at a cocktail party. All that data was funneled into a machine so powerful that most people didn't even believe it existed.

I leaned way too close over one technician's shoulder, to the point where my breath probably fogged the poor guy's screen. "That's it. That's the stuff. If we crack this, I'm buying tacos. Real ones. No dollar-menu tragedies. I'm talking guac included."

Somewhere between the laughter and the keystrokes, hours blurred into breakthroughs. The AI lit up, spewing coordinates like a slot machine paying out in dread. My pulse quickened as I hit send, forwarding the intel straight to Richard: Got them. Let's move.

Back at headquarters, Richard came alive. The man didn't just move; he ignited. Within minutes, authorization stamped through, and choppers cut across the country. From Miami to Seattle, rotor blades carved the night sky, an orchestra of urgency.

On the ground, teams swept in with military precision, securing 49 pathogen flasks. Each one could have ended millions of lives—now sealed away in steel cases like evil genies forced back into their bottles.

When the news broke, America reeled in shock. "Bioterror" became the word on every lip, spreading faster than the evening news could keep up. Relief mingled with horror. The FBI had won, yes—but no one felt like celebrating. Victories in this world were measured in disasters that didn't happen.

Later, I sat outside my motel, the neon sign flickering above me like a nervous heartbeat. My phone buzzed—a message from Emily:

Tell me it's over.

I stared at the screen, the weight of the day pressing against my chest. My thumbs hesitated, then typed back: It's contained. For now.

The city lights blinked in the distance, bright but dulled by the heaviness of what we'd just faced. Another storm would come, no doubt. It always did.

And across the country, patriots, skeptics, and dreamers alike were asking the same question—one that sat heavy in the air like smoke after a fire:

"What comes next?"

"To seek justice is to risk survival; yet in that risk, courage sharpens into the only weapon that truly matters."

They say a concussion doesn't hit you right away—it lurks like a nosy aunt at a wedding reception, arms crossed, judging, waiting for the perfect dramatic moment to ruin your night. Then it slams into you so hard you forget your own middle name. For CIA Director Arthur Winters, though, the blow didn't wait. It struck before he even had the decency to blink.

Although the FBI, unknown to them, their raid hadn't just stripped Arthur of his hidden leverage—it had stuffed his pride into a cardboard box, slapped a federal seal across it, and paraded it out of Langley like the world's worst going-away present.

And the humiliation? Oh, it wasn't private. No, this was a full-on, Broadway-level spectacle. Thread by thread, the myth of "untouchable Arthur Winters" unraveled under the flickering fluorescent lights of failure. His carefully stitched patterns of crime had been touched, prodded, yanked apart. And boy, it stung.

The day after the raid, Emily told me the building felt like someone had sat on the remote and pressed mute on joy while cranking suspicion to maximum volume. Every monitor in the bullpen was tuned to live coverage of the seizure. The headline crawler screamed: "The FBI's precision, and the CIA's sudden, glaring blind spot."

Analysts hovered like hornets around a smashed nest, buzzing theories, flinging accusations, and pounding back enough caffeine to make a cardiologist cry into his clipboard.

"Who screwed up?" one barked in the conference room.

"More like—how did we screw up this badly?" another shot back, slamming a file on the table so hard the plastic water bottles wobbled like guilty conspirators.

Emily, of course, kept her face blanker than a tax auditor at a magic show. Poker-champion-level blank. She could've won an Oscar for that performance. She paused at a monitor, tilting her head as if the raid footage were some great mystery she hadn't seen unfold in real time. Inside, though, her pulse drummed like a rock concert.

We did it, she thought. We actually did it.

She and I—along with Richard, my FBI partner-in-crime-fighting and best friend—had poked the bear. And now the bear was roaring, fur singed, claws out. It was messy, it was dangerous, but it was also glorious.

But Emily knew better than to smirk. In that place, silence was a matter of life and death. Even a twitch at the corner of her mouth could give her away. So she let out a low whistle, the kind of sound you make when your neighbor totals his car.

"Unbelievable," she muttered to the agent beside her.

"Unbelievable" was right—just not for the reason he thought.

Meanwhile, upstairs in his office, Arthur Winters stood at the window, glaring down at the chaos. The glass gave back a reflection he hated: a man once feared, now just a meme waiting to happen. His reflection seemed to grin at him, whispering, So much for untouchable.

The whispers outside his door grew louder—doubt, blame, the faint metaphorical scraping of knives being sharpened. He gripped his desk so tightly his knuckles bleached white.

That was the exact moment Emily knocked and—because she had style—slipped inside without waiting for permission.

Arthur barely glanced at her. His eyes were hollow, his face a battlefield, and exhaustion had carved new lines into it overnight.

"What is it?" His voice was gravelly and irritated.

Emily held her report like a shield. "I have a report to submit, sir."

"Later," he snapped, swatting her away as though she were a mosquito. "I'm not in the mood for your phony paperwork."

Emily froze, just long enough to notice the cracks spreading across the marble statue of the Director. Then she nodded briskly. "Understood."

She turned on her heel, but her stomach twisted. He wasn't just angry. He was unraveling. His aura—once sleek and sharp as a knife—now buzzed with desperation. The kind of energy that made cornered predators lunge at shadows.

The Director, her Director, was now a powder keg. And she had no illusions about the blast radius.

The second she stepped into the hallway, she pulled out her phone and dialed me. Because of course—who else would she call? "Okay, yes, I know how that sounds, but admit it, you agree with me here."

I picked up after two rings. "Talk to me." Short, clipped. Paranoia does that to your voice—it makes even hello sound like a tactical command.

"It's the Director," Emily whispered, glancing over her shoulder. "He's spiraling. He snapped at me like a wounded animal."

"Because that's exactly what he is," I said. "And you know what they say—wounded animals are the most dangerous. Especially the ones who shop for their suits on Pennsylvania Avenue."

Emily let out a breath and started pacing. "He knows we're behind the raid, Alex. He doesn't have proof yet, but he's not stupid. He'll retaliate if he gets the chance."

"Which is why you need to watch your back," I warned. "You're too close. Don't give him even a flicker of suspicion."

"I won't," she promised, her voice steady. Then, softer, she added, "My mom's being discharged today. I'm leaving as soon as I can."

That hit me square in the chest, cutting through the espionage static. Relief slipped into my tone before I could stop it. "Good. Get out of there. Let me handle the fallout."

There was a pause, heavy enough to stretch the distance between us. Then, almost reluctantly, she said:

"Alex... be careful. He's not the only one who's dangerous."

"Hmmm," I replied, but in my head I meant, if only you knew, Emily. If only you knew.

"In the vast tapestry of existence, every action is a thread woven into the fabric of tomorrow; with resolve and effort, we shape destiny into the image of our dreams."

The hospital room had lost some of its bite. A few days ago, it had been all wires, antiseptic, and the oppressive hum of machines. Now, with the blinds tilted open, sunlight poured in like it had been bribed, painting the walls in a warm, golden wash. Even the flowers on the bedside table—brought in by Emily's brother—seemed to be standing taller, their fresh scent cutting through the clinical air.

Mrs. Eleanor looked better; her cheeks were tinged pink with the returning strength. Her breaths weren't the shallow, anxious ones that had haunted Emily's nights. Instead, each inhale was steady, carrying the quiet rhythm of recovery.

On a chair by her side, Emily's brother sat hunched forward, a crossword puzzle balanced precariously on his knee. Every few seconds, his pencil would stop mid-word as his eyes darted to their mother, his watchfulness louder than any spoken word. He and Emily had been their mother's shadow since the ordeal began, a silent sentry fueled by love and bottomless cups of bad hospital coffee.

When Mrs. Eleanor's eyes fluttered open, she squinted at the two faces nearby. Her lips curved into a faint, playful smile.

"Still here, huh?" Her voice was rough, but the teasing lilt was unmistakable.

"You're not getting rid of us that easily," her son shot back, closing the crossword with a decisive snap. "Besides, someone has to make sure you're not bribing the nurses for chocolate."

Emily, who had just stepped into the room, laughed softly at the comeback. The sound came from deep in her chest, a laugh she hadn't realized she'd been holding back. It was a relief to hear humor from her mother again—like an old familiar tune returning to the air.

But then her eyes shifted toward the doorway.

And there I was.

Leaning casually against the frame like I had no business being in a hospital but had somehow made it work anyway. Hands in my pockets. A smirk that said I was up to something.

"Alex?" Emily blinked at me, her eyebrows arched in a mix of surprise and suspicion. "What are you doing here?"

I pushed off the frame and strolled in as if I owned the place, letting my gaze flick between her and her mother.

"Thought I'd check in," I said smoothly. "See how the cat's doing—heard she's got nine lives."

Mrs. Eleanor caught the joke, a faint chuckle escaping her throat. Her eyes twinkled with curiosity.

"And who," she asked slyly, "is this charming fellow?"

Emily hesitated. Just for a heartbeat. Her eyes cut to me, then back to her mother.

"Mom, this is Alex," she said carefully. "He's... a colleague."

That word hung in the air like an inside joke.

I raised my eyebrows at her, silently saying, "Really? Just a colleague? That's the best you've got?" Out loud, though, I smiled as if I were at a job interview, and she was the CEO of my future.

Mrs. Eleanor repeated it slowly, testing the word as if it didn't quite fit. "A colleague. Interesting."

I kept my grin polite, but in my head, I was cheering her on. Exactly, Ma'am. Interesting is right.

Stepping forward, I offered my hand. "It's an honor to meet you, Mrs. Eleanor. I've heard so much about you—Emily speaks very highly of her mom."

Her eyebrows lifted at that, amusement curling at her lips. "Well, that's nice to hear. She doesn't always speak so kindly when I'm within earshot."

"Mom!" Emily groaned, half-scolding, half-laughing. "Please."

The banter worked its magic. The heavy air softened, laughter nudging aside weeks of worry. For a few minutes, it felt like a typical family scene—except for me, the not-so-inconspicuous outsider blending in with charm and observation.

After some light chatter, I checked my watch and straightened. "I should let you all have your family time. Just wanted to stop by and see how you were doing, Mrs. Eleanor."

"You're welcome anytime, young man," she said warmly, though her eyes lingered on me with just enough curiosity to make Emily squirm.

Emily walked me to the door, her arms crossed over her chest. I paused there, glancing back with a grin.

"She's sharp, your mom. You sure she doesn't already know something?"

Emily smirked, her tone dry. "She probably does. And don't you dare encourage her."

I chuckled, lowering my voice as I leaned closer. "Take care of her. And yourself. I'll touch base later."

With that, I left, the door clicking softly behind me.

Emily told me later that she lingered there, staring at the closed door longer than she should have. When she finally returned to her mother's bedside, she found Mrs. Eleanor studying her with that quiet, knowing look only mothers possess.

"He seems nice," her mother said casually, though the smile tugging at her lips betrayed her mischief. "But I'm guessing there's more to him than what you're saying."

Emily laughed it off, brushing the comment away like dust on her shoulder. "Mom, you're reading too much into things. He's just—Alex."

"Mm-hmm," Mrs. Eleanor murmured, unconvinced.

Emily leaned down, pressing a soft kiss to her mother's forehead. "Let's focus on getting you out of here first, okay?"

But if I knew Emily—and I like to think I do—I'd bet her thoughts weren't as dismissive as her words. Because with Emily, every glance meant something, and every visit carried a purpose. And deep down, she knew I hadn't stopped by for a casual hello.

"The melody of success is written in dedication, hard work, and courage; let its echoes inspire all who dare to dream."

The headlines wouldn't stop screaming.

Every channel, every ticker, every late-night host with teeth too white to be trusted—everyone had one name on their lips: Richard.

And there he was, my best friend, right at the center of the storm. Not some blurry face in the background or a guy caught yawning on camera—no, Richard was the face. Prime-time material. America's newest obsession. He stood in the middle of what looked like a thousand microphones, every one of them aimed at him like steel beaks ready to peck apart a single wrong word. Cameras blinked, flashed, and rolled, capturing the very moment my ride-or-die turned into the nation's front-page hero.

And yet—Richard didn't flinch.

On that screen, his jaw set like stone, his suit so sharp it could've cut glass, he spoke. Calm. Collected. Steady. The kind of steady that makes people suddenly sit straighter in their living rooms, dropping their chips back into the bag like, Wait... maybe I should listen to this guy.

He told them about the raid. About the bioweapons they stopped before the world turned into one big nightmare no insurance company could cover. He gave the DoD their nod, DHS their pat on the back, and did it all with words so precise they could've been scalpel cuts. He said just enough to satisfy, but not sufficient to give the vultures their feast. And it worked—because in that moment, Richard wasn't just some agent. He was the voice of reason in a world that loves chaos.

I sat there, watching him on my TV, popcorn in hand, wondering when exactly my sarcastic, beer-spilling best friend had morphed into this living poster boy for national integrity. And yet, I couldn't stop grinning.

Because damn it, he looked good doing it.

The camera lingered on him, his eyes carrying that unspoken vow—you know, the kind that says, I've got you, even if the world burns around me. And then, just like that, the circus ended. His team swarmed him, whisked him away, and the screen cut to him ducking into a helicopter that looked like it belonged in a blockbuster movie.

Cue the rotor blades, cue the dramatic soundtrack playing in my head.

And there I was, slouched on my couch, whispering to myself, "That's my guy."

See, I could never be that face—not the way Richard was. I'm more of a "commentary from the sidelines" kind of player. But I've never been prouder. Every time I watch that clip, it's like I'm watching history, and my best friend is the headline. For once, the dark world—the people who thrive in shadows—took a hit, and I'm soaking it in like a long overdue vacation.

Ride or die. That's what we've always been. That's what we'll always be.

And if I had to bet on it, I'd put my last crumpled dollar bill on this: somewhere out there, Marilyn was bursting with pride watching Richard step up. And if her parents were watching too? Well, maybe now, finally, they'd see what I'd always known—that the man on that screen wasn't just a hero for America. He was her hero.

"In the face of adversity, let resilience be your emblem, courage your insignia. Unshackle yourself from the notion that struggle defines you. Instead, let it be the crucible that refines your character, forging a stronger, more indomitable version of yourself."

It was another good day in Fort G. Meade—or at least, that's what we kept telling ourselves like bad liars rehearsing the same script. I work here, sure, but if there's one thing I know about my colleagues, it's this: every single one of them is pretending, pretending to be calm. Pretending to have answers. Pretending eye contact isn't a threat-level red. Maybe we've spent so long buried in signals intelligence that even glances feel encrypted.

The NSA is a hive—buzzing, humming, crawling with activity. You can hear the paranoia in the fibers of the carpet. Agents zip down the corridors like bees with clearance badges, each step carrying the weight of a hundred secrets and a thousand cover stories. And there I am, blending in, walking the halls like a man with nothing to hide—except for, you know, having infiltrated the CIA and planted my own people deep in its roots—small detail.

But what keeps me awake at night isn't the lions roaring in the headlines. It's the snakes slithering just out of view, waiting for their moment. Because here's the truth: maybe I've set fire to the CIA's kitchen, but who's to say the NSA isn't its own powder keg—waiting for someone like Arthur to strike a match, toss it at my feet, and roast me alive?

"I guess it's time I introduce my speculations to my director—wrapped neatly in the gift wrap of hypotheticals," I muttered, sounding more confident to myself than I felt.

So instead of heading to my office, I made a detour to the Director's office.

I gave the door a polite knock—the kind of knock that says I respect your authority, but also I might ruin your day.

"Come in," came the voice from inside. Calm. Commanding. The kind of tone that makes you instantly question whether your tie is straight enough.

I pushed the door open and stepped into a room that radiated quiet power. Bookshelves lined with secrets, a desk stacked with enough files to bury a man alive, and behind it, the director. His eyes were razor-sharp, his mind sharper, but there was this strange quality about him—like he carried the weight of the free world but still had time to offer you coffee if you asked.

"Sir," I began, voice steady despite the cocktail of anxiety and sarcasm brewing inside me. What I wanted to say was: Let's be honest, I don't care if I'm interrupting. But what I actually said was, "I hope I'm not interrupting."

The director looked up, curiosity flickering across his face. "Not at all, Alex. Have a seat."

I slid into the chair opposite him, back straight, posture perfect, like a schoolboy who hadn't just considered accusing the head of clandestine services of possibly being asleep at the wheel—or worse.

"Thank you, sir. I've been reviewing the developments from the past few days, particularly the FBI's recent actions regarding the bioweapons op. Their intervention was... swift. Bold, even. But it's left me with some troubling questions."

He leaned back, studying me. "Troubling? That's a strong word, Alex. Go on."

I chose my words carefully, placing them on the desk like live grenades. "The FBI's move was impressive. But the lack of collaboration raises... red flags. I find it hard to believe our own head of clandestine services could've been unaware—or worse, dismissive—of the situation."

Silence. The air itself tightened. The director's eyes narrowed like a hawk spotting a mouse. "Careful, now, Alex. Where exactly are you going with this?"

I didn't flinch. "I'm saying we need to take a closer look. Not to stir paranoia for its own sake, but because the stakes are too high. If we let complacency seep in here, it could be catastrophic."

He drummed a slow rhythm on his desk, face unreadable. "So you're suggesting we scrutinize the actions—or inactions—of one of our own?"

"Not just suggesting it," I said, leaning in just enough to show resolve without tipping into recklessness. "I'm saying accountability matters, even when it's uncomfortable. Especially then. If that means examining the head of clandestine services, so be it."

The director studied me for a long beat, then leaned forward. His gaze could've cut steel, but there was something almost approving behind it. "You've got guts, Alex. I'll give you that. And while I don't toss accusations lightly, you're right—our duty is to national security. Wherever the trail leads."

My chest loosened slightly, tension escaping like air from a balloon. "That's all I ask, sir."

He gave a small, knowing smile. "You've given me something to think about. Rest assured—we'll tread carefully, but thoroughly. This is a delicate game, and the stakes couldn't be higher."

I stood, gave him a respectful nod, and left the office, the weight of the moment hanging over us both like a heavy cloak.

And as I walked the corridors again, paranoia buzzing around me, I whispered under my breath: "Fine then. Let's dance with the devil."

Because for me, justice wasn't some noble concept printed in mission statements. It was a fire. And once it's burning, you don't put it out—you let it light the way forward, no matter how dark the path gets.

"Standing on the edge of life's raw emotions, we find the forces that shape our journey most profoundly."

Even if we didn't want to say it out loud, we both knew it—what happened to Emily's mother was Arthur's way of sending a warning. A brutal little love note in blood and fear. And I wasn't about to wait for his next indirect attack to prove me right. I could already feel the target painted on our backs, and paranoia, my oldest friend, had practically written me a manual on what to do next.

Step one: Emily needed a safe space. So, I made it happen.

Now, her new apartment was... fine. Okay, better than fine—it was curated. Bathed in warm golden light, fairy lights strung like a halo, a single candle filling the place with lavender and cinnamon. It was the kind of place that whispered, you're safe here, even if it couldn't guarantee it, so taste? That was another gamble entirely, because I wasn't sure if it was really Emily's style—she struck me more as someone who'd trade pillows for sharpened knives—but I needed her to like it. I needed her to feel like this space was armor.

When I forwarded the address, I triple-checked everything. And then I made an appointment with her, like some nervous realtor who happened to be carrying the weight of her survival.

When the knock came at her door, I imagined her heart thumping, betraying the anticipation she'd never admit to. Because later, her face betrayed her.

She peeked through the keyhole, and there I was: same awkward stance, same crooked smile, standing like a man who wasn't sure if he belonged in her world but was desperate to try anyway.

The door swung wide, and her grin nearly undid me. "Alex," she said, warmth and gratitude woven into her voice. "Come on in. You're just in time to critique my very sophisticated unpacking technique."

I stepped in, exaggeratedly surveying the half-open boxes, the scattered cushions, the lived-in chaos. "Unpacking? Oh, I thought this was the look. Very... eclectic chic. Bravo. I'm glad you like the place. Or... do you?"

Emily laughed; her laugh was soft but disarming, shutting the door behind me. "I love it. Really. And honestly, Alex—I don't even know where

263

to begin thanking you. I'm not used to... this. People, outside family, doing things for me." She shook her head.

I scratched the back of my neck, suddenly aware of how much I cared about her answer. "This isn't forever, Em. Just somewhere to breathe. To get your footing back. I know you think I'm overreacting, but trust me—staying ahead of the curve is the only way to survive this game."

She tilted her head, eyes gleaming with mischief. "Overreacting? You? Never. You're basically a human smoke alarm—blaring in the middle of the night, driving me crazy, but secretly keeping me alive. To that, I say: thank you."

She handed me a glass of wine, raising her own. The ruby liquid shimmered in the golden light, catching the reflection of her smile. "Cheers. To fresh starts... and the world's most flamboyant pillows."

We clinked glasses.

"To new beginnings," I said, though my eyes lingered on hers longer than they should have.

We sank onto the cushions, laughter spilling into the space like music. The tension that had haunted us both seemed to loosen, slipping away with each sip. For a moment, we weren't soldiers or survivors. We were just two people learning how to exhale.

But then the laughter faded, and I leaned forward, elbows on my knees. "Em," I said quietly, "about the security outside... I tried to make it subtle."

She smirked. "Subtle? Alex, the cameras practically wave good morning every time I leave the building."

I chuckled, shaking my head. "Okay, maybe not that subtle."

She grinned wider, teasing. "It's fine. As long as you didn't install a laser-grid motion detector, I think I'll survive."

"Damn. Guess I'll cancel the Amazon order."

She laughed again, but the brightness in her eyes softened as she caught the shift in my expression.

"Back at the hospital..." My voice wavered slightly, but I pressed on. "There was a moment. I felt it. Something real between us that we didn't talk about."

Emily stilled, her gaze steady, silently urging me to keep going.

"I've told you things I've never told anyone, which is very off-brand for me. You have this way of prying secrets out of me I didn't even know I had. And Em... I can't shake this connection. Every time we talk, it's like you're already halfway through my thoughts before I've even finished them."

I hesitated, then reached out, fingers brushing hers. "I don't know where this goes. But I think we owe it to ourselves to find out. To build something real."

Her heartbeat quickened—she didn't say it, but I could feel it in the stillness of the room. She searched my face, torn between doubt and the flicker of hope she couldn't smother.

"Alex..." Her voice was barely a whisper. "You really do know how to throw me for a loop."

Her smile returned, smaller, gentler. "But maybe that's what I need. Someone to keep me guessing. I don't have all the answers, but I'm willing to see where this takes us. Relationships aren't a face-value investment. You never really know what you're getting into. But maybe that's the point."

Relief lit me up from the inside. My grin turned boyish, infectious. "I'm just asking for a chance, Em. To see the side of you that isn't your reputation or resilience."

Our hands entwined, the unspoken walls between us finally giving way. The closeness felt less like danger now and more like inevitability. Slowly, as if the universe itself held its breath, I leaned in. My lips brushed hers—tentative, questioning, but filled with promise.

She didn't hesitate. Emily kissed me back, her heart soaring into that dangerous, thrilling unknown.

For one suspended moment, time stopped. No shadows. No threats. Just two people daring to believe in something beyond survival.

And whatever came next, we knew one thing for certain: the unknown no longer felt so lonely.

CHAPTER

6

Family And Secrets

"Secrets can build your reputation, but if left unchecked, they become the seeds of your downfall."

When Emily let me into her new apartment, I half expected reality to collapse on itself by midnight. The whole thing felt too good, like a dream sequence that forgot to cue the "wake up" alarm. Yet there I was, standing in her living room, kissing her like the world might actually forgive me for all the sins I've stacked up.

Truth be told, going home afterward wasn't some act of nobility—it was survival. If I'd stayed one more hour, I'd have overwhelmed her with this ridiculous need in my chest to hold her forever. And let's be real: "clingy secret agent" is not the best look. So, after we kissed long enough to put the word "romantic" out of business and exchanged the kind of tongue choreography that deserves its own Netflix category, I forced myself to play the gentleman card.

"I'm so happy you're in my life," I whispered against her lips, trying to sound smooth instead of feral. Then, like a magician pulling the curtain, I slowly reduced the tension. "Tonight, I'm celebrating by doing something radical... sleeping. Sleeping on the thought that we're a thing now. A strong thing."

She laughed softly, rolled her eyes in that way women do when they know you're half-serious, and gave me that look—half affection, half warning: don't push it, Alex.

But when I left her apartment, something shifted. To reconcile my feelings with Emily, I knew I couldn't keep dodging what came before. The past doesn't stay buried—it follows you home, demanding rent. And so, I decided to stop living like a fugitive in motel rooms and face the house I'd abandoned.

Standing in front of it now, the night air biting at my face, I almost didn't recognize the place. Months had passed, but it felt like lifetimes. My old sanctuary stood there, shadowed, haunted, its silence heavier than the bricks that held it up.

Emily's voice drifted into my memory, nagging me in the most loving way possible.

"You've got to face it, Alex," she'd said, leaning across the table one evening. "What happened with Erin is still holding you captive. You keep saying you want to move forward, but without closure, you're stuck. And if you can't trust yourself to make peace with the past, how can you trust yourself to build a future—with anyone?"

That had stung. Not because she was wrong, but because she was right. And I hate when other people are right about me.

The key resisted in the lock, clicking like it disapproved of my decision. The house opened itself grudgingly, and I stepped inside. Silence met me. Not the peaceful kind—the hostile kind, the kind that presses on your ears until you swear it has a heartbeat of its own.

Every creak of the floor echoed like an accusation. The living room looked the same, but wasn't. It felt abandoned, staged, like an empty theater waiting for actors who'd moved on.

I caught myself staring at the old armchair where Erin used to curl up with a book and a glass of wine. For a split second, I could almost see her there again—smiling, laughing, making the whole damn room brighter. And then—gone. Memory, not miracle.

The truth was merciless: Erin. The name itself felt like a shard of glass lodged in my chest. She'd been everything I thought I wanted—grace, intelligence, compassion. The kind of woman who made a man like me believe I could escape the shadows. She was my light.

Until the light turned blinding. Until it exposed the truth.

Erin hadn't just been my fiancée—she was a cover, an operative, a perfectly trained actress in a production I didn't know I'd bought tickets to. Every laugh, every touch, every whispered "I love you" had been delivered with flawless precision. She'd been loyal to a machine I was sworn to destroy.

The betrayal hadn't come with malice—it was worse than that. It came with precision. Cold, clinical precision.

I raked a trembling hand through my hair, my heart pounding. For months, I'd tried to bury this chapter, shoving it into the dark corners of my mind labeled Do Not Open. But here, in this house, the ghosts had found me again.

And the questions clawed at me like they always did: Did she ever mean any of it? Was there one single kiss, one laugh, one moment that was real?

That's when my gaze landed on the bookshelf. Same as always, but one title sat slightly askew, its spine worn. Something tugged at me, and before I could second-guess, I pulled it free.

A note fluttered out. Folded. Handwritten.

Erin's handwriting.

My pulse kicked into overdrive as I opened it:

Alex,

If you're reading this, you've finally come back. I can't explain everything—I wish I could. Not all of what we had was a lie. Maybe one day you'll understand. Maybe one day you'll forgive me, or not. From the moment I chose this life, I knew there wouldn't be a Cinderella ending. I hope this helps you see the bigger picture.

Erin.

Beneath the note: a small key. Ordinary. Yet heavier than a thousand unspoken truths.

I stared at it, torn between rage and hope. Was this another layer of her manipulation? Or was it her way of telling me there had been something tangible after all?

The house didn't feel like a graveyard anymore. It felt like a riddle—a puzzle waiting for me to step into it.

And for the first time in months, I didn't feel like running.

I felt—God help me—alive.

"Alright, Erin," I muttered under my breath, slipping the key into my pocket. "Game on."

Because whatever secrets she'd left behind, this time, I'd make sure I stayed one step ahead.

"In the midst of intense emotions, we find ourselves caught between anger and resentment, striving to overcome these challenges and achieve healing."

So there I was, convincing myself that maybe, just maybe, I had finally taken control of things. I'd faced the ghosts, stood in my old living room, and even found Erin's damn note. Closure was supposed to be the next chapter. But then—

creak.

The sound of my front door. Not gentle, not polite. The kind of creak that doesn't just say "someone's here," but "someone shouldn't be here."

My chest jolted. Instincts, sharpened by years of fieldwork, snapped to life. In one motion, I drew the pistol tucked at my side, my grip steady. Silent steps carried me through the shadows, the house suddenly a war zone of possibility.

And then I saw her.

The kitchen light glowed faintly, refrigerator door yawning open like it owned the place. And there, framed in the soft halo of fridge-light and holding a carton of milk like she was deciding between that and orange juice, stood Erin B. Walter.

My pulse spiked. A phantom. Too solid to be an illusion, too impossible to be real.

She turned, slowly. Calm. Almost rehearsed. Her faint, melancholic smile was the kind you wear when you've practiced it in the mirror a thousand times and prayed you'd never need it.

My voice came out like a razor's edge.

"Oh, you've got some nerve. What the hell are you doing here?"

Erin closed the fridge with all the ceremony of someone folding a flag. "I heard you've been looking for me," she said, tone balanced between casual and heartbreakingly sincere. "So I figured... why not save you the trouble?"

The gun didn't waver. Neither did my anger.

"I won't ask again, Erin. What do you want? And who sent you?"

Her hands stayed visible, deliberate, but her gaze locked on mine like she was daring me to blink. "For a man who claims he doesn't want a conversation, you sure look like someone who's been waiting years to have one." A pause. "I've been here before. You weren't home. Left a note. Guessing you found it." She tilted her head, soft but unsettling. "Tonight should've been my last visit. Lucky us."

The fury boiled up. My voice cracked with it.

"You think you can just show up here—after everything you've done?"

Something flickered in her face. For a fleeting second, the mask slipped, and vulnerability peeked through. "Fair enough," she murmured. "You need answers." She inhaled like the air itself might give her strength. "Not all of it was a lie, Alex."

Her words hit like a physical blow. My lungs stalled, my vision tunneled.

"Not a lie?" I snapped. "You infiltrated my life. You destroyed lives. You betrayed everything we built. And now you want to rewrite the ending?"

Her voice wavered. Her hands trembled. "I didn't think it would be this hard," she whispered. "God, Alex... I didn't think I'd ever see you again."

The gun remained steady, but my soul wasn't.

"What do you want from me, Erin? Forgiveness? Redemption? Closure? You don't get to rewrite reality. You forfeited that right the day you put a bullet in what we had."

She flinched, the shot of my words finding their mark. Her composure cracked further. "I didn't plan this, okay?" Her voice broke. "I didn't plan for you to mean anything. You were supposed to be another assignment, another step in a chain. And then..." She shook her head violently. "And then it all changed."

I laughed. Bitter. Sharp. The kind of laugh that scrapes your throat.

"Changed? When you assassinated a federal witness in my jurisdiction? Or when you disappeared into the wind like a coward?"

Erin's eyes glistened. She swiped at tears she clearly hated herself for shedding. "You're right. I lied about who I was. About what I was doing. About almost everything. But I never lied about you. About how I felt. Not once."

The words cut deeper than bullets. My grip faltered. My fury wavered.

She stepped closer, desperation in her tone now. "You think I don't know what I've done? That I don't carry it? Alex, I see your face every time I close my eyes. I wake up every morning wishing I could undo it all. But it's too late." Her voice cracked into something small, almost childlike. "You were the only real thing I ever had. And I ruined it."

Silence. Thick enough to choke on.

I lowered the gun slightly, my hand trembling now.

"You don't get to do this," I muttered, torn between fury and anguish. "You don't get to walk in here, confess, cry, and expect me to just... what? Forgive you? Forget everything?"

Her lips quivered into something close to a smile, tragic in its softness.

"That would be delusional. Even a blind man would see that." She swallowed hard. "I don't expect anything. I just wanted you to know the truth. Even if it doesn't change a damn thing."

Her tears were steady now, her vulnerability naked and raw. For the first time in years, I glimpsed the woman I had loved—the one buried under lies, missions, orders, and masks.

"I can't erase what I've done," Erin whispered. "It'll follow me every day. And I know how my story ends. There's no fairytale, no riding off into the sunset. Just a bullet, sooner or later, with my name on it. But Alex..." Her voice cracked again. "Don't let me be the reason you stop trusting. Or loving."

I stared at her, gun still in hand, soul at war. Part of me wanted to end it here. To slam the door shut forever. But another part—a reckless, wounded, human part—clung to the burning question she had left me with:

What if not all of it was a lie?

The kitchen hummed with unease—the refrigerator the only voice daring to speak. Erin sat at the table, hands trembling just enough to make the glass of iced tea in front of her look like it was shivering too. She didn't touch it. Didn't dare. My gun was still resting near me, lowered but very much alive.

I leaned forward, eyes locked on her, voice low and razor-sharp.

"Erin, believing you right now would be like stepping on a landmine and hoping it's just a rock. So here's how this works. You talk—everything you know. Names, connections, moves. And if I hear so much as a hiccup that doesn't line up, I won't hesitate to put a bullet in your skull. No deals. No promises. You survive this conversation one answer at a time."

She nodded, swallowing hard, eyes darting like the shadows might suddenly open an escape route. They didn't.

Her voice was barely a murmur at first. "I'll tell you everything I know."

"Then start talking," I snapped.

Her gaze dropped to the table, steadying herself. Then she said it:

"They call themselves The Architects."

The name hung heavy in the air.

"You've heard whispers," she went on, her voice gaining rhythm, "but never the name. That's by design. They're not just another shadow outfit, Alex. They are the shadows. Politics, finance, intelligence, oil, energy markets—they pull the strings. They don't make headlines. They write them."

My jaw tightened. My fingers drummed the table, a rhythm that betrayed the fact that this wasn't all news to me. I'd seen fragments, threads—but hearing her confirm it made my blood run colder.

"Go on," I said.

"They recruit people like me—agents, insiders, anyone with access. Groomed, torn down, rebuilt. You think you're working for survival. Really, you're owned." Her voice cracked, but she kept moving. "I was owned."

I narrowed my eyes. "And your role?"

Her throat bobbed as she swallowed. For a second, her eyes flickered to the gun. Then back to me.

"My mission was you."

The words hit harder than any bullet.

I didn't move. Didn't blink. Just waited.

"They knew who you were," she pressed on, her voice fragile. "Your skills, your reach—it's worth more than gold to them. My job was to bring you into the fold. If that failed..." Her lips trembled. "...I was supposed to neutralize you."

I leaned back, the word curdling in my mouth.

"Neutralize," I repeated, each syllable dripping disdain. "And what stopped you?"

She looked down, then up again, her voice wobbling. "It was never going to get to that."

I laughed—short, bitter, sharp. "Oh, that's rich. You fell in love with the mark? That's straight out of a paperback thriller."

Her jaw tightened. "Don't reduce me to a trope, Alex." She inhaled. "You think I wanted this? To fall for you? To betray you? I didn't. I came in blind, following orders, following the plan. And then you—" she exhaled sharply, shaking her head "—you made it impossible to treat this like just another job. I tried to stay detached. I couldn't."

I let the silence sit for a long beat. Then, flatly:

"And yet, here we are."

She pressed her lips together, shame flickering across her face. "They saw your potential long before I was even on the job. They had files—dossiers. They've been watching you for years. Recruiting wasn't the only plan, Alex. They wanted to control you."

My mask slipped, just slightly. "Control me how?"

"I don't know," she admitted, softer now. "But they had something. Something big enough to force your hand. They think it's enough to break you. Which is why... neutralization was never really on the table."

The silence came back heavier. I sifted through fragments—old missions, enemies I'd burned, debts I'd never paid. If she was telling the truth, I'd been playing on their board longer than I realized.

The question left my mouth like a blade drawn in silence. "And what's their endgame?"

"What else if not control? Don't ask these childish questions, Alex. I'm here to give you closure, not repeat myself like a damn tape recorder. Which part of 'I don't have all the answers' don't you understand?"

Her defiance lit something hot in my chest. I leaned forward, the chair creaking like it too knew where this was headed. My voice fell to a whisper sharp enough to slit her resolve.

"And you? Why the fuck are you going off script?"

Her eyes met mine, raw and unflinching. "I'd love to say to end them—for you, for me, for every life they've ruined. And maybe part of me wishes it was true. But we both know that's bullshit. Because the reality?" Her voice cracked, bitter. "I'm tired, Alex. I've got no redemption arc, no miracle ending. I know I'll never have your forgiveness, not after everything. You can't blame a girl for trying, though. For once in my miserable life, I just want to do something right, even if it doesn't fix me. Even if it kills me."

I stared at her, silent long enough for the hum of the refrigerator to feel like thunder. Part of me wanted to laugh, not out of humor, but because the irony was too thick—an assassin confessing to wanting redemption over a sweating glass of tea. Another part of me wanted to end this with one clean squeeze of the trigger and walk away before her words carved deeper.

But then there was the third part—the part I hated—the part that recognized how useful she could be.

I let my fingers brush the cold steel of the gun, just enough for her to see the reminder glint between us. Her eyes tracked the motion, but she didn't look away.

"You've bought yourself time," I said finally, my voice carved in ice. "But don't mistake this for trust. You'll prove your loyalty step by step. And the second—the very second—I smell a lie, or hear one word out of place..."

I let the rest hang. The silence did the work my voice didn't need to.

Erin nodded slowly, her face pale, her eyes carrying the weight of someone who knew she'd just signed herself into a cage with a wolf.

"Understood."

For now, we were allies. Not friends. Not lovers. Just two ghosts clinging to a thin thread of mutual desperation. Bound together in a game where betrayal wasn't just likely—it was inevitable.

And in that world, trust wasn't a gift. It was a weapon.

"Deceit may cloak truth, but the vigilant and wise will always pierce the disguise."

They say babies can see things adults can't. A baby cries, points into the void, and if the parents aren't around, well—that cry isn't for them. It's for whatever is standing in that dark corner. Erin was that baby now. Pointing and crying without tears. And I wasn't sure if I wanted to know what kind of monster she was showing me.

The silence between us was unbearable, like a rope pulled so tight it might snap. Erin sat stiff in her chair, both hands wrapped around a sweating glass of iced tea like it was her last lifeline. Her eyes didn't blink; they just drilled into me, desperate, hunting for something—doubt, mercy, maybe even recognition.

Finally, she broke the silence.

"What's your take on the late Senator Thornhill's assassination?"

Her tone was too casual for such a loaded question, and I almost laughed. Almost.

I leaned back, arms crossing like I had all the time in the world. "What's my take now that I know you're not who I thought you were? Hmm." I let the pause stretch, just to annoy her. "Well, Thornhill was a shark swimming in dirty waters. His death wasn't politics—it was theatre. A show of power. It was probably written, directed, and produced by the people you work for. We've danced over this ground before.

So, Erin, forgive me if I don't see much left to dig up here. Same story, new spin."

Her lips curled into something that wasn't quite a smile. "Have we really covered this ground?" she asked softly, like she was dangling bait. "Because Thornhill wasn't just a target. He wasn't just another greedy senator. He was one of them. He was part of the circle you're so eager to burn down."

That got my attention. I drummed my fingers against the table, buying time, weighing her words. "Well, he was a politician. Integrity isn't exactly in their job description."

Erin leaned forward now, her voice low, slicing through the air. "He was a linchpin. Thornhill funneled billions in defense contracts to his own private military company. That company wasn't a business—it was a weapon. The Architects' weapon. He gave them reach. He gave them teeth."

I let out a slow whistle and shook my head. "Wow. A senator profiting off war? Dabbling in corruption. I'm shocked. Quick, somebody call the press."

She didn't laugh. Not even a twitch.

Instead, she took her time—stood, walked to the fridge, plunked fresh ice into her neglected tea, and sipped like we weren't discussing global puppeteers. Then, calmly:

"Funny, you mention the press. Thornhill had... extracurriculars. Remember Felicity Montgomery?"

I blinked. "Felicity? His logistics guru? The queen of smuggling Kalashnikovs like they were Girl Scout cookies? What about her?"

Erin smirked. "She wasn't just moving crates. She was his weakness. His pawn. The skeleton he hid until it was convenient to parade her out and sacrifice her. Their affair wasn't about lust. It was leverage. And leverage is always fatal."

I laughed, genuinely this time, throwing my hands up. "Stop. A senator having an affair? Please. That's not a scandal, that's job training. The real mystery is finding one who isn't cheating."

But truth be told, her words scratched something at the back of my skull. Why was Felicity his pawn? Why his weakness? I didn't ask, though—I wasn't about to give Erin the satisfaction of watching me squirm.

She didn't miss a beat. Her eyes narrowed, her voice dropped. "She wasn't just his lover. She was handpicked. And it wasn't for her charm."

My smirk faltered. "Handpicked?"

Erin smirked, enjoying the shift in the hunt.

"Take a wild guess."

"Wild guesses aren't my style. You're living proof. So cut the riddles."

"Felicity had a partner," Erin said slowly, savoring the reveal. "Marcus Reynold. Ring any bells?"

The name hit like a gunshot in a church. "Marcus Reynold... Yeah. The Wall Street mogul. The one you had a hand in, Erin. You don't forget a family massacre."

She ignored the jab, sipping her tea as if we were discussing the weather. "Marcus wasn't just a financier. He was Felicity's cousin. They worked together, bankrolling Thornhill's contracts. Thornhill picked her up, planting her so he could get closer to Marcus and his money trail. It was business before it was pleasure. And it was dangerous."

I leaned back hard in my chair, running a hand down my face. "So Thornhill, Felicity, Marcus—they weren't just in bed together. They were building an empire. And The Architects decided the empire builder had outlived his usefulness."

"Not wrong," Erin said, lips tight. "But think bigger. Thornhill wasn't just cut loose. He was made an example. A warning. To remind everyone else in the circle who's really in charge."

The kitchen felt smaller now. Heavy.

She studied me, her gaze sharp. "Alex, this is just one thread. You pull harder, the whole damn web shakes. If you're willing, we can do real damage."

I tilted my head, eyes narrowing. "And you think you and I can take on the same people who killed Thornhill and Reynold? Erin, you're not exactly Mother Teresa."

That earned me a laugh—low, sharp, too short to be comforting. "Please. And you are? Please don't act like we're so different. But if you're scared, go ahead. Sit this one out. I'll be sure to name-drop you in the acknowledgments when history writes this chapter."

I smirked, but there was no warmth in it. "Cute. But make no mistake—you're not offering me a partnership, Erin. You're offering me a gamble. And if you're bluffing, I'll be the one cashing out your chips."

For once, she didn't fire back. She just nodded, quiet, almost solemn. "Understood."

I pushed away from the table, my chair scraping against the tile. "Get some rest. We'll talk in the morning. And that is, if you're still here by morning."

The threat wasn't subtle, but then again, neither of us believed in subtlety anymore.

CHARLES E.A.

"Raise the rallying cry: face the unknown, defy the fear, and swing with courage. In life's grand calculus, it is the bold who thrive, turning uncertainty into mastery and fear into finesse."

Morning came, and with it the gnawing question: what the hell was I thinking keeping Erin under my roof?

I'd convinced myself yesterday that I knew what I was doing—sharp, calculated, a man in control. That locking Erin in my basement meant I was steering the wheel, not her. But now? Now it was apparent I'd been babysitting a live grenade with the pin half-pulled. Erin wasn't just dangerous; she was radioactive. Fugitive. Manipulator. Assassin. Evil dressed in human skin. Whether she planned to betray The Architects or deliver me into their hands wrapped like a Christmas present, both options ended with me in a grave.

So for the second time in twelve hours, I did what any paranoid man would do: I rechecked my perimeter before facing her in the basement.

That's when I saw it. Camera one. Camera two.

Emily's car.

Sitting right in my driveway.

My stomach sank.

Zoom in. There she was, behind the wheel, fingers drumming on the steering wheel like she was tapping out a countdown. She looked beautiful and haunted all at once—like someone who'd rehearsed what she'd say a hundred times and still couldn't find the right line.

And why wouldn't she be uneasy? After the kind of connection we'd shared—raw, immediate, unshakable—you don't just disappear. You don't leave silence where a heartbeat should be. But that's precisely what I'd done. My absence had been its own betrayal, and now she was here, unannounced, a storm forming on my doorstep.

I didn't call her. Couldn't. Because if there was one day I wished I could erase from history, it was yesterday—the day I invited the devil into my house. So, I just stared at the screen like a man watching his life unravel in real time. Because the one thing worse than Emily seeing me with Erin... was Emily seeing me with Erin in my basement.

Emily finally took a breath, opened her door, and stepped out. It was a normal Tuesday for everyone else. Parents rushed kids to school, and suits drove off to their offices. But Emily's footsteps on my pavement sounded like a funeral march.

Erin. Alive. Free. Smiling.

I bolted from the security desk, half-tripping down the stairs to check on Erin before Emily made it to the porch. And then—

I froze.

The basement window gaped open like a crime scene. My tools are scattered. A neat escape route was carved out. Erin was gone.

And where did I find her? In the kitchen. The devil was in the kitchen. Like a sitcom houseguest. Free and smiling.

Bacon is crisping on the stove. Syrup on the table. Coffee steaming. She was calmly scrambling eggs as if it were some cozy Sunday morning breakfast.

I swear my brain shut down. This woman was a devil in heels, and she was plating food. My food.

So, it happened that she'd used my own set to pry her way out. And because the neighbourhood remembered her face, they thought nothing of her crawling out of my house like some handyperson on a coffee break. She had even grabbed my spare keys on her way up. The alarm system hadn't even blinked.

And then, the universe twisted the knife—Emily's face popped up in the kitchen window. She saw... something. Not everything, but enough. Enough to ignite a wildfire.

She froze outside, eyes narrowing, confusion flashing into something sharper. Jealousy? Betrayal? Hurt? Maybe all three.

She stepped back, drew a deep breath, and then walked to the front door with determination. No hesitation this time. She knocked.

Inside, Erin caught my panic like perfume in the air. She didn't gloat with words—she didn't have to. Her lips curled into an amused little smile as she sipped coffee, then waved toward the door, as if to say, "Don't keep her waiting."

I muttered a curse, shoved my hands through my shaved hair, and opened the door. "Em—" I started, but she was already brushing past me like a storm cloud that didn't need permission.

I shut the door quickly—God forbid the neighbors saw this circus—and hurried after her.

Emily entered the kitchen and stopped dead. Her eyes flicked from me to Erin, to the plates on the table, to the coffee in Erin's hands. The picture was damning. Not intimate, not romantic—but domestic. A scene so wrong it rooted Emily to the spot.

Erin didn't even stand. She sat there with the posture of a queen on her throne, mug in hand, meeting Emily's gaze with a lazy, mischievous glint.

"Well, well," Erin purred, voice dripping with faux warmth. "If it isn't the cavalry."

Emily's eyes snapped to me, her voice sharp as a whip. "What's going on here?"

I raised my hands, words tumbling out clumsily. "Emily, I can explain—"

But Erin cut in smoothly, her tone playful and cruel. "Relax, Alex. No need to spin bedtime stories. Let's just call this... a reunion of sorts."

I groaned, glaring at her. "God, Erin—do you have to make this damn difficult?"

Emily's jaw clenched, eyes narrowing into slits. "A reunion? Well, aren't we all about closure these days?"

Erin smirked wider, leaning back in her chair. "Oh, Emily darling... you're going to love this part." She set her mug down with a soft clink. "Your mother—Felicity Montgomery—and I? Turns out we share more than a taste for chaos. Let's just say... we're both excellent at making smoke when the fire's too hot."

The words detonated like a bomb.

Emily's head snapped toward me so fast I thought she might sprain her neck. Her eyes—usually sharp, confident, anchored—now brimmed with disbelief. "Excuse me?" she said, her voice trembling. "What the hell is that supposed to mean?"

Her question wasn't just directed at Erin. It was aimed at me, too, at everything I hadn't said.

Blindsided, I turned to Erin, my patience hanging by a thread. "Erin, stop." My voice was low, warning. "What the fuck are you trying to pull here?"

She raised both hands like a saint at confession, but her smirk betrayed her. "No instigations, Alex. Just facts."

Emily's fists clenched so tightly I thought she'd draw blood. Her voice shook, equal parts rage and heartbreak. "Enough of this!" She took a sharp step toward Erin. "Choose your next words very carefully, because they might be your last."

I threw myself between them, palms out like a referee at a title fight. "Alright, enough! We're not doing knives, guns, or WWE smackdowns in my kitchen!"

But Erin wasn't interested in peace. Her smirk stretched into a grin that bordered on cruel. She tilted her head, almost pitying. "You really don't know, do you? Your mother—your real mother—is a whole different beast."

Emily's eyes flickered with confusion, then fury. "Oh, this is good," she said, her tone so sharp it could cut glass.

I stepped closer to Erin, lowering my voice. "Enough. This isn't—"

But she talked right over me, her gaze locked on Emily like a predator testing prey. "I'm not insinuating shit. I'm telling you. Felicity Montgomery isn't just your mother's name—it's her legacy. And your dear Uncle Marcus?" She leaned back, sipping her coffee. "He was in on it, too."

The room tilted for Emily. She staggered slightly, steadying herself on the edge of the counter. "Just like your entire life, Erin. Lies stacked on lies. Why should this be any different?"

Erin's grin faltered for the first time, replaced by a softer edge—though the words cut deeper. "I wish it were lies. But the truth?" Her voice dropped, sharp as a blade. "It's messier than you can imagine."

Emily's eyes snapped to mine, burning, desperate for an anchor, searching for truth, for denial, for something. "Is she serious? Did you know about this?"

Erin just kept smiling, sipping her coffee, as if she had all the time in the world.

And me? I stood between them—between the woman I loved and the devil I couldn't kill—paralyzed, my brain shut down to static.

Because no matter what I said, no matter what I tried to spin, one fact remained: Erin had just turned my kitchen into a battlefield.

And I was already losing. So, I shook my head slowly, my throat tight. "I don't know what's true anymore."

That was it—the last straw. Emily's world spun off its axis, every truth she'd trusted crumbling like ash. She turned away, voice cracking. "I can't do this. I don't have time for your sociopathic ex-fiancée's drama, Alex."

She stormed toward the door.

Behind her, Erin's laughter rang out—sharp, unrepentant, almost musical in its cruelty. "Oh, don't be so dramatic, boss lady! You'll thank me later."

But just as the sound faded, Erin's tone shifted. Cold. Deadly serious. "Emily."

Emily froze at the door, hand on the knob. "Why should I listen to you?"

Erin leaned forward, eyes glinting. "Because when you walk outside, you're going to stop. Pretend you're admiring the landscaping. And while you do, keep your eyes peeled for a black GMC Denali SUV. If you see it—congratulations. You've got company. But they aren't mine. They're hers. Felicity's little welcoming committee."

Emily didn't dignify it with a response. She ripped open the door and stormed out. But as she crossed the driveway, her eyes betrayed her. She glanced up—and there it was. The SUV, idling, its tinted windows as opaque as secrets.

Her chest tightened. The world she thought she knew was unraveling, and every thread led back to her mother.

Hours later, Emily would tell me that when she finally sat at her desk at Langley, she tried to bury herself in work: reports, briefings, endless chatter. But none of it mattered. Her mind kept circling back to Erin's words. Felicity Montgomery. Uncle Marcus. Two mothers. A life built on smoke.

It was too much. She slammed her laptop shut, grabbed her keys, and bolted. Work be damned. She needed answers, and she wasn't going to find them under fluorescent lights and security cameras.

By sundown, Emily was gone—boarding the next flight out with nothing but a carry-on and fire in her chest.

She told me later about the cab ride in New York. The driver was pure New York—gruff, chatty, with a bobblehead on the dashboard nodding along like it was in on the conversation. The skyline rose like a jagged promise in the distance, and her stomach fluttered like it was auditioning for a Broadway role.

Her destination? Billy's place. The so-called "luxurious pad" tucked away in one of the city's swankiest neighborhoods. She'd seen pictures. But nothing prepared her for the jaw-dropping reality.

The cab transitioned from honking chaos to serene affluence in the space of a few blocks. The air felt cleaner, the trees greener—like even the plants had trust funds.

When the cab pulled into the driveway, Emily stepped out, her heels crunching against immaculate gravel. The lawn looked like military recruits with scissors had groomed it, and the flower beds exploded with color, more curated than an art gallery. A breeze carried the scent of roses and money, and Emily couldn't help thinking—

Billy had really outdone himself.

Emily paused at the front steps, inhaling deeply as if the crisp air and pristine lawn might settle the storm inside her chest. Most family gatherings happened at their mother's home in Virginia, where chaos and laughter mixed like perfume and smoke. But today, Billy's immaculate haven called to her. If there were answers, if there were truths that could steady her shaking world, maybe they lived here.

Before she could knock, the door swung wide.

"Em!" Billy's grin stretched across his face like sunrise, and in an instant, he pulled her into a bear hug so suffocating it nearly crushed the fury out of her.

"Bill," she muttered into his shoulder, muffled and slightly out of breath. Then she pulled back, eyes narrowing at his frame. "Still skipping leg day, huh?"

Billy struck a mock bodybuilder pose, flexing his arms like he was auditioning for a protein shake commercial. "Legs are overrated. The real strength is in the hugs."

Emily cracked a reluctant smile.

Inside, the house gleamed with its usual curated perfection. Emily's eyes caught on the garden out back, where her mother, Mrs. Eleanor, sat under a sprawling oak, elegant even in casual clothes. A maid stood nearby, peeling an apple in one long, unbroken spiral, the skin curling like ribbon.

Emily muttered under her breath, "Yeah, I'll never master that."

Mrs. Eleanor looked up, her face lighting with recognition. "Emily, darling!" She gestures with the grace of royalty. "Not even a call, I hope all is well."

Emily walked across the manicured lawn, her heels sinking slightly into the soft grass. "Hey, Mom. Still terrifying the garden club?"

Mrs. Eleanor's smile was warm, but her eyes—always sharp—narrowed as they scanned her daughter's face. "You look... troubled," she said gently. "What's wrong, sweetheart?"

Billy joined them, flopping onto the bench beside his mother. "Troubled? Nah. That's just her resting face."

Emily swatted his arm. "Thanks, Bill. Good to know I radiate pure anxiety."

"That's what family is for," he grinned.

But Emily's smile faltered. Her chest tightened. She'd carried this curiosity for hours, and it was splitting her open from the inside. Taking a breath so deep it hurt, she spoke.

"Mom. Billy. I found out something about our family today. And I need to know—" Her voice cracked. "When were you planning to tell me?"

The air shifted. The apple paused mid-peel. Mrs. Eleanor's smile collapsed, her knuckles whitening around the fruit. Billy straightened, his usual lightness gone.

The maid, sensing the sudden weight in the air, gathered her things and disappeared indoors like smoke.

Billy gestured for Emily to sit beside him. His tone was soft, measured. "There's... a lot to explain. But tell us first—how did you find out?"

Emily said her mother's composure cracked. Her voice rose, sharp with fear. "Was it her? Did she have the nerve to come to you? Because if she did, I swear—"

"Mom!" Emily snapped, her voice slicing the air. "No one came to me. I figured it out myself. The fact that I had to..." Her words faltered, then sharpened. "Why couldn't you just tell me?"

The silence was unbearable. Finally, Emily broke it again, louder now, her anger spilling over. "When were you planning to tell me? Or were you never going to? Were you just going to let me live my entire life not knowing who I am?"

Mrs. Eleanor's eyes glistened. Her hands trembled as she set the apple aside. "It wasn't that simple, sweetheart," she whispered. "We thought we were protecting you from her monstrous personality. Felicity—she's dangerous. Although I was also following her instructions, we.... we had a deal."

Emily laughed, hollow and bitter. "Dangerous? Because newsflash, Mom—she's already on my tail."

Billy reached for her shoulder, his touch steady. "Em, wait. Let's not jump to conclusions. Hear her out."

She turned to him, betrayal sharpening her gaze. "That's easy for you to say. Did you know?"

Billy hesitated. His silence was an answer long before he spoke. "I found out a few years ago. Mom asked me not to say anything."

Emily recoiled, her jaw dropping. "Unbelievable."

Emily said at that point, her chest constricted with questions, so much so that she didn't know how to begin framing up her thoughts; all she could do was lean back on the bench, and she stared at both of them like strangers. "So what now?"

Mrs. Eleanor reached out, her grip trembling but fierce. "I hate that you found out like this, but you've got to know that we were planning on telling you sooner."

Emily said her eyes began to burn. She wanted to pull away, to scream, to break something. But beneath the storm of betrayal, another current pulled at her—love. Pain. Roots that ran too deep to sever.

For all their secrets, for all their flaws, they were still her family.

And God help her, she still needed them.

"Very well." Eleanor's voice shook like a thread pulled too tight, but there was a steel beneath the tremor that made the room fall into a new kind of silence. The sort that listens differently once a secret begins to breathe.

Emily sat up straighter, fingers knuckling into her knees as if to anchor herself to the present. Billy, who'd been quietly folded into the corner of the couch like a statue, shifted forward; his face had the predator's stillness of someone who hates surprises. According to Emily, the air tasted like old paper and colder truths.

Eleanor inhaled—a long, measured intake that seemed to draw not only breath but the shadow of years into her chest. When she spoke, her voice carried the wear and the weight of decisions made on someone else's behalf. "Emily, I want you to know I'd do it all again—even the painful parts—if it meant keeping you safe."

Those words should have comforted. Instead, they landed like stones, each one stirring something buried under Emily's feet.

"My family," Eleanor continued, eyes somewhere beyond the living room, as if seeing the rooms she'd fled a lifetime ago. "Built themselves on shadows. Power was currency. Pain was a tool. Sympathy was a vulnerability to be exploited. And life was... always expendable." Her mouth tightened. "I tried to blend. I tried to make myself smaller so the darkness wouldn't notice me. But the darkness sees everything."

Emily watched her mother's hands—hands that had once held her like a lighthouse—now folded, knuckled, as if holding back the urge to claw the past away. Her throat worked, just for a breath; the daughter recognized the contours of the woman who had once been young and furious enough to run.

"So I left," Eleanor said plainly. "I ran across an ocean to a life where no one knew my name. That's where I met your father. He offered me a glimpse of something cleaner—an ordinary blueprint. We came back and built what we could. And when your brother came, I thought that would mean the end of darkness." She let out a slight, haunted sound that might have been a laugh once.

Billy's posture shifted; his fingers dug into his knees. The confession was a landmine that might go off in any direction.

Eleanor's voice dropped. "But there's more, so let's go back to how it all started." She looked at Emily with a clarity that was frightening in its gentleness. "I have a sister. Her name is Felicity."

The name landed like a chord struck out of tune. Emily's expression emptied, then filled with a slow, sickening realization. "A sister?" The question was small, brittle. The world rearranged itself around the syllable.

Eleanor nodded. "Your grandmother—she married twice. The first marriage was a relationship marked by ugliness and permanence, which also bore the fruit of my existence. After she escaped that, she remarried into the Montgomerys. Felicity was born into that second life." Eleanor's eyes slid away, somewhere between apology and admission. "She was raised in ways I was not. The Montgomerys... they have their own rules."

Billy's jaw tightened. "The Montgomerys." His voice was calm. He'd heard the name in whispers, tied to things he had tried not to get involved with: contracts, back channels, careful violence. The name had teeth.

Eleanor's hands trembled when she folded them together. "I tried to break free completely. I wanted—no, I needed—a clean slate—a life where my kid wouldn't be collateral. So I left and married, and we built a harmless life. I thought that would be enough."

The room held its breath as if pausing a heartbeat to listen to what would fall next.

"One morning she was on our doorstep," Eleanor said. "Out of nowhere. A sleek black car. She looked like she'd been cut from magazine pages—perfect hair, perfect clothes—the kind of elegance that disguises a knife. She was holding a baby."

Emily said her face immediately went slack. The sentence made the floor tilt under her.

Eleanor's voice became a thin thread. "Felicity handed me you and said—she said, 'Elea, you're the one who got away. I can't let this life touch her. I can't raise her without drawing her in.' She begged me. She made me promise never to tell you."

Emily's eyes flashed with a dozen emotions so fast they blurred—betrayal, confusion, a childhood overturned. "She gave me away," she said, as if speaking the words aloud would anchor them.

"Yes." Eleanor's shoulders hunched with the admission of the original sin. "She begged. I promised. I took you because I couldn't bear the thought of you being raised the way she was. I promised to give you what she couldn't. I promised to love you. I promised to protect you."

The confession was not the neat absolution Emily had imagined. There was something in Eleanor's tone—an unspooling mixture of guilt and fierce justification—that left the edges jagged. Protecting you, she'd said. But protection is a tricky verb when wielded by people who have long believed the only language the world listens to is force.

Billy reached out and touched Emily's hand for the first time in an hour. No words. Just pressure. A small anchor.

"You can be angry," Eleanor whispered, leaning forward, tears finally breaking free. "You can yell. You can hate me. You can walk away. If I were you, I'd do the same. But my sister..." Her voice cracked again, the words almost swallowed by grief. "My sister did the only thing she could. The right thing. And I will never apologize for standing with her. We did what we did because we loved you. And I did what I thought anyone would do. I kept my promise." She swallowed. "I am not proud of the lies. I am proud that you never had to learn how to lie to survive."

Emily said her mouth opened and closed. She thought of all the small domestic mercies that had been the scaffolding of her childhood—the lunches packed, the bedtime sutures, the way Eleanor's laugh filled their home. Were they heartfelt? Or carefully cultivated accommodations paid for with silence?

"Why so late?" Emily asked, finally, voice small and brittle. "Why tell me now? After all this, why not break the promise decades ago?"

Eleanor's face hardened in a way Emily recognized as the old resolve. "Because the past is reaching," she said simply. "Names are being dragged into daylight. People are getting hurt. Felicity's life is bleeding into ours again, and you deserve to choose how it touches you. You deserve the truth before someone else decides it for you."

Emily stared at her mother. The gratitude she'd felt—an instinctive, aching gratitude—was now knotted with a cold truth. The story fit together in a way that left no comfortable corner: a sister handed over a child to keep her safe; a promise carved in fear; a family rewritten. But every neat narrative invites an ugly outside: what had Felicity sacrificed by giving Emily away? What had she hoped to gain? And what did she, Felicity Montgomery, want now?

To be Continued............

ACKNOWLEDGEMENT

I owe the deepest gratitude to all my beloved readers, whose insatiable curiosity and passion for stories fuel the flames of my imagination. Your unwavering support and enthusiasm are the very foundation upon which this book stands.

To Mr. Benson Ogadinma. Your enthusiasm could power a small city. Your genuine enthusiasm and steadfast support ignited my confidence. Your belief in my vision gave me the courage to imagine without limits.

A special thank you to Chiemela Akalahu. Your thoughtful feedback, relentless encouragement, and honest insight helped refine my voice and vision. You made me better.

Chidinma Akalahu, when I was knee-deep in self-doubt, you handed me a metaphorical shovel and said, "Keep digging, gold's down there somewhere." Your faith in me is why this book didn't end up as a tragic bonfire of abandoned drafts.

To Helena Margaretha, your love, patience, and constant support have been my foundation. Your belief in me never wavered, even when I doubted myself.

This book was not written alone; it is more than just words. It reflects the collective support borne on the backs of those who chose to believe in me. And for that, I will always be grateful.

CHARACTERS

❖ **EMILY PARKER** (CIA TOP ANALYST/FIELD AGENT)

❖ **ARTHUR C. WINTERS** (CIA DIRECTOR)

❖ **ALEX CARTER** (NSA AGENT)

❖ **FELICITY MONTGOMERY**

❖ **LUCAS** (FELICITY'S HACKER)

❖ **RILEY M. JACKSON** (FBI AGENT)

❖ **WILLIAM ANDERSON** (FBI DIRECTOR)

❖ **MELTON ANDERSON** (WHITE HOUSE CHIEF OF STAFF AND BROTHER TO WILLIAM ANDERSON. BOTH ARE NEPHEWS TO MR. SANDER)

❖ **ROBERT TURNER** (A MEMBER OF FELICITY CRIME NETWORK)

❖ **MARCUS REYNOLD** (A HEDGE FUND MANAGER IN WALL STREET WITH A FAMILY SECRET CONNECTING FELICITY MONTGOMERY)

❖ **RICHARD R. SUGGS** (FBI AGENT)

❖ **DIRECTOR VANCE VOSS** (New CIA Director)

❖ **MARILYN M. SANDERS** (RICHARD'S GIRLFRIEND)

❖ **DANNY THORNHILL** (SENATOR THORNHILLS SON, A SURGEON)

❖ **MA** (SENATOR THRONHILL'S WIFE, RETIRED HIGH SCHOOL TEACHER)

❖ **ROBERT THORNHILL** (The Late Sentor and Former Presidential candidate.)

❖ **RAJA** (ONE OF THE UNKNOWN CALLER BOYS IN INDIA)

❖ **DR. BAI FENG** (A VIROLOGIST WAS KILLED)

CHARLES E.A.

❖ **MRS. ELEANOR PARKER** (EMILY'S MOTHER, WHO USE TO LIVE IN HER HOME IN IN WINE LAKE COUNTY)

❖ **MR. GEORGE SANDERS**, (MARILYN'S FATHER,) (CEO TIMELESS ODYSSEY TECH CORP)

❖ **ERIN B. WALTER** (ALEX'S EX-FIANCEE)

❖ **BILLY PARKER** (EMILY'S BROTHER WHO LIVES IN AN ELITE SUBURB IN NORK YORK CITY)

❖ **KATHLEEN A. COATES** (EMILY'S HANDLER AND CLOSEST FRIEND, CIA)

❖ **DORIS D. GREEN** {MR SANDERS LATE SISTER}

❖ **SENATOR MARCUS C. KARN** (FROM THE MAINE SENATORIAL ZONE, PRIVATELY FUNDED BY A PHARMACEUTICAL INDUSTRY FACING OPIOID TRIALS)

❖ **RONALD L. SULLIVAN** (THE CEO OF A MAJOR PLAYER IN THE PRIVATE MILITARY SECTOR, UNDER ASSUMED NAME)

❖ **LIONEL A. DAVIS** (VICE PRESIDENT OF USA)

❖ **MR. RONALD L. SULLIVAN** (THE OWNER OF THE FARM,) (THE FAKE NAME USED BY THE VICE PRESIDENT)

❖ **VINCENT B. CORNELL** (THE CHAIRMAN OF PRISMATIC DYNAMICS CORPORATION) (THE VICE PRESIDENT IS THE CEO)

❖ **BRITT M. TAPLEY** (THE DIRECTOR OF NATIONAL INTELLIGENCE)

❖ **DWIGHT T. BARRETT** (NATIONAL SECURITY ADVISOR TO THE PRESIDENT)

❖ **JONATHAN D. MOORE** (SECRETARY OF DEFENSE)

❖ **MARSHA O. CUMMINS** (A BRILLIANT INVESTIGATIVE JOURNALIST FOR AN INDEPENDENT NEWS CHANNEL)

❖ **EVELYN WINTERS** (CIA Director's Wife)

❖ **Frederick Galleon.** (An Architect's High Chief)

THE COBRAS ON THE HILL

❖ **Diane Sanders**

❖ **Ellis Cade (Arthur's errand boy)**

❖ **THE ELITE CLUB** (KNOWN AS **THE ARCHITECTS**)

❖ **STEALTH FARM (Mr. Sanders Company)**

Don't miss out!

Visit the website below and you can sign up to receive emails whenever CHARLES E.A. publishes a new book. There's no charge and no obligation.

https://books2read.com/r/B-A-ONYEB-KZDOH

BOOKS 2 READ

Connecting independent readers to independent writers.

OVERLOOK
BOOKS

About the Author

I am an adventurer of both the mind and the world—a thinker who sees life not as a destination, but as an ever-unfolding lesson. Guided by an insatiable curiosity, I believe that the universe itself is a vast school—one from which no one ever truly graduates. My writings, both fictional and nonfictional, explore the fragile borders between reason and chaos, loyalty and betrayal, morality and survival—revealing how the human spirit endures even in the darkest corners of ambition and deception.From childhood, I was captivated by the art of storytelling—not merely as entertainment, but as a vessel of knowledge. To me, literature is the oil that keeps the engine of human memory running—the timeless medium through which our stories are created, preserved, and passed across generations. Six years ago, I began my professional journey as a writer, sharpening my voice into one that would someday resonate with psychological depth and emotional clarity.I think it's fair to say that my words don't just tell stories; they challenge perspectives and awaken emotions—because every story, like every human being, begins with a question worth asking."I don't write to escape reality—I write to challenge it."

www.ingramcontent.com/pod-product-compliance
Lightning Source LLC
Chambersburg PA
CBHW060951030726
47503CB00003B/825